Morningquest

Morningquest

JOAN AIKEN

St. Martin's Press
New York

Library of Congress Cataloging-in-Publication Data

Aiken, Joan.
Morningquest / Joan Aiken.
p.   cm.
ISBN 0-312-09339-X
I. Title.
PR6051.I35M67   1993   93-18508.   CIP   823'.914—dc20

First published in Great Britain by Victor Gollancz.

First U.S. Edition: May 1993
10 9 8 7 6 5 4 3 2 1

BT 17.95/9.82 - 4/93

TO JULIUS

and in memory of his grandmother

BESSIE MASHORES

I

'I'd like you to come with me to Boxall Hill this afternoon, when I go collecting signatures,' my mother said, in the extra-brisk tone she always adopted if not fully confident of success – as a horseman thumps his mount to an inciting speed while on the run-up to an obstacle.

Of course I scowled, and sighed, and hunched my shoulders over the handful of spoons and forks that I was drying. 'Why?'

'Because I think the young Morningquests might be interesting friends for you. And you for them.'

That suggestion was in itself enough to damn the project.

My mother was not in any way a snob. I would like to make this perfectly clear. But – looking back, with pity, with empathy – I can see that for almost all her life she was insufficiently supplied in her thirst for intelligent talk by my father and the people around her. *Insufficiently*. That's putting it in a minor key. She had a first-class degree in European languages and literature, won at God knows what cost. She ought to have been teaching. But here, in Floxby Crucis, not a soul had any ambition to learn about European literature. And my father, once home from his daily round, wished for nothing more than to slump silently into the *Milk Producers' Weekly Bulletin and Cowkeepers' Guide*. (My father was not a farmer, but the interests of farmers and vets frequently coincide.) He did not even wish to converse in English, let alone French, Spanish, German, Hungarian, or Russian.

Floxby Comprehensive, which I attended, was not a bad school, in its upper reaches at least. But my coevals were a dull enough lot, and my mother, I now understand, suffered a corroding anxiety that I might slip into such a life as hers: collecting for the Congregational Jumble Sale, or the swimming-pool fund, the annual coach trip to Stratford as the most notable event. And the orange lipstick and loud laugh of my friend Veronica, let alone the way Veronica had of crossing her legs diagonally with a display of high heel and long shiny nylon shins, grated dreadfully on my mother and struck a chill into her heart.

'Come along,' said she. 'The walk will do you good.' And she muttered something about frowsting indoors. 'Put on your shoes.'

But there I balked. This was at the time when everybody of my age

7

(except Veronica) went barefoot, unless the ground was actually coated with snow.

Mother sighed, accepting that my physical company was all the victory she could look for: bare feet, jeans, duffel coat, ravelled navy sweater and shaggy hair had to be part of the deal.

In fact, once resigned to the plan, I went along biddably enough. Mother could be excellent company, had read all the books I'd ever heard of, including Homer in Greek, and was able to supply answers to any questions I cared to put – from Napoleon's trouble with piles to the psychiatric problems of bluetits.

But, on this particular Sunday afternoon she was withdrawn, silent, and preoccupied, sighing frequently as we walked up Boxall Hill Lane, one of the five narrow roads that radiate from our small town.

For me, the walk made a soothing regression to much earlier childhood when I had accompanied her on countless such outings, canvassing for the Labour Party, selling Remembrance Day poppies, or Alexandra Roses, carrying petitions related to overhead power lines, opencast mine projects, oil prospecting, or the closure of bus services.

'So how many Morningquests are there, exactly?' I demanded in a calculatedly glum tone, just to get a conversation started, for I did have a rough idea.

'Seven children.' She had the information pat. 'The boys are at university, I think they are older than you. I'm not sure of their names, I think one is Barnabas. The girls are Dorothea, Selene, Alethea, and Elvrida.'

'Cripes,' I muttered.

'I should think Dorothea would be the nearest to you in age,' my mother added. 'And don't say cripes, it's ugly.'

Sir Gideon Morningquest was a conductor of world renown. Hardly ever to be seen in our town, for the Morningquests also inhabited a house in London (Cadogan Square) he spent most of his year elsewhere, on the other side of the world, in Buenos Aires, Sydney, Rome, or Tokyo, presiding over foreign orchestras. His aquiline profile on record sleeves or the cover of the *Radio Times* was far more familiar to us than his bodily presence; during my entire sixteen years I had probably not laid eyes on him more than three or four times. (It did seem quite remarkable in view of his far-flung habits that he had managed to father such a large brood.)

Lady Morningquest also was a celebrity in her own right, a singer, a soprano. Mariana Tass had been her professional name. Some years ago she had stopped taking operatic parts, but she still gave recitals, taught at the Royal College, and sat on educational committees. She and my mother

8

were somewhat acquainted, I vaguely recollected; they had met over the organisation of a Floxby Music Festival and struck up a friendship.

'I suppose all the family are dead musical,' I muttered apprehensively.

'Oh, certainly. I think she said that each of them plays a different instrument.'

My mother spoke wistfully, and sighed again. It struck me that she was walking rather more slowly than usual. Brought up in Scotland (though not a Scot), she had acquired strong views about the importance of air and exercise; she despised cars and car-owners, and her customary gait had always been a long, raking stride. As a small child, I had to trot to keep up with her; I must have jogged hundreds of miles before the age of ten, pursuing her about the local lanes and commons. But now she seemed to be having trouble keeping pace with *my* stride; dimly I supposed that people, parents, did grow older and less athletic; it must, I reflected, be a necessary stage of life.

'Don't we go in by the lodge?' I asked, a little surprised, as she turned right, and slowly climbed a stile in a hedge.

'No. This way is a short-cut.'

Mother had a passion for short-cuts, would often go substantially off her course when tempted by some promising diagonal path. ('Come along; we may as well try it; it might be quicker. And we've never been this way.')

The path beyond the stile took us upward through a little coppice-wood, the kind where, in May, there would be bluebells; on this autumn day the narrow track was rustling, ankle-deep in large crisp chestnut leaves.

I was secretly quite eager to see Boxall Hill House, which occupied a large wedge-shaped tract of land north-west of our town, a small park really, protected on all sides by a belt of woodland. The house itself was not visible at all from any point close to the town; you had to go to the next height of land, about five miles off, to catch a distant glimpse of it. Sir Gideon valued privacy, and this secluded situation within fifty miles of London had been one of his main reasons for acquiring the place, then derelict, as a weekend retreat, some twenty years earlier. But he had never mixed in local society. And the county gentry, when he first arrived, were in no particular hurry to make his acquaintance: 'Not really our sort.' Of course he was much less famous in those days. The culture-hungry of the town – there were only a few of those – at first hoped for great benefits from his presence, but were soon disillusioned. He came for curtailed weekends, arriving after midnight on Friday in his Bentley, gone again by Sunday evening. His children all attended distinguished London schools; they rarely took part in local events, except occasional summer fêtes, when the boys would appear, looking nervous and diffident, then proceed to win all the races. They were tall, fair, handsome, reserved, godlike; unapproach-able. I could hardly recall ever having seen their sisters in the town; I would not know them by sight. Presumably they came down at weekends and for school holidays; but since I was full of touchy pride, intensely anxious not to seem to be trying to scrape acquaintance, I had always kept well away at such times from the neighbourhood of the Boxall Hill estate.

In consequence this tract of land, so close by yet so completely unknown, kept for me the mystery of Xanadu. 'Twice five miles of fertile ground, With walls and towers were girdled round . . . '

I did not particularly hanker for gardens bright with sinuous rills; though people in the town did sometimes murmur that it was a shame, Boxall Hill used to have beautiful grounds in Major LeMercier's day (but he, poor man, had shot himself after the Stock Exchange crash); it was a wicked waste that Sir Gideon did not throw the gardens open sometimes in aid of the Cottage Hospital or the swimming-pool fund. But he was deaf to all hints or requests. What *I* really hoped for was a deep romantic chasm – not entirely an impossible dream, for the estate sloped up to a ridge of land, then dropped steeply through beechwoods on the far side. There was a tower, or folly, or gazebo: that I did know. My father had seen it. For he, of course, as a vet, went where nobody else was permitted, down private lanes, over remote farm properties; but, characteristically, he could not remember what it was like. My father was not interested in follies. 'Built of brick, perhaps,' was as far as he would go.

Our path wound upwards through the little chestnut-coppice, my mother walking ever more slowly, sighing ever more frequently. At the upper boundary of the wood another stile in a cleft between the saplings offered a gleam of grey sky and a narrow vista of ascending meadow.

Mother, when she reached the stile, leaned her elbows on it and went into a deep abstraction. Coming up alongside, I looked over her shoulder (being now a head taller than she) and gasped with astonished pleasure.

The meadow sloped up to a saddle, between two wooded shoulders of hill. On the left, exquisitely perched, like a butterfly on the lip of a bowl, was the house, a rectangular Georgian block of delicate pinkish-white stone: three storeys, arcaded ground-floor windows, three upper windows, pedimented, and the whole crowned by a small saucer-dome supported by a drum. The white drive ribboned leisurely towards the house, following the curve of the hillside; a stone wall encircled the property at a lower level so that it was protected but not screened; and below the wall, halfway down the saddle, a ha-ha gave additional protection.

On this windy, cloud-flecked autumn day the house seemed to glitter in the fitful sunshine, offering back reflections, like a stone that absorbs and returns radiation from light.

'Oh, my goodness!' I said.

After a pause, my mother remarked, 'I knew you'd like it.'

Her tone baffled me. It was accepting, but dry; rather like, I thought, remembering later on that evening, the reaction of a cook who knows that a dish has been left too long in the oven, and receives effusive and hypocritical compliments with an ironic nod.

But at the time this passed me by.

'Oh I do like it!' I agreed with fervour. 'I really do!'

One of the basic essentials for a building is a proper relationship with the ground on which it stands. From an early age I had always felt this strongly. Raw new suburbs and housing estates fill me with almost physical distress because of the way the blocks are strewn about, not planted, there is no link between horizontal and vertical. Our own house, though small, dark, and inconvenient, did at least sit among trees which gave it protection and dignity. To me, the situation of Boxall Hill house seemed perfection itself, like a smile on the landscape.

Looking back now, with hindsight, I believe it may have been my first view of the place which – as with Elizabeth and Pemberley – was to set the mode for my relationship with the whole Morningquest family.

'Are you all right, Ma?' it then occurred to me to ask. 'You look a bit pale.'

'Just pensive,' she said.

I hopped over the stile and gave her a hand. She followed slowly.

'Now we cut across the corner of the hill to the drive,' she said.

Doing so, we were given a view down into the bottom of the saddle, where willows, now shedding yellow leaves, encircled a pond. On the water, which reflected a blue coin of sky, two swans idled.

We climbed to the drive, negotiated a cattle-grid, and threaded a beech-grove. Beyond this lay the encircling wall; there was a door in it through which we passed.

'The back way is quicker,' said my mother. 'The drive loops all round the house.'

'Another of your short-cuts.'

Now I was nervous, ill at ease, unprescient of the many future times that I would be taking this path. We seemed to be under observation from all the fourteen large front windows, which overlooked a wild-garden area of short turf studded with shrubs and a few clumps of late-flowering lilies. Rambler roses smothered the inside of the wall. Two white-painted iron seats were placed so as to catch the last rays and command the huge view southwards.

'From the terrace up there you get the north view,' said my mother, waving a hand upwards. 'We go round to the kitchen door.'

'They must catch the wind frightfully up here,' I said, peevish and affronted, and relieved. So, kitchen-door status, were we? (But it was also true that most of the people we knew in the villages round about – proper country people, not the pseudo-gentry of Floxby Crucis – never used their front doors at all, were always approached from the back. And they were the nicest people I knew.)

The back door, viewed across a cobbled courtyard, stood open; voices could be heard from inside. In the centre of the yard there was a fountain. A low collar of moss-grown brick wall encircled it. The jet, no more than a two-foot needle of water, emerged from a somewhat phallic lump of bright-green moss in the middle. It was charming, absurd, rather touching in its humble, workaday uselessness.

My mother walked unhesitatingly through the open door and turned right along a short passage, no more than a couple of steps in length. Following, I suddenly found myself in a huge kitchen with a stone-flagged floor. The first thing to strike me was its antiseptic lightness: it was a long room with great arched windows at each end. The walls were painted white. And my next impression was that it seemed to be inhabited by giants, who were all conversing at the full pitch of their lungs.

But they fell silent after we entered, except for a male voice which was proclaiming: 'Scientific knowledge is bound to be shaped by social and political factors— '

To which another male voice retorted with equal emphasis: 'Bosh, that is total bosh! Facts are facts.'

Somebody else had been saying, 'Stravinsky wasn't at all pleased when his publisher asked him to write a violin concerto— '

As they fell silent, all eyes turned on us.

I suppose there must have been fifteen or sixteen people gathered round the long, scrubbed kitchen table which extended from end to end of the room. The eaters sat on wooden kitchen chairs, and the empty plates in front of them contained nothing but crumbs. Boards in the middle of the table held ends of brown loaves and remnants of cheese; there were also wooden bowls of apples and catering-size boxes of Shredded Wheat.

Shredded Wheat? Yes, Shredded Wheat.

It appeared that we had arrived towards the end of Sunday lunch, which seemed quite peculiar to me since it was nearly four o'clock. Lunch in our house, invariably meat, two veg, and pudding, took place at one sharp, since my father's long active day often commenced in the small hours.

'Hélène, my dear!' exclaimed a welcoming voice – female, this one. 'What a pleasure to see you. And this must be Pandora—'

Lady Morningquest was greeting us. But how in the world did she and my mother come to be on such affectionate terms as, plainly, they were – kissing, continental-style, first one cheek, then the other – then sitting close together at the near end of the table, falling into immediate, low-toned chat. Meanwhile I, paralysed with terror, stood where I was until Lady Morningquest, glancing up, said, 'But Pandora – ah, that's right, Dolly dear, pull in another chair, you can easily make room for Pandora beside you.'

'Not all *that* easily,' put in a boy's voice, heavy with brotherly sarcasm, and there was a general guffaw at which Dolly shrugged with maternal indulgence. She was not really so fat as to justify the teasing: big and solidly built, she had a round, amiable, freckled face with slight double chin; brilliant red hair, twined, unbecomingly, in two large coils over her ears; and large blue-grey eyes.

She gave me a reassuring, slightly patronising smile. 'Would you like some cider, Pandora?' And she poured from a massive earthenware jug into a blue-and-white striped mug. All the china was very plain, farmhouse stuff.

How could they eat *Shredded Wheat* for lunch?

My mother was declining cider. 'No, thank you, Mariana, no, really—'

From the start, I was totally hypnotised by the beauty of Lady Morningquest who sat just across the corner of the table from me. Her hair, exquisitely fine and snow-white, had been swept back and gathered into a loose bun, but stray wisps fell around the high, moulded brow, in no way reducing her dignity. Nor did the deep-set, bruised sockets detract from the brilliance of her blue eyes. She had on a plain grey loose garment, the kind that porters wear in hospitals, and smoked a cigarette in a long ivory holder. I thought that she looked like the Sibyl of Cumae.

'But, poor Pandora, you don't know anyone here, do you? Well, that's my husband down at the far end . . .'

Sir Gideon, full-face, was not as hawklike as his profile on record sleeves; in fact he had a very sweet, saintly look. Enormously tall (he was standing up, at the moment, to draw another jugful of cider from a cask on a shelf), he appeared as skinny and muscular as a Leonardo drawing. A fillet of downy greyish hair ran round the back of his head; the front was bald. His face was shaped into an interlocking series of triangles by a massive nose and deep grooves on either side of his mouth. I itched to make a drawing of it.

'You *know* it's not the slightest use expecting Pandora to get us all sorted out, Mar,' one of the boys told his mother in a patronising voice.

Why not? I thought, annoyed at once.

'Why not?' said Lady Morningquest, and, to me, 'Those are the three boys down there at the left-hand end of the table – Barney, Toby, and Dan. The friend sitting this side of them is Alan, from Scotland, and beyond him is Garnet, who helps with the garden, and then Dave Caley, from Louisiana; next to my husband at the end is his friend Luke Rose. Then on this side, but you can't see them so well from where you sit, are the girls. (Girls and boys always seem to take opposite sides in this family.) First, Dolly, by you, then Ally and Elly, the twins. Then Tante Lulie would be next to them, but she has gone into the garden to get some tea-towels – and my darling Leni, beyond her, and then Uncle Grisch on my husband's left-hand side . . . '

Someone at the far end of the table rose and bowed formally to me. He was a little shrimp-like elderly man with coal-black eyes. He had not shaved for days. He wore blue dungarees and his shirt was unbuttoned at the collar.

Naturally I had not, in fact, managed to take in or remember most of these names, or their application to the people at the table. But I did (from seeing them at summer fêtes) recognise the three sons of Sir Gideon who sat on his right-hand side, and know them for Barnabas, Toby, and Dan. They were uniformly handsome, hawklike, and fair-haired, as I supposed Sir Gideon must have been in earlier days. They had straight noses and brilliant blue eyes like their parents (though Sir Gideon's were somewhat faded now) set at a slight tilt, sloping downward at the outer corners. This gave them, to me anyway, a very beguiling look. They talked loudly, confidently, and continuously, interrupting and contradicting each other.

'Chromosomes have nothing to do with it!'

'You simply can't *draw* that kind of analogy— '

'Nicholson has already proved that's not so, in his paper on sheep glands. Sheep only— '

'*Please*, Barney. Not at the lunch table!' begged Lady Morningquest.

Her voice, like all her other attributes, seemed perfection itself: clear, pure as that of a thrush. It issued from her with effortless power and made itself heard all over the room.

'This is a good moment to remind the boys that it is their turn to wash the dishes,' said her husband.

The boys at once stood up, never for a moment breaking off their argument, and began to pile plates and mugs into the large stone sink behind Sir Gideon. The small unshaven black-eyed man stood also, but Sir Gideon pulled him down again.

'Not you, Grischa my dear; there are quite enough workers. And you do so much all the week.'

'Besides, you aren't a boy, Uncle Grisch,' affectionately said the red-haired girl sitting beside him. Which was she? Selene perhaps. She had a pale, pointed, Pre-Raphaelite face, and her hair was a paler red than Dolly's; it stood out in a fuzz round her face.

'Ach, what you say has the ring of truth, Leni my dear.' Uncle Grisch sat down again. He had in front of his plate, I noticed, two little pots: a copper coffee-pot like a milk-churn, and a flask wrapped in basketwork. He sipped from them alternately. They seemed the only sign of self-indulgence in the room, which was otherwise severely functional: closed cupboards and shelves all round the walls, white paint everywhere, limp blue-and-white gingham curtains at the windows. Plainly, nobody ever drew them.

Two of the girls now moved from their seats beyond Dolly to chairs vacated by the boys across the table and, plumping themselves down opposite me, began to interrogate me.

'Where do you go to school? What's your best subject? Which university will you aim for? Dolly wants to go to St Vigeans—'

'Oh, why?' asked my mother, breaking off her talk with Lady Morningquest, who answered the question.

'Gideon likes to encourage new universities. Barney's at Cumberland, Toby at Hay-on-Wye; and then a friend of ours, Tom Goodyear, is musical director at St Vigeans. He says the standard there is first-rate...'

Meanwhile I was taking stock of the girls opposite me, who must be the twins, Alethea and Elvrida. They were an extraordinary-looking pair, undersized and plain; the boys had certainly scooped the looks in the Morningquest family I thought. It did seem unfair; but the two elder girls at least had clean-cut features and hair of a colour that could be called striking even if you didn't like it. Also their eyes were a pleasant blue-grey, whereas the twins had black hair of an uncompromising straightness, cut to unflattering jaw-length and hanging lankly round their ears. They wore dental braces to correct violently protruding teeth, which caused the poor things to spit when they talked, and their eyes were a muddy-greenish colour. They had loud, grinding, confident voices, a total contrast to that of their mother. None of which disadvantages seemed to have impaired their self-esteem in the very least; and that, I thought, spoke well for the kindliness and tolerance of the Morningquest family.

The twins reminded me of something. I struggled to think what.

When I said that my favourite subject was art, they exclaimed together: 'Art? That's not a *subject*! I'm going to do biology and Elly's going to do physics.'

'Not yet for a while, surely?' I suggested.

But Lady Morningquest turned to me. 'They have both reached university standard in mathematics, they work with the sixth form in their school; but Gideon is opposed to their starting university life till they are at least seventeen because it would mean so many special arrangements. And in other ways, of course, they are not so advanced . . . '

In other ways, I thought, they seemed positively retarded. How old could they be, twelve, thirteen? They poked each other like eight-year-olds, stuck out their elbows, shouted, insulted one another and contradicted even more than the boys. Their voices were like a flock of geese.

'Please be quiet, you two!' called their father and eyed them, I thought, with dislike.

'Darlings, why don't you take Pandora and show her the grotto. And the folly, and the tree-house,' suggested Lady Morningquest. 'Dolly, you go along too, and make sure they don't wear her out.'

'All right, come on!'

The twins clawed me from my chair with skinny hands. Dolly, wearing what seemed a habitual expression of indulgent readiness to go along with anybody's wishes, got up likewise. I would much rather have remained in the kitchen listening to the adult conversation.

Sir Gideon had now moved round the table into Dolly's vacated chair, and my mother was saying to him: 'But how can you possibly stand Elgar's pomposity? He's worse than pompous, he's *sanctimonious*!' and he was laughing at her. 'Our business, my dear Hélène, is not to like music or dislike it; our business is to know it.'

Ma! I thought, in total astonishment. Where does she *get* it from? First, the assurance; second, the know-how. I had never heard her like this in my life, never.

But the twins hauled me off. Their grins, glittering with metal, were like the Cheshire Cat's.

'The grotto was designed by Lutyens,' they were saying, 'and the folly was built by a student of Flaxman.'

'Do you like reading?' I hastily asked Dolly, who was strolling by my side while the twins scurried ahead self-importantly.

'What kind of reading? I'm going to read Social Psychology at St Vigeans – of course the twins would say that's not a *subject*.'

'No, I meant just ordinary books – fiction.'

I had recently discovered Penguin books and was voraciously devouring all I could lay my hands on, from *South Wind* to *The Catcher in the Rye*. My favourite at the moment was *The Horse's Mouth*. I had read it at least seven times. Floxby Crucis did not boast a bookshop – the newsagent kept only a few popular thrillers – so I was obliged to bicycle fifteen miles to Crowbridge where there was a secondhand bookshop, but the journey was well worth it.

'*Fiction?*' said Dolly doubtfully. 'Well I read *Gone With the Wind* – but it was awfully long — '

'But when you were younger?'

She looked vague, but presently recalled the Arthur Ransome books which, she said, she had preferred to fairy tales and that kind of thing. 'Tante Lulie used to read fairy tales aloud when we were sick, but I never enjoyed them much.'

At this point we encountered Tante Lulie, who carried a bundle of rough-dried laundry. On seeing my bare feet she exclaimed in utter disapprobation: '*Kriech nicht darum at borvas!*' Or that was what it sounded like. '*Borvas! Borvas!*'

'I beg your pardon?' I said, startled, since she was plainly addressing me.

She pointed again to my bare feet. '*Borvas!* Where are your shoes, child?'

'At home. I never wear shoes.'

'Ach!' She flung her hands to Heaven. 'Pneumonia! Polio! Tetanus!'

'Really, I go barefoot everywhere,' I pleaded.

And Dolly, in her creamy indulgent tone, said, 'Oh, come on, Tante Lulie! She is sure to be full of antibodies by now. She looks quite healthy, you must agree. This is Pandora Crumbe, by the way.'

Tante Lulie suddenly gave me a shrewd and friendly grin, tossed the laundry over her shoulder, and held out a wrinkled paw which, surprisingly, encased mine in a grip of iron. 'And I am happy to meet you now, so late, Pandora. Your mother is already a dear friend.'

She, like Uncle Grisch, had a foreign accent – Austrian, perhaps? Was she his wife? Later I discovered that they were in no way connected; Tante Lulie was the aunt of Sir Gideon's first wife, long since dead. Grisch was called 'uncle' by courtesy only, he had come to Boxall Hill for a visit nineteen years ago and remained ever since.

Tante Lulie wore a white crumpled tam-o'-shanter cap crammed on her head, and wonderfully elegant suede boots on her feet; the rest of her clothes were so dishevelled and nondescript that, even while looking at her, it would be hard to give an account of them. Her appearance, like that of the twins, was puzzlingly familiar to me. Had I seen her face in the streets of Floxby? Or at church? Broad, wrinkled, tolerant, resigned, her face was like the moon, untidy and full of secrets; it was only weeks later that, coming across a reproduction of one of Rembrandt's self-portraits in a book, I realised why, with characteristic self-mockery, she wore the white beret tugged over her brow.

'Is your dear mother here also? Then I go ask for the recipe for her wonderful quince preserve. Do not lead Pandora too far into the wilderness, children,' she told the twins. 'Tea will be soon.'

'*Tea?* We only just finished lunch!' Dolly called after her, and she responded with an indescribable flourish of one hand conveying her opinion of such habits.

I was interested and attracted, if alarmed, by the glimpse that I was being given of this large, complex household. My own minimal, scanty family unit – Father so taciturn, Mother so subdued and reticent, I myself the product of their silences – what a total contrast we presented to this intricate conversational clan. My father's habit of saying, 'Be quiet, Pandora, you know nothing about this,' had a quenching effect on me which it would take years to eradicate.

The girls were leading me along a path, across a walled rose-garden still filled with warm late scents, past a yew-hedge maze, where I would have liked to stop, but – 'The maze is a frightful bore,' said Ally, or Elly; through a rhododendron shrubbery and into a little grassy dell. Along its bottom meandered a brook which, doubtless, fed the willow-bordered pond we had passed coming up.

'That's where we swim,' said Dolly, waving a hand towards a wider reach of the brook with a dam across it. 'We dammed the stream and dug the pool three years ago, that was our summer project. It's rather cold, but nicer than the willow pond, which has leeches. Colonel Venom was furious, of course, at the time when we did it. He created like mad, to Mar, said we were spoiling his view and generally distracting him.'

'Colonel Venom?'

'Don't you know him? He lives up there in the house called Aviemore.' I looked up the brow of the hill where she pointed, and saw a small neat red house, quite close, framed by monkey-puzzles and garnished with mock Tudor gabling and fake lead windowpanes. 'It's just over the edge of Gideon's land. He loathes almost everything we do, the Colonel does. Lieutenant-Colonel Sir Worseley Venner. Old Miss Findlater died and the house came up for sale ten years ago, when Gid was doing his Latin-American tour – which lasted almost a year – and he was in such a rage with Mar for not snapping it up. But that was when Dan was having polio, and she had other things on her mind. So the Colonel got it, and he's been a pain in the neck ever since. He hates all our projects.'

'Projects?'

'We've always had one, every summer. Mar likes us to do things together. She has strong views about the importance of family ties. And Gideon plans them. Gid's a great planner.' Did I detect a note of indulgent irony in Dolly's voice? She ticked on her fingers. 'There was the Roman fort. We excavated it. Then there was the World War One dugout. We dug it. Then the year we did falconry, Toby almost got his ear pecked off. Then canoeing down the Aff to the coast and making a map. Then digging the pool. Then building the Argo – that was a bit of a disaster. No one quite seemed to agree about it, and it turned turtle and sank at the launching. Then we wanted to repair Matilda's Tower, but Gid said it was too dangerous; Uncle Grisch had a surveyor in to check it.'

'Matilda's Tower?'

'Up there behind the beech trees. A brick tower. We'll show you another time.'

I was slightly unnerved – but encouraged also – by the way in which she seemed to take it for granted that there would be another time.

'Then we built a kiln for Silly. She's going to be a potter. She makes lovely things. Last summer, when we couldn't agree, the boys wanted to build an organ. But we didn't think there would be enough in that to keep us all busy. We wanted to go rock-climbing. But Gid likes us to do things in the summer that keep us here. He says, what was the point of getting Otherland if we don't come here. And anyway it was a horrible wet summer last year. So we wrote a book.'

'*Wrote a book?*'

'We all worked together,' broke in one of the twins, who had been visibly champing at the bit during Dolly's discourse, 'and concocted a fake eighteenth-century journal. Barney had lots of good ideas. He'd been reading Defoe and James Hogg, *The Confessions of a Justified Sinner*; and Dan was a big help, he got hold of some really old paper in a furniture store, that made it seem authentic; and we all thought of things to put in. We pretended it had come to light in an old ice-house, and got a publisher to look at it. Dan did that, too.'

'It was actually *published*? What was it called?'

'*The Journal of Mad Murgatroyd.*'

'But I remember that! It got reviewed.'

'Mar says we can't touch the bulk of the money till we're twenty-one,' said Dolly complacently. 'But it did do quite well.'

I felt absolutely floored by all this talent and industry. On the surface they were so unassuming: freckled Dolly in her plain blue cotton pinafore dress (which looked mighty like school uniform to me); the twins, who wore brown-and-white checked shorts, grey jerseys, and draggled black-velvet bandeaux restraining their stringy locks. As they grinned at me, they resembled gargoyles.

'This is what we've brought you to see,' Ally (or Elly) told me. 'Here's our this year's project. It will probably be our last. The boys aren't so keen any more. They have *adult interests*. And this sort of thing does begin to seem a bit childish.'

Just the same, there was a wistful note in her voice.

We were approaching a grove of ilexes, holm oaks, centred on the northern slope of the little valley we had entered. There were twenty or so trees, large old ones, and their branches dangled around them in mannered, elegiac swags and fronds. The grove would have been distinguished in itself, a piece of natural sculpture on the grassy slope, with its dark, baroque outlines; but into the very middle of it led a staircase.

'Toby was terribly fussy about getting the right kind of wood,' explained a twin. 'It had to be Canadian red cedar and it cost us a fortune, but we managed to persuade Gideon to let us use some of the *Mad Murgatroyd* money. Toby has worked about twenty hours a day on it all summer.'

'He worries *all the time* in case old Venom does something horrible to it while we are in London,' said the other twin.

'Old Venom nearly had apoplexy over it,' Dolly told me. 'He was down here the very first morning we started work, telling us that he was going to get lawyers' letters and file writs and lay injunctions, that we were wrecking his view and undermining his health. His letters about it to Gideon would fill a suitcase.'

'What did Sir Gideon do?'

'Well, one weekend we had Sir Gervas Mostyn staying (the attorney general, you know?); he and Gid like to play oboes together. So old Gervas went and called on Venom and told him he was wasting his time. It was *our* grove, *our* land; we had got planning permission, we weren't hurting the trees, we were not blocking his view. In fact Sir Lucian Hawke, the president of the RIBA, you know? He's another musical chum of Gid's, he said the staircase was a unique piece of work, outdoor sculpture, and might well win a Landmark Award.'

'Did it?'

'We never got round to applying.'

'What holds it up?'

The staircase, made of golden wood, looped upwards in an elegant curve, disappearing among the dark green swags and fronds.

'Something to do with cantilevers, I think,' said Dolly vaguely. 'You can't see from here.' The twins grinned at her with younger-sisterly malice. I suspected they knew a good deal more about cantilevers than she did. 'The wood will weather in time, of course. It will go grey. I suppose that may appease old Venom, if he doesn't die of fury first. In the meantime he's retaliated by putting up a gate at the end of our north drive, where it passes his house, and locking it.'

'Can he do that?'

'His house is on the site of a lodge, you see, which is what it was in LeMercier's time, but that bit of land was sold off when he was in straits, and the old lodge pulled down, and that horrible little bijou residence built.'

'But can he put a locked gate across your drive?'

'Gid's lawyer thinks he can, because that strip of land belongs to him now, though we have a right of way across it. But that may not apply to cars. It's only a footpath right of way. Anyhow Gideon says he doesn't want a lot of *schtuss*. He hates unpleasantness. So when we drive we go out the other way – it's not much further. But we climb over Venom's gate as often as we can.'

'It's a foul gate,' put in one of the twins. 'With diagonal bars. He looked for a kind that was as difficult to climb as possible. You can't help sliding down the bars. The boys just vault over.'

I supposed that any clan as close-knit and remarkable as the Morningquest family must have enemies, simply because of their cohesiveness; their very unity would attract anger and ill-will. But it seemed rather sad.

Two young males were clambering about on the stairway and inspecting it; as we came closer I saw that one was a fair-haired Morningquest brother, but I did not know which; the other was the short, dark man who had sat on Lady Morningquest's left hand and been introduced as somebody from Louisiana.

'Toby can't stay away from the stair for more than a couple of hours,' said Dolly tolerantly. 'It's his baby. Now he wants to get started on the next part.'

'Can Pandora come up and see?' she called to her brother, who was up at the top of the stair where it curved into the trees.

'Have you a head for heights?' he shouted down at me.

'Oh, yes.' In fact I adored climbing trees, and up to the age of nine or ten had almost lived in them. Even at sixteen, tree-climbing was one of my secret joys.

'All right. Hold the rail, though. Someone's broken leg would be just the ammunition old Venom is looking for.'

'Need a hand?' inquired the dark man. His accent was languid and drawling, with flat vowels. He sounded patronising; I didn't care for the way he studied me with his greenish eyes, faintly amused, wholly unimpressed. I took an instant dislike to him. What was he doing here, anyway? I wondered. Whose friend was he? Too old for the boys, too young for the adults. I supposed he might be about thirty.

'No, thanks.'

There was a tough, graceful hand-rail of curved wood. 'We moulded it in a steam-bath,' Toby explained. 'It took ages to get right. I was afraid it might warp. But it seems OK so far. Come and see what we are going to do next.'

He led on up the steps, which now rose between dangling clumps of foliage, and we arrived at a skeleton platform built into the fork of the tree that grew in the centre of the grove. This platform, at present, was formed merely of criss-cross joists, with a hand-rail round the circumference. It was an irregular shape, governed by the five branches radiating from the fork. Toby and the twins, who had followed me, at once fell into an impassioned argument about the shape of the structure, a kind of tree-palace, I gathered, which they proposed to erect on this base. Dolly, down at ground level, listened to them with a calm maternal smile. While every now and then some cynical remark was inserted by the green-eyed man, who was called Dave. I liked him less and less.

The day had turned grey and grim. From our precarious perch, twenty feet up among thick foliage, we could not see the sky, but presently cold drops of rain began to patter among the small evergreen leaves.

'Damn,' said Toby. 'I hoped there'd be time to put in a bit more work on it today. Now it will have to wait till Christmas.'

'You poor hard-working little student,' said Dave. Now there was a definite sneer in his voice.

'But, darling Toby, it's only about three weeks till the end of term,' Dolly pointed out.

A bell began to clang from the direction of the house.

'Oh God,' said Toby, 'it's nothing but meals at weekends.'

Dave, the American, ran smartly down the stair, disdaining the use of hand-rail, and made off towards the house; Toby and the twins lingered, looking yearningly up at the grove.

'Weekend meals are practically Gid's only chance to talk to us,' Dolly pointed out piously.

'Whose fault is that? He doesn't have to go trailing all over the map. He doesn't have to accept every invitation.'

'He could retire and live on his savings,' said one twin.

'But then he'd be round our necks all the time.'

'He'd probably go senile and die.'

'It's his work that keeps him alive.'

Ally and Elly laughed together like hyenas. They looked a bit like hyenas, I thought.

A small man came towards us over the grass, saying 'I am sent to hurry you.'

'Uncle Grisch, why you? Why not one of those lazy boys?'

'I elected myself. I needed the air.' He spoke English with the exquisite correctness which few natives can ever achieve. He wore carpet-slippers and, over his dungarees, a black velvet waistcoat, unbuttoned.

'Uncle Grisch, don't you think our tree-house ought to be a pavilion, like Prinny's at Brighton?' The twins attached themselves each to an arm.

He firmly removed them and came to walk at my side. 'So this pair of revolutionaries have been showing you the estate. I hope that you will return on many more visits?' he said to me with kind courtesy. I said I hoped so too.

'We'll all be here for the Christmas holidays,' graciously announced Dolly. 'And the twins break up a week before the rest of us.'

The twins gave me sharp, measuring looks.

'It is sad for me and Lulie that the family are here only at weekends,' said Uncle Grisch.

'*Har, har,*' said the twins, and one of them added, 'You know you can't wait for us to take off on Sunday evenings so you can have the place to yourselves and fraternise with old Venom.'

Ignoring them, Grisch asked me questions about my school, and my plans for university. I told him these were uncertain as I wished to study art, but my father, unfortunately, disapproved of further education for females.

'So? You are an artist?' Grisch said with what sounded like real interest.

'Uncle Grisch is a painter,' Dolly explained in her queenly manner.

The twins burst out in chorus: 'He's a *great* painter. You ought to show Pandora your stuff, Uncle G.'

'Well, well,' he said. 'She may not want to look at them.'

I said that I would love to, if he could spare the time.

'We shall see.'

'*And* he is also rewriting English literature,' injected a twin, now with a note of satire.

I would have liked to ask about this, but we had arrived back in the great kitchen.

Most of the people who had been sitting around the table were still there. With more assurance, now that I had talked to some of the family and found them neither superhuman nor especially contemptuous of me, I glanced about.

The room still seemed just as barnlike and cheerless. But, after all, it was merely the kitchen. Perhaps the rest of the house would be furnished with more attention to comfort and appearance. Later I found that this was not so; no room in Boxall Hill was provided with more than the bare minimum of tables, chairs, and beds, all of a severely utilitarian kind. Sir Gideon's plan was that his family, at weekends and holidays, should accustom themselves to the austere and comfortless surroundings of their peasant ancestors. I do not believe this was due to a streak of parsimony in his nature, or puritanism; or even that he expected adversity in the future and thought they should be prepared for it; simply, he wished them to be adaptable. I was quite startled when, later, visiting the house in Cadogan Square, I found it cosily, even sumptuously furnished with glowing colours, soft fabrics, ornaments, and articles chosen for looks rather than basic need. His family seemed to go along, unrepining, with this dichotomy, though the boys sometimes mocked it. 'But,' as Dan said, 'at least, here at Otherland, you don't have to worry about scratching the furniture.'

They called Boxall Hill Otherland; I never found out who had invented this name.

Tea was being dispensed by Tante Lulie from a massive contraption (a samovar I later learned); one could have it with slices of lemon or milk from a huge blue-and-white striped jug. 'Your mother and Mariana take theirs in the West Room; will you perhaps be so kind as to carry it to them,' she said, handing me a battered metal tray with two mugs and two ginger-biscuits. (Ginger-biscuits were the only kind ever consumed by the Morningquest family.)

'Where do I find the West Room?' I took the tray, pleased at this promotion to family status.

'Out that door and first on the right.'

A stone-flagged passage led away from the kitchen. On the right lay what had probably been a steward's or housekeeper's room; it had a brick floor, bare wooden shelves, large hooks in the ceiling, and sepia photographs of bygone laundrymaids, footmen, and gamekeepers in stiff, unsmiling groups. It was furnished now with a small folding card-table and two osier basket-chairs. My mother and Mariana Morningquest were seated here, talking in low affectionate tones; both looked up amiably at my entrance, but I could see that I was not expected to linger in the room a moment longer than was necessary.

'Tante Lulie says, come back soon for the singing.'

'We will, we will! But I so seldom get a chance for a good gossip with your mother.' Mariana gave me a smile that seemed created expressly for me and for nobody else. Her smiles were *ravishing*; they completely dissipated the slightly formidable, nutcracker quality of her face. It became suddenly radiant, refulgent.

I beamed back, thinking, what a pity her daughters had not inherited this beauty. Perhaps there was a trace of it in Selene? She, so far, had studiously ignored me. She seemed to talk only to Toby.

In the kitchen, the rest of the party were chomping ginger-nuts (I noticed Barnabas crunch up five in quick succession) and talking about disarmament, Cuba, reconnaissance flights of U2s and inspection zones. Since my father was antagonistic to any discussion of this kind, especially at mealtimes (his views on political matters were deeply entrenched and unshakable), I sat silent, as at home, but quietly fished out the little sketch-pad I carried in my jeans pocket at all times and began making notes of faces in it.

'But we are boring our newest visitor,' said Sir Gideon suddenly, sending me a smile from the far end of the table. I blushed, feeling I had been caught out in a breach of manners. Sir Gideon's smile was quite different from that of his wife: it had a sweet, benign quality (rather like that of Sir Malcolm Muggeridge), but I felt it was a public smile, suitable for all occasions. There was nothing in it for me personally.

'No, no, I'm not bored, not at *all*,' I protested fervently. 'It's just that I don't *know* much about inspection zones. And I like to draw faces and don't often get such a lot of new ones.'

'Inspection zones can wait their turn,' said Sir Gideon. 'What we want now is to hear you sing the Siamese national anthem.'

'I'm sorry – I don't understand.'

A bored, pitying expression, I noticed, had closed down over the faces of Dolly and the twins. Selene looked faintly nervous, Tante Lulie impatient, while the boys were simply waiting with resignation for the business to be over. Uncle Grisch gave me a nod and shrug.

'It's a small test of their vocal chords that all our guests have to undergo,' Sir Gideon went on genially, scribbling in a pocket notebook about the same size as mine, on a page which he then proceeded to tear out and despatch in my direction.

One of the twins passed me the square of paper together with a vigorous wink. (It is odd how some people are unable to wink without a convulsion of the whole face.) I thought again, as I had in the ilex grove, what a very strong likeness they bore to the grinning stone heads that peer down from cathedral cornices. How could beautiful Mariana have given birth to such a plain pair? Did she mind?

The writing on the paper in my hand was unintelligible. OH WA TA NA SIAM. I looked up, puzzled.

'You must sing it,' Sir Gideon instructed me. 'To the tune of God Save the Queen. Sing it to us, nice and loud.'

'*Now?*'

'Sing!' the whole family chorused, and so, seeing no help for it, I chanted out the words as boldly as possible. And of course they all fell about laughing.

'Oh, what an ass you are!'

I felt myself grow scarlet again, and wished that the stone-slabbed floor would open and swallow me.

'*Schon genug*, that's quite enough,' scolded Tante Lulie impatiently. 'Who is for more tea? Gideon, you must leave in one hour's time. Why not start the singing now? We should be sad to miss that. Selene – go and fetch your mother and Mrs Crumbe.'

'You sang very well – very well indeed!' Sir Gideon called to me kindly and reassuringly down the table. 'Don't take it amiss, we have these little rites of passage; we always tease our guests. You are by no means the first. But your voice is better than most.'

'Gid is really a pain in the gut,' one of the twins hissed at me. '*All* his jokes are a hundred years old.'

But I thought the twins had laughed as loud as any.

Mariana and my mother came back into the kitchen and resumed their places at the table. Sir Gideon glanced round the group and said quietly, 'The Georg Christoph. *Siehe, wie fein*. Mariana, my love, give us a note.'

Mariana gave one, very pure and clear.

I glanced at my mother. She seemed expectant, but vague, as if trying to remember some obscure item for a shopping list. She was still excessively pale.

The Morningquests started to sing.

Whatever one might think, or come to think of them, as a group, about their singing there could be no adverse opinion. Listening to any of their Sunday song sessions – and in course of time I listened to many – has always ranked among the best experiences of my life; not only because of the sheer quality of the sound they created, but also from the strange exhilaration of knowing that such an oddly variegated group of people was capable of producing such unity, such harmony. I sat in a transport of pleasure and astonishment, but had enough attention to notice that Tante Lulie sang with them in a thin, true thread of voice; that Uncle Grisch did not sing, but listened hard, his black eyes very heedful; that Dave from Louisiana did not sing, and looked bored. Dolly took an alto part, the other girls were soprano; two of the boys were tenors and one, Dan perhaps, a counter-tenor. Sir Gideon conducted with a breadknife, singing loudly himself as he did so. Luke Rose, his friend, had a powerful bass.

When they reached the conclusion, Sir Gideon glanced at his watch and said briskly, 'That must be all for today. I have to set off in twelve minutes, *no later*. Who is riding in my car?'

And that was the moment at which my mother gave a curious little sighing moan, and leaned forward until her head rested on the table. A thread of blood trickled from her mouth.

II

The sudden death of my mother from heartfailure in the kitchen at Boxall Hill had, for me, momentous and far-reaching consequences.

My father's anger was one of the first and most noticeable. In fact it took him years to get over the event.

'If she felt off-colour, why the deuce did she have to go out?' he kept demanding. 'Why couldn't she stay at home and let it happen there? Instead of subjecting us to all this ghastly publicity? What was she *doing* there? At Boxall Hill? Anyway?'

The fact that I was there too only added fuel to his indignation and helped to push forward the whole subsequent train of events.

'Suppose I'd come home that night? And found nobody in the house? Both of you missing? What would I have thought?'

'I don't know what you would have thought, Father. But the point is, you weren't at home.'

He had been away, out of touch, unobtainable, at a weekend conference on Swine Fever, in Skegness. He had said, previously, that he might be home on Sunday evening, or he might not; therefore, it was no particular surprise to me that there was no reply when, that Sunday evening, Mariana rang my home number.

'Well,' she said, 'you most certainly cannot return to an empty house. In any case I think it better, much better, that you spend the night here with Lulie and Grisch.'

The flashing ambulance, the doctor, the kind, caring, concerned people had all come and gone. Sir Gideon, with overpowering, exquisite sympathy, had made a whole variety of statements which I had not at all taken in, had kissed my hand, then my cheek, and had swept himself away, exuding self-reproach, at great speed. 'One thousand, thousand apologies, my dear child, but I fly to Tangier at six a.m. tomorrow with the Parnassus Ensemble. So very, *very* sorry to leave you thus; but Mariana will look after you, and we shall help you in every way that lies within our power.'

He vanished down the drive in his huge car, taking most of the family with him. But some went with Barnabas, who had his own Volkswagen. And Dan went on a motorbike. Mariana, too, had her own car, a Peugeot, but she remained until after midnight, sitting, condoling, discussing, helping to ease me through the unbelievable shock of sudden death.

28

Lulie and Grisch were there too. We had moved to Lulie's room, which was a total contrast to the rest of the house. For a start, it was warm, with a delicious hot scent of paraffin, since she kept an oil radiator burning there, night and day, during eight months of the year. Furthermore the room was lined, layered, packed with her own possessions, so that it resembled some sea-cave of treasure, or a dragon's lair, with shawls, patchworks and tapestries dangling, mats piled on carpets, cushions in every corner, sequins winking in dim lamplight, countless little stools waiting to trip the unwary foot. Every chair and couch was draped with brocade or cashmere, every shelf and table dense with boxes, framed photos, and bits of jewellery that needed mending.

Grisch kept me topped up with powerful coffee and armagnac. At the moment of my mother's collapse I had discovered that these were the contents of the two little pots in front of Grisch on the table, for he had leapt up, faster than anybody else in the room, and brought both to administer to Mother; finding this impracticable, he had insisted on giving me a slug of armagnac which supplied me with just enough command to see me through the ensuing hours.

'You have to remember, you have to understand,' said Mariana later that night, not once, but over and over, 'that your mother died, probably, at a moment of great happiness. To listen to music was one of her supreme pleasures.'

Was it? I had never known this about my mother.

'Therefore, what a very blessed way in which to go! We could all ask for ourselves such an end.'

'Fortunate lady,' agreed Grisch. 'And we can guess that your mother may, for the last months, have been feeling very unwell, very anxious about your future. The doctor said it was a massive heart attack. She must have expected such an event, feared it. Now she has these cares no longer.'

With a pang of guilt, I supposed this was so. It was true that lately she had looked haggard, she had looked preoccupied ... For my part, I had simply assumed that Father was being more of a trial than usual. But she had married him, hadn't she? She knew what she was doing when she took him on.

'It is for your poor Papa that we must feel sympathy,' Tante Lulie remarked in a detached tone.

'Oh,' I said. 'Well. Not too much. They didn't – they hadn't really much to say to one another. She gave up talking to him long ago, because he never answers.'

'He may, nonetheless, miss her quite severely. Her cuisine, perhaps? Her housekeeping? Especially after you go off to college.'

I mumbled something to the effect that this was by no means a strong probability, even if I succeeded in getting a place, as my father was quite capable of vetoing the project. He might easily insist on my remaining at home to housekeep for him.

'No, no,' said Mariana serenely. 'Of this, we shall take care. We hope that when Dolly enters St Vigeans University, your father may agree for you to go there too; we, my husband and I, are very happy to help with any problems and expenses. It will be a comfort for Dolly to have a friend when she goes for the first time so far away from her family – right up in the north of Scotland! And for you, too, we hope it will be a comfort to be with somebody that you know a little.'

'Oh, but – my goodness! I didn't – I hadn't— '

'This very plan I am discussing with your mother over tea. And I think she liked the idea.'

'She would, of course – she went to a Scottish university herself – it's so *kind* of you,' I stammered. 'But how do you know – suppose I don't get a place— '

'Not much doubt of that.' Mariana smiled her forked-lightning smile. 'We hear that you are Claud Rigby's pride and joy.' Rigby was my headmaster. 'And there is a very excellent Art School at St Vigeans. We have heard fine things about its Principal. He is a Czech. And Grisch has stolen a peep at your little book of portraits which was on the kitchen table.'

'You have a sharp eye, young lady,' said Uncle Grisch calmly. 'A sharp eye and a good line. I see that already you have noticed this distinguishing difference between the twins ... And Daniel's unaligned tooth ...'

'He is going to have it straightened,' said Mariana absently. Something about this remark had not pleased her. Did she feel proprietorial about the twins – that she ought to be the only person who knew the difference between them? Or was it Daniel's tooth? My mind wandered to the extraordinary prospect of university life in Scotland, in the company of Dolly Morningquest. But did Dolly really need such a back-up escort from home? She seemed so much more mature than I was. Dolly so maternal, so self-possessed, so imbued with condescension and confidence, so tolerant, so gracious? Was this merely a kindly pretext for my benefit, on the part of her mother?

Had that conversation really taken place?

'The child is dead tired and must go to bed,' pronounced Tante Lulie. 'And you, Mariana, should be off. You have a meeting at the Menuhin School tomorrow at nine-thirty.'

'So I have.'

'There is a flask of coffee and sandwiches already placed in your car. And Grisch has taken out your bag.'

'Life without you two would be insupportable,' said Mariana. She hugged them both warmly, and then embraced me – a lightning, tingling, fragrant contact. 'Dear girl, grieve for your mother, but worry about *nothing*. We shall take care of you. I shall phone your father tomorrow. And of course Gideon and I will come to the funeral – whenever it is – Lulie will keep us posted about that.'

We accompanied her to the back door. At some point she had changed from her grey wrapper into a 'little' black velvet suit that seemed moulded to her thin shape. Two enormous moonstones shone in her ears.

Dave, the young American, came yawning from the hammocky sofa of the ping-pong room to accompany her. I was rather startled at the sight of him, not having known he was still in the house; I assumed he had gone off with Barnabas, long since.

But Mariana said, 'Ah, there you are, Dave,' comfortably.

Perhaps he was her chauffeur? But no, he lit a cigarette while she herself got into the driver's seat.

'Straight to bed now,' she called to me, and the car murmured off into the dark.

'I have placed a hot-water bottle in Dolly's bed,' said Tante Lulie.

Dolly's room, on the first floor, shared as well, when they were at Boxall Hill, by Selene and the twins, had all the comfort of a dormitory in a workhouse: bare wooden floor, four iron bedsteads with white cotton spreads, two unpainted wooden chests-of-drawers, four cane-seated chairs. Four hooks on the wall. Enormous, uncurtained windows, sheets of black glass, looking north over the beechwoods. In the distance I could hear pheasants cranking themselves up, the shriek of a vixen, the far-off whinny of an owl. This was much further into real country than our place on the edge of town.

'Goodnight, my dear,' said Tante Lulie from the door. 'Think only of your mother that she has now no more to trouble her. I will leave this candle and you will blow it out when you are ready.'

I knew that electricity at Boxall Hill was supplied by a generator, which Uncle Grisch had switched off at some point during the preceding hours. 'Goodnight, and thank you so much for all your kindness.'

'*Gornischt, gornischt,*' she said. 'Sleep well now, *bubeleh.*'

I crept into the hammocky nest, glowing warm from the bottle, but with a thin lumpy mattress and light, scanty coverings. Well, I could always borrow blankets from the other three beds . . . I slept.

*

The next day was dreadful, of course.

When my father arrived back from Skegness, at midday, irritable already because of troublesome traffic, he flew into a surly rage.

'Dead, *dead*? How do you mean, dead? How can she be dead?'

I had just returned from filling out forms at the doctor's. Grisch had very kindly driven me there, then brought me on to our house, talking all the way in a rambling, inconsequential, instructive monologue as he guided his ancient Minor through the streets of Floxby. I had felt boundless gratitude to him. All night long, even through my sleep, one prospect had weighed on me painfully: the thought of walking back down the sloping field, over the stile, through the little wood, on my own – without Mother. But, of course, in his car, we went decorously along the drive, and down the lane.

'Who's that?' barked my father, just arrived home, glaring at Grisch. I explained.

'Ho. One of the Morningquest's pansy wops.'

Grisch bowed, in polite silence.

'Dr Skinner wants to see you as soon as possible, Father,' I said hurriedly. 'And Pengellys want you to call them about arrangements for the funeral. And ought we to put a notice in the paper? And, if so, which paper? And Mr Martindale rang up to ask if Mother had left a Will. I didn't know.'

My father looked beleaguered. 'Look, how can I possibly – I'm very *busy*, can't you see that? I've got all kinds of things to do at the practice – you can't expect— '

News had of course travelled as fast as thistledown blowing on the wind. Already neighbours were tapping at both doors with pies and quiches, and offers of help.

Grisch said peacefully, 'If it would be of any use, Lulie and I could put the notice in the paper for you. We are well used to such routines. For many years we have handled all Gideon's publicity.' My father gave him a glance of scornful dislike which he ignored. He went on in the same comfortable tone, 'And if you care to give me a list of addresses, we could also inform people – relatives – there are always so many who have hurt feelings if they are not told.'

My father growled, 'Dunno what good getting a note from *you* would do 'em. Anyway, there's nobody. M'wife had no relatives. None.'

This was true. It seemed that my mother had always been a loner, perhaps from force of circumstance, perhaps from choice. I knew nothing about her parents who, left behind somewhere in eastern Europe, had died before she was twelve. She had spent her early years in Geneva, at school.

After her parents' death a cousin of her mother's, a surgeon in Scotland, had adopted her, and she had crossed the Channel and grown up in his house in Edinburgh, attending school and then going on to university there. But Cousin Mark, a bachelor, had contracted hepatitis and died when she was not much more than my age.

Apart from these meagre facts I knew remarkably little about my mother's life before she married my father, which she had done soon after taking her degree. She was a woman who never, ever, talked about herself, who apparently found it impossible to believe that any other person could be interested in her affairs.

When I came to dispose of her personal belongings, I realised for the first time their Spartan scarcity. Three or four dresses in plain, unobtrusive colours. Three or four pairs of shoes: outdoor, indoor, slippers. A coat, a raincoat. A drawer of scarves and cardigans, a drawer of underwear, neatly folded. A few belts, a flask of cheap eau de Cologne, some plain talcum powder. A Bible, a one-volume Shakespeare in tiny print, with her name on the flyleaf in youthful handwriting. Racine, Goethe, Sophocles, clasped between a pair of stone bookends.

My father had a cubbyhole of his own, his office, where he transacted veterinary practice left over from the surgery, or read *The Countryman* and the *Milk Producers' Weekly Bulletin and Cowkeepers' Guide*. But my mother had not even a desk of her own; when she transcribed the minutes of her various local committees she opened up her flimsy little Empire portable typewriter on the dining-room table, and she kept all her papers in an old cowhide suitcase which lived under the bed in the spare room. She had accumulated none of the clutter that follows me wherever I go: letters, answered or unanswered, books, clips torn from newspapers, maps, magazines, dried flowers, photographs, sketchbooks, portfolios, rolls of canvas, stretchers, broken necklaces. She could have been a nun, or a prisoner in a cell. Half an hour sufficed to parcel up her residue – her whole life – and pack it away for Oxfam. The room she had shared with my father was now his alone, and there seemed hardly any change in it. I asked if he would like her twin bed removed, and he said it might as well stay; he could throw his clothes down on it; had done so already, in fact.

I began to think of Mother as one of those canny redskins in Westerns, who elaborately obliterate their footprints by sweeping behind them with an armful of twigs; she seemed to have that sort of skill in abolishing her tracks. On purpose? I wondered. As if in atonement for something?

It would be no use asking my father about their first meeting, courtship, marriage. That would be to invite a slashing rebuff. I did vaguely know that the original encounter had been in Scotland while he had been up in those parts collecting information about cattle disease on some offshore island, and he, apparently, had been impressed by her prowess on the golf course.

'You have to play golf in Scotland in order to stay alive,' Mother had once remarked to me.

They got married in Edinburgh and then he returned to his job in the South and she gave up whatever she had been doing and accompanied him. That was seventeen years ago. She seemed to retain no friends of her own from earlier times. And made very few in Floxby Crucis.

'She was a very private kind of person, your mother,' remarked Uncle Grisch.

Since my father seemed to have no particular use for me at home, after dealing with Mother's personal belongings I returned to Boxall Hill to help Grisch pick a late apple crop. This, he suggested, would stop me moping, and also be a help to him. 'Lulie is growing too arthritic. And gales are forecast for the weekend.'

'How did Mariana come to know my mother so well? I was hardly aware that they were even acquainted,' I asked him as we worked.

'They met on a committee for the Music Festival. And then discovered, I believe, that they had areas of background in common. You will have to ask Mariana.'

'I'd like to. Very much.' I was longing for another glimpse of Mariana. Her smile, her voice, her flint-like beauty shone in my mind like a lighthouse ray. She had sent a message that she, and perhaps some of the children, would be down for the funeral. Sir Gideon, still in Tangier, would make it if he possibly could . . .

The orchard at Boxall Hill was a sloping field running up the height of land behind the house; it commanded a wide, windy view. The apples were hard yellow russets.

'Too sour yet,' said Grisch, taking a bite from a bruised windfall. 'They will be sweet later. We could have left them on the trees another week, but they would all blow down in the bad weather that is to come. Then they would soon rot.'

We were picking into large grey canvas buckets, then transferring the crop to open crates. Every now and then Garnet, the wizened, one-eyed man who helped on the estate, would drive round the perimeter in a battered farm truck and collect the boxes we had filled.

'Some to keep, some to sell,' Grisch explained. 'Mariana arranges all that. She is an excellent administrator. When Gideon bought this place, he had a romantic notion of it as a rural hideout. But Mariana makes it pay for itself.'

He chatted on, as we worked, keeping up a pleasant, rambling monologue, for which I was immensely grateful. I was still in deep shock, unable to reconcile the huge painful gap in my own life with the almost invisible crack that Mother had filled.

A lark twittered above us.

'Hail, ecstatic presence,' said Grisch unexpectedly. 'Never feathered friend, That of Heaven's essence, Spares enough to lend, A noble draught for us, of music without end!'

'I beg your pardon?' I said, startled. The subject, the metre, sounded familiar, and yet . . .

'Shelley's *Ode to a Skylark*,' said Grisch complacently. 'Terrible, terrible stuff. "Hail to thee, blithe Spirit, bird thou never wert. " *Mawkish*. I rewrite all, in better language. It is one of my evening occupations. Slowly, by degrees, I work my way through the whole of English literature.'

I recalled the twins mentioning this. Grisch, they had said, lived over the stables, part of which had been converted to a flat and a studio for him, where he wrote, painted, and composed.

'Tell me some others that you have done.'

'I leaned upon an orchard gate, when frost was ghostly grey . . . The frozen brambles crossed the sky, like strings of broken cellos, And all the folk who lived nearby, Were blowing on their bellows.'

'No, no, that won't do,' I said firmly. 'That won't do *at all*.'

'No?' he said, disappointed. 'Well, I am still working on that one. But cleaned up it must be. The theme of the poem, the aged articulate thrush, is beautiful and touching: "Some blessed Hope, whereof he knew, And I was unaware." But the language! Where does Hardy get these grisly, pretentious words – *bine-stems*, *illimited*, *fervourless*? He must have used a dictionary of archaisms. "All mankind that haunted nigh!" I *ask* you.'

From a discussion of language, we moved naturally on to the twins.

'Mariana has plans for them to study philosophy at Heidelberg as soon as they are old enough to go off on their own.'

'Do they like the idea?' I inquired cautiously.

'Oh yes, argument is their favourite sport. And they are never going to win any beauty competitions,' said Grisch, his black eyes reflective, 'so they may as well sharpen up their other faculties.'

This, I felt, was rather a male chauvinist attitude, but I lacked confidence to say so; after all, I scarcely knew these people.

'And Gideon will be glad to have them away,' Grisch went on. 'He finds them exasperating.'

'Their own father!'

He shrugged. Unacknowledged between us, I supposed, lay the fact that my father visibly found me exasperating and would no doubt be relieved enough if some respectable means could rid him of my presence at no cost to himself.

Tante Lulie brought us mugs of cider. 'Good, *noch?* We make it ourselves from the windfalls.'

It was very good; stronger, less sweet than commercial cider.

'I have been thinking, *bubbe*,' she said to me, 'about your mother's funeral. Have you a dress to wear?'

I had been thinking about this also. Worrying. The only possible garment I had was a grey school pinafore dress, unworn for the past year since I had been elevated to the sixth form and consequent exemption from wearing uniform. By now it was probably too tight and too short. And the only clothes shop in Floxby catered to customers in their fifties and sixties who were looking for pleated crimplene and floral house dresses.

'There was material left over last Christmas when the children had a theatre and acted a play in the ping-pong room,' recalled Tante Lulie.

Instantly I thought of *Mansfield Park* and 'Lovers' Vows'. 'What was the play?'

'*Twelfth Night*,' said Grisch. 'The twins took the parts of Viola and Sebastian. It was quite one of the most amusing productions of *Twelfth Night* that I have ever seen,' he added after some thought.

'The costumes were all black and white, doublets and ruffs, farthingales and petticoats, shirts and tights. There is plenty of the material left. Black bombazine. I will make you a dress.'

'Oh, but that's a lot of—'

'I like to make dresses,' said Tante Lulie placidly. 'All Mariana's clothes I make for her, and she is the best-dressed woman in the West End of London.'

Not only was this true, but also, I subsequently discovered, Tante Lulie's materials were invariably acquired at second-hand shops and furniture auctions. She kept a gimlet eye on all the Cancer Concern, Oxfam and Nearly New shops for miles around, scanned the local furniture sales, and made shrewd purchases of old curtain materials, brocades, felt, velours, velveteen, baize, tapestry, and cotton bedspreads. '*Es kommt a mohl zu nützen* – it'll come in useful for something,' was one of her most frequently used phrases. From these troves, Mariana's stunning wardrobe was put together, at a cost of about twenty pounds a year. Not counting Tante Lulie's time, of course.

'I would make for the girls, too, but they are not interested,' Tante Lulie told me, scooting her scissors across thin black woollen material. ('Somebody's blackout from World War II, no doubt.') 'The twins, maybe I will dress some day, they have the instinct for elegance.'

'The *twins?*'

'Yes. You will see. By and by. But Dolly, just at present, is puritan to the backbone. She does not think it right to plan her everyday clothes to please the eye. Only for special occasions will she take trouble. And Selene – who can tell what is in the mind of that one?'

'Tell me more about the twins,' I said, putting away pins.

I had an idea of the Morningquest family as a lofty citadel perched up on a crag, with dangerous access and impregnable walls. The males, I assumed, were wholly above my reach, lost to me in distant university realms of music and science, no doubt with swan-like London girlfriends. The plan to send me and Dolly to St Vigeans together could not be one to take very seriously; I foresaw any number of obstacles. And if we did arrive there at the same time it seemed plain to me that she would go her way in circles far distant from mine; Dolly had been kindly and gracious to me, but I guessed that was her usual means of keeping the rude rough world at arm's length. I did not expect to become her friend. While Selene, as Tante Lulie had said, appeared to live in a universe of her own. She had not even looked at me yet.

No: if I was to burrow my way through the outer defences of the Morningquest clan, it must be by way of the twins. I was not greatly attracted by the prospect, but they were definitely the most approachable of the group.

'Oh, the twins?' said Tante Lulie. 'When they were smaller, a real pair of *nudniks*. Always complaining, always sick.' She sighed. 'Not their fault, perhaps. Mariana didn't have much time for them. Their birth spoiled a Far Eastern operatic engagement. And Gideon has never— ' She stopped, knotted a thread, and said, 'Come, try on this *schmatte*.'

We tried it. It was a perfect fit. For years afterwards I wore Tante Lulie's bombazine dress to parties, to concerts, interviews, oral examinations, openings, all formal occasions and plenty of informal ones. I never had a garment I loved better. And when the day of Mother's funeral arrived, the knowledge that my appearance, at least, was unexceptionable made a profound difference to me. Otherwise, really, the occasion would have been unbearable.

Father, of course, had kicked up a terrific fuss beforehand. 'What's the point of all this?' he kept asking. 'Who cares what happens to a person when she's dead? When *I'm* gone, I hope you'll just shovel me underground the quickest and cheapest way possible.'

He gave me a belligerent look. I would dearly have liked to retort that my personal inclination would be simply to deposit his remains on the compost heap; but I managed to restrain the impulse. In fact my feelings about funerals closely matched his. I hated the social ordinance that my private grief for Mother must be swamped by a great public ceremony. But I was given no choice in the matter as I rapidly discovered. The Townswomen's Guild, The Ladies' Choir, the International Friendship Association, the Town Twinning Committee, the Boy Scouts, the Girl Guides, and various other bodies, were all anxious to play a part, and the piles of wreaths and enormous bouquets that arrived, both at our house and at Pengellys' Chapel of Rest, were extremely daunting. It was going to take me at least a week to acknowledge them all. I knew that Father would be no help.

Mother's funeral was held on Saturday, in order to allow all the people who wished to attend it to do so; and by then the promised rain and gales had arrived with ferocious force. A force-eight wind whipped around the shins of the mourners and blew their umbrellas inside out as they scurried up to the church, and the Reverend Willis' eulogies were almost drowned by the moaning and keening of the blast outside. I had thought – hoped – that not many people would brave it to the cemetery, but a great many did nonetheless, and stood clutching their hats and ballooning mackintoshes while the grave filled with water and the floral tributes were dashed to soaking shreds. Mother, who relished almost any kind of weather, would have enjoyed the occasion thoroughly, I thought.

As it had become plain that our small house would be hopelessly inadequate to entertain the numbers who had to be catered for – some of whom had travelled half-way across the county – a buffet lunch at The George Hotel had been organised by the Floxby Orpheus choir. So to The George we all repaired, and its cramped Ladies' Cloakroom was jammed with sodden matrons scrubbing their stockings, combing their maltreated coiffures, and dabbing frenziedly with tissues. Mariana, very sensibly, had skipped the grave-side and was in better case than the rest, elegant as always.

'This will be the worst, the very worst part for you, my poor darling,' she told me. 'Just keep remembering that,' and I did, and she was right. Dolly was there with her, and Lulie and Grisch; none of the others. Why should they trouble? They had met my mother only once. It seemed to me the height of kindness that Mariana had made the effort, and that Gideon had telephoned a message. And, of course, Mariana's presence made the occasion for many citizens of Floxby Crucis. They were all dying to have a word with her.

Father was the centre of another cluster of guests, and so was I.

A buffet lunch of cold ham and quiche and The George's terrible Orange Trifle had been laid out on a long table, but I never succeeded in getting anywhere near the food, and could not have eaten it if I had. People continually surged at me, squeezed, patted, told me what a wonderful person my mother had been, how lonely it was going to be for my father now, and what was I planning to do?

Over and over I said I was not certain, hoped to go to university, would have to wait and see.

Over and over I was told that my place, now, was to stay with my poor father, he would be so lost without Elaine. (That was what most people called her.) By the time that weak Nescafé was being poured, and people were starting to find their umbrellas and take their departure, the vision of St Vigeans – so unknown, so challenging, but above all so far off, hundreds of miles away in the North of Scotland – glimmered and beckoned like a beautiful mirage. I found myself beginning to reply to people, 'I'm hoping to go to St Vigeans University, it's in Scotland.' I was startled to find myself saying it to my own headmaster, Claud Rigby, who looked even more startled, but said heartily, 'An excellent idea,' before patting my shoulder and moving on.

'Scotland?' remarked a bearded man, whom I had vaguely noticed moving in my direction for the last few minutes, as the crowd filtered towards the door. Now he stood beside me. 'Was that your mother's wish?' he asked.

Did he have a slight Scottish accent? Perhaps. He was nobody I knew. Glancing around anxiously for Mariana who, I could see, was on the point of departure, wishing I could leave with her, knowing I must not, I paid little heed to this stranger, but answered him carelessly, 'Yes, I think Mother thought that it might be a good idea.'

'I was your mother's first husband, you know,' said the bearded man. And then he was carried away from me by a sudden swirl of the crowd, and I lost sight of him.

But his words cleft my mind like a lightning stroke. 'Wait!' I called. 'Please wait! *Hey!*'

But he was gone.

I began searching about for him, eagerly, desperately; saw him at length in the doorway, made for it myself, but was intercepted several times on the way; glimpsed him over the banister, down at the foot of the stair, and then he vanished through the street door.

Jeffrey Martindale, Father's lawyer, was saying to me, 'Would this be a good time, Pandora, to have a word with you?' and a couple of ladies behind him were waiting politely but eagerly to tell me how much they would miss my dear mother.

The bearded man had disappeared. I had never laid eyes on him before, I was quite certain of that. But his brief announcement had an impact that went on affecting me for years, all my life really.

I made a drawing of him that evening from memory, and showed it to Lulie and Grisch. Grisch said he recalled having seen the man talking to me.

III

The twins arrived for the Christmas holidays in a disgruntled frame of mind.

'Why have you two come home a fortnight early?'

Mariana was not giving them her full attention. She always had a huge pile of mail at breakfast, charitable appeals, requests for talks or recitals, and fan letters which even after fifteen years of semi-retirement continued to pour in. With the help of a secretary she liked to have all this despatched and out of the way by nine a.m.

'Inhuman practices,' mumbled Elly through lumps of marmalade.

'*What?*'

'Not practices, practising,' corrected Ally. 'We've been working on the Bach double violin. They didn't like it.'

'*When* were you doing it?'

'Four a.m. It's the only time in that place when you don't get a whole stream of background noise.'

The twins attended the progressive school of St Monica's, Mildenhall, as weekly boarders. It seemed likely that St Monica's was about to follow the example of the half dozen or so similar establishments which had borne with them for a period and then lost patience. One of their less desirable traits was the fact that they required less than four hours' sleep a night.

'There's a letter for you in the post from Fergus McQuitcham,' said Elly, spreading more marmalade. 'It explains why they don't want us back.'

'I don't doubt it. Well,' said Mariana, blocking her mail together into a neat stack, 'for the moment you had better go down to Otherland. Lulie and Grisch will find plenty for you to do there. And you can be company for that poor girl. They are seeing a lot of her. I understand that her father is giving her a hard time at home.'

'Poor girl?'

'Pandora Crumbe.'

'Oh. Ah.'

The twins consulted with one another non-verbally. Their closed mouths were stretched over the protruding teeth like skins of fruit about to burst. Their eyes were bright with unspoken plans.

'Now then, you two!' admonished Dolly, taking a tray of dishes to the serving hatch (in London the family life style extended to servants, but the young were expected to do their share), 'don't *you* go giving Pandora a hard time, as well as her father. She's got no family at all, remember; while we've all got each other.'

'So we have,' remarked Ally pensively.

'*So* we have,' echoed her twin.

'We won't give her a hard time, Doll. On the contrary.'

'*Au contraire. Gegenteil. Helemaal niet. Nada. Nient'affato.* We'll make her *welcome.*'

Friday was always a busy day for Dolly. She had her fencing, her choir practice, her cello lesson, and coaching for the university entrance English papers (English was a subject in which she took little interest, and some added attention in this area had been thought advisable by the headmistress of the superior London day school she attended). With a mind concentrated on this programme, and a meeting of the school prefects' committee, she paid less than her usual heed to her younger sisters.

'Just don't make her *un*welcome, that's all,' she said, gathering up her music.

'I'll get Miss Halkett to telephone Grisch and say that you'll be on the eleven-o-seven,' said Mariana, doing likewise.

'So here we are, all ready to help you trim the maze,' the twins told Grischa, when he met them at Floxby Crucis.

'Oh; thank you, my dears, but in fact Pandora has helped me do that already,' he absently replied, manoeuvring the aged Minor down the right-angled hill from the station. 'But I don't doubt you have many other modes of employing your time – the double concerto, your Chinese studies, the tapestry . . . '

When not engaged intellectually, the twins worked on an immense wall-hanging, which was kept suspended in the disused ballroom at Boxall Hill, the only space large enough to house it. No one had dared inquire to what use it would be put when completed.

'Oh; so Pandora's been helping you, has she?'

'Kind, helpful Pandora.'

Grisch maintained a diplomatic silence while coaxing the car up the steep lane towards the South Lodge.

'Wasn't that Thelma Venom?' remarked Elly as they passed a dejected-looking female figure walking a large grey poodle.

'I gather that Thelma is visiting her parents, yes.'

'Wonder why?'

'Filial devotion, perhaps?' Grisch pulled up in the stable yard.

'With those parents? Not likely.'

'Maybe she came to grief in what she was doing,' suggested Elly. 'What was it?'

'A social service course?'

'*Social service*!' The twins had no time for those who engaged in such activities, arguing that this must denote a lack of individual purpose and inner resources. Work in such a field was deemed by them the most degraded possible form of human activity.

'I'm afraid she may want to see Dolly,' said Grisch neutrally.

'Ah yes. Wasn't she one of Dolly's dotes, a couple of years back?'

'Didn't last long,' said the other twin, lugging her violin and duffel bag from the boot. 'Where's Tante Lulie? We'll help her with lunch.'

'*Tut mir nicht kain teuves*, don't do me any favours,' said Tante Lulie, appearing at the back door and hugging the twins with a nicely balanced blend of affection and tolerance. 'So! We have you for an extra two weeks. That is very nice. If unexpected.'

After lunch (it was tacitly understood by the Morningquest children that if they visited Boxall Hill without their parents, the Shredded Wheat regime gave way to the preferred diet of Lulie and Grisch – vegetable soup, yoghurt, and apple cake), the twins went out to scoop sodden willow leaves from the surface of the pond.

'Where, by the way, is dear Pandora?' inquired Ally, detaining Grisch as he made off towards his studio.

'Oh, she has gone for an interview. In Scotland. She will not be back until tomorrow.'

'Ah, has she so? How very nice it will be for Dolly if Pandora gets a place at St Vigeans,' remarked Elly blandly, and then the twins went off to ransack the miscellaneous shed where dredging nets and long rakes were stored. They put on waders and canvas trousers.

Tidying the pond for the winter was, in fact, just the kind of messy task they enjoyed while conducting one of their long unheated arguments – arguments which lasted sometimes for weeks, or months.

This one was about Sir Gawain and the Green Knight. It had been going on since October. Structuralism. Good and evil. Levi-Strauss. Winter and Summer.

'It is just like double-entry book-keeping,' said Ally patiently. 'What you put on one side, you have to put on the other side also. Then it adds up.'

'Hold it, what's with the sheep?' Tante Lulie had an arrangement with Silkin, the neighbouring farmer who rented the grazing. He kept

Highland sheep, and she bought the wool from him for her weaving co-operative.

They were all pouring in a manic rush towards the pond. The patter of their feet on the grassy hillside above was like the drumming of giant hailstones. They were bumping each other and bleating loudly in evident terror. And above the bleating could be heard a dog's bark – shrill, snarling, furious.

'Oh, Jesusgod – look at that!'

Most of the sheep had managed to get away, had circled the pond, and were panicking up the opposite slope, and out of sight over the skyline. But one had been behind the others and was on its back, crying out in a high whimper that was horribly close to the wail of a human infant. Something – another animal, grey and furry, nowhere near as large as the sheep itself – had struck like a javelin, thrusting, boring, and savaging. The sheep screamed in agony.

'It's a bloody *dog*!'

'That beast of Venom's! Knock it off with a rake!'

It was not an easy process for the twins, weighed down by their heavy boots, to hoist themselves from the steep slimy verge of the pond and go to the rescue of the struggling sheep. By the time they had done so, two more people had arrived, one well ahead of the other. A young woman in Wellingtons, grey flannel skirt, waterproof jacket. And an older woman in a long grey coat, black hat, and plastic overshoes, who cried out shrilly, 'Jumps! Jumpsie! Jumpsie! Heel, boy, *heel*!'

'Heel, my foot!' growled Elly, belabouring the poodle with her long wooden rake. It broke away, snarling, whining with unappeased excitement, then abandoned the stricken sheep, and made off up the hillside after the rest of the flock.

'What the *devil* do you think you are doing, letting your goddamn dog go for Mr Silkin's sheep?' demanded Elly, lowering her dripping rake.

But the two women, taking no notice of her, turned wildly on each other.

'You utter fool, Mother! Why don't you keep the wretched dog under proper control?'

'I like that! I really like that! Who saddled me with the dog in the first place? Did I ever ask for a dog? Did I? You know your father never takes the least— '

'The dog was perfectly well trained when I left it with you last spring. If you only— '

'How can I be expected to take a dog out three times a day?'

'If it was properly exercised . . . '

44

The twins exchanged looks and shrugs. A shot on the hillside above made them spin round and stare upward. The shot was followed by a dog's yelp.

'Oh, no!' cried the older woman. 'If he's shot Jumpsie – if he's hurt him—'

The dog could now be seen, going off at a limping run in the direction from which it had first come. A man carrying a gun strode down the hill.

'Did you shoot at my dog?' demanded the woman.

'Mother, you *saw* him!' snapped the girl.

The man made no reply till he had carefully examined the quivering sheep. Then, with one brief, angry muttered comment, he shot it in the neck. The sheep stopped quivering and lay still.

After that, the man looked up at the two women. 'Broken leg *and* its belly gouged. You ask did I shoot at your dog? Yes I did, and I'm sorry I didn't finish him off. But I will! That dog's got to be destroyed, Lady Venner. It's not under proper control. *I* saw what happened. So did you two, didn't you?' he addressed the twins.

They nodded, silent for once.

'You've absolutely no right to shoot someone else's dog,' said the girl hotly. 'Whatever happened, *that*'s not right!'

'Oh? And I'm to take no notice of this? And how do I know what's happened to the rest of the flock?' Without waiting for an answer he strode off up the hill, following the scattered flock.

'What about my dog? Mr Silkin! What about my Jumpsie?' the woman called after him.

'I'll look for him later,' he shouted and then, turning, 'Don't you mistake, Lady Venner! I'll be round at your house very soon!'

He vanished over the skyline.

The four people at the pond's edge looked at the dead sheep, not at each other.

'I suppose he'll come back later with the Landrover,' muttered Elly after a moment. 'Sheep are heavy things.'

In silent agreement, the twins turned back to their unfinished task.

'Well,' said Lady Venner irresolutely, 'we'd better hurry home. If your father – if your father sees—'

Completely ignoring Ally and Elly, she turned and started plodding up the hill.

The daughter – she was in her early twenties, but seemed younger because of her red, untended skin, roughly bobbed hair, and graceless, abrupt manner – rounded suddenly on the twins, and cried, 'Well, *you* didn't help much, did you? Try to stop the dog—'

45

They looked at her in silence, their mouths for once closed over the shining bridgework.

She said, 'Oh, I'm sorry, I'm sorry, I didn't mean . . . ' And then, lamely, after a pause: 'I don't suppose – is Dolly at home?'

'No,' said one twin.

'She isn't,' said the other.

Thelma Venner turned away from them and climbed the hill.

'And won't be, to you,' added one of the twins, after another pause.

'Getting back to the Green Knight . . . ' said her sister.

IV

I travelled back from Scotland in a fizz of exhilaration.

I had enjoyed the spare briskness of the little fishing town. The air smelt clean, as if it had been delivered that very minute from the North Pole; and the houses ended so abruptly that grass from the surrounding farmland seemed to be edging its way into the town centre. The red-brick campus, though new, was already silvered over with sea-lichen, and the sea could be heard and smelt everywhere, hurling itself against crags to the North, purring in orderly ranks of white breakers over a huge flat sandy bay to the South. All this was a wonderful contrast to the inland suburban cosiness of Floxby Crucis where, I now realised, I had felt suffocatingly enclosed, encapsuled, imprisoned. Had Mother felt so too, I wondered as I fidgeted about the train on the boring endless night journey southwards. Had she, too, longed for escape? Had her death been a welcome way out?

The return to home and Father quickly put a stopper on any feelings of exhilaration.

Mrs Budd had been in, dusted and cleaned, and carried away some of the superfluous quiches, but the place had a neglected, shut-in smell, as if nobody really lived there any more, and things that I had been using – books, papers – lay in exactly the spots where I had dropped them. Our household had lost its mainspring, the active spirit that caused change, created growth and movement, stirred currents of air. I could not wait to get away. The house had died, even though my father remained there, using it merely as a launching pad.

'Oh – you're back then,' he offered reluctantly, coming forth from his den. 'Can you make tea? I think Mrs Whatsername has left things ready; she usually does.'

She had; and we sat opposite one another, drinking it.

I would dearly have liked to fantasise that I was not my father's child, that I had been begotten in some earlier epoch by that unknown bearded man who had come to the funeral; but unfortunately two factors stood up implacably against this pleasing theory: first my age, and the bald truth that my parents had been married over a year before I was born; second the discouraging evidence, impossible to deny, that I closely resembled the man sitting across the table from me. I had his wide, straight mouth, like a letter-box across the face, his bracket-shaped countenance, high forehead, long nose, obstinate chin, greenish-grey eyes, and rough thicket of black, bristly, unmanageable hair. No amount of brushing seemed to tame it, and I had never yet discovered a cut that did anything to enhance my appearance.

'Well,' remarked my father, when he had drunk three cups of tea and eaten two slices of Granny Brown's Manor House Madeira, 'what was the point, pray, of that expensive excursion to Scotland? Took you long enough to get there and back; seems madly unpractical to me. If you go to that place, you certainly can't keep running home for weekends.'

Shan't want to, I thought, but suppressed that. I said: 'Well, they say they'll have me if my A' levels are all right.'

He shrugged, looking past me out of the dining-room window at the towering laurel hedge outside. 'Up to you, then. If those Morningquests really stick to their offer of paying your expenses . . . I certainly can't afford to. But, I daresay, when it comes to the point, they'll find some reason for backing down. Wouldn't blame 'em. Much better take a typing course like your pal Whatsername. Those Morningquests are in a spot of trouble, by the way, with the Venners; Venner's dog got shot.'

'*What?*'

'I had to go up there to put the beast down; shot in the head, part-blinded. Came crying home, all over blood; not very nice for the Venners. Remarkably silly woman that, mind you; always thought her a bit ninepence in the shilling. Can't understand why she ever had a dog in the first place – one of those giant poodles, stupid, gross beast.' My father tended to be more observant of animals, on the whole, than of humans.

'The dog belonged to Thelma Venner in the first place,' I said, unclenching my jaw. 'She dumped it on her parents when she and her boyfriend split up.'

'Oh? Stupid of them to take it.' Father, not interested, helped himself to a slice of bread.

'But why – who – which of the Morningquest family could have shot it?'

'Wasn't one of the family – tenant farmer, Silkin. Dog was worrying his sheep in Boxall Hill meadow; had killed a ewe. And Silkin had lost several before, suspected it was the same beast.'

'Well, surely in that case the Venners haven't a leg to stand on.'

'Ah, but nasty, though; seeing your dog come home in that state. Venner's a hot-tempered chap. Can't blame them for getting indignant. Shouldn't take the law into your own hands. Will you wash the plates?'

My father, having spoken more in the past five minutes than in the preceding five weeks, went back to his study and the *Milk Producers' Weekly Bulletin and Cowkeepers' Guide.*

I made haste to tidy away the tea things, then dashed for my bicycle and the road to Boxall Hill. It was a Saturday; the family would all be there. Most of all I wished to see Mariana, to tell her of my provisional acceptance. And Grisch and Lulie too, of course.

The phone rang in the hall, as I was on the point of leaving. My friend Veronica. Oh God, I thought.

'Haven't seen you in ages,' came her reproachful voice.

'No; well, I went for an interview at St Vigeans.'

'Interview go all right?' she inquired, carefully casual. I knew she had been hoping, planning, that she and I would have larks together at the secretarial school in Crowbridge.

'Not bad,' I said cautiously. 'The Art Director there is terrific.'

'How about a film this evening? Bobby and Lin say they're on. It's a— '

'Oh, I'm sorry,' I said falsely. 'I promised the Morningquests I'd go up and tell them about Scotland.'

'Mighty thick with *them*, all of a sudden, aren't you? Never away from that place,' she said with discontent. 'Well – how about tomorrow? We could get up a group and go to The Hay Mow.'

The Hay Mow was a pub far enough out of town for its owners to be unaware, or make believe to be unaware, that Veronica and half of her group were under the legal drinking age.

'I'll see – phone you tomorrow. Have to fly now. Very sorry. 'Bye.'

Curdled with guilt, I got on my bike and began the toilsome ride up Boxall Hill Lane. When I reached the north gate by the Venners' red-brick gabled villa (which bore the name 'Aviemore' on its oak-shingle gate), I was embarrassed to find both Venners out in their front garden, talking to a policeman. His car stood in the road. He was PC Chinnery. His daughter Daphne was in my form, and he had promised to give me driving lessons. We nodded to one another.

He was saying, 'Well, I'll do what I can, sir, but I'm afraid the chap was within his rights. The – er – animal should have been under restraint, not running loose across pastureland.'

'But it's a public right of way, dammit, along the drive through the park!'

Colonel Venom – I had fallen into the Morningquests' name for him – was a short, pear-shaped man with rough red skin, scanty whitish hair, and an expression of permanent outrage. He wore tweed knickerbockers and a deerstalker cap with flaps, and was never seen out of doors without a stick. Indoors, too, for all I knew. His wife, tall, thin, wispy, and stammering, seemed born to be his victim.

My embarrassment was caused by the fact that having approached Boxall Hill by the northern route, I was now under the necessity of getting my bike past the high locked gate. The hedge on the left, or Otherland, side of the lane was low and skimpy, though threaded through with barbed wire. It was not too difficult to hoist my bike over this.

'I would prefer that you did not do that,' shouted Colonel Venom, when, bike safely dumped on the far side, I had vaulted over the gate.

'I would prefer that you kept the gate open,' I said mildly. 'It is a public footpath, after all, isn't it? As you just said yourself.'

He spun away, turning his back on me. His face had turned several shades darker, to a purplish colour. I wondered if he was likely to have a stroke. I knew he had never liked the dog, Jumps, which it had always been his wife's task to walk. It seemed perverse of him to get into such a rage about the beast.

'Well, if you persist in being deliberately unhelpful, I shall consult my lawyer,' he snarled at PC Chinnery.

'Yes, sir, that would be my advice,' I heard Chinnery reply in a soothing voice, as I thankfully bestrode the bike again and started on the downhill glide round the curved saddle of hillside that would take me to Otherland on the further brow. Early winter dusk had begun to thicken, and the house was all lit up. Sir Gideon's country austerities did not extend to electricity, since that was home-made by the generator. Light streamed from every window. Music did too – Barney's piano, Dan's bassoon, Dolly's cello, the violins of Toby and the twins. It was like approaching a musical beehive. Gliding towards it on my bike, I thought how uniquely lucky I was to have the the entrée to this hive of harmony. Why, why, had Mother not introduced me there long ago? Hastily I suppressed the painful knowledge that I had only my own pig-headedness to blame, that I would have refused, very likely *had* done so. Instead I wondered how it came about that all the Morningquest children, who had inherited their parents' proclivities, who breathed in music like air, should none of them have chosen to follow it as a profession.

I had heard all about this from Lulie when I'd helped her make quince jam, and from Mariana, down on midweek visits to replenish her wardrobe. 'Too much like hard work,' said the twins. 'Practice, practice, all the time.' They practised anyway, but it was for pleasure. 'Too demanding in the wrong way,' said Dolly vaguely. 'I prefer pots,' said Selene. 'Music is for pleasure, not for a living.' And the boys, sighed Mariana, all seemed to have their noses stuck firmly into science; though

50

Danny showed an alarming tendency to move, by way of physics and electronics, towards an interest in the media. 'If he became a journalist it would just about break his father's heart.' Dan had that kind of slickness, the ability to grasp the basics of any subject on a superficial level, that would serve him well if he went into the media.

As I parked my bike in the yard beside the frosted fountain, Tante Lulie, wearing her white tam-o'-shanter, emerged from the back door accompanied by the twins.

'But what do you want out of the deep-freeze?' she was asking suspiciously.

'Ice, Tante Lulie.'

'What for? It's not cold enough out here for you already?'

'It's for our photography,' Elly reassured her.

'Oh, very well! But do not, I beseech you, make a great muddle in there. Put things back the way you found them. Ah – here is Pandora. So, how did you get on, my dear child? Is it all decided? Are you and Dolly to go together?'

The twins hurled themselves on me.

'Just the person we wanted!'

'Why?' I said, suspicious as Lulie.

'We'll explain. All in good time. You *can* stay the night here, can't you?'

'Well – I'll have to phone Father,' I said, but fully intended to. I had my toothbrush in my pocket.

'Oh, your father won't care. He'll never notice. Did you pass the Venoms on your way? There is *such* a feud building up,' said Ally gleefully. 'It's like those Sicilian vendettas. Old Venom is really ready to murder Gid – which is totally unfair, as the joke is, poor old Gid hardly knows what it is all about.'

'Is that my Pandora?' called the golden voice of Mariana from an upstairs window. 'How did it go in Scotland? Leave those hoydens for later, and come up to my room and tell me *all* about it. Dolly will be cross – but she's practising her cello in the attic, so her turn must come later.'

'Chellous,' said one twin to the other. 'Tolly will be chellous.'

Ignoring this, I ran up to Mariana's narrow, bare, nun-like little slip of a room, where she was trying on a cocktail dress made from a piece of stuff found by Tante Lulie in a trunk after a local estate was sold up. Lulie thought it might have been an altar cloth. It had a deep red glittering border.

'Help me off with it, there's a love, the pins are sticking into me all over,' said Mariana, turning sideways at the glass. 'It needs taking in here

– and here.' She was as thin as a sapling; I could easily see why Tante Lulie enjoyed making clothes for her.

Once the dress was safely back on its hanger she gave me a cool, fragrant embrace. She was wearing a plain silk slip and looked no more than thirty-five in spite of her white hair.

'So how did it go? A' levels? Of course. No problem there. Dolly will be over the moon. And the town – the place? Did you like it? Hélène was always homesick for Scotland, she once told me; it said something atavistic to her. Oh, my darling, *how* much I miss your mother! Never mind: I am lucky to have found you instead. Come along, let's go down and tell everybody your news.'

'There's really none to tell at this stage,' I demurred, anxious not to tempt Providence. (Why, I wonder, should we credit Providence with such a spiteful disposition? Why expect it to reward any foolish sign of confidence with a rocket attack?)

'Well, come along anyway. Everybody will be dying to see you.'

This I well knew to be one of Mariana's flights of fancy. When we entered the kitchen where most of them were already seated round the long table, and she cried, 'Here is darling Pandora!' as if bringing the good news from Ghent to Aix, I received no more than a series of casual nods from the boys, who were deep in argument as usual, and a cold blank stare from Selene. From the twins, eldritch grins. Dolly, it was true, had a big hello for me when she came down later from her cello practice.

'Why didn't anyone tell me you were here? How did it go?' She gave me a plump, pneumatic hug. Dolly always smelt very hygienic, of Wrights Coal Tar soap and lavender water.

'Not too bad, I think. The Art Director is wonderful. He's a Czech.'

'Good-good,' said Sir Gideon from his end of the table. Suddenly I recognised the source of Dolly's bland graciousness; she had inherited it from her father.

'Good-good,' repeated Sir Gideon benignly, nodding. That was his invariable statement of public approval. And he began serving out vegetable soup – a concession to the bitter dry frost which now held the country in its grip.

We all ate soup, the boys fell into their usual argument about inflation, deflation, and reflation, and the twins into theirs about Sir Gawain and the Green Knight.

'The poem is about doing things the proper way. And about keeping your word,' said Elly. 'In the fourteenth century that was considered important.'

52

'Not any more, it isn't,' said Ally, giving Dan a sour look. I wondered what he had done, or not done.

The rest of the family were discussing the affair of Silkin's sheep and the Venners' dog. The twins, I learned, had actually been present at the scene and witnessed the whole affair.

'"Thenne such a glaver ande glam of gedered raches Ros that the rocherers rungen aboute,"' said Elly.

'Do stop showing off,' said Dan irritably.

I now knew the brothers apart: Dan was the stockiest, though certainly not fat; Toby the thinnest and fairest (and for some reason he nearly always looked rather worried); Barney the tallest and handsomest. But, still, they were remarkably alike. Barney was studying pure mathematics, Toby was reading biology and Dan, at London University, was doing physics. Barney was his mother's favourite. Toby was the youngest, but taller than Dan. It was like one of those puzzles: Mr Smith is on the right of the surgeon; the man at the end of the table is married to the doctor; Mrs Jones is the one with false teeth...

'Venom can't really expect to enlist everybody's sympathy just because his revolting dog got shot in the eye,' said Toby, turning from his brothers.

'Oh no? You'd be surprised at the morals of the English Tory countryside,' said Dan.

'It's all perfectly horrible,' shivered Mariana. 'I just hope it doesn't mean that we become the target of a hate campaign. And I hope that it will have blown over before the next Music Festival. Oh, if only your Mother were still alive, Pandora! She would be such a help. I wish that revolting old Venom would die of a syncope.'

Uncle Grisch walked into the kitchen carrying a large heavy water container, which he deposited on the counter by the sink. Then he sat down and started eating soup amid a chorus of indignation and surprise.

'Uncle Grisch! Why were *you* fetching the water? Wasn't it Dan's turn?'

'Grischa, my dear fellow, why in the world do you go on that cold, tiring errand when there are all these healthy young males in the house?'

By now I knew that the family preferred to fetch their drinking water from a spring that bubbled out in the upper valley beyond the ilex grove. During the week, Uncle Grisch replenished the house supply every two days or so, and made nothing of the errand; he was as stringy and tough as an old bramble. But at the weekend one of the boys was supposed to take care of it; they had a rota.

Dan made a great demonstration of charming contrition, and vowed that he would undertake the task for the next five weekends.

'*Tut mır nicht kain teuves,*' muttered Tante Lulie.

Sir Gideon's whole face flowed downwards in triangles of grief.

'But I'll tell you a thing,' said Uncle Grisch, ignoring all the distractions. 'There was somebody in the ilex grove.'

'There was?'

'Doing what?'

'What sort of a somebody?'

'How do you know, Uncle Grisch?'

'I have ears, don't I?' said Uncle Grisch. 'I was on the way to the spring, so the jug was not heavy, and I was walking quietly through the little wood with my eyes well used to the dark. I could see the moonlit hillside ahead of me through the trees, and then – all of a sudden – I became aware of a rustling and a scrunching. And I saw something, a dark shape, moving among the tree trunks.'

'Could it have been a badger – a deer?'

'Too big for a badger. The wrong shape for a deer. It dodged behind a tree. Your deer would not do so. A deer would simply run away.'

Two of the boys, Barnabas and Toby, impulsively jumped up. Sir Gideon impatiently waved them to sit down again.

'Whoever it was will be long gone by now,' he said. 'And we do not want any confrontations. That is the last thing we want.'

'What do you suppose the guy was doing?'

'That we shall discover tomorrow,' said Sir Gideon.

After the conclusion of the meal – apples, cider, ginger-nuts, Shredded Wheat – and after the girls' washing-up rota, the twins collared me.

'Come on now, phone your father, tell him you are spending the night here, and then we want to have a *serious* conversation with you.'

So I phoned him – he raised no objection – and they dragged me off to Grisch's studio over the stables.

'But what about Grisch?'

'Oh, he's playing triangular chess with Gid and Barney; they'll be at it for hours. Do come on!'

I loved Grisch's studio. Approached up a kind of companion-ladder, it was over the old tack-room, now used as an apple store, so that the loft above was imbued with the scent of apples. A litter of paper, paints and drawing-materials lay on several paper-hangers' tables in the room, which was formed from two large garrets thrown together and lit by skylights. English literature, still awaiting the process of revision, was ranged on shelves across the two ends. And a series of black-and-white satirical drawings had been tacked on canvas screens which stood in front of the sloping roof. They showed pairs of people in various unflattering juxtapositions: cuddly girls ogling lecherous old men; fat ladies eyeing soldiers in uniform, glances of matrimonial hate being exchanged over breakfast tables, looks of despair and triumph as the wedding ring was pushed into place. I found them somewhat depressing, though brilliant and skilful; they represented a side of Grisch that I hardly knew; I much preferred his watercolours, which were mysterious undefined landscapes in wild dramatic glowing colours.

When I once said this to him he replied, 'But, my child, the world is always so much better than the people in it.'

The twins plainly relished these acid sidelights on human nature.

'Sharp old Grisch,' said Elly, glancing at his work with admiration, then dragging forward a tiny electric heater to a spot on the floor covered by a small Turkish rug, and switching on the heat. Grisch, unlike Tante Lulie, treated cold weather with Spartan disregard, preferred it in fact: 'My mind functions less intelligently if I am too warm,' he said.

So we huddled down on the icy floor in front of the heater.

'Now,' said Ally, 'you won't know this, but we have a kind of crossing-the-line ceremony in our family.'

'Like the Musgrave Ritual,' put in Elly.

'The Musgrave—?'

'Oh, *you* know,' said Ally impatiently. 'In Sherlock Holmes. "Whose was it? His who is gone. What shall we give for it? All that is ours."'

By now I had discovered that the twins, unlike their elder sister Dolly, were surprisingly well read in many odd corners of English literature.

'Oh yes, I do remember,' I said hastily. 'It was something to do with the crown of the kings of England – or was it the Holy Grail?'

'Well, never mind that. The point was that members of the family had to go through a special rite when they came of age. We do it, too, in our family, but ours is at the age of ten.'

'It was the boys who invented it in the first place,' interrupted Ally. 'They started it on Dolly, to make her an honorary boy, because they said she was always moaning about being left out of their games. And then of course *she* wanted it done on Silly, when she was ten; and then they did it on us.'

Elly grimaced at the memory.

'*Did* it?'

'So now,' explained Elly, 'as Mar and your mother between them have—'

'Have infiltrated you into a kind of honorary position in our family, we decided to ratify the situation by giving you a formal initiation,' said Ally.

My reactions to this announcement were mixed. Indignation came uppermost. 'Thanks. Thanks very much. Very obliging of you.'

They gave me their pussycat grins.

'Do the rest of the family know about this?' To me, it all sounded undignified. Childish and undignified. Embarrassing.

I was relieved when Ally said, 'No, we didn't mention it to Dolly and the boys. Silly wouldn't be interested anyway. She thinks of nothing but her old pots. You can tell the others afterwards, of course – if you want to.'

'The ritual is always administered by the two next above in age,' Elly explained 'The girls did it to us when we were ten. Toby and Dolly did it to Sil.'

'But I'm older than ten. And older than you two. A lot.'

'Well, we can't help that, can we? The point is, you've only just arrived in the family.'

'By the avalanche,' agreed Ally, nodding.

'So it couldn't be any sooner.'

'And there is no time like the present.'

'Oh; very well,' I said, capitulating with an ill grace. 'So what do I have to do?' envisaging some kind of gipsy-brotherhood process, cutting wrists, mingling blood, mixing with wine.

'Ah well, we've got it all set up.'

'But not here. We just brought you here to get you used to the idea.'

'First you have to be blindfolded.'

'Oh – for Heaven's sake!'

'We had better go down to the tack-room first,' said Elly. 'It'll be easier to start with you on level ground.'

So they switched off the heater and we went down to the tack-room where, among the shelves of sharp-smelling apples, the twins capably wound my head in a voluminous old India-cotton shawl (doubtless from one of Tante Lulie's rummage sales). Then I heard the light click off and they led me out of the stable, into the cold night.

'Lucky it's not raining,' mumbled one twin aside to the other. (I was interested to discover that, with eyes bandaged, it was hard to tell their voices apart.)

'"When the cold cler water fro the cloudes shadde, And fres er hit falle might to the fale erthe,"' declaimed the other twin, so then I recognised Elly.

They led me a long way, first stubbing toes over cobbles, next along a gravel path, then over an area of rough grass. I heard a door unlatched and creakingly opened – toolshed, garden store, summerhouse? The place that we entered smelt of earth, oil, roots – the mower shed or the greenhouse, I guessed.

'Kneel,' commanded one of the twins.

As they grew more confident, their voices acquired resonance; or perhaps it was the acoustics of the new surroundings.

I knelt on a stony, gritty surface, relieved that I had changed into thick sweater and a comfortable pair of old corduroys before the bike ride up to Boxall Hill. Some article of furniture was shoved with a rasping sound across the floor and against my stomach.

'Now, you will be given various items to eat and drink,' I was told. 'You must take them willingly, and after you swallow each one, you must repeat, *I share the solemn ancestral food of the tribe of Morningquest; I acknowledge their forbears as my own kindred; I take their troubles and glories as my own.*'

Wow! I thought, and then wondered did the twins invent this rigmarole specially for me? Somehow I could not imagine Barnabas or Danny devising it for the benefit of Dolly. Nor Dolly passing it on to Selene. I was willing to bet that their ceremonies had been much simpler.

Kneeling with eyes blindfolded makes it difficult to balance; I gripped the ends of the wooden bench before me and concluded that it was one of the wooden slatted tables from the potting shed. Behind my back I could hear a subdued clinking and shuffling. Then, with a soft thump, something was deposited on the board in front of me.

'Before you on the table,' intoned one of the voices – now they were really getting into their stride – 'before you on a dish lie three sheep's eyes. One for the past, one for the present, one for the future. Swallow these one by one, and, after each, repeat the ritual phrase.'

Sheep's eyes? I thought incredulously, where the devil would the twins get hold of sheep's eyes? Was this all a grotesque leg-pull? But then, with a grisly quake, I remembered the slaughtered ewe. Did I really have to put up with all this nonsense? Were they serious? I decided that they were.

Resigned to going along with their game, I groped with cautious fingers and found what felt like a plastic saucer with three globular objects on it, swimming in thick slime the consistency of egg-white. With a slight shudder, I put one in my mouth. It was freezing cold and tasted salt. Without attempting to chew, I swallowed the slimy thing – an olive, perhaps? – and heard a sigh from behind me. If it was an olive, I hoped that the stone had been removed.

Suppressing a strong urge to laugh or expostulate, I began reciting the formula: 'I share the solemn ancestral food of the tribe of Morningquest; er – um— '

'I acknowledge their forbears as my own kindred; I receive their troubles and glories as my own,' someone prompted.

Twice more I gulped through the ritual. Three eyes? But only one sheep was killed. A sheep has two eyes. Hang on, though – is it possible they could have come from the butcher?

The slimy saucer was removed, and was replaced by a cylindrical object. A mug.

'In the chalice now before you,' chanted the voices, 'there is ritual wine mixed with blood, herbs and spices. Drink it unfalteringly and repeat the mystic formula.'

I did so, hoping they had not laced the potion with a hallucinogen. The taste was unbelievably noxious: heavy, oily, strong, it could have been a combination of ink, blood and castor oil. But the residual impression was alcoholic and slightly sweet. A dash of cooking sherry? With a fierce effort I controlled my heaving oesophagus and clamped my tongue against the roof of my mouth, drawing deep cold breaths through my nostrils.

'Recite the oath.'

I recited it.

'Now,' said the voice on my right, 'we adjourn to another place. But first you must be ceremonially anointed, and you must yield a portion of hair— '

'Symbolic of your readiness to share all your worldly goods with the family.'

'Here, hold on— ' I protested, but then reflected that, in fact, matters were the other way round. The family was generously preparing to help me on my way through college; so, all right, it was the least I could do to submit to this preposterous mumbo-jumbo. All the time, though, my conviction grew stronger that Mariana and Sir Gideon knew nothing at all about the family 'passing-out' ceremony, had nothing to do with it. Thinking this, I suddenly felt a cold gooey liquid dolloped on to the top of my head, from where it ran down, soaking into my blindfold. Then, with what felt like a large pair of garden shears, one of my mentors snipped the hair on top of my head. Wet tufts fell on to my hands, on the table, and I jerked uncontrollably.

'Hold still!' ordered a voice.

'What the devil are you doing?' I demanded.

'Quiet, please! Now we lead you to the Place of Aspiration.'

With muscular claw-like hands clamped on my arms, they urged me upright and turned me round. We went out of doors again and walked for what seemed like ten minutes, mostly over grass. By now I was becoming very impatient indeed with the whole affair, and resolved that I would put up with another five minutes of this nonsense, no more. A joke was a joke, but I had had more than enough. I felt slightly groggy, probably from the effects of the drink. Cold trickles ran down my head and neck. I wanted to be indoors, preferably with Mariana, listening to her sing. But first, a hot bath and some coffee to take away the taste of that foul potion.

The chill night air was a relief. It helped reduce the nausea. But my gorge still rose at the memory of the sheep's eyes – *could* they have been olives? – and my slight dizziness was not helped by the effect of having my eyes bandaged for such a long time.

'Now,' said one of the voices, 'you are going to climb a stair. Set your right hand on the rail.'

Two hands raised my arm, placed my right hand in position.

And, of course, the moment I grasped the rail, I knew exactly where I was: at the foot of Toby's staircase leading up to the tree-house. Below the blindfold I grinned a private grin. Very likely the twins had no notion at all of the many times I had climbed up to the platform during quiet weekdays when the family were all away in London. The ilex grove (which contained a melancholy little group of pets' graves: 'Blackie, Ann's first pony'; 'Bonzo, a Faithful friend'; 'Saladin, Tom's hunter for seven years') and Toby's wooden framework, high and secret among the branches, had become my favourite haunts. I had grown thoroughly familiar with the smooth sweep of the hand-rail and the curve of the stair; knew exactly how many steps there were; I could – as the saying goes – walk it blindfold.

I set my foot confidently on the bottom step.

'Wait! Wait for instructions!' ordered one of the voices. 'You will now climb exactly fifteen steps – *very slowly*. Counting aloud as you do so. On the fifteenth step you will stop. Stand still there, hold tight on to the rail, and await further instructions. Do not move *at all*, or you will be in danger.'

'OK', I agreed cheerfully. And I began to climb.

Now I thought I could guess what they had in mind. The cunning little beasts. I bet they plan to go back to the house – maybe they have sneaked away already – and they want me to stand palpitating for twenty minutes on the top step before I realise they have left me. Well, this was the point at which I was going to stop co-operating. I would take off the bandage the very minute I got to the top. With a light heart and assured – though appropriately slow – step I ascended the stair.

The fifteenth step, I remembered, was actually the platform itself. I knew Toby had nailed a few planks across it. His moulded banister ceased to be the stair-rail at the top step and bent around to the right, becoming the deck-rail of the platform.

Under my hand, sliding smoothly upwards, I felt the rail bend to the right. 'Fifteen!' I called, stepping on to the platform.

And then my plan to toss off my blindfold, and the twins' plan to surprise me – whatever that had been – both went agley, for the joist under my feet split and dropped away below me, and I plunged downwards with it. Luckily, with my right hand, I still had hold of the rail, and clutched it. That helped break my fall, because I was given a moment to shove the shawl from my head, and then to grab at other branches and bits of tree as I tumbled past them.

Just the same, when I hit the ground, it was with enough impact to knock me out – and just before that I had felt an ominous cracking pain in my left leg.

V

All hell broke loose, naturally, when the twins were discovered hauling me across the stable yard on an old sleigh.

My black-out had been very brief, but my leg was so painful that trying to walk was out of the question. Lord Newbery, Sir Gideon's friend and doctor, who happened to be spending the weekend at Boxall Hill, pronounced the break to be a simple fracture, but I had to be ferried off to Floxby General to have it set. The Morningquests, I thought despondently, were always being obliged to summon ambulances for members of my family.

Mariana rode in with me.

'Please, *please* don't apologise!' I kept begging her. 'And don't blame the twins. It was just an idiotic accident, I'm sure – probably my fault. I don't understand what can have happened, but I'm absolutely sure they didn't plan it.'

'But what were you all *doing*?'

'It was just – just a game,' I said rather hopelessly, and then we arrived at the Casualty Department and I was whisked off to have my leg tidied up and set in plaster.

Next day – Sunday – I was pronounced fit to be sent home from the hospital, and, given my father's widowed circumstances and active professional habits, it was thought best, by all, that I should return to Boxall Hill.

I had talked to my father on the phone, of course, and received a terrific scold from him. 'Idiotic tomfoolery – climbing trees at night – what *can* you expect?'

I certainly had not expected sympathy from him, and didn't get it.

Barney came to fetch me in the Daimler. 'Just so you can stretch out your leg,' he said, establishing me in the spacious back seat. 'And we thought it would be a smoother drive than Grisch's Minor.'

It was like being wafted through the air on a velvet wing.

'I do hope the twins haven't been massacred by your parents?' I said anxiously.

'Well, they did get a bit of a wigging. Childish behaviour; considering their mental endowments they ought to have known better; and so forth. But they are in such constant hot water at their schools that I think they aren't much affected – it just slides off them.

'Gid and Mariana hadn't ever known, you see, about our coming-of-age ritual. So it helped a bit when Dolly and I told them that. Though I must say the twins seem to have carried it a fair way beyond anything that *we* ever dreamed up. Inventive little devils,' he said morosely.

I thought of the sheep's eyeballs.

'But the main thing was,' he went on, 'that of course they never had the least intention of having you fall out of the tree-house.'

'No, I hadn't supposed so. That must have been pure accident.'

'No. It wasn't accident. Quite the reverse. Somebody had been there, in the grove, and had sawed through the joist in two places, leaving just a millimetre of wood to hold it together.'

'No!' I said, startled to death. 'How absolutely wicked!'

'Toby and I went down there as soon as it was light and had a good look round. We found the sawn-off piece of joist where it had fallen, and dents in the ground, three of them, where a fruit ladder had sunk in under some-body's weight. We found sawdust, too, scattered over the fallen leaves down below. So it must have been done recently, since the last shower of rain.'

'I was in the grove last Thursday in daylight,' I said, not adding that I had climbed up on to the platform, 'and I certainly didn't see any sawdust then. Who could possibly have done it?'

'Oh, not much doubt; it must have been old Venom – crazy old fool. In a rage about his dog, I suppose. The problem is, what line to take about him. Gid is terribly anxious not to get involved in any local unpleasantness if he can possibly avoid it. This place is such a refuge for him.'

'But malicious damage on that scale is a bit much. Somebody might have been killed.'

'You, for instance,' said Barney.

'Oh, well, it's just lucky that I have such a lot of primal ape in my make-up. I've been falling out of trees all my life.' After thinking some more, I asked, 'Have the police been told about this?' remembering PC Chinnery outside the Venners' house.

'Gid is waiting to talk to you about that. He doesn't want to bring the police in. But it's up to you, really. After all, you are the one who got hurt,' he ended soberly, and I reflected that I had never held so long a conversation with Barney before.

He pulled up in the stable yard. 'Tante Lulie has fixed you a bedsitter in the housekeeper's old room; we thought you'd better be on the ground floor.'

'"He hipped over on his ax and orpedly strides, Bremly brothe on a bent,"' declaimed Ally, appearing in the back doorway and helping me out with my crutches, to such a degree that I nearly toppled on to the cobbles.

'Take it easy!' I gasped.

'And not so much bloody Sir Gawain, do you mind,' said Barney, backing the Daimler away into shelter. She grinned at him in a friendly way, and I pondered on the interesting and complex hierarchies of family life; the twins had, I knew, a better rapport with Barnabas than they did with Dan or Toby, or the intervening sisters.

'Oh, you poor, poor darling!' cried Mariana, running out of the back door in her grey smock. 'Come along, come in, and let's get you settled.'

With maximum fuss and commotion, during which I was several times nearly knocked over and trampled underfoot through sheer solicitude, I was finally established on a chaise longue in the housekeeper's room.

'Danny lit a fire in here for you,' said Mariana, looking fondly at the leaping flames.

Danny had indeed done so, but since he'd forgotten to provide more than a handful of fuel, the fire soon went out; ungratefully, I would have preferred an oilstove.

'Now Lulie shall bring you some of her marvellous coffee; and let's take your jacket and get this thing off your head.' She twitched off my turban-scarf and let out a yip of astonishment. 'Your *hair*! What happened to it?'

'*Oy veh!*' cried Lulie, nearly dropping the coffee tray. 'Never in all my days did I hear that a broken leg turned a person's hair green!'

They had been pretty startled in the hospital too, and had kindly done their best to eradicate the colour by scrubbing with surgical shampoo, but with minimal result.

'I think it must have been the stuff the twins put on it last night,' I explained weakly.

'Ach, those twins. Meshugge! Wait till Gideon sees!'

'My poor Pandora, it is outrageous!'

'Oh, I expect I shall soon get used to it. And I suppose by and by it will grow out. Or fade.'

'Maybe we should *geblonde* you,' meditated Tante Lulie. I could see her inventive eye light up, as she considered the challenge of the situation. 'But what a terrible, terrible cut they have given you. You look like a crested grebe. That, we can certainly set to rights.'

Tante Lulie's expertise with scissors extended to hair-cutting, and she performed on most of the family, male and female alike.

Dolly soon came swanning in. She, like Mariana, was ready to exclaim, and cluck and commiserate over my plight; but I was interested to observe that when she actually came face to face with it, it was more than she had bargained for and she seemed mortally embarrassed – especially by the green hair. Perhaps it was because I had been reduced to this state by her naughty younger sisters? Whatever the reason, having come in, she could not wait to get away again. So much, I thought, for our great future friendship at St Vigeans. Selene, on the other hand, who had never hitherto addressed me directly, displayed a surprising amount of sympathy and concern, offering to fetch a back-rest that Toby had made her when she hurt her spine, lending me a mohair stole to wrap round my shoulders and providing a little posy of winter jasmine and holly berries in one of her tiny elegant ceramic pots.

Sir Gideon paid a state-visit of condolence. 'My dear child, I do not know, I truly do not know what to say.'

'Please, please, don't give it a thought,' I besought him. 'Honestly, it was just as much my fault as the twins'.'

'Indeed, I am deeply touched that you were prepared to go through all this ritual rigmarole to become part of our family – from now on you must feel that you belong to us absolutely.' His eyes kindly ignored my green hair.

'Oh, thank you,' I said, mortally embarrassed. 'I'm tremendously grateful for everything you— '

'Nothing, nothing, it is entirely our pleasure.'

Here we both ground to a standstill. Then I said, 'But what are you going to do about that monstrous old man, Colonel Venom?'

A wary look came over his face. 'Ah, there my dear, I must admit that I am not in agreement with the boys. They are so Old Testament. An eye for an eye, a tooth for a claw.'

'But you don't agree?'

'It solves no problem. And I see too many difficulties ahead. What could we prove against him? Probably nothing. And there would be much acrimony.'

Yes, and I can see that all you really want to do is to get on with your life, with your music.

I had a sudden flash of empathy. Even those three handsome boys, I realised, must, to Sir Gideon, have seemed rather a distraction, a bit of an intrusion. I gazed at him with affectionate awe. He was so like an elongated angel beside a church door, abstracted and benign. How very different from my father, who rushed about disagreeably, getting things done. (Though it was true that Sir Gideon did get a lot of music done.)

'Shall you be comfortable here, my dear, at Boxall Hill, do you think?' he was asking solicitously.

'Oh yes, thank you, I shall be in Heaven! I can get on with reading for my A' levels.'

'And our dear Lulie and Grisch will keep you company. Mariana, too, says that she plans to stay down here for a couple of weeks.'

'Oh, that will be *wonderful*!' I breathed fervently. My times of contact with Mariana were always so tantalisingly few and short. Two whole weeks of her company sounded to me like a dream of Paradise.

'Yes, well,' a shade of displeasure passed over Sir Gideon's brow, 'Dave is to accompany the twins to Harvard.'

This sounded to me like a non sequitur, and an astonishing one at that. '*Harvard?*'

I was so surprised I nearly rolled off the chaise longue.

'Mariana will explain – we had this offer – it is all most complicated. But, so you are not too cast down, my dear Pandora? You go along with these arrangements? And you do not mind that I do not pursue the matter – take legal action?'

'No, no, I shall be only too glad to forget it.' (Though what Father would think . . .)

'Good-good,' he said, smiled his serene, ineffable smile, repeated, 'Good-good,' and sailed out of the room, humming one of Brahms's variations on a theme of Haydn.

The twins reappeared with my lunch on a tray (bread, cheese, apples, Shredded Wheat) and remained to laugh like hyenas at my green hair.

'Oh, we never, never thought that it would take so well! But don't you think it quite suits you, Pandora dear?'

'No, I do not! It makes me look like a potted palm. The only virtue of my dark hair was that it provided a kind of Doric capital. Never mind. Maybe I'll just stay in this room till the colour grows out. But tell about you. What is this Harvard caper?'

'Well,' said Elly, 'it seems that Gid and Mar had this offer which they'd decided not even to mention to us; it was from some old flame of Mar's, who is now in the Chair of Psycho-Kinetics at Harvard. He wanted us to go over there and form part of a research project for six months.'

'And at first they weren't even going to consider the suggestion, let alone tell *us* about it.'

'But as St Monica's has thrown us out, and what with one thing and another, and we can't start at Heidelberg for at least another year, maybe two—'

'—And then Dave said he wanted to go and visit his great-aunt in Baton Rouge, and could just as well drop us off at Harvard on the way, where some old dragon of a para-psychology professor who is the sister of Mar's old flame will keep an eye on us.'

'*Chaperon* us—'

'Not that we believe for a moment that Dave *has* a great-aunt in Baton Rouge.'

'We think he just wants to get out from under for a bit.'

The twins looked at me smugly, limpidly. Then Elly said, 'I knew that fire would never stay in. Dan is really hopeless. It's all shop-window with him. He is a total louse.' She snatched up the log trug and carried it away.

Ally said, 'We were really sorry about your fall from the tree, you know, Pandora. Not at all what we intended. We just meant you to turn round and come down again, after we'd given you a bit of indoctrination. And you'd been doing so well, up to then!'

'I never thought you planned for me to fall. Honestly, don't worry.'

'It's the old monster in Aviemore we want to get to grips with. Dan is with us there. We and he are going to put our heads together—'

'For Heaven's sake, *don't*!' I exclaimed, horrified at the thought of what they might get up to. Especially with Dan. 'Just leave the old wretch to stew in his own juice. He's sure to come a cropper and end up in Davy Jones' locker,' I gabbled on, mixing metaphors in my urgency, like fruit in a Christmas pudding. But, with luck, they would be swept off to Harvard before they could think up some suitable retribution for the Colonel.

Elly brought in more logs and re-lit the fire.

Uncle Grisch followed her in to take my tray.

'Go, go!' he said to the twins. 'You have dyed her hair green, you have broken her leg, now go to your violin practice and leave the poor girl in peace.' Grinning like alligators, they went. 'What *were* those sheep's eyes?' I called after them. But they did not reply.

'How long must your leg remain in plaster?' Grisch asked.

'Two or three weeks, depending.'

'I shall show you some exercises that will help. Once I was a dancer and I had my leg broken; so I shall be glad to pass on to you the benefits of my experience.'

'You were a dancer, Uncle Grisch?' I said, surprised. Though – now I came to think of it – he had the physique of a dancer: nimble, stringy, tireless. And the dancer's expressive, economical, bony face.

'Oh yes. You smile at the improbability. So, my dear Pandora, let that be a lesson. To find nothing, ever, surprising. Once, even, I danced with Fonteyn!'

'*Fantastic*!' I breathed, believing him totally. 'What was she like?'

He thought. 'It was like dancing with God. You *knew* that she would never let you down; that she would always be, to the last hair's breadth, just where she should be; that single experience in my life I knew would be worth any trouble and terror that might come later.'

'And was it?'

'Yes. I was in Auschwitz later, you know. Did Lulie or Mariana tell you

66

that? No? Well – I was there. A young man, a dancer, only twenty. I had performed before crowned heads, even the English king. And with Fonteyn in London. And then to come to this place.'

'Why didn't somebody pull strings – get you out?'

'And leave all the rest behind?' He gave me a look so bleak that I was glad of the layer of quilts covering me. 'They asked if I would give a performance before the Commandant. I said no. They said they would give me special privileges: better food, a place to practise. I said no again. So they broke my leg to teach me better manners. But luckily there was a doctor among my fellow inmates. She set my leg, and she taught me these exercises. So now I teach you.'

'How did you get out?'

'Oh, the war ended. We all got out. Well, those that were alive.'

'How ... extraordinary,' I said slowly. 'Do you ever wonder – why? Why you? Why not the others?'

'Yes,' he said. 'Very often. Very often I wonder that. And then, so as not to go mad or fall into despair, I decide that I must have been preserved for some useful purpose. To take care of the Morningquest family, maybe. Or to look after you. Or to rewrite the whole of English literature in reasonable, intelligible language.'

'What did you do when you first got out?'

He grinned. 'I sold a pen which guaranteed that the writer would pass his exams. And it worked. A real example of sympathetic magic! On the profits from that pen, I made my way to England.'

'You didn't dance any more?'

'No,' he said. 'No. Like Mr Elton, my dancing days were over. But then – then I met Gideon.'

'And your troubles were over?'

'In a way. I began looking at people's faces. You too, I notice, do that.'

'Looking at them, what for?'

He said, 'Once I met an Indian holy man who tells me, when people die, if they have had anything of value in them, it travels further, to join the Whole Being, this great endless torrent of spirit that pours on, without rest, for evermore. Do you believe this?'

'I don't know,' I said helplessly. 'Yes. Perhaps. Possibly.'

As usual, I thought of my mother. Had part of her been swept away to join that tremendous torrent? Which part, if so? And which part had been left? And left, in that case, where?

'All does not go,' said Grisch, echoing my thought. 'Part – fragments – may remain behind: confused, forlorn, unhappy, *waiting*. This is what we describe as ghosts. Have you ever been into that building up on the hilltop, the one they call Matilda's Tower?'

'The Folly? No, I never have.'

The way to it was across a disused pig-field, grown high with brambles; the derelict, though interesting brick structure seemed not quite worth the effort.

'Well,' said Grisch, 'do not go there at dusk. It is a most unhappy building. Some ghost waits there to be liberated. I suppose that for people who die by violence or in distress, this process of separation takes longer. Decades, centuries. Like froth on the surface of the water. I hope I do not die in such a way: alone, unhappy, afraid.'

'Oh, Uncle Grisch, I hope not! But why should you? Lots of people love you.'

'Anyway,' he said, 'it is all froth. And, in the end, absorbed. But that is why I look at faces: to see which part of the person will break free and soar away; which part will stay here, hanging around like a street-corner boy. And so I am occupied. Also with revising English literature.'

'Who are you working on now?'

'Still on Hardy. He drives me mad, poor Hardy; this mumbling gloom in which he lives; the way he cannot make a statement without beating about the bush until the bush is all trampled flat.'

'Perhaps he was afraid of dying, too. And wanted to make some kind of statement first? Better than not making any statement at all?'

'It is so wasteful of energy.' Uncle Grisch gave me a sudden flashing grin. 'I tell you another thing I discovered in Auschwitz. We are all the time, all our lives, spending, paying out money, breath, energy. As soon as you are adult, it begins. Every breath costs money – for gas, for electricity, rent, tax, food. All of life costs, everything costs.

'Only, if you read a book for instance, that does not cost.'

'Yes it does. You bought the book.'

'One payment only. Now it is yours. Or you borrow it from the library. And you can read it many times. Each time you learn a new thing from it. Free! Or you look at a picture, a self-portrait, say, by Rembrandt. It teaches you all there is to know about resignation and suffering. Also free. So, art does not cost.'

'Should not cost,' I said, thinking about it.

'That is why art is better than science. But you are tired,' said Grisch. 'I go now. Tomorrow I begin to teach you exercises.'

VI

I still measure those weeks that I spent at Otherland after my fall from the tree-house against any subsequent height of happiness in my life, and nothing has yet surpassed them.

Sir Gideon was out of the country for two months, conducting orchestras in Germany, Sweden, and Finland. The boys were at their respective universities and, because the weather was wintry and forbidding, preferred not to return home at weekends. Dolly, busy at her crammer, passed weekends with friends in London. Selene had come down with a severe case of flu – Selene was a delicate girl, much more liable to illness than her siblings – and remained in the London house, nursed there by the housekeeper, Mrs Grove. I was quite surprised that Mariana did not elect to stay in London with her – Selene was accepted by all the rest as being her mother's favourite – but she explained this quite calmly.

'You see, I always have to take especial care of my throat; I am particularly susceptible to that type of virus. Gideon has begged me to remain out of range until the poor girl is quite convalescent. Also I am a bad sick-nurse, while angelic Mrs Grove is a very good one. Toby is coming down from Hay to keep Selene company; that is not too hard for him, and she loves him best of all. Much better than me!'

This was true. I had noticed it.

'But you are not a bad nurse, Mariana! Look how wonderful you are to me.'

'But you do not need *nursing*, my darling child!'

This was so. I was not ill or feverish once I had recovered from my slight concussion. I could hoist myself from bed, to sofa, to table on my crutches; though nobody thought it worth the effort to transport me daily to Floxby Comprehensive. Assignments of work were sent to me and I remained at Boxall Hill, living, not in luxury certainly, for the diet was unvarying – vegetable soup, Shredded Wheat, home-made bread and apples, but in serene, idyllic happiness.

Lulie and Grisch went calmly about their lives, stopping by my couch many times a day to give me the respective benefit, Grisch of his system of muscle exercises and encyclopaedic knowledge, Lulie of her uncompromising, unjaundiced, unsparing view of existence. *'Es ist zu hilfen wie a toyten bankes,'* was one of her favourite expressions. 'That's about as much use as bleeding a corpse.' And another: '*A fleckl herein, a flekl heraus, und the meisse ist aus.*' Or, 'A scrap of this, a scrap of that, and it's all over.' 'Everything is somewhere else,' she said.

Dave and the twins had gone off, respectively, to Baton Rouge and Harvard. The twins were not pleased at the aura of disgrace that accompanied their departure, arguing stoutly to the last that they had meant me no harm in the world, that old Venom was the real culprit, and that it was grossly unfair that he should be allowed to get away with his crime. But Tante Lulie told them not to get their bowels in an uproar, Sir Worseley was absolutely certain to come a cropper sooner or later. 'The way he continually quarrels with people and tyrannises over that poor *yenta* of a wife; I have seen her, often, in the Maxi-Market, looking absolutely *oysgematert*, exhausted, with that trolley-basket of hers, staring about her as if she didn't know an egg from an apple. They make their own bad luck. You go off to Harvard, and try not to get up to any more mischief than you can help.'

So the twins departed, protesting, and commanding me to write to them at least once a fortnight. Much to my relief, they and Dan had failed to hatch up any plot of revenge on the Venners.

To the last, also, they refused to make any disclosures about the provenance of the sheep's eyeballs, or divulge the ingredients of the potion that had turned my hair green; when questioned they assumed enigmatic expressions and said they had never expected that it would work so well. It would probably wear off in six months or so, they predicted.

As soon as they had left, Tante Lulie applied herself to the problem. She snipped away so much of my green and gluey locks that what remained – no more than a couple of inches – could quite easily be disciplined and made to lie flat by brushing until my scalp felt like a roller-skating rink, and by the application of numerous tinctures, balms and embrocations which Lulie brewed herself.

'I just wish that my hair would grow again straight,' I said. 'I'm tired to death of this fuzzy bush.'

'We see, we see,' said Tante Lulie. 'Keep brushing, *bubeleh*. One thousand brushes, at least, both night and morning.'

She put in a lot of time brushing herself, and so did Mariana. Peaceful, sociable mornings we passed, quiet, industrious afternoons during which I read aloud from my A' level set-books – Goethe, Nostromo, *King Lear*, Kafka, Dostoevsky, Chaucer – while one or other of the ladies brushed away diligently at my reduced crop until it felt more like nap or fluff than the old rough crinkly growth. In the glass, now, I could hardly recognise myself, I seemed to have such a huge expanse of forehead and such large earnest eyes, like those of some nineteenth-century female social-reformer.

Grisch had created a felt pad glued on to a rubber base, and with this Mariana or Lulie would rub my head, much as one curries a horse.

'Maybe, *kinahora*, it will also stimulate your brain,' Lulie suggested.

As well, she vigorously attacked the problem of the hair's immutable, obstinate greenness. Lulie had a deep interest in colour and, if she bought materials at her auctions and rummage sales whose hue did not please her, would often mix dyes, trying out different combinations, and might dip stuffs once, twice, or three times, in a fanatical search for some rare tint that she wished to achieve.

At first these efforts were unavailing. Brew after brew ran, like water off a duck's back, inoperatively through the verdant crop.

'I look like a statue that has been out in bad weather for twenty years.'

'We do not give up so easily,' declared Tante Lulie.

Each night she sent me off to bed with a cap of muddy paste strapped over the top of my scalp. This, one morning, proved to have turned my hair a smokey greenish pewter colour.

'Well, I certainly prefer it to that very bright green it was before,' I said doubtfully, surveying it in the glass.

'Interesting,' pronounced Grisch. 'It matches her eyes, but does not agree with the rest of her appearance.'

Mariana concurred.

'No? You don't like it?' Lulie was disappointed, but by no means defeated. 'We go on trying.'

In two or three weeks, after more experiments, she found a shade that was approved by all: a dark tangerine brown which, by some chemical miracle, seemed able to hold its own against the puissant green.

'It *looks* dyed, though,' objected Mariana.

'I don't mind that one bit. Lots of people my age have dyed hair.'

'Striking it certainly is,' said Grisch. 'And, yes, it suits her. Though it makes her look older.'

'I don't mind looking older. I *feel* older.'

So the tangerine brown was allowed to stay.

One day my father dropped by (he was going on over the hill to the Silkins' to deal with a calving problem) and left a load of books for me that had been mis-delivered. I answered the door (Lulie was at the races, Mariana working on her top-notes upstairs in the ballroom, Grisch over at the coach-house tending the generator) and, even though I was supported on my crutches, for a moment Father did not recognise me at all.

Then, vaguely surprised, he said, 'Oh, it's you! You've done something to your hair – haven't you? I brought these books, some fool left them at the house. Thought you might need them. Are you all right here?'

'Oh yes, thank you. I'm fine. My cast is supposed to come off in a week or so; then I can come home,' I added sadly.

'All right.' He gave me another puzzled, not unfriendly glance and departed. I forgot him at once.

Of course what I wanted to do with Mariana, more than anything else, was to make her talk about my mother. The fact that they had been such friends, so much more closely acquainted than had ever been apparent (to me, anyway), created a tantalising Bluebeard's chamber of potential mystery and revelation. Yet the facts, when produced, seemed simple and straightforward enough.

'We attended the same school in Geneva for a while,' said Mariana. 'I was an orphan, sent to it from a convent in Bratislava. Your mother was younger than I. But we learned from the same piano teacher.' *Piano* teacher? I thought. I never knew that my mother played. We didn't even have a piano. 'Then, of course, when your mother left to live with her cousin in Scotland, we lost touch. And then she married ... As Mrs Crumbe, in Floxby, I did not at first recognise her. But then, when we did realise – oh, what a great pleasure! She was a dear, dear friend. She would come back here, sometimes, after meetings of the Festival Committee, and we would just talk. Since we had both lost our families, you see; one does not know, now, so many people from the old days.'

Of course I asked if Mariana knew anything about my mother's first husband, the bearded man at the funeral. But no, she did not.

'Your darling mother was a very compartmented person,' pronounced Mariana, brushing away at my burnt-marmalade hair. (The brushing, Lulie said, should be maintained for many months, preferably for ever, to compensate for the drastic chemical assault on the hair's natural flexibility and oils.) 'She once told me, without going into particulars, that in the past some total disaster had befallen her, because of an indiscreet revelation that she'd made.'

'Who to? What about?'

'Ah, she never told me that. There were some things that she would not disclose. She did on various occasions admit that her relationship with your father was terribly hampered, if not altogether overturned, vitiated, by her habit of reticence. But she said that, nonetheless, this was preferable to the alternative.'

'*What* alternative?'

Mariana shook her head.

72

'No use to ask. Some knowledge that she felt would distress your father very greatly. She did not dare to take the risk.'

'But what could it possibly have been?' I worried. 'That she had done something wicked? Been to prison? Murdered somebody?'

'Oh no, no. Never, never!' Mariana was half-shocked, half-entertained. 'Darling, what priceless, melodramatic ideas you nurture! I am certain, quite positive, that it was nothing of such a kind.'

'But how absolutely tantalising to think that I shall probably never know.'

Mariana gave me a long, clear look. Afterwards, I was to remember the enigmatic expression in her deep-set blue eyes. Sometimes the twins had that look, too; it was the only way in which they resembled their mother. But their eyes were a dark-green mud colour.

'However you remember her, my angel, let it be always with love. She was a superlative person, your mother; she could, given other circumstances, have done tremendous things with her life. I shall always be happy to think that she was my friend. And she had huge hopes for you. Which you will justify, I am sure!'

One of the things I loved most about Mariana – because it was in such total contrast to the habits of my parents – was her proclivity for extravagant admiration. I spent hours egging her on to talk about the many famous people she knew, or had met, and savouring her lavish descriptions of them. She had a funny turn of colloquial English, very upper-crust in its inflections and adjectives. Odious, priceless, scandalous, too killing, too appalling.

'Schweitzer: the most *brilliant* man. Yes, yes, I met Garbo; she was *staggeringly* beautiful. It was the eyes that chiefly haunted you. Like twin moons. Leslie Howard? Such a sweet, sweet person. The Windsors? They were a queer, appealing, faded pair. Sad, you know, but somehow glamorous, touching.'

Not only the famous came in for her eulogies. 'Such a plain, shy boy, but the inside of his mind was like the most wonderful Eastern bazaar – one would wander in it for hours together.'

I could certainly wander in Mariana's mind for hours together; she was my Xanadu. Of course I was helplessly in love with her: the planes of her wonderful bony face seemed perfection to me, the slight jerky ungracefulness with which she moved, walked, or sat was more to my taste than any possible felicity of motion; her funny, gruff shout of laughter was the most heart-warming sound that had ever gladdened my ears. And she laughed so often! My feeblest attempts at wit served to throw her into stitches, and she encouraged me to come out with many more, to give utterance to anything that came into my head; in those weeks at Otherland it is likely that I talked more, laughed more, than I had during all the preceding years of my life.

Lulie, meanwhile, taught me dressmaking.

'*Es kommt a mohl zu nützen*,' was her credo. 'Nothing must be wasted. You may use your *un*-broken leg to operate the machine.'

It was an ancient treadle Singer, kept lovingly in tiptop condition by Grisch, and on it Tante Lulie made his denim overalls and velvet jackets as well as Mariana's celebrity wardrobe. In four days she taught me more than Miss Sykes, the head of Domestic Science at Floxby Comprehensive, had achieved in four years. I can still hear Lulie's shriek of exasperation:

'Ach! You have it all wrong *gethreddled*! *Tension*! You must understand that tension is the most important part of sewing. The pattern? *Narrishkeit*. Unimportant. We use it only as a basis.' And she would toss away most of the pattern pieces and, with her scissors, slash recklessly at a breadth of material in a way that made me turn cold with fright; but she always produced the exact shape she wanted, to a hundredth of a millimetre.

In the same way she flew at the papers. She and Grisch took three between them, *Times*, *Guardian*, *Telegraph* ('*Telegraph* is best for news coverage,' said Lulie, 'though I do not agree with its views'). Having scrupulously waited until Grisch had read them, Lulie tore into them like a terrier, ruthlessly slashing out news stories, leading articles, background features; what she did with these I had no idea, but by the time she had finished with the papers they were in ribbons, fit only for lighting the fire.

She had done excellently at the races lately, and so attended several furniture sales. By now I had learned that when Lulie vanished for a day, it was to make for one of the three race-tracks that were within commuting distance of Floxby; a friend of hers, Roger Patcham the market gardener, another betting enthusiast, drove her over. She studied form assiduously and followed her own system; almost invariably she returned from such excursions with handsome winnings. All these were devoted to the needs of the Boxall Hill household, or the wardrobes of Grisch and Mariana. On herself she spent next to nothing.

'*Nu*? What should I need? Here I pay no rent. I want for nothing. Why not put the money where it will be of use? *Kinahora*, it is all tax free.'

At the last sale she had bought a pair of enormous, chestnut-brown velour curtains, and from about a third of one of them she was helping me make myself a coat.

Tante Lulie did her sewing in the ping-pong room on the ground floor. Vast and cavernous, it contained a table-tennis table and a snooker table, a battered bookshelf with copies of old scientific magazines, a piano which

Grisch kept tuned and in good order like the other six or seven pianos scattered about Otherland, some beat-up armchairs and a hammocky old sofa. Next door was a utility room with a huge sink, a washing-machine, and a cumbersome old airing-rack composed of four long wooden slats suspended from the ceiling by a pulley; 'Heavy enough to crack your skull if you let go of the rope. Always take care, *bubeleh*,' said Tante Lulie.

Mariana never came near the ping-pong room because she said it gave her the horrors. One end of it, the end where Lulie kept her Singer machine, backed on to the kitchen with its solid-fuel stove, and so remained always mildly warm; but we did also make use of a little paraffin stove with a glowing ruby eye.

On one occasion the telephone rang as we sewed. There was an extension in the kitchen; Tante Lulie went off to answer it. Though I was fairly mobile now, having progressed to a rocker on the base of my plastered foot, my best speed was still nothing to boast about.

When Lulie came back, she said, 'That was Dolly. She plans to come down next weekend.'

I had not seen Dolly since she'd bolted out of the housekeeper's room after my accident. I said a little blankly, 'That will be nice. Er – how will she come? Will one of the boys drive her down?'

'No, she will catch the train and Grisch can meet her at the station.'

'Of course.'

I looked up and found Lulie's broad, benign, illusionless face regarding me over the spine of the sewing-machine.

'Your cast comes off tomorrow, *nu*?'

'It does. I shan't know myself.'

'Then, I think, *bubeleh*, it might be a good plan if you were to return home, say, on Thursday.'

'Yes,' I said slowly. 'I expect you are right.'

Just the same, her suggestion gave me a frightful pang. What! Exchange this heavenly, free, cherished, talkative existence, living on terms of equality with three intelligent, interesting adults whom I loved and respected – exchange all this for the narrow trammels of home, for my father's mumchance lack of attention, or gloomy disapproval, for the company of Veronica and her cronies?

'Maybe, now you have your father to yourself,' suggested Lulie kindly, reading all this in my face with perfect ease, 'maybe now you will find out more about him.'

I rather doubted this. Anyway, what was there to find out?

'It will be nice for Dolly, I think, just now, to have her mother all to herself.'

'Of course. Of course it will.'

I had felt, from time to time, that to the other Morningquest children I must seem an interloper, a cuckoo in the nest. Really I was in the house on false pretences. Or so it might seem.

'Dolly has feelings for her mother that you would hardly suspect. They are very deep and hidden,' Lulie went on, looking at me carefully.

It was true that Dolly's public manner to her mother was one of rather carping mockery administered with a petulant, little-girl manner. No one who did not know that Mariana was a world-renowned soprano would have guessed it from Dolly's behaviour, which suggested that she was slightly absurd, and needed continual admonishment.

'More than Selene?' I said.

'Oh, Selene has Toby. They constitute their own *mishpocheh*. Their own society. No need to worry about Selene.'

'I'll certainly go home on Thursday,' I said to Tante Lulie.

'We shall finish this coat for you before then. But anyway,' she said comfortably, 'you will be coming back at weekends, as before, many, many times, I hope. *Nu?* Only, perhaps *not* next weekend, hmn? Indeed your visit has been a great, great pleasure for all three of us; and for Grisch and me, you have been like the child we never had.'

'You and Grisch—?' For a moment I gaped at her, aghast, the ground slipping sideways under my feet. She laughed heartily.

'No, no, you misunderstand me. I do not say that Grisch and I were ever lovers. No, indeed, *au contraire!* Women are not his métier. But we have known each other so long and so peaceably that sometimes we regret we did not have the good idea in time to set ourselves up such a comfort and support for our old age! Grisch worries a great deal about dying old and forlorn, in solitude. And in any case, when we first came here, first met one another, it would already have been too late; I would have been past child-bearing.'

I had no idea what Lulie's age might be; she seemed ageless.

'You could have adopted a child?' I suggested.

'*Es loinsacht nicht!*'

'What does that mean?'

'Not worth the bother. An adopted child – who knows what a time-bomb that may be, ticking away? Even the children one bears oneself are enough of a hazard, God knows— ' She broke off suddenly, looking down at the machine, and said, 'You are running that seam too close, *bubeleh*; go back six inches and do it over.'

*

76

Grisch drove me to the hospital to have my cast removed. The break had healed well, and the surgeon told me I should have no problems, though he advised me to walk with a stick for a week or two.

'So, tonight we go dancing,' said Grisch, as we drove back to Boxall Hill.

'Uncle Grisch, you and Tante Lulie have been so kind to me. I've been so happy here—'

'Ah, sha, sha,' he said. 'You have been our little ray of sunshine.'

'Come off it, Uncle Grisch!'

'No, I mean it,' he said. 'When you grow old, like Lulie and myself, the end begins to lie in wait. You have it in mind.'

This was particularly true of Grisch, I knew. He was not exactly parsimonious, but when buying anything – instant coffee, adhesive tape, toilet paper, whatever – he always chose the smallest possible size. 'In case I die before I finish it. I *hate waste*.'

He worried about waste a great deal of the time. And, although his latter end did not seem to be at all near – he was in excellent health – it was plain that he had it constantly in mind.

'There is always some threat,' he said plaintively. 'Just now, I am threatened with cancer of the throat. I feel a certain something – just *there* – ' he laid a finger below his ear – 'when I swallow. I keep thinking, what a horrible, horrible way to die. Like Freud.'

'His was cancer of the jaw, I think?'

'So what? Equally unpleasant.'

'And Freud smoked a lot of cigars. Have you been to a doctor?'

'Not yet,' said Grisch. 'I wait a week. Generally, by the end of one week, the symptom disappears. Something else will take its place. Ulcers, angina, paralysis. *But one day a symptom will persist for longer than a week*. And then I will know that my time has come. That will not be *so* bad,' he went on, glancing sideways at me as he drove. 'Of death itself, I am not afraid. It is just the uncertainty, not being sure how it will make its approach known; that is what keeps me constantly in a state of troubled anticipation. You see?'

'I think I do. Yes.'

Had my mother, I wondered, experienced this state? Or had she known for sure? Had she watched it approach?

I felt for Uncle Grisch's thin arm and gave it a squeeze.

'I'm really sorry about your cancer of the throat, Uncle Grisch. But you might be wrong. It's not as if you smoked a lot of cigarettes like Dave.'

'How Mariana can bear to have him about the place – and she a singer.'

'But anyway I think you should see a doctor. Maybe you have a throat ulcer and he can give you penicillin for it. Or Vitamin C.'

'It will pass,' he said. 'What I am really saying – do not interrupt me, please – is that while you have been here at Boxall Hill, talking and working and keeping Lulie and me busy and cheerful, my cancer of the throat has been much less obtrusive; so also with the prostate gland, heart palpitations, skin melanoma, varicose veins, bone disease, and Alzheimer's disease. All have abated considerably.'

'Well, I'm really glad of that. Anyway,' I suggested, 'you can hardly die of *all* those things. That ought to be some consolation? Alleviation?'

'You think so?' He pulled up in the stable yard. 'Ought and is are not good neighbours.'

'Talking about neighbours, what has been done about Colonel Venom?'

'Done? Nothing. I got Garnet to repair the tree-house. And we informed the police in case anything of a similar kind should happen again. But nothing has. Gideon is away, the children have not been down, there has been nothing, you see, to inflame Venom's wrath. Or not here. Probably, instead, he turns it on that poor persecuted wife. Marriage,' said Grisch, helping me out of the car, 'is a truly terrible institution.'

That afternoon I went for a walk in the ilex grove. It was a clear, tingling, ice-cold day. The little fountain in the yard was capped with a neat dome of ice. All morning the frost had not melted off the grass, in spite of sunshine. The shoe on my mended foot seemed perilously thin and flexible after the rigid cast, and the ground below that shoe remarkably hard and lumpy.

With a stick borrowed from the miscellaneous household supply of umbrellas, canes, hockey sticks, racquets and bats, I set off across the crisp grey grass. The ilex grove rose ahead of me in dark classic curves, and Toby's staircase made its elegant sweep before plunging into the foliage. I had sworn to Tante Lulie that I would not even *think* about climbing it.

'All we need is for you to break the other leg. Do me a favour, stay strictly on the ground.'

As a matter of fact I did not even want to climb. The memory of my fall, its frightening unexpectedness, my loss of control, and the painful snap of the bone, all that was much too recent and vivid. Perhaps I would never have the impulse to climb trees again? But in the meantime I did have a strong wish just to be in the grove by myself, to listen to its silence, sniff the cold, musty, smoky scent of the ilexes, and shuffle luxuriously through the slippery dead leaves.

'Sheba: our best hunt terrier.' 'Tammy: Alan's favourite hack.'

Who had put up these records to long-defunct dogs and horses? The dates on the small tombstones were back at the beginning of the century, so presumably it was the LeMercier family.

For me, the ilex grove held the essence of Otherland; perched high on the hillside, a long way from the town, silent and contained inside its own solitude. I loved the Morningquest family and what they represented, but this place they inhabited was of equal importance to me. Here I felt I could understand why, in so many early religions, groves had been held to be sacred places, how it came that altars and temples were established within them, oracles and sibyls visited, sacrifices celebrated, the dead interred.

Grisch had a picture-book of graveyards; it seemed an odd subject for a book, but many of them were very beautiful, and I particularly admired the Turkish habit of burying their dead in small woods where, during the heat of summer, the graves would be kept cool in shade, and the spirits, if restless, could float and refresh themselves amongst leaves and branches.

Toby had set up a rude bench in the centre of the grove, a resting-spot for workers on the tree-house: two up-ended logs and a plank nailed across them. Finding that even after the short walk, my mended leg ached, I made my way to the bench and sat down. From here, through the tree-trunks, I could see to the willow-pond, and beyond, over the top of the little chestnut copse through which my mother and I had walked, to where the wide landscape stretched mistily to the horizon.

The melancholy of parting had me in its grip. Which, I told myself, was perfectly stupid. I was not going into exile, but to my own familiar home, not three-quarters of a mile away. I could return here whenever I chose, in two days' time if I liked. And Dolly had a right to her mother's undivided attention.

There were over forty ilex trees in the grove, so the twins had told me. The family, they said, believed the grove to be slightly haunted, in that it was never possible to count the trees and get the same total twice running. For my part, I had never tried, and did not intend to. The trunks were pale grey, but delicately greened over with lichen; straight and plain like temple columns, they soared upwards. Rough grass covered the ground between, sprinkled with leaves, here and there a clump of brambles. Every now and then Grisch, or Garnet, or one of the boys, would cut down the brambles. But this had not been done for some time, and the clump just behind Toby's bench was now three or four feet high.

I heard something stir beyond it, perhaps a footstep, and because of my lameness and inability to move quickly I felt a sudden and rather unreasonable qualm. 'Is somebody there?' I called, standing up, leaning on my stick, glad that I had brought it. Nobody answered.

'Who's there?' I called again, remembering suddenly that on the night of my fall, Uncle Grisch, fetching water, had said he'd heard something in the grove.

What I heard was a sort of snuffle.

Limping round to the far side of the bramble clump, I was astonished to find Lady Venner down on her hands and knees by one of the trees.

She presented a ludicrous and pathetic spectacle. The clothes she wore – grey tweed coat, long tubular tweed skirt, grey ribbed stockings, highly polished black ankle-strap shoes – were all at least twenty years behind the times, rigidly respectable upper-class ladies' clothing, very much at odds with her position and behaviour. She must have got them by mail order, long ago, from Dickins & Jones. She seemed to be grubbing about in the short grass as if she had dropped a hairpin. She wore on her head one of those very upright hats, black velvet in several tiers, with a feather. It had been tipped slightly sideways by her odd activities.

'Lady Venner! What on earth are you doing? Have you lost something?'

Leaning on her grey-gloved hands she peeked up at me through a black mesh veil. 'Hush!' she hissed. 'Someone might hear you!'

And she returned to her search, combing with her fingers through the grass – under the trees it was not frosted, but it must have been extremely cold. What she was doing reminded me of Lulie's operations on my hair.

'Have you lost a brooch – a ring?'

'No, no!' she whispered urgently. 'It's very important. But I mustn't tell you, I can't tell you. Nobody must know.'

She went on urgently grubbing about.

It seemed pretty plain that the poor lady had taken leave of her wits. I supposed that life with the Colonel might easily have such an effect on a person who, perhaps, was not mentally robust in the first place. Otherwise, why marry him?

'Come along, Lady Venner,' I said with compassion. 'Let me take you home. I don't think you are going to find whatever it is that you have lost. It's very cold, and it will be dark fairly soon. Come along. Let me give you a hand. See, you have got your gloves all dirty.'

Leaning on my stick, using it as a brace, I managed to hoist her up. It was like hoisting a scarecrow; the poor creature's arms and legs felt like curtain-rods. She was painfully thin.

'That's the ticket! Now let's go,' I urged her, half pushing, half pulling.

I supposed that, as the crow flew, it would be only a quarter of a mile across the park to Aviemore, but we were no crow, and it was going to be a long laborious trek up the frosty, grassy slope.

Lady Venner began to gabble. 'It's not having servants, you see? All I have is a daily woman. That's not enough. It's by no means enough. It is not what Burly is used to. That's what I call my husband, Sir Worseley, you know. It is a pet-name. But he is accustomed to a cook and a parlourmaid, and a valet. *How* can we manage? You seem like a strong girl. Would you come to us? Would you like a job? The house is modern. Can you cook?'

At this moment I began to hear distant echoes. A voice was shouting, 'Prue? Prudence?' Faintly at first, then louder.

'I think your husband is coming looking for you, Lady Venner,' I said with considerable relief.

She started to shake. 'Please don't tell him where I was! Don't! But he's sure to guess. And he'll be angry.' She pulled off her gloves. 'Here, take these, and put them in your pockets. Then perhaps he won't guess.'

The Colonel came striding down to us. 'Prudence! I told you *not* to go down there!'

Her lips, her chin, her whole face quivered. She cringed. Supporting her, I felt her legs crumple. I said, 'Look, Lady Venner isn't a bit well, Sir Worseley. She's going to need a lot of help to get home. Can you take her arm, please?'

He gave me a belligerent stare, and then his look changed, marginally, and he said, 'Oh, it's you. Aren't you the girl who got hurt falling out of a tree?'

'I broke my leg, yes. That's why I'm staying with the Morningquests. I just had the cast off today.'

'I know your father, don't I?'

'Tom Crumbe, the vet, yes.'

He said abruptly, 'You shouldn't be heaving my wife about. Here, let me take her off you, she weighs no more than a sack of potatoes.'

He put his hands under her armpits and lifted her bodily. She let out a little moan, which was half fright, half the breath being jerked out of her.

'All right, thanks, I can manage her now.'

But she began to squawk and mumble. 'My shopper, my shopper. It's by the tree. I can't go without it, I can't.'

'What does she mean?' I asked Colonel Venner.

He said furiously, 'She must have brought her shopping basket on wheels with her, she takes it everywhere. She's a bit confused, you know.' He grimaced at me over her flailing arms. 'Do you think you could be a good girl and very kindly find it? If you take it as far as the drive, I'll come back and pick it up when I've got her indoors.'

And he plodded away with his wife in his arms. Her wordless wailing cries sounded like some sad sea bird.

I went back into the grove and easily found her wheeled basket by a bramble clump. I now remembered I had seen her with it, many times, pecking nervously about in Floxby shops. I had a look inside, hoping that whatever she had lost might be there, but it held nothing except a handful of grass and moss, and a few dead leaves. Poor thing, I thought. No wonder the Colonel tends to be irascible.

Then I wondered if she could have been responsible for my broken leg. Had she sawed through the joist? But no: whoever cut so neatly through nine-tenths of that joist had skill, co-ordination and cunning; it seemed to me that Lady Venner was signally lacking in those qualities. If one of the couple had done the deed, it was indubitably the Colonel. Perhaps he was sorry, now, that I had been the unintended victim of his act, but that left me a long way still from feeling that I was required to forgive him.

I wheeled the basket up to the tarred driveway, and then thought I might as well take it as far as the gate of Aviemore, only another five minutes along the road.

I put the basket inside the fancy oak-shingle gate, with Lady Venner's gloves done up in a ball. And was puzzled, because the voice I could hear crying from the house appeared to be much younger than hers. It sounded like that of a young child.

I had intended to tell Lulie, Grisch and Mariana about the incident, but, when it came to the point, I kept silent. Afterwards I asked myself why I had not said anything, why I had abandoned my new habit of communication? Something about the poor distracted lady, her evident terror of her husband, made me feel sad and sick. I just did not want to discuss it.

Grisch, most unexpectedly, had produced two bottles of champagne for supper. 'Your last evening with us, your leg almost back to normal,' he said. 'We make a feast.'

Lulie, who had been off at a sale in Affmouth buying cotton bedspreads, had also brought back a basket of cheese, fruits and patés. So it was a feast indeed.

Grisch, lit up by champagne ('And it is the real stuff, I wish you to observe,' he said proudly, 'none of your miserable mousseux.') gave us a demonstration of how to draw a person in one line.

'Watch this, Pandora, because for you it is most important: always you must start with the hand, right hand is best, but depending also on whether the subject is a right- or a left-hander; hand first, then up the arm, round the neck, jaw, ear, other side of face, neck, shoulder, down arm, hand, up inside arm, drop from armpit to foot, around legs, up other side of body, and so back to the hand on which you began.'

And there, springing from the paper, was a portrait of Mariana, like some slender mountain deer seen across a ravine, with the skin stretched tight as silk over her bony face. He must love her very much, I thought, to catch her so exactly.

'You do it so fast! All around her in three seconds like a guided tour.'

'Like the weather forecast,' said Grisch complacently.

'The weather forecast?'

'Every morning I am listening to this recitative, beginning at Berwick-on-Tweed, a fast spin around the coast of this island. Most exhilarating. But why always start with Berwick-on-Tweed, I am asking myself?'

'It's because—'

'No – don't tell me, I prefer it should remain a mystery.'

Mariana, talkative, relaxed in a way that I had seldom seen her, expounded her view that only in very small units might the human race be saved. 'Only families are small enough; that's why I work so hard at this one.'

'You do not say much, Pandora,' Grisch told me, at one point.

'Your family likes to argue over meals. Mine tends to go to sleep.'

Oh, why did I not listen to them more carefully? Now I feel, sometimes, as if I had been short-sighted and deaf among the Morningquests; I missed so much. So much.

By this stage of the evening I felt even less inclined to mention the Venners. Especially when Grisch related – to Mariana's consternation – a notion he had heard being discussed among the boys to tar and feather the Colonel and ride him on his own gate.

'Of course I forbade it,' he said. 'It was Dan's idea.'

'It would be. Thank you, Grischa,' Mariana said faintly, huge-eyed with horror. 'Thank Heaven they have such respect for you.'

In the end, flown with champagne, which I had never tasted before, I did manage in a halting way to express my love and gratitude to the three of them.

'*Eppes, eppes,*' said Tante Lulie.

And so we all reeled off to bed without, for once, washing the dishes.

And later that night, a thing happened to me which, at the time, seemed so earth-shakingly important and transforming, that I got up next morning a different person – a new me, severed and disconnected in every way from the one who had gone before.

Still, events can alter, wholly, in retrospect – as the apparent shape of an object changes while it approaches, passes by, and recedes into the distance. So, too, with happenings. And this one, so momentous at the time, began almost at once to change, in receding vision, and to lose its importance, as a mountain top diminishes when seen from the train, becomes smaller, equally beautiful but less significant, then dwindles to a pin-point, and at last is lost entirely – unless its memory is recalled by some external stimulus, notes of a Schubert song, or a glint of moonlight seen across a curtain.

That was another self. I don't have any connection with that person now.

Barney would say, of course, that we can never entirely amputate our past selves.

At breakfast – which Lulie and I took alone together, for Grisch had gone off early to help Silkin with a tractor problem, and Mariana was not yet awake – Dolly telephoned to say that she would not be coming by train next day. Dan was going to drive her down. Selene and Toby might come along as well.

'*Uber gor, uber gornischt*, all, or nothing,' Lulie said. 'Grisch will be pleased he does not have to meet the train. But we must buy some more Shredded Wheat.'

I felt sorry for Dolly, missing the chance to have her mother to herself. But I suppose that is always a hazard in a large family.

Cycling home – with caution – I decided that I would go and call on Lady Venner in a day or two. I felt sorry for the poor woman. Perhaps I could do something for her. It must be pretty grim in that house with no other company than the Colonel.

Next week, meeting Grisch in the WI market hall off Floxby Square, I learned with astonishment that Mariana had flown off to America on Friday. By the time Daniel and the others arrived, she had gone.

'To Boston? To see the twins? Did they have a crisis?'

'I really do not know. She went to London first. And now Gideon tells us of this departure.' Grisch seemed wholly unsurprised.

'Poor Dolly must have been so disappointed.'

'Ah well,' he said, 'they are accustomed to Mariana's sudden comings and goings. The Venners are gone away, also.'

'I know.'

When I went to the house, nobody answered my knock. The postman told me that the Colonel and his lady had gone to Brightlingsea for some bracing air.

Mariana did not return to England for nine months.

VII

The next time I saw Dolly was at the end of the summer.

Having achieved the needed A' level results, and having come to the conclusion that, despite Lulie's hopeful prediction, my father and I were going to take a long time for our relationship to progress to a level of chatty rapport, I had found myself a job in the theatre restaurant at Crowbridge. That way, outside working hours, I could take in some art classes. I was able to lodge in Crowbridge with the family of a girl I had known at school who was now training as a nurse in London, so her room was going spare. And, as a bonus, I got to see a lot of plays and scraped acquaintance with the set designers. Dolly, meanwhile, had been despatched to a family in Chartres to improve her French. So, though I spent weekends at Otherland, we did not see each other for six months.

She came bouncing into the theatre restaurant one Friday evening with five friends, and they made a great business of having two tables pushed together. There were three boys, two other girls in the group, all wearing festive summery clothes. Dolly, I was interested to observe, had changed her image during the summer, perhaps under French influence. Gone were the ugly red coils of pigtail clamped over her ears; instead her hair, which had been cut short, rose in a brilliant crest from her brow and was caught in a clip at the back. Much better. Also, she had grown an inch or so, or lost five or six pounds in weight. Almost elegant, she looked, wearing a plainly cut white, flowered chintz dress – people did wear chintz around then; not a striking costume, but it brought out the tones of her pale freckled skin and red hair. She also wore bright vermilion lipstick, which was a mistake.

Despite her fine new plumage, she was not at ease. I could sense that immediately. She was talking too much, too loudly, laughing too frequently – the kind of high, giggly laugh that is called 'infectious' as if it were a rash; I could hear her using many of Mariana's words: 'killing, priceless, scandalous, divine, odious, grotesque.'

'Oh, how absolutely priceless,' she kept saying. 'How killing.'

I could see that the real leader of the group was a small, self-possessed girl with soft silver-fair hair, a pale mouth and calm grey eyes. Her name seemed to be 'Vision'. Everybody deferred to her, all the time. 'Don't you think so, Vision?' 'You were there, Vision, you saw what happened.' 'What do you say, Vision?'

The three boys in the group were well and conventionally dressed with collars and ties and nice clean hair, not too long. They were the same age as the girls and, as is so often the case, appeared a couple of years younger. The third girl had dark curly hair, a patchy skin, wore glasses, and was no threat to anybody.

I went to receive their order and, when she saw me, Dolly's mouth fell open a yard.

'*Pandora!*'

'Hallo, Dolly,' I said. I was used to friends from Floxby turning up, or their parents; this was old routine to me. 'What can I get you and your friends? The Swiss salad is good.'

Dolly was still staring at me in total amazement. 'You are so different! Good heavens, what a transformation. Why, you look *wonderful!*'

'So do you,' I said.

And then, to her friends, suddenly realising what a social asset I was going to prove, Dolly explained, 'The last time I saw Pandora she had bright green hair.'

'Just the colour of this,' I said, nodding resignedly, accepting the rôle. And with my pencil I tapped the gruesome frilly apple-green heart-shaped apron which was Crowbridge Theatre waitress uniform that year.

One of the boys hooked on. 'Hey, you must be the girl who fell out of the tree!'

Evidently Dolly had made use of the story – which was fairly bizarre, after all – to entertain London friends.

'But,' said another of the boys, plainly a well-educated one, 'I thought Pandora opened a box, not fell out of a tree.'

'Oh, Ben, you are a goon!'

Amid the general laughter, Dolly made scanty introductions: 'These are my friends Ben Russell, Suzanne Mayer, Vision Plunkett-Smith, and so on. This is Pandora Crumbe.'

Plunkett-Smith, I thought. Why haven't I the luck to be called Pandora Plunkett-Smith. 'I'd better take your orders,' I said. 'Or they'll fire me for loitering.'

'I cannot, simply cannot, get over the change in your appearance,' Dolly kept repeating when I came back with their prawn cocktails.

She was staring at me with frank, undisguised admiration. And I contrasted this with her original gracious patronage and remembered, too, how after the accident she had shouldered into the housekeeper's room, given one embarrassed glance at my green hair, then beat a retreat in horrified dismay. That was the last I had seen of her. Seemingly appearance, for Dolly, was of primary importance. Not surprising, I supposed; with such handsome parents, her own plain looks must have made her miserable for so long. I remembered how the boys teased her about her girth and called her 'Jolly Dolly'. It must have been a trial. Now she was riding high; but still, I could tell from so many of her tones and gestures, not quite high enough.

As they left to go to the play (a Noël Coward revival) Dolly said, 'Pandora, we *must* get together! Do you realise that in a month's time we shall be sharing a room?'

I did, and was not very cheerful about it. I had begun to feel that I might cope reasonably well with the old Dolly. About this new one I was not so sure.

'How long are you going to be working here?'

'Another two weeks.'

'Oh, then you must come up to Otherland and we'll make plans. Gid gave me a car for my nineteenth birthday, so I'll be able to drive us up to Scotland with a load of our things.'

And there yawned the gulf between us, I thought glumly. No doubt before the eye of God I and Dolly were indeed equal; but before the eye of Mammon we certainly were not, and never would be. Not in a month of yesterdays would my father be giving me a car for my next birthday.

In the end I sneaked off up to Scotland on my own, by train, ahead of Dolly. I did not feel equal to that long drive in her company. My books and belongings had been sent in advance by carrier (my father was perfectly helpful and instructive about practical details of that kind) and the two tea-chests were there, waiting for me, in the nasty little room on campus which had been assigned to Dolly and me. It was L-shaped with one skimpy bed in the window looking out on to the quadrangle, and the other bed across the end of the 'L', a narrow cul-de-sac looking on to nothing.

Of course I politely waited for Dolly to arrive and make her choice, hoping that, as she was so well brought-up and imbued with kindly graciousness, she would take the bed in the dark corner; and of course she did not.

'Which bed would you prefer?' I said when she arrived loaded down with skates, skis, a fur coat, her cello, a tennis racket and a record player. Without hesitation she appropriated the better berth. I suppose that's what having three elder brothers and coming from a large, privileged family does for you: you know when to make a rapid decision.

87

At the time I didn't mind a bit. I was feeling so cheerful that an inferior bed occupying a dark corner in a small poky room seemed a trifling blemish in a future that otherwise spread before me as a broad, sunny panorama. I had just been over to the Art Department, refreshed my memory of its delights, and renewed my acquaintance with Tom Dismas Yindrich, its acting Director.

The usual head of the Art Department, Fergus Ruaridh Mackay, remained almost permanently elsewhere, communing with Nature on an island called Egilsay. He was a white-haired, noble old patriarch who had been briefly in the college at the time of my interview, patted me benignly on the head and told me he had na doubt, na doubt at all, that I would do some grand, interesting work while I was at St Vigeans. I had not expected to have many personal dealings with him, but the sight of his deputy had certainly been a bit of a startler.

Tom was from Prague; his father had been a Czech pilot stationed in Dornoch during World War II, who had fallen in love with a Scots girl, Flora Dalgairn, and swept her back to Prague with him after the war. Later their son had crossed the North Sea to meet his Caledonian aunts and grandparents. The air of Scotland had agreed with him.

'Not to live here for ever,' he said. 'But I like the cool dry Scottish humour, and the granite rocks, and all the things baked in Scots ovens – bannocks and baps, Birlins and Clods, Derrins and Meldars, Nackets and Smoddies and Tivlachs.'

'Good Heavens,' I said, 'where did you come across all those?'

'My grandmother makes them. Or some of them, at least,' he added scrupulously.

Tom seemed young to be the head of a Department – and he was young, only twenty-five – until you studied him more closely and noticed the deep lines round his eyes. I think he worried continuously about his family. His parents were both doctors, back in Prague, and his sister was a teacher. Their views were always likely to involve them in trouble. Tom was skinny and bony, had a long narrow clown's face, a thin, lively mouth and deep-sunk dark-brown eyes that bored into one like drills. His darkish hair was long and unkempt – romantic, I thought. He had made a powerful first impression on me. And the second impression was equally powerful.

The Art Department – smallest, newest, and least-favoured adjunct of St Vigeans – had been housed in Army huts on a windy headland.

'It seems like home to me,' said Tom. 'My grandfather had once a boot factory in Prague. Now, no longer. It stands empty because it was closed by the communists and nobody can think of a use for it. I used to creep in there and make plans, all by myself. That is art, no? Making plans.'

'What kind of plans did you make?'

'Well – for instance – this film on which we work.'

It was a film about socks and gloves. Not a documentary, I mean; the socks and gloves did deeds, led active emotional lives, betrayed each other, underwent religious conversion, fell ill, died, were buried and resurrected. Its spectacularly low budget was laid out mostly on cups of tea to stop the technicians dying of frostbite. Subsequently it won an award at Cannes.

Tom was also encouraging his students to collect wheels from all over Scotland.

'They are sure to come in useful for something,' he said vaguely.

I thought of Tante Lulie's *Es kommt a mohl zu nützen*. She and Tom, I felt certain, would get on like a house afire.

In the meantime the wheels piled up higher and higher around Tom's Army huts and, as he pointed out, provided quite a substantial barrier against the Arctic wind.

In his kilns, exquisite pottery was baked. None of your crude primitive earthenware. I wished that Selene could meet him. But she could never be dragged far from home. He also ran an active Theatre Club in a cellar called Merlin's Cave. He arranged showings of Japanese and Swedish films, sent his students out through the blast to photograph the wealth of sea-birds up and down the coast, and persuaded art dealers far-flung all over the British Isles to lend him paintings that brought people flocking from equally far to see his mixed shows.

'The Czechs are good at ceramics, films, exhibitions, dumplings and mushrooms,' he said. 'In these areas we show our particular genius. In other fields our main skill is to appreciate others and enjoy ourselves. We are not gourmet cooks or sculptors or, on the whole, world-shaking playwrights. Others lead in those spheres. But ah! how we enjoy their skill. That is what I plan to teach my students here. For – let's face it – in this small new university we are not likely to attract very many young people of genius. But what I shall show them is how to extract the maximum value and excitement from all their experiences.'

So – on that first day of term – I danced back to our narrow dark room, and Dolly's displeasure and disgruntlement, in such an exuberant, optimistic frame of mind that her low spirits did not trouble me in the least.

I took her on a tour and showed her the amenities, the showers – our room had only a hand-basin – the ironing-room, students' kitchen, and the common room with sagging armchairs and cigarette burns, which reminded me of the ping-pong room at Otherland.

'Why did Mar ever send me to this awful place?' cried Dolly disconsolately, gazing at the cigarette burns. 'It is unfair! None of the boys' universities are anything like so dismal. And Selene's in clover, going to St Martin's every day. This place is like Belsen!'

'Externals aren't the main thing,' I comforted her priggishly – we seemed to have reversed rôles. 'Wait till you've been to a lecture or two. Then I expect you'll feel differently.'

She seemed unconvinced. She said the Social Psychology professor – his name was Grindley-Schimmelpenninck – reminded her of a sheep.

But luckily he, from the first, was deeply impressed by Dolly, and there were several earnest young men in her department who looked up to her, and solicited her good opinion and often asked for her comments on their essays.

During our first university year, my path and Dolly's did not cross much. And perhaps this was just as well. I was deeply, happily involved in art, drama and literature; nearly all my spare time was passed in the pottery studio, the film workshop, the disused warehouse that we were converting into a theatre, or the freezing art studio. Whereas Dolly lay in bed till all hours, I leapt up at six a.m. and worked late; I was absorbed in gulping down instruction, ideas, points of view, like a donkey indiscriminately munching thistles, grass and dock-leaves. I really had no time or energy to spare for grumbles and homesickness. In which I was lucky, for the conditions at St Vigeans were certainly Spartan and the climate frigid. Also, Dolly's habits as a room-mate were far from ideal.

She, like her brothers, especially Barney, had never in her life been made to tidy up. She left her garments in heaps on the floor as she peeled them off. With the exception of bloodstained knickers, which were hopefully deposited to soak in the bedroom basin (for days on end, had I not kicked up a fuss). Likewise, in the communal kitchen, she would optimistically pile up greasy frying-pans, plates crusted with bacon-rinds and eggstains, burnt toast crumbs, kipper-reeking grill pans, swamps of dank tealeaves, oily sardine-cans and stained coffee-jugs in the sink, strong in the faith that an overnight immersion in cold water would somehow put all to rights.

'Well, *I* left the dishes in soak,' she would proclaim next day, smugly and righteously. 'Now all somebody *else* has to do is wash them.'

For the first time I began to realise what a protected life the young Morningquests had led, with Lulie and Grisch keeping the wolf from the door at Boxall Hill and Mrs Grove with her band of assistants in the London house.

The trouble was that if I reproached her it seemed to have a shattering effect on Dolly's spirits; she would turn on me the eyes of a stricken deer, her mouth would quiver, she would breathe out contrition and guilt, and creep about silently, failing to meet my eye and piling up her scattered belongings into little heaps as a kind of hopeful preliminary to putting them away; but that was as far as her atonement ever went. Not once did she ever proceed to do something about the situation that had caused me to expostulate in the first place – wash the dishes, clean the cigarette ash off the floor, remove the dirty towels from my bed, hang out the soggy wash; she simply took on the air of a poor faithful dog, savagely chidden for some unwitting fault; and she could keep this up far longer than I could keep up my indignation.

It became plain to me after a month or so that Dolly was not going to change, that she was never going to change; either I must resign myself to living in squalor, or I had to be the one to wash the dishes. Further, in order to keep Dolly cheerful, I had to connive at the pretence that she was a big help, or she would eye me with mute reproach and spare no pains to make me notice that she had emptied the ash tray or slightly adjusted the clothes that I had washed and hung out on the communal line. Dolly, I began to see, was a past master at arousing guilt in others; I felt sorry in advance for her husband and children, who were going to lead hunted lives if they did not swiftly get her measure.

She had also found a made-to-measure method of playing on my feelings of culpability and intrusiveness.

'Of course you have completely stolen my mother's affections from me,' she announced, fixing me with huge, wounded grey eyes. 'I know it's not precisely your fault – but you have displaced me, and it will never be the same again.'

'Oh, what rubbish, Dolly.'

'No, it isn't rubbish. Mariana's feelings towards me were never very strong. She's never been very maternal, you know, at any time. Fond of the boys in a way, but she never *doted* on them. And the twins she only just tolerates. Selene was always her favourite, and the funny thing is that Sil has never had any time for Mar, never seemed to feel the need for mother-love. So long as she and Toby have each other, all the rest of the world can go hang. I've often seen Mar looking quite rebuffed. But I've always bored Mariana,' said Dolly sadly. 'She has never made any secret of that. "My good, dull girl," she once called me. It was on my eleventh birthday.'

'No, Dolly, that must be a ridiculous exaggeration. People aren't bored by their children – especially not people so intelligent as Mariana.'

But I recalled my sudden insight into the workings of Sir Gideon's mind: that he would be perfectly happy to dispense with the whole brood of charming talented children and concentrate exclusively on his music. And I thought of my own father.

'Oh, aren't they?' said Dolly. 'That shows how little you know. Think of the Venoms, they were bored rigid by Thelma. They sent her away to learn crafts, and that only made her more boring. Sometimes I think Mar deliberately manipulated me into *being* boring, just so there'd be no risk of my competing with her.'

Privately I felt there could never have been any danger of that, but diplomacy kept me silent.

'And then Mar met your mother and had her as a kind of secret friend. And had even less time for us. Now she's kind of putting you in your mother's place.'

Naturally this accusation aroused in me all kinds of wayward feelings and questions, unresolved doubts and terrors, which I was not about to divulge to Dolly. Instead I said bracingly, 'Dolly, there's not a word of truth in what you say. Mariana has been wonderful about my mother's death – she knew what a shock that was for me, and how my father wasn't much help because my parents lived on such chilly uncommunicative terms. My mother was a very secretive sort of person, I'm only now beginning to discover *how* secretive—'

As a sop to Dolly I told her about the man at the funeral, and that I had asked Mariana if she had known anything about Mother's first husband, and that she had not. But that they had been to school together, and Mariana had known things about Mother of which I was ignorant.

'So you see, it's not that I've displaced you – that would be preposterous; just that Mariana can help me by telling me things I didn't know, filling in gaps for me.'

'There you are, you see, you are more *interesting* to Mariana than I am, because of all these mysteries,' Dolly wailed piteously. 'Everything about me is just so obvious and dull to her. I tried to change my appearance while she was away, I tried to look more glamorous—'

'And you did a terrific job,' I said.

'But what's the use? She still thinks I look as dull as rice pudding. Whereas you – when the twins poured green dye on your hair and broke your leg, you'd think somebody had thrown acid at a Mantegna in the National Gallery. The commotion! And all the changes in your appearance after that were like a work of art that she was helping to create. She never even noticed when *I* had my hair cut off.'

'That can't be true!'

'Well, I'll tell you. When she came back to England she said, "Why,

Dolly, you've had your hair cut off. I do hope you don't regret it later."
And that was all.'

Unfortunately this quotation had the authentic ring of Mariana's incisive delivery.

I took another tack. I said, 'Dolly, you're nineteen. Twenty in two months. You don't *need* a mother any more. You should be looking for different models. Striking out on your own.'

But hewing out a solitary path was by no means Dolly's forte. At St Vigeans she became the nucleus of a large, animated group of well-heeled girls and sporting young males who accepted her good-humoured gracious sisterly image at its face value; they all danced into the small hours every night, wherever they could find a floor to dance on, they listened to Beatles records and when winter laid its grip on the town and the surrounding countryside, they skated, snowballed, and arranged long cross-country skiing excursions. (Dolly of course had learned to ski at the age of four as Mariana sent her brood to Klosters every winter.)

'Dolly seems quite happy,' I wrote to Mariana. 'She is the centre of a huge social group involved in nonstop activities. I can't think why you ever worried that she would be lost or homesick.'

And Mariana wrote back (but not until after a two-month interval; the ratio of her letters to mine was about one to five): 'I would rather you told me that Dolly was applying herself to work. As I have no doubt that you, *mein leibstes hertz*, are doing, solitary and indefatigable, encouraged no doubt by your Tom, who I must say does sound a charmer.'

Tom Yindrich did, at this time, occupy about eighty per cent of my life and thoughts. He was so instructive, so well-informed; like my mother, he seemed able to supply the answer to any question I cared to put to him; also he was funny in a dry, deadpan way that reminded me of Uncle Grisch.

After the daily life-classes (how those models contrived not to die of exposure in the freezing barn that was our studio I will never know), he was egging me on to turn out a flow of portraits. Wizened, gnarled fishermen, crofters, shepherds and grandmothers from the villages around were persuaded in turn to come up to the studio and give us the benefit of their seamed, weathered countenances and ingenuous Nordic blue eyes. For me, it was a continual feast.

Tom was laconic about my work; with other students he would go into lengthy detailed encouragement, suggestion, criticism; but with me it was always one of two remarks. 'Much better,' he would pronounce, after a long, pregnant pause; or, alternatively, '*Much* worse.' And then he would dig me between the shoulderblades and continue on his round.

I had never learned to ski and one essay at cross-country skiing with Dolly and her boon companions had been enough to convince me that if I wished to travel through snow-filled woods, I much preferred to do it at my own pace, in solitude, and not in a file of shrieking, giggling merry-makers who continually fell over tree-roots and had to have their skis adjusted by male helpers. Skating I had learned, however, at age seven, from my mother during a couple of extra-cold winters at Floxby. So I borrowed Dolly's skates and went off to St Vigeans Moss, inland from the town, which had first flooded and then frozen, to enjoy the Breughel-like scene of the townspeople diverting themselves. There I encountered Yindrich, taking pictures with his Nikon, and we attempted a waltz together, accompanied by bagpipe music and guitar from a mixed duo on the rushy bank. That prompted me to tell him about the music at Boxall Hill: the different instruments practised in all the different rooms; the Sunday-afternoon choral practices; the six pianos (or was it seven?); Toby and two of his sisters playing flute trios, Barney working at Beethoven's *Opus 109*, the twins and their formidable Bach programme.

'Morningquest,' he said. 'Ah, I see. That is your friend Dolly, the one with the red hair? I have seen her at a distance, always the Queen Bee, setting the table in a roar.'

His tone was more than a touch derogatory, so I quickly gave him more information about the Morningquest family: how kind they had been to me at my mother's death; how unique was Mariana; how impressive Sir Gideon; how remarkable Lulie and Grisch; how talented their brood of children. And his interest was aroused.

'What a saga! It is like the Bach family. Tell me more. And your friend? What instrument does she play?'

'The cello. But I'm afraid she's been neglecting it since she got here.'

In truth Dolly, once released from family bonds, had cast many of their ways behind her. Except, of course, the confidence that comes from wealth and security; that is not so quickly relinquished.

Christmas, back at Floxby, was a fairly muted affair. I was rather sorry I had gone home at all, since my father was not pleased to see me; he had adjusted very comfortably to a solo existence. Sir Gideon was in New York, conducting a series of concerts; and Mariana was giving a set of song recitals in San Francisco; so their children remained in Cadogan Square, and Lulie and Grisch had Boxall Hill to themselves. I went to see them, of course, and had lovely long talks. They told me that the twins were enjoying a great success in the project at Harvard and had been invited to stay on for another period. 'Those two have remarkable telepathic facility, it seems.' 'I wouldn't doubt it,' I said.

Barney had moved out of the family home and now occupied a flat of his own in Pimlico with his cat Mog, and his girlfriend who was beautiful, intelligent, and rich, Lady Mary Flyth-Wardour, an editor at Schmit, Ponsonby, Power, and De Croux, the art publishers. 'How lovely for Barney,' I said sadly. I had always nourished a hopeless unrequited passion for him, ever since he had been so kind to me after my fractured leg and green hair. But I knew that he was far above my aspirations (and also had a terrible reputation in the family for fickleness; he was said to have broken the hearts of three or four girls already). He had a very good job at USU and was expected to go far.

Dan was working on his doctorate (something to do with silicone chips) and Toby, coming up for finals, was scheduled for the Civil Service. 'But we're worried about Selene. What is she going to do when Toby is permanently away from home?' Toby, from Hay, still spent most weekends in Cadogan Square.

'That Selene is like a mole,' Lulie told me mournfully. 'She goes to her classes, Mariana tells me, comes home, shuts herself in her room and sees nobody. What will become of her? She has no friends, nobody.'

'She needs psychiatric help,' said Grisch, 'but Mariana will not agree.'

Grisch at this time was engaged with Wordsworth.

> 'I wandered lonely as a ghost
> That floats among the dales and hills
> When all at once I saw a host,
> A crowd of golden daffodils.'

'For, after all, to say, "I wandered lonely as a cloud," is preposterous. Clouds are not lonely. Wordsworth was unquestionably a great poet, but in his young days slapdash, careless.'

'Why should a ghost be floating among the dales and hills?'

'Why not? Ghosts have to float somewhere.'

Talking to Grisch and Lulie was my real homecoming. I culled more and more news and gossip from them, while helping Lulie cut out her daily press-clippings, mending a broken window with Grisch in the saddle-room, stacking logs while watching him dismantle and repair the aged mower, ready for next summer, watching Lulie make me a tiger-skin hat from a tattered rug bought for ten pence at a mixed auction.

'Mariana writes that she is anxious about Dan. He does brilliantly at his work, but he has got in with a very joking set.'

'Joking?'

'Practical jokes they play on people. Not nice. Dan belongs to a club where they gamble. One man was found to be cheating. So they say nothing to him, but when they are playing roulette, two of them move up beside him and fill his pockets with kidneys – raw, bloody kidneys. Only a *momzer* would do such a thing,' said Tante Lulie disapprovingly.

I thought this behaviour accorded pretty well with what I had observed of Dan. He had always been my least favourite of the three brothers.

'What other news?'

'In the town a scandal – or a mystery, at least. A girl lost her baby.'

I remembered that Father had mumbled something about that, too.

'Lost her baby? Lost it how? What girl?'

'A red-headed girl. Buckley.'

'Oh yes, I know her. Ginge Buckley. She was in my form at school.' I had liked her. She had left, ultimately, just before her A' levels to have the baby.

'Well, there was some gossip because after it disappeared people said perhaps she had made away with it, because she did not wish to keep it.'

'*Ginge?* She would never do such a thing. *Never.*' I was appalled. 'I'll go and see her.'

'Do that,' said Lulie placidly. 'She was a *good* girl. She came up one year to help Grisch pick apples when I had an infected bee-sting. I liked her. And I met her with the baby once, at a church sale; he was a fine, pink-cheeked *bubele* and she plainly loved him to distraction. It would be in no way likely that she would have lost him on purpose.'

I did go to the Buckleys' house in Station Road, but Ginge was away, her mother told me, staying with cousins in Norwich. 'For the sea air.' I was shocked by the change in Mrs Buckley; she had been a brown, friendly, laughing woman who enjoyed making her small front garden into a bower of scent and colour. Now she seemed to have aged by twenty years and her once well-cared-for clothes looked neglected and draggled. 'Well, Ginge couldn't stand all the talk, you see,' she said, sighing. 'And I don't blame her. We all loved Kirk. It just broke her heart when he was took.'

'How – how did it happen?'

'In the Maxi-Market. She was queuing at the cold-meat counter for tongue, left him in his stroller over by the bread; he was right under the covers, see, he always did snuggle down like a little dormouse when he was asleep, bless him. When Ginge got home, she went to take him out of the stroller and he was gone!'

'How *awful*. Poor, poor Ginge. It wasn't Kirk's father who did it?'

'Alan? Oh no. He felt just as bad as us. They didn't reckon to get

96

married, him and Ginge, too young, you know; but he used to give her a bit, now and then, when he could, for the kiddy ... No it wasn't him.'

'And the police couldn't help?'

Mrs Buckley thinned her mouth. 'Made it plain they thought she done it. Couldn't prove anything. But I reckon they didn't make more than a show of looking.'

I was glad to escape from Floxby, back to the Arctic air and exhilarating company of St Vigeans. This time I travelled up in the train with Dolly. (She had left her mini in Scotland before Christmas, daunted by the prospect of the long wintry drive south.)

Previous to the journey I spent a night in Cadogan Square and a day in London, following Yindrich's instructions to look at every picture in the National Portrait Gallery, and to take in also the National and Tate Galleries. Greatly to my surprise I found myself accompanied in this project by Toby, Dan and Barney. They all happened to be about the house that day, and were attracted by my plan.

'Why isn't Barney in Pimlico with Lady Mary?' I asked Toby as we crossed Trafalgar Square.

'Molly? Oh, she's in Pau with her stepmother – left Barney to mind the cat. He does go back to Pimlico at night. But anyway that relationship's on the rocks,' said Toby judicially. 'He's selling the flat to her.'

'What went wrong?'

'Molly was too possessive. Wanted to know where he was every minute of the one thousand four hundred and forty.'

I did some silent mental arithmetic.

'Where will Barney go?' I asked then. 'Back to Cadogan Square?'

'No, USU have asked him to go to Chicago and run things there.'

'But what about the cat?'

As well as heartbroken girlfriends, Barney left behind him everywhere a trail of deserted cats; somehow (as in this case) there never seemed to be a satisfactory solution for the cat. And yet Barney loved cats dearly – more than girls, perhaps? – always had to have one. No doubt he would have another in Chicago.

'If Molly doesn't want it, I expect they'll give it to the cleaning lady,' said Toby callously. Dan and Barney were walking some yards ahead of us down Whitehall. We were making for the Tate.

'Listen, Pandora,' Toby said. 'I want to ask your help.'

'What for?' I was very astonished that any member of the Morningquest clan should require any help from me.

'It's Sil. I'm worried about her. Soon I'm going off on this six-week course to Geneva and I'm afraid that without me to stir her up a bit every few days, she'll just go into retreat. She doesn't pay attention to any of the family. She says Gid is nothing but an old fraud. And she really seems to hate Mar. Anyway Mar won't be back for several months. I wondered if you could talk to Sil a bit, try to persuade her to see somebody – a doctor, maybe?'

'Oh gosh, Toby, I don't think she likes me much. Why would she take any notice of anything *I* said to her?'

'She doesn't like anybody,' said Toby sadly. He gave me a straight look. 'But she does respect you. She said once that you have guts.'

Guts ... A glum expression. I was visited, suddenly, by a full-scale cartoon-like vision of a self-portrait – myself, with a random, perplexed expression and my guts being pulled in a dozen different directions like the ribbons outflowing from a maypole. At once I was possessed by the frantic urge to get it on to paper or, preferably, canvas. This is one of my chief problems. I have an impatient nature. I find it very hard to bear the necessary period of waiting while the image of a picture enters my mind and solidifies; and yet I am obliged to wait. I know it is useless to start without a certain plan. And the plan, of course, always tends to arrive at the least convenient moment.

So, now I knew that I must carry this plan inside me for at least another twenty-four hours (one thousand four hundred and forty minutes, according to Toby); and, in fact, did so all the time I was careering round London with the Morningquest boys, lugging it like a heavy briefcase loaded with magnetic nuggets. Yet this fidgety burden inside my skull played its part in making that a memorably happy day. We went to the Tate, we went to the Courtauld; sometimes we walked, whistling tunes from the *Serenata Notturna*, sometimes rode in taxis (the Morningquest boys had a rare gift for raising taxis) and we ended up watching Victorian music-hall under the arches at Charing Cross. Barney sat on one side of me, Dan on the other, and I held a hand of each. Even for Dan, on this occasion, I was prepared to feel less dislike than usual, euphoric as I was on white Bordeaux and crab sandwiches.

'Dearest Pandora,' said Barney, 'I wish *you* could live with me and be my love.'

'And be left with another orphan-cat? *A schenem dank*, thanks a bunch, as Lulie would say. An orphan cat I need like a *lochenkopf*.'

'You are a heartless, hard-hearted girl.' But still he kissed me.

I had of course given my word to Toby that I would try my persuasions to make Selene seek professional help, but today there was no time. Dolly and I had berths on the night train to Scotland and we only just managed to make it, driven to Kings Cross at top speed by Barney after my late return with the boys to Cadogan Square.

'But I'll be down again two weekends from now for the ballet,' I told Toby. 'I'll see what I can do then. Maybe she'd allow me to paint her portrait.'

'That might be just the thing.'

Dolly, who had spent the day shopping with schoolfriends in Knightsbridge, was extremely cross with all four of us. When she and I were tucked in our red-blanketed bunks, after Barney had hugged us goodnight and gone back to the orphan-cat in Pimlico, she burst into a furious tirade.

'Gadding about – having childish fun – very irresponsible – poor Silly, left alone in Cadogan Square. Didn't think of *me* – didn't ask me if I'd rather look at pictures than do boring shopping.'

'But, Dolly, you hate looking at pictures!'

'How do *you* know? I might have enjoyed it. Hardly ever get a chance to go out with my brothers.'

'But you hate your brothers— '

'Of course I don't!'

And on and on she went, scolding and repining. While I, heartlessly happy, hypnotised by my visionary self-portrait, drugged with exercise and white Bordeaux, fell fast asleep.

VIII

The arrival of the twins, back from Harvard, was unheralded and unexpected. When their taxi dropped them at the house in Cadogan Square with a great mass of luggage and books, they found the downstairs rooms empty and tidy, the house apparently unoccupied except by Mrs Grove the housekeeper who came up from her basement quarters to investigate.

'Oh, it's you two!'

'So where is everybody?'

'Your dad's in Bergen, your ma's in Mexico City ... Barney's in Chicago, Toby's in Geneva. Dan's here, but never in the house till all hours. Dolly's in Scotland.'

'What about Silly?'

'Oh, Selene's here. She moved her room up to the attic, Barney's old quarters. You'll find *her*.' Mrs Grove's delivery was always flat; now it was markedly so. 'Yes; she's here. That girl's making a painting of her.'

'What girl?'

Mrs Grove was already beginning, in a martyred way, to peck at the mountain of luggage.

'*Leave* that, *don't* do that, we'll take it. What girl?'

'Crumbe ...' came back Mrs Grove's faint voice from the landing as she carried up two bags.

All agog, the twins abandoned their luggage in their bedroom and scurried up more stairs.

The attics, during Barney's incumbency, had been transformed from four little servants' cubicles into one largish, odd-shaped room with skylights and sloping ceiling. Barney had covered the walls with red hessian. Selene had replaced the red with a bleak pale grey, and painted doors and windows to match in a slightly darker shade. The floor was glossy white, uncarpeted. Furnishings were minimal. Books and belongings, if any, were behind cupboard doors.

'Hmmn,' commented Elly. 'Very monastic.'

'After Bronzino, I see,' remarked Ally, who had walked straight across to look at the portrait on the easel. '*Lady in a Yellow Dress*.'

'It is customary,' said Selene coldly, 'to *knock* before entering a person's bedroom.'

She spoke without breaking her model's pose, upright in a straight-backed chair, one slender hand across her thin bosom clasping a stalk of rhubarb.

Pandora, at the easel, gave the twins a more cordial welcome. 'But what happened? When did you get back?'

'This instant minute. We found the house depopulated and came looking for signs of life. Why aren't you up in Scotland with Dolly?'

'Oh, I am, for most of the time. I just stayed down for a few days to finish this.'

'Not bad,' pronounced Ally judicially. 'Bronzino lends himself to Silly's toffee-nosed air.'

'But why have you two come back from Harvard? I thought you were fixed there till the summer.'

'We outwore our welcome,' airily explained Elly.

'We discovered that our sponsor had pinched most of his doctoral thesis from an unfortunate Polish professor who was in no position to remonstrate because he was in jail in Cracow for his political opinions.'

'And we made it rather plain that we didn't think much of that.'

'You've been very quick about acquiring American accents,' said Selene. 'Don't you think that's a piece of affectation?'

'Protective colouring over there,' explained Ally. 'During the period of adjustment while we found our feet, you know, and learned to project ourselves, and invested in a spot of orthodontics.'

'You certainly seem to have done *that* to some purpose.'

'Oh, we were a *succès fou*,' said Elly complacently. 'No question of that.'

'Tante Lulie will be over the moon with your transformation. She always said you might become very chic.'

'Except she will be sorry she didn't do the job herself. Like your hair, darling Pandora; what a truly magnificent job she made of that. You look like one's conception of what the Winged Victory would be if the poor dear lady happened to have a face. But why is our sister Silly clutching a stick of rhubarb, pray?'

'Oh, that's only temporary. It will be replaced by a yellow rosebud. But at this time of year they are so expensive.'

'Chintzy,' remarked Ally to Elly. 'Cheeseparing. But what could you expect?'

Ally carefully studied the brushwork. 'You want to watch out for inherent vice, you know, Pandora dear.'

'Inherent what?'

'Aha! We've been making a study of Albert Pinkham Ryder. A most engaging and worthy painter. You should take a careful look at his work, Pandora my love.'

'Why, for Heaven's sake?'

'Amn't I telling you? Inherent vice. Albert used some very funny combinations of paints. Mixed them with jam, you know, or rhubarb juice, or mayonnaise. Whatever lay handy. The result has been quite queer. All those nice paintings are beginning to buckle and mildew, and change colour.'

'Like Vincent's *Sunflowers*,' Elly put in. 'Going green.'

'*Inherent vice*,' repeated Ally thoughtfully. 'It's a really useful expression.'

'Make a nice title for a novel. Or an ice cream. Fifty-seven different flavours. Try our Inherent Vice with raisins.'

'You are very silly little girls,' remarked Selene calmly. 'Just because you come back from America with a lot of slick clothes and a phony accent doesn't give you carte blanche to – to cut any ice in *this* family. You had better remember that!'

'Do you really think our clothes are slick?'

'What about our hair? Don't you even like our hair?'

'Oh, go away, stop bothering us, and get Mrs Grove to give you some lunch,' cried Selene impatiently. 'Let Pandora get on with her painting.'

The twins gave each other resigned looks.

'It's because she has such a strong sense of hierarchy,' said Elly.

'You always *do* get that in big families,' agreed Ally. 'Now, in China – with this one-child tradition they are trying to set up – nobody will have any sense of hierarchy at all. That may be quite disastrous, of course. Indeed, how can society operate without it?'

'On the other hand,' observed Elly pensively, 'it may be that Selene derives her feeling of superiority not from the fact that she is older than us, but because her father is classy old Gid, whereas ours is merely dicey Dave. Though whether – on balance – one would prefer to have old Gid, rather than Dave, for a father, is a moot point. Quite critically moot, if you ask me.'

Pandora, who had continued to work throughout this conversation, here dropped her loaded brush on the white floorboards.

'Oh,' said Elly. 'See, you have dropped your brush on the nice white floor. Why don't you have a dustsheet, I wonder? Where do you keep the turps, Pandora dear?'

'I believe you have surprised her,' said Ally. 'Didn't you know, Pandora, that Dave was our father? It's no secret, truly.'

'They met while Mar was on tour in the Southern States, way back in the fifties,' explained Elly, mopping the floor, 'and she brought him home as a trophy, you know the way people bring back conch shells and strips of cactus. Gid didn't mind, or not very much. Or, if he did, he didn't say.'

'Not that he *likes* Dave much,' observed Ally pensively. 'About the house.'

'But he's a great one for live and let live, old Gid.'

'Anyway, maybe Dave has left and won't come back.'

'The thing is, Mar has to have a bit of time off from Gid every now and then.'

'Well, anybody would.'

'Gid is a bit too saintly for day-to-day consumption.'

'Like our sister Selene. Now she *is* Gid's daughter, and you can see how she takes after him.'

'Unlike Dolly. We aren't so sure if *she*'s Gid's.'

'*We* don't take after Dave one bit,' said Ally. 'Now our teeth have been fixed there will be no link at all.'

'I think you are wrong,' said Pandora, cleaning brushes.

'About our teeth?'

'No. About Dolly. I'm sure she is your fa— Sir Gideon's daughter. Sometimes she is exactly like him. And I ought to know. I've had plenty of chance to study her while we've been sharing digs.'

'That's true,' said Ally.

'And a very interesting viewpoint,' said Elly.

'And Pandora has a painter's eye.'

'She certainly has. She is entitled to her theory.'

'*Will* you two get out of my room!' screamed Selene, flinging the stick of rhubarb on the floor.

'Sorry, Selene dear. We'll leave you in peace. But why don't you come and have some lunch too?'

'*No!*'

IX

In the spring of our second year Dolly and I moved from our cramped and unpleasing college accommodation to a flat in St Vigeans town. The flat, two huge dark rooms and a courtyard on the ground floor of an eighteenth-century merchant's mansion, would without doubt be glacially cold in winter, but it had various signal advantages so far as I was concerned: the chief one being that now I would have a room of my own to which I could retreat if I chose while Dolly was entertaining her train of cronies. And it would not matter how loud they played their Rolling Stones records, for our landlady was deaf as an adder. And the little paved courtyard with a plane tree was charming and shady during our second, unexpectedly hot, Scottish summer. I put in many hours painting peacefully in that yard, and we ate out of doors all the time.

Of course Dolly washed no more dishes, swept no more floors here, than she had done in college, but it didn't show so much because of the darkness of the rooms, and we had a dank cell-like lean-to kitchen where her greasy crumby plates could pile up until I impatiently dealt with them.

In truth I would have preferred to be on my own; I was beginning to realise that solitude was my chosen state, but Mariana's letters (which were, however, becoming very rare) still exhorted me to 'please keep an eye on poor Dolly' and reiterated her joy that we were still together.

By now I was beginning to realise that she considered this a matter for surprise, and by now I did not wonder. During the period that we had been sharing digs I had found Dolly, simply, hard work; one could not with justice accuse her of selfishness or inconsideration, or bad temper, or moodiness; on the contrary, she was unremittingly cheerful and gracious, but nonetheless under that rippling surface I always sensed a reverse current of suppressed discontent, displeasure, dissatisfaction; she was like a child whose birthday treat has failed to come up to expectation. Some aspect of St Vigeans had let her down – the place? the people? me?

I often felt that, if it were not for Mariana's exhortations and the generosity of the Morningquests, there was remarkably little to hold the two of us together. When we left university we would certainly go our different ways. We had very few tastes in common. And Dolly's single means of demonstrating affection (if affection it were) consisted of what her sociological tutor might have termed the Playful Scold, or Joking

Relationship. With a pouting, little-girl expression, eyes half-closed, a smiling frown, and a cross, cooing tone, she habitually found fault. She continually grumbled. This, I knew, had also been her habit with her brothers, who bore it with exemplary patience. The only defence against her fault-finding, elder-sisterly manner lay in calm silence; to argue was fatal. For my birthday Mariana sent me a pair of filigree silver earrings shaped like leaves; this gift evoked a perfect torrent of jokey, sub-acid comment which lasted, on and off, for weeks ... I quickly learned to escape as fast as I could, or to assume an indifferent, absent-minded demeanour while to her friends she criticised my habits and views – or described my paintings as 'Pandora's nasty Picasso messes.' Or, if they chanced to be representational, as with the portrait of Selene, 'Much too warts-and-all for *my* vulgar taste.'

I had brought the picture of Selene back to Scotland to show Tom Yindrich.

'It's a step,' he said calmly. 'Mm, a decided step. Now we get away from Bronzino, no?' And he gave me a hug.

Ah, now it makes me sigh with impatience at my younger self to recall how incensed I used to get with poor Dolly; I have been in much worse company since. She had her own hang-ups, after all. Selene, during the painting of the portrait, had unbuttoned with me to some degree (though not as much as I had hoped). Sooner than talk about herself, she had let loose a few cloudy confidences about Dolly's difficulties.

The information so artlessly relayed by the twins concerning their parentage had come to me as a staggering shock. Even a year later I was still absorbing its impact. I had to revise my basic estimate of Mariana, of Sir Gideon, of the boys, of Lulie and Grisch – of the whole Morningquest ménage. For so long I had viewed them as a single structure, one organism; suddenly I was obliged to understand that this romantic notion had been simplistic and mistaken.

How – I asked myself again and again – could the boys endure to have Dave about the house? I had never liked him. Now the very thought of him curdled my blood. I tried to imagine a situation in which my own mother brought home a much younger lover and installed him in the guest-room; my imagination simply buckled at the first attempt to picture my father's behaviour in such a scenario. Mariana and Dave? No, no, impossible. And yet it had been possible, was possible.

Dave came, I knew, from a distinguished Deep South family, steeped in courtly tradition and mint juleps. His grandparents, parents and siblings were judges, district attorneys, state governors, deans of colleges. Dave was an abnormality on the family stem. The rest of the family, Grisch told me, were tall, rugged, monumental, and impressive in appearance, with craggy brows and jutting noses. He was short and dapper. But, more fundamental than this difference, he was bone idle. He had obviously inherited his family's intelligence – he could complete any crossword in four minutes, solve logical or mathematical puzzles in the flick of an eyelash – but he had a total aversion to any kind of work or public service, and no intention of using his mind to earn his living. And this basic laziness dwelt with a powerful strain of spite; having searched out for himself another family of achievers, equal and similar to his own; having settled snugly, parasitically into its midst, he was imbued with an urge to tease, annoy and harass his host environment.

Luckily for him the Morningquests, especially the males, were on the whole good-natured and ignored his jibes as they would a buzzing bluebottle. They seemed to accept him as a kind of licensed jester, a court teaser. Dan was the only one who ever showed active dislike.

The twins simply ignored him.

'But didn't anyone mind? Didn't anyone object?' I asked them both when we chanced to be alone together at Easter, working rather half-heartedly on a project to drill a tunnel from the capacious Boxall Hill cellars to the grotto at the heart of the maze. (The original plan for this, and the impetus, had come from Dan. 'So useful,' he had said, 'supposing all the citizens of Floxby suddenly stage an anti-Morningquest riot and come with sickles and shotguns to burn us in our beds; it would make a very good escape route.' But then Dan, typically, had receded from the scheme, being now greatly occupied with a plump girlfriend called Topsy Ponsonby, who made patchwork quilts and sold them to Liberty; so he seldom appeared at the rock face, preferring to pass his time above ground engaged in an activity described by Grisch as 'spooning'.)

One thing about the twins; I knew I could always rely on them to be utterly objective.

'Mind?' said Ally. 'Of course everybody minded. Or so we were given to understand when we were old enough to comprehend the situation. Barney and Toby and Dan had all sorts of lethal plans for disposing of Dave. But Grisch persuaded them not to take action, told them it would be uncivilised. So everybody settled down as best they could.'

'And I will say for our dear siblings,' added Elly, 'that they have never held our paternity against us.'

'Any complaints have been on a strictly empirical, pragmatic basis.'

'Well, and there had been some ambiguity also about Dolly's origins—'

'No, no,' I said. 'Dolly must be Sir Gideon's child. The likeness is marked. There's not a shadow of a doubt.'

'Just the same,' said Elly, 'we have it on good authority . . .'

'Whose?'

'Lulie.'

'Oh.' Lulie, I knew, would never transmit false or unreliable gossip.

' —Good authority that before Dolly's birth, Mar and Gid were on the brink of splitting up. She was proposing to take off with this Somebody and leave Gid with the three boys; and Gid's sister (Tante Sidonie) was going to come over from Paris to live with him and look after the boys. Only that plan fell through because Tante Sid got polio travelling in Albania and died.'

'But who was the Somebody?'

'History doesn't relate. Mar played her cards really close to her chest that time.'

How tantalising it was to recall those winter weeks of what had seemed unclouded intimacy with Mariana, and to realise what huge realms of sequestered territory she still kept fenced away from public intrusion (or mine, anyway); it was like being a tourist in a palace where the zenana, occupying more than half the premises, is kept forever locked and inaccessible.

'Do you think Dave was perhaps a consolation, a rebound, after the Somebody?'

'Perhaps. We have no idea.'

'And conjecture is vain.'

'Why don't you write to Mar and invite her to come up here and visit us?' Dolly urged me, over and over. 'She'd never come if I suggested it, she might for you.'

'Why are you so anxious to have her up here? She wouldn't like your friends.' Dolly never invited her friends to Cadogan Square or Otherland.

'She'd like this flat. She'd admire your taste. And she'd impress old Grindley-Schimmelpenninck. And she'd get on with Mrs D.'

Our landlady, Mrs Dalgairns, was Tom Yindrich's Scottish grandma; it was he who had told me about the flat, that it was available. Mrs Dalgairns was short, frail, but energetic, with snowy hair neatly plaited and shrewd blue eyes; although not in the least resembling Mariana, she reminded me of the latter in that they shared an intensity, a ferocious, indomitable quality. It was easy to imagine either of them riding to the guillotine on a tumbril in petticoats, head high, looking neither to left nor right; this was a quality that Dolly lacked entirely.

'Yes, they might get on, it's true,' I said slowly.

'If only it were possible to talk to Mrs D.'

Communication certainly was impeded. She was so impregnably deaf that we could only transmit a message by writing in a notebook that she carried in her overall pocket (by day Mrs D invariably wore a blue-and-white print overall while presiding over the small but magnificent sweet-shop which occupied the front part of our ground-floor premises. At night, upstairs, she was formal in dark brown with a large Cairngorm brooch). To any written statement or question her usual reply was one gnomic syllable: 'Hmn,' or 'Aye'. Tom was the only person who seemed able to get her to converse. *His* voice, mysteriously, she could hear; it was tuned to her range.

Tom and she were devoted to one another; in fact I thought she was the main reason why he remained in Scotland. Often he seemed homesick for Prague. It was Mrs D who had told me about his poetry, unpublished in Czechoslovakia of course. They were terse poems, ironic little statements, some of which he had translated for the entertainment of his grandmother, not for any other purpose it seemed. For her, he was a link with her greatly missed daughter.

'You could persuade Mar to come to Scotland,' Dolly repeated obsti-nately. 'You know she is putty in *your* hands— ' with so much emphasis that I knew this must be the reverse of what Dolly really believed. And it was quite untrue, as I also knew full well; Mariana had not answered my last three letters. I had a strong suspicion that I would not be hearing from her again. She had recently gone off to Brazil where, the twins reported, she was due to meet Dave and then come back to London with him.

By what means the twins got their information, I was never sure; perhaps they were in telepathic communication. At present they were in London, polishing up their German in preparation for Heidelberg; they wrote to me regularly.

'You could invite Mar to come to the end-of-term ball,' Dolly suggested.

'Dolly, that's idiotic; you know she would detest the ball!'

At St Vigeans it was the social climax of the academic year; Dolly looked forward to it with natural enthusiasm, I with natural dread. Though in fact, this year, it might not be so awful as I gathered it had been on former occasions; this year it was being billed as the Arts Ball, and Tom Dismas Yindrich was playing a major part in its organisation. Thanks to him, instead of the College Hall, a gloomy Victorian barrack abandoned by a long-defunct dissenting sect, the ball's venue would be a capacious prefabricated hangar, the charitable donation of some fly-by-night oil prospectors. This would have the advantage of departure from all former tradition since it was located on the headland alongside the other Arts buildings a mile out of town; for which reason the Dean and Provost, and older members of faculty, might be deterred from attending the party.

It was to be fancy dress; Dolly had already contracted with me to make her costume. She was going as Mary Queen of Scots.

'But why her?'

'She was tall, like me, and had red hair.'

'Dark chestnut, to be accurate. And her eyes were brown, not blue. But let that pass.'

As a matter of fact, I had a good time constructing Dolly's black-and-white costume with its fetching little headdress. And she looked a knockout in it.

'*Please* write and ask Mar to come,' she besought me.

It was because – poor thing – she wanted Mariana to see her in the Queen of Scots costume. I knew that full well. Dolly always hoped – as thwarted lovers forever do and forever will, I suppose – that some happening, some transformation, would magically throw the course of events into reverse, and change boredom back into love.

Dolly loved to argue. It was one trait that all the Morningquests had in common. So we used to conduct these debates while I was working on her costume. I hate to waste time, always have; argument seems to me a hopelessly unproductive occupation, unless it can be combined with some form of creation, or some necessary and useful task such as making pastry or tidying one's workbox. I can't argue while I paint, though.

In the end I did write and invite Mariana, and, of course, had no reply. Meantime I made my own costume for the ball. I was going as a bat.

The reason for this choice was that shortly after we had moved into our new quarters, Mrs D came downstairs one morning in a state of unusual disarray with a handkerchief tied tightly over her silvery plaits. She asked for help in expelling 'a gilpy wee flittermouse' which had invaded her bedroom and was whirling nervously about, apparently unable to find the exit. I caught it in a bath towel and, charmed by its elegant trick of folding striated wings like leaves over its furry head, made several drawings of it before releasing it into the courtyard where it then perversely decided to take up residence. So I was given plenty more chances to study its gait and habits.

I showed my drawings to Mrs D, hoping to persuade her that bats were not 'clarty wee hallions' but, on the contrary, interesting and lovable. She refused to be converted, affirming that to see them 'flittering ava' gave her the 'mirligoes'. But she did, from then on, take a keen interest in my sketchbooks, which were mostly full of portraits, and would pore over them absorbedly for half-hours at a time, exclaiming, 'Eh! yon's the postieman!' or 'Hech, sirs! it's auld Maggie Sempill to the life. Ye've a farrant wee talent there, my dearie.'

I succeeded in keeping my bat costume – pewter-coloured tights and tunic, dark crepe wings boned with old umbrella ribs, and a buckram mask covered in plastic fur – secret from everybody, even Dolly, by carrying out the construction work upstairs in Mrs D's parlour on her sewing machine. Dolly was never much interested in other people's concerns. 'Have you done yours yet?' she might vaguely ask, and if I said, 'I'm giving it some thought,' she asked no more.

I had assumed we'd be able to drive out to the hall in Dolly's mini, but it was never any good placing dependance on Dolly. She had left the car unserviced and untended for months (Dolly was hopeless with machinery), and when the day came it was in McDonalds' Motorworks having a blown sprocket repaired. So Dolly said, instead: 'Can I borrow your bike, Pandora? I want to go before the College coach sets off.'

'You mean to cycle out to the headland in long white skirts? And how am I supposed to get to the ball? In a pumpkin?'

'Oh,' she said artlessly, 'I supposed you'd be out on the headland all day, decorating. Some of us plan to take our costumes and change out there, in the darkroom.'

'Oh, very well; yes, you can have the bike.'

'And then,' she said, 'We'll come back on the coach, and you can have the bike to ride back on.'

'*A schenem dank*!'

In fact I had private hopes that Tom might drive me back afterwards in *his* mini; but I was not about to divulge such an idea to Dolly, it would set her on the warpath at once.

And of course it was quite true that I did spend most of the day out at the headland, or ferrying back and forth in the Art Department pick-up, fetching the food (Dundee cake, bloater-paste sandwiches, mini-choc rolls) the soft drinks, stereo equipment, and large boxes of crinkled crepe-paper streamers, kindly proffered by the Women's Institute and rudely rejected by Yindrich.

'Thank you *very* much, crinkled crepe-paper streamers we do not need.'

To avoid offence the boxes had to be deposited in the Art Dept store and returned two weeks later, the contents carefully repacked in different boxes. Nonetheless, word got round. It always does.

In the event, Dolly's striking appearance proved slightly counter-productive. She was so dazzling that quite a few of the boys were scared off, afraid to ask her to dance. Still, she did well enough and seemed satisfied with the effect she created. And quantities of pictures were taken.

Her costume was the sensation of the evening and featured lavishly next week in the St Vigeans *Friday Herald*.

I managed my own change at the very last minute in a deserted corner of the store-room behind huge rolls of canvas and paper. Nobody saw me slip in, and only one person – one of Dolly's cronies – saw me come out. She gave a loud yell of terror and bolted, which was quite satisfactory.

Nobody recognised me during the party. That was satisfactory, too. Because of this anonymity I had a far better time than I'd expected, feeling quite relaxed and out of my own persona. The enjoyment culminated in a fast waltz with Yindrich which – to me, anyway – brought back our encounter on the ice of St Vigeans Moss. To him also, apparently, for though at the start he seemed unaware of my identity, after three or four minutes he suddenly said, 'Good Heavens. It's you!'

'No it's not, no it's not,' I cried hastily.

He gave me a sharp look, piercing the buckram-and-fur carapace.

Alone of all the males there, he had made no concession to the childish urge to dress up, still wore his everyday garb of jeans and grey cotton shirt. His long black hair flopped about his head even more messily than usual, his narrow clown's face was pale and cross and smudged with fatigue. He looked as if he might be coming down with one of the shattering migraines which sometimes overwhelmed him after a period of intense effort. He had been at work, organising and arranging, nonstop for several days. All of the female art-students were dying for love of him. Dolly, who hitherto had taken very little notice of Tom, had danced with him twice; the second time – I observed – she swooped sideways and cut in as he swung by with somebody else, and he laughed at her as if he quite enjoyed being the object of somebody's predatory pounce.

Our decorations were huge sculptural thistles, hanging round the walls like halberds. We had made them from purple, white and silver packing materials, vulgar but festive, wheedled out of the local bottling plant. The lights, too, alternately purple and white, kept dimming and brightening, which had the effect of making the laughter and music (bagpipes, fiddle, and accordion) appear to come in gusts. Spiked shadows of thistles went snaking back and forth across the floor. The plaintive squawks and wails of the fiddles brought Toby and Selene to mind, and the twins, grimly practising their Bach. But I felt a long, long way from Boxall Hill.

'Your Dolly Morningquest is certainly a jolly lady,' pronounced Tom, neatly slicing into my process of thought. 'Jolly Dolly Morningquest.'

The music bounced to a stop and a kilted boy grabbed my hand, plucking me away from Tom. Energetic regional dances had been planned to bring the party to a close: Lancers, Strip the Willow and the Dashing

White Sergeant. Pounded by stamping feet and lashed by whirling kilts, the hangar began to shudder and thrum and vibrate as if it might easily fly apart. Huge sparkling whiskers began to come floating down from the flimsy thistles.

'Hoo aboot a chappin, when this pirn's over?' suggested my kilted boy. 'I'm dreigh. There's a wee bar out ben.'

He was no student, I could see. There must have been, I realised, a certain amount of infiltration from the town.

The bar out-ben was supplied with far stronger tipple than the college shandy and innocuous white-wine cup. I choked on my mugful.

'What in the world is it?'

'Och, it'll be a hantle of Uncle Murdo's masking. Have another, for a bonally.'

It tasted suspiciously smooth at first; then liquid lightning.

'No, thanks, no more. That was grand. I'd better go and help close down.'

He showed a disposition to hang on to me, saying that a flittermousie should be a' richts be out of doors, but I gave him the slip and tottered back inside the hall.

The effects of Uncle Murdo's brewing were becoming apparent in here too; loud stamping, laughter, and yodels almost drowned the pipes and squeeze-box.

'We'd best start chasing them oot,' howled Angus Hastie in my ear. He was Tom's Assistant Tutor, a tough, limping, sandy-haired Glaswegian. 'This building's no' goin' to take much in the way of rough-housing.' And he began briskly shoving and sweeping the merrymakers towards the exits. 'Everybody oot! Everybody oot! The caley's over. Walk yer ways, walk yer ways, lads and lassies, the fun's done.'

He encountered some slight resistance at first, but the students were on the whole a douce, law-abiding crew, and they began obligingly to bunch and shuffle and straggle, like bullocks, towards the exits; a few couples went on pertinaciously dancing but as the lights came on and the music died they succumbed to persuasion and reluctantly crept off.

'That's the lot, then.' Angus began hurling plastic cups, which were rolling all over the floor, into waste-bins. I helped him, wondering where Tom had got to.

'Are ye no' goin' in the coach?' said Angus. 'Dinna fash about all this. Tomorrow's time eneugh.'

'No, my bike's here. I don't have to go in the coach.'

And thankful I was, to Dolly, for providing me with exemption from the inevitable singsong and jollity. 'Your bike's behind the store,' she had shouted to me over her shoulder as she left with a bunch of her mates.

But – of course – the bike wasn't. No doubt she had forgotten to padlock it. And by the time I made this depressing discovery the two coaches had left, and a whole-hearted Scottish downpour was battering on to the prefabricated roof and streaming down the flimsy windows, and combing the scrawny headland grass.

Angus had already departed on his motorbike, ripping out some Glaswegian expletive as the water blew under his oilskin cape. Tom was nowhere. Given a choice of walking back into town or spending the night in one of the Art Dept buildings, I had no hesitation. In my pocket was a key to the store, because we had kept all our provisions there. And from the hangar to the store was no more than a three-minute sprint along a lit concrete path.

I did the sprint, unlocked the door, and hurled myself inside.

'And who invited *you*?' said Tom.

It took me a minute to locate him in the patchy light that filtered through the window. He was sprawled out on a white beanbag of parachute nylon, part of some bygone sculpture project. He looked terrible, with a hard crease down the middle of his forehead. Plainly he was in the grip of a migraine.

'Tom! I thought you'd gone home.'

'Would have,' he said harshly, 'but some joyrider absconded with my car.'

'So they did with my bike. I planned to spend the night here.'

He made no demonstration of welcome. A long pause ensued.

'This beanbag is not big enough for two.'

'I never suggested that it was,' I said, trying to sound neither plaintive nor irritable, though, for a moment, at a loss to think of anything else in the place that might serve as bedding. The rolls of paper and canvas were much too hard, and all stored on end, vertically. But then, by a happy stroke of fortune, I recalled the WI loan of crinkled crepe-paper streamers. There were masses and masses of them, thick and bunchy and rustling, packed in large coffin-like cartons, all standing together at the far end of the store.

'Don't worry about me, I'll be fine,' I called, burrowing myself a dry, scratchy nest like a hedgehog. Poor Tom, I thought, overtaken by a migraine and obliged to spend the night in this dismal spot, what an undeserved piece of misfortune. I had seen him before in the throes of one of his attacks, sick, shivering, and speechless. There was no remedy. Nothing could be done for the sufferer.

"Tis a fell deray,' said his grandmother. 'My puir Oe.' Oe was what she called him. 'Syne my man had it, and so did my son Tammas, that was shot down over Dusseldorf. Ye canna do aught against it. The aunly cure I e'er heard tell of was tae remember a' yer birthdays, back to the faurst. But wha's the yin could dae that?'

Wondering if she had ever mentioned this piece of folk advice to Tom, I called, 'Try to remember all your birthdays,' and then, succumbing to exhaustion and Uncle Murdo's hooch, I tumbled into a bottomless pit of sleep.

I was startled awake, some hours later, by another human body burrowing into my nest.

'I'm *freezing*,' said Tom.

He was. His teeth were chattering audibly, and his feet, hands and face all felt like something straight out of a butcher's cold room.

'I shall die if I don't warm up.'

He did seem to be almost in a rigor. I became quite alarmed. 'Perhaps we should walk back into the town? That might warm you?'

'B-but it's still p-pissing with rain. And the w-wind has r-r-risen,' he said, stuttering with cold.

It had. We could hear it booming over the roof in great wuthering swoops, and the thrash of the waves, down below the headland.

'Just a minute, then.'

'Hey! Where are you g-going?' He clung to me as if I were his life-support machine.

'To get the beanbag.'

I hauled myself out of the rustling lair, fetched the beanbag and laid it on top of us both, dragging it up like a coverlet, while I snugged myself back down beside Tom.

'That ought to be some help. OK, now just hold on to me. Tight.'

No need to urge. He clung like an octopus. Gradually his teeth ceased their death-rattle.

'That's a b-bit b-better,' he gasped.

'What about your migraine?'

'How queer. Perhaps the cold k-killed it. It has g-gone.'

'Well, that's one good thing. Or did you remember your birthdays ...?'

I yawned. I was very keen to get back to sleep, but this process was hampered by my position of frightful discomfort, with Tom's bony knobs and joints weighing down on all my pressure points until I seriously thought my circulation might come to a stop. Two feet and one arm were already numb.

All those romantic phrases, I thought, about falling asleep in your lover's arms, are totally misleading.

I had no idea that anybody could be so bony.

In the end, however, I did begin to sink towards sleep by slow degrees, as the temperature in our crepey nest slowly started to climb. After a while, Tom let out a mumbling sigh, which at least sounded closer to contentment than desperation. I could feel for myself that his hands and feet were warmer, so I began to try and withdraw, to rearrange myself in a less crippling position.

'Hey! Don't go away!' he said, and followed after.

'It's just that I don't want to die of gangrene.'

'No risk of that.' And he thrust an arm under my back and hugged me to him. Then with the other hand he removed my earrings – they were the clip-on sort – and stowed them somewhere. Then he began to stroke my back.

What followed after that was, to me, completely unexpected. True, I had woven some fantasies about Tom, but their scenarios were all set far ahead in the future. And they had certainly never been like this. Unwelcome? No; I can't say it was that. Not precisely. But – somehow – I felt taken at a disadvantage, as if I were sitting for an exam for which I was unprepared, had done no revision. I needed more notice. And then, he was so *very* bony. Not at all what I had bargained for. Not a bit like *The Eve of St Agnes*. 'Into her dream he melted as the rose . . . ' Or something. Nobody was doing any melting hereabouts.

Was this really what it was all about? Sex? Or was it nothing but a great confidence-trick?

But still I was, in the end, bound to acknowledge, that it had its points.

Just the same, I muttered, 'I didn't mean this to happen.'

'Oh, nor did I,' said Tom. 'Not for at least another two years . . . '

'Two years? What chutzpah!'

When day broke, I was somewhat exercised in mind as to the best course of action. Walk back along the road to town hand in hand? God forbid!

Tom solved the problem by leaping out of our nest and vanishing. (I later learned that he had climbed down the headland, swum for five minutes in the freezing sea, then walked back along the beach.)

I was still in process of tidying myself, the beanbag and the paper streamers when Angus Hastie reappeared. By now a gloomy, damp, grey regulation Highland post-gale morning was under way.

'Goodsakes! Pandora! What are ye doing here?' said Angus, greatly startled.

'Someone pinched my bike. I spent the night here.'

'Och, what a peety. If I'd known I could have taken ye on the Honda.'

'It was OK. But,' I said, 'I'd be very grateful if you'd take me now.'

'Nae trouble at a'.'

So he whizzed me back into town. It was still early; only half past eight when I made an unpretentious return to the flat. Naturally I'd assumed that Dolly, never an early riser, would still be in bed, fathoms deep. But to my great surprise she was up already and entertaining three other people to breakfast – Cordelia Gray, Hugh FitzMaddon and Eric Potter. Somebody – two people? – had slept in my bed. And they had used up all the bread, butter, bacon, eggs and coffee supplies which, having laid them in yesterday, I had planned on lasting at least a week. A huge pile of dirty plates toppled sideways in the sink. The place was blue with cigarette smoke.

'Pandora!' cried Dolly indignantly, accusingly. 'Where have you been?'

Attack is the best defence, so I came in powerfully on the subject of my missing bike. Not to mention the inclement weather, though that, true, could hardly be laid to Dolly's account.

She looked flushed, guilty, triumphant and condemning, all together.

'We were so worried about you!'

'Very kind of you,' I said sourly, rummaging about for something to eat, finding an overlooked rasher of bacon and the heel of a loaf.

Hugh, Eric, and Cordelia soon melted away, with abashed apologies.

Later on that day, when I was out, Mrs D brought down my silver leaf earrings which Tom had wrapped in his handkerchief and put in his pocket. She gave them to Dolly, who handed them to me when I returned with more bread, bacon, and coffee.

Mumbling a vague acknowledgement – by this time I was feeling the effects of a late, and singularly disturbed night – I tucked them into my jeans pocket and flopped on to my disorderly bed for a nap, intending to close my eyes for no more than a brief ten minutes. For I found myself exceedingly anxious to see Tom again. There were various matters that needed to be straightened up and sorted out between us regarding last night's episode. To my mind, a calm, objective discussion appeared essential. And for this reason it was necessary to see Tom.

Well, I just wanted to see him, really. All of a sudden there seemed to be a huge gap in my life, unless he were there to fill it.

Unfortunately my ten-minute nap extended itself to three hours. When I woke, the urgent priorities were to wash my hair and find a clean pair of jeans. Dolly was nowhere about. As usual, she had nicked one of my favourite garments, a grey-green shirt with black-and-white spiders; she had an unpleasing habit of doing this and, as she was a size larger than me, stretching whatever it was so that it only hung limply on me thereafter. Annoyed, I found a clean black shirt and climbed the stairs to Mrs D's quarters. Often, of a Saturday, Tom dropped in to share her tea.

But – 'Och, he's no' here the noo,' she told me. 'He's awa' tae the studio tae finish the tidy-up and, forbye, haud one o' his adult classes; he's obleeged to dae it the day, for he's awa' tae Enbro the morn's morn.'

'Oh yes, now I remember,' I wrote on her slate. 'Thank you, I'll go and find him there.'

Politely declining her offer of Nackets, Snoddies and Tivlachs, I took leave of her (she gave me two funny, quick little pats on the shoulder), reclaimed my bike, which some guilty soul had parked in the entry with a flat tyre and a slow puncture, and made my way back to the headland.

By now, late afternoon, the weather had ameliorated, as it sometimes will after a Scottish gale, and a wooingly sweet evening sun cast gilded lustre over the austere coastal landscape. Slanting tinselly rays of yellow light filtered through the studio where Tom himself was posing for his extra-mural class as, at such short notice, he had failed to induct any of his regular pensioners. They were all doing their Saturday shopping or watching the footba'.

He was up on the dais, seated in a wooden armchair, in the position of Van Gogh's postman Roulin, elbows on the chair arms, hands lying loosely, eyes fixed on distant space. His clothes were rumpled, his hair untidy. He had an absent, mournful air, as if trying to remember where in Heaven's name he had put down the book he was in the middle of reading. Lozenges of gold light showed up the dust on his old green corduroy jacket and his uncombed hair, and the stubble on his jaw.

This new discovery of him, abstracted, unaware of me, wrapped in his own preoccupations, whatever they were, suddenly brought me up short. In a flash I realised that none of the things I had intended to say to him were at all possible. There was no way of saying them. Not for me, at least.

Looking across the room, over the heads of the intent students, I saw him as a piece of landscape, a natural phenomenon like Malham Cove, or Coalbrookdale. And you can't *own* a piece of landscape; it belongs to the world. All you can do is love it.

Absently, I took up a stick of charcoal, pinned a sheet of paper on a board and began to draw, following Grisch's routine as I always did: right hand, up to the head, around and down. All in one smooth clear line, never lifting the tip of the charcoal from the paper. And as the shape of the figure followed my moving hand, I thought, This, what I am feeling, this must be love. It has nothing to do with my comfortable, confident expectations. This total perception of him, besides an almost unbearably painful engorgement of the heart – so that I feel I might suffocate at any moment – this is what they all talk about. This is what they mean. But how can I bear it, at this intensity? For the rest of my life?

Tom ordered the class to pack up, just as I had completed my outline. They had, of course, been working for two hours already by the time I got there.

Still, I felt in some degree satisfied with what I had done. Of course I had made many previous drawings of Tom in other classes; but this single line-sketch was, I thought, a good deal better than most of my former attempts. Something essential had been caught: the turn of the head, the fall of the hands.

He was moving around now among the students, commenting, criticising. At this moment he caught sight of me and appeared visibly startled. He became a shade paler than he was already, and stared at me gravely. I stared gravely back. It did not seem the moment for cheery salutations.

He began working his way in my direction, not with any impetuosity, but deliberately, by degrees, pausing here and there en route to inspect, to comment, to praise or find fault. Now and then he picked up a piece of chalk and drew a few lines on somebody's paper. He was a good teacher. People listened to his words with ardent attention.

Finally he reached me. Without a word, I exhibited my hasty drawing. He frowned, as if it surprised him.

Then he muttered, in a low voice, 'You have to forgive me. I did not realise – I had no idea – that you were committed.'

'Forgive? What can you possibly mean?' I muttered back. 'There's nothing to forgive. On the contrary. It was—'

'We won't speak of it any more,' he said quickly. Then he looked at my paper again and added, '*This* is what you have been searching for. Hold on to it!'

To my profound dismay, and dissatisfaction, I now saw Dolly's face appear over his shoulder. She was wearing my shirt (it suited her very well) and a green chintz dirndl. Never before, to my knowledge, had she attended one of Tom's drawing classes. But she was laughing her infectious laugh and exhibiting a stiff, laboured little drawing – it was cramped, in the middle of the paper, done in many heavily indented lines, like a child's picture.

'I've a long, long way to go to catch up, haven't I? It's terrible, isn't it? Oh, go on! Tell me it's terrible.' She stared at Tom challengingly.

Dolly had absolutely no idea of drawing; none. It had never been one of her interests. Now she stuck her arm vigorously through Tom's. 'Come on, Thomas! We're going to be late for the film, unless we start *at once*. Pandora will see to the locking up – won't you, Pandora?'

And she hustled him away. He turned to give me one more look – puzzled, intent, almost accusing. I found it impossible to comprehend. What had made him so angry with me? It was unfair. Outside, I heard Dolly's car start up, saw her drive off with him. Evidently in the course of the day she had managed to get the motor fixed.

So I saw to the locking up.

Tom went off early next morning to Edinburgh, where he was arranging for a show of college work, and I did not see him again.

I gave the drawing I had done of him to Mrs D, who exclaimed lovingly over it.

'Eh!' she said. 'Eh! Yon's the very marrow of him! My certie! 'Tis his very self, a' in one canny line. I'm blithe tae have it, hinny, if ye daena want it yersen?'

'No, you have it,' I wrote. 'I'd like you to have it.'

I travelled home early, a week before the end of term, because my friend Veronica (who now worked as an editorial secretary on *Ton* magazine) wrote that they had an opening in the art department there, and that if I landed it I could share her flat in Shepherd's Bush.

I applied for the job, got it, and removed myself to London.

Dolly followed Tom to Edinburgh, and they were married there, later that summer.

Oh, Tom. What a bungled business.

X

Before travelling south, I endured a painful scene with Dolly.

She accused me of unkindness, insensitivity and of snubbing all her friends. 'Look how they ran from you!'

'But, Dolly, it is just the other way round. They are all so upper-crust, they think nothing of me. Most of them hardly know I am above ground.'

She paid no heed to that or, indeed, to anything I had to say.

I was busy tidying the flat, packing up my last odds and ends. I had given the kitchen its final clean-out, but discovered, going in again, that Dolly had dumped a used glass in the sink. If there is one thing that exasperates me, it is when somebody leaves an article that *one single rinse* would dispose of, cluttering up the clean empty sink and waiting for some other person to wash, dry and put away. Silently I proceeded to do this while Dolly, following me in, went barrelling on in a passionate tirade. My hard-heartedness, self-absorption, disloyalty and cynicism were its chapter heads. When she was angry her eyes narrowed and tilted down at the outer corners. At these times she looked remarkably like Sir Gideon.

'All you ever want to do is paint! When I think of all our family has given you! And it was I – I – who begged Mar to get to know your mother because I so wanted to meet you, get to know you—'

'*What?*'

I was utterly taken aback. Could this possibly be true? Or was it a pure piece of Dolly-invention? She was quite capable of it.

'I was in love with you!' she said, tears pouring straight from her tilted eyes like Hokusai waterfalls. 'I always wanted to get to know you. I used to see you with your mother at town concerts. I *longed* to meet you. I used to think about you – dream about you—'

'Oh, my dear Dolly . . .' I was really aghast. It is almost impossible to imagine oneself figuring in somebody else's dreams.

This is all just too preposterous, I wanted to protest. It can't be true. But what would have been the use? My objections, my disbelief, would only exasperate her further. And perhaps – just conceivably – what she said was the truth. I recalled her gracious, patronising air when we first met, her alarmed and horrified retreat after the twins had lamed me and dyed my hair green. Her visible jealousy of my relations with Mariana. And she was, after all, Mariana's daughter . . .

'But you just aren't what I'd hoped!' she finished furiously. 'You are not the person I took you for! You are hard – and cold – and selfish – and sarcastic. I hope I never see you again!'

I rather hoped for this, too. If what she had said was the case; if, all along, I had been the object of her hopeless adoration, my weight of guilt-packed memory was going to be hard enough to support without constant reminders from her vengeful presence.

But Dolly was quite capable of a good round lie, I had discovered. Had it really been she who'd persuaded Mariana to make friends with my mother? Mariana did not readily submit to anybody's persuasions. I resolved to ask her about this the next time I saw her.

Whenever that might be.

Tom's name never came up at all.

Parting from Mrs Dalgairns was very sad. And she seemed sorry too.

'Och, hinny, it's a peety ye have tae gang awa',' she told me. 'I'd hoped ye and my Oe wad make a match of it. I'd be blythe if he'd settle here; I'm aye feared he'll gang awa' back tae Prague. And I thocht ye were juist the lass for him.'

'Perhaps he'll find some other lass here,' I wrote in her notebook.

But she shook her head doubtfully. 'He's gey hard tae please.'

Another thing that fretted me was that Mrs D left a frustrating riddle unsolved. Once, when leafing slowly through one of my sketchbooks which contained drawings of the Morningquest family and Floxby citizens, she had paused at a portrait of a bearded man.

'Now yon's a familiar face. Syne I've seen him somewhere . . . '

'Where?' I scribbled, full of excitement.

It was the bearded man who had spoken to me at my mother's funeral, drawn from memory the same day.

'Och, 'tis a long time ago. Maybe when I was living in Enbra', whiles . . . ' She frowned, then shook her head. 'Would he have been a preacher now, at the West Kirk? Somehow I feel he was in Orders. Na, na, it's clean slippit from my recollection. If I call it to mind, lassie, I'll tell ye.'

But she never did. Several times, later, I showed her the drawing again, hoping to stir the buried memory, but it remained tantalisingly out of reach. She continued to think it might be connected with the period when she had lived in Edinburgh, twenty years ago.

So how did that advance me? Was I to go to Edinburgh and stand in the street, showing my picture to the passers-by?

*

The offices of *Ton* magazine were in Curzon Street, ancient, inconvenient and elegant. Each tiny separate room was up or down three or four stairs.

I had arrived early, so as to be primed by Veronica. Veronica these days wore a Sophia Loren look: swept-aside fringe, eyes made up to look slanting, inch-long lashes and a mini-skirt. Immensely long legs, pointed toes, sling heels. 'Bunions,' I could hear my mother's ghost growl. She's laying up bunions for herself. Wafts of Blue Grass filled the minuscule office.

'Sorry I couldn't offer you a bed last night, ducky,' said Veronica. 'But Roz will have married her ghastly pansy photographer by the time you want to move up to town, so then you can have her room.'

I said it didn't matter a bit, I had stayed in Cadogan Square; and I sighed at the recollection of my mother, heroically restraining herself, suppressing the urge to denounce every aspect of Veronica, from shoes to syntax.

'Now *don't* be afraid of standing up to the old trout, she likes the ones who aren't scared of her. *And don't forget* – ' Veronica hissed as the editor's secretary came to conduct me to the Presence, 'she pronounces her name *Bo – sh'm* – not "Beecham". And— ' But I missed her last exhortation as I was led away, up and down four more flights of stairs.

'Of course the Art Department is tucked away up in the attics,' Mrs Beecham told me. 'Candida will take you up there presently.'

Mrs Beecham at first sight was not alarming, a comfortable, grey-haired bulk in a floral dress; but presently you began to notice that the floral dress was from Paris, the grey was blue-rinsed and she had an eye like a dagger.

'Ah, and you have been studying art in Scotland ... our Mr Heron seems to think well of your portfolio. You will, of course, go on studying in London?'

At the Southampton Row School, I said, wondering what this had to do with a fashion magazine. But I was to find that Mrs Beecham liked to fill her stable with what she called 'highly creative spirits'. How different from my father, who thought all this modern urge to be creative was a lot of pernicious nonsense, that led to cluttering up the place with nasty things people had made that they had much better not.

'What are you working on at present?' asked Mrs Beecham, assessing my suit, which Tante Lulie had whipped together from a piece of dark-brown deckchair canvas.

'A portrait,' I said, playing my ace, 'of Sir Gideon Morningquest.'

He had liked *Selene in Yellow Dress*, which I had varnished in Scotland and brought back to Cadogan Square. He was in London for a few days, between Rejkiavik and Managua, and had himself suggested the sittings.

At first I demurred. 'I've just had an awful row with Dolly, Sir Gid. Won't it be a bit awkward if she comes home?'

But he had waved a dismissing hand. 'Nonsense, what nonsense. Children's quarrels ... Mariana tells me that you have been a very admirable influence on Dolly; and I suspect that a quarrel with somebody is just what she needs. Dolly always makes *such a point* of being sweet and gracious.'

He smiled at me sweetly and graciously. I will paint him with just that syrupy look, I resolved at once. Toying with an hour-glass in his fingers, perhaps.

'In any case Dolly informs us that she has gone to stay with friends in Edinburgh. And that she plans to go on to Skye,' he added. 'So there will be no risk of an encounter.'

In fact at that very moment Dolly was getting married to Tom Yindrich.

'Oh then,' I said to Sir Gideon, 'I'll begin right away.'

'Good-good.'

The person I was replacing on *Ton* had a month to work out, so I would not be wanted there until September.

I finished the portrait of Sir Gideon in a week, painting with frenzied speed so as to get the figure done before he went off to Managua, completing the background after he had left. I had him in a standing pose, leaning nonchalantly against the banister post, with the rail spiralling up behind him and the stairs rising like a stave. How I longed for Tom to come up behind me and say, 'Much worse,' or 'Much better.'

How I longed for Tom, period. But Toby (now back living in Cadogan Square, as he could not persuade Selene to move with him to a mews flat in Paddington) was encouraging and kind, and told me that it was my best work yet. I made use of Toby a good deal for the standing figure, wearing Sir Gideon's velvet jacket, as he and his father were the same tall skinny height and shape, and it was too much to require a man of Sir Gideon's age and eminence to stand for long periods – though, to be sure, he was quite capable of conducting three-hour concerts.

In the evenings Toby and Selene and I listened to records, Handel operas, for which we all shared a passion. Or they, on violin and piano, played Schubert chamber music, gruff introspective stuff; like shovelling cement, I sometimes thought. It was a calm, not unhappy time. Selene was peaceful, undemanding company and, of the three brothers, I'd always found Toby the most approachable. Dan was still too competitive, spiteful, and pleased with himself. Barney, though friendly enough, too remote, living most of the time on a mental plane far beyond my reach.

Or so I thought.

My father at this time was away on his annual month's leave from the practice, domiciled in Cannes with his sister Freda. So, when the portrait was done and drying, it seemed natural for me to return to Boxall Hill rather than camp by myself in an empty house.

I took down with me a bundle of back issues of *Ton*, which I had been instructed to study, and of course I had a wonderful time leafing through them with Tante Lulie and the twins.

'*Sharpen up your line for spring*,' Lulie would read out. 'Just look at that *schmatte*! What's to *kvell* over that?'

And the twins were merciless in their criticism. 'Can't they even write proper grammar? This pidgin fashion-lingo is like a chipmunks' chorus.' Having polished up their own grammar to a high level in preparation for Heidelberg, the twins just now were very strong on sentence construction.

'Really, Pandora, it's a good thing you are going to work on this terrible little journal. In three years' time, when we're through at Heidelberg, when you have pulled it into shape, you can give us jobs as Philosophy Editors or Art Directors.'

'Hey, look, there's Mar at Salzburg! That was the dress you made from the blue silk curtains at Cluny Park, Tante Lulie.'

'Ach, so it is. With all the pleats. I wonder who is that *yenta* she is talking to.'

Combing through ten years of *Ton*, we found quite a few pictures of Mariana.

'Naturally!' said Tante Lulie. 'For, thanks to me, she is always the best-dressed woman in any assembly.'

'Not forgetting that she can sing a bit, too,' said Elly.

I yearned for Mariana to come back to Boxall Hill. But, of course, she did not. It seemed an eternity since I had seen her. I badly needed to confess and be absolved for the crime of my breach with Dolly and the fact that I had quitted St Vigeans never to return. Forlornly, I now began to suspect that Mariana was deliberately avoiding me, that I might never see her again – or never, at any rate, on the terms of our last meeting.

I could not wholly believe in Sir Gideon's reassurances about my abrupt departure from St Vigeans.

'My dear child, it is of no consequence, none. One of my dear wife's more far-fetched plans. She had a notion it would benefit Dolly. That Dolly! She has always been a most fidgety character – she and Danny both. A truly tiresome pair. But you – my dear Pandora – of *course* you must make your own way as you think best. Art school in London, and a job on this magazine – wholly praiseworthy, wholly practical. Why do you not take up your quarters in this house, in Cadogan Square? Now that Danny has moved out, and with the twins away in Germany, there will be ample space.'

'Oh, that's so kind of you, Sir Gid, but a girlfriend in Shepherd's Bush has offered me a share of her flat.'

'Good-good,' he said, not very interested. 'Whatever you choose. Good-good.'

But still, he seemed pleased with the portrait. (The previous one of him, now in the National Portrait Gallery, was by Graham Sutherland, and he hated it. He said it made him look constipated.) I was pleased with my picture, too; I liked the treble-clef banister rail, and felt I had done a good job in catching my subject's creamy, satisfied, pussy-cat look.

On his final evening I had rather hoped that he might take me out to dinner to celebrate, but he didn't; he had to pack for Managua, and was always, anyway, rather careful with his cash. He probably felt, with perfect reason, that I'd already received sufficient free board and lodging in London and Scotland; besides, after all, even my recently acquired improvement in painting technique sprang from his beneficence.

Matters at Boxall Hill were tranquil and productive as usual.

Grisch had moved on to the works of A. E. Housman.

'"The troubles of our proud and angry dust, Are from eternity and shall not fail." Quite good that, yes, not bad at all. But why, just tell me why does he have to finish with zis terrible last line – "Shoulder the sky, my lad, and drink your ale." *Ale!* So phony! So fake-archaic.'

'So, OK Uncle Grisch, what do you suggest as an alternative?'

'Well, in the first place, it would have been better to finish with a trisyllabic word.'

'Nightingale? Martingale? Farthingale? Anyhow, Uncle Grisch,' I said, 'how come you are so far on in English literature, already at the end of the nineteenth century? Haven't you been skipping rather? There must be dozens of writers that you have missed out. What about Shakespeare, Milton, Blake? What about Browning?'

'Now you are teasing the old uncle, my dear Pandora. Shakespeare, Milton and William Blake don't need my attentions. They are high up in the pantheon. Not a word of Blake would I tamper with.'

'Oh, *I* would! "When that heart began to beat, What dread hand, and what dread *feet*?" Who ever heard of *feet* twisting sinews?'

'Like on a treadle spinning-wheel,' said Ally at once. 'You have to remember about Blake that he was looking out of his window *all the time* at the Industrial Revolution. I used to worry dreadfully when I was younger about the dark satanic mills; I thought he just put them in for the rhyme. But, of course, they were right there in his back yard.'

'Browning I shall come to in due course,' said Uncle Grisch. 'Browning is going to give me a great deal of hard work. I have to brace myself for Browning.'

'"Needs its leaden vase filled brimming? Hell dry you up with its flames."' quoted Elly. 'That could certainly have been better phrased.'

The twins had shed their American accents even faster than they had picked them up.

I asked about local news. Ginge Buckley was still away, had got herself a job in Norwich. Nothing had ever come to light about her lost baby.

'And Garnet? And the Venoms?'

'Garnet is just the same as ever. The Venoms have gone.'

'*Gone?*' I was thunderstruck. 'I thought they were fixtures for life. Till Judgement Day. That nothing but death would free Sir Gideon from their baneful presence.'

'Well,' said Grisch, 'it seems you were wrong. Lady Venom suffered from something that her husband called a nervous collapse. And they have moved away to the west country, to Torquay, "for her health".'

'Well I never! What about Mon Repos? Aviemore?'

'Oh, Danny is buying it. Didn't you know?'

'*Danny* buying it? No, I certainly did not! Sir Gid never said a thing about that.'

'Oh, well he is quite annoyed about it, of course,' said Tante Lulie placidly. 'Naturally he is happy indeed to see the last of the Venoms. But he is furious about Danny's having wasted all his university career and made such a lot of money in what Gideon considers a most disreputable manner.'

I did know that Danny had written a pop song. Selene had told me. I had been exceedingly careful not to allude to this in Sir Gideon's presence because, apart from defecating in public, there seemed nothing any of his family could do that would disgust him more than such a departure from what he called *real* music. That Dan should have done this must have been excruciating for him.

The song went, approximately:

> When the wind stops blowing
> and the trees stop growing
> only then is when, then is when
> I'll stop lovin' you
>
> When the sun stops rising
> that won't be more surprising

126

than that I should stop stop stop
stop lovin' you

There are guys who leave ladies
after they've kissed 'em
but my love for you is permanent, yes, permanent
as the solar system

When the wind stops blowing, etc, etc.

It went to one of those inevitably memorable tunes on the level of 'Twinkle, twinkle, little star', the sort that Mozart, and Sullivan and Gershwin tossed up all the time, and other composers sometimes manage on their lucky day. Due to that (and also perhaps to Danny's many friends and acquaintances in the upper fastnesses of advertising and the media) it had winged straight to the top of the charts; deservedly so, I reckoned, whilst reserving the right to go on disliking Dan and finding him a conceited mischief-maker. No doubt Salieri felt the same about Mozart.

'I must say, it does seem quiet here without the Venoms,' said Elly. 'I miss that ever-present sense of ferocious ill will and impending trouble. But it certainly eases life. At weekends Toby and Garnet are building a beautiful perspex palace roof on to the platform of the tree-house. And they do get on much faster without old Venom always prepared to raise Cain and send in writs.'

'And the tunnel?' I had my own reasons for inquiring about that.

'Oh, it's coming along. You can give us a hand. Dan, of course, has lost interest; he's all wrapped up in plans to adapt Mon Repos from Stock-broker's Tudor to Pop Person's Gothic. But he still keeps *us* up to the mark. He seems to want the tunnel finished, for some reason of his own. Maybe he wants private access from the cellars to Aviemore. As the crow flies, the pavilion isn't very far from his house. Perhaps he's planning to smuggle Chinese LPs.'

Grisch lost interest. 'I must find Garnet. The downstairs wc does not flush as it should.'

As he pottered off, Lulie looked after him indulgently. 'Always he is worrying about the plumbing. He is obsessed by pipes. I think it is a kind of transferred anxiety about his own bowels.'

'Why?' At once I was anxious, too. 'Don't they work?'

'Oh, perfectly. He takes such good care of them. Just now he is eating all his vegetables in strict alphabetical order, so as to miss none. From alecost to zucchini.'

'What is alecost?'

'Ach, it is a kind of chrysanthemum herb with a bitter flavour,' said Tante Lulie, who, though despising the fashionable craze for 'herb gardens' grew, scattered among her vegetables, dozens of herbs the average person would never recognise, of which she made daily practical use.

I spent a happy fortnight at Otherland, dug parts of Lulie's veg patch, did a bit of plumbing for Grisch (plumbing was one branch of learning which, at St Vigeans, I had tackled thoroughly, for the system in Mrs D's house was mainly eighteenth century), constructed (with Tante Lulie's help) a wardrobe to see me through my first months at *Ton*, and worked with the twins on extending the tunnel.

I had been uncertain whether my one-night event with Tom might lead to a pregnancy, and in consequence was in a state of moderate, though publicly suppressed terror until the question was resolved. But a week's garden digging and vigorous hacking in the tunnel was enough to set my mind at rest. Whereupon, profoundly relieved though I was I felt a perverse sense of sadness that any last possible link with Tom was broken.

Now came Dolly's bombshell.

'Married Tom Yindrich in Edinburgh, honeymoon in Skye,' she telegraphed her family, sending duplicate wires to Boxall Hill and Cadogan Square in hopes of hitting the target somewhere. In fact she missed: her parents were still away on the other sides of oceans.

'This Yindrich, who is he?' demanded Lulie. 'Will Mariana be pleased?'

'I – I really don't know. Yes. Perhaps. I hope so. He is very intelligent and – and lively, and creative. Yes. I'm sure she'll like him. And be relieved that Dolly has made such a sensible choice.'

'What does he do? You have turned very white, *bubeleh*, are you ill?' inquired Tante Lulie, looking at me closely.

'No, thank you, it's just that I have stomach cramps. Menstrual,' I explained hastily. 'Nothing out of the common.'

'Camomile tea is best for that,' said Tante Lulie, and made me a mugful directly, and it helped.

'So tell more about this Yindrich,' commanded the twins.

I told all I knew – about his Prague background, his granny, that he was the virtual head of the St Vigeans Art Department.

'Ah, so he was your professor, not Dolly's. Was that why you had the quarrel?'

'No; no it wasn't. We quarrelled simply because Dolly said I was unkind to her.'

The twins cast up their eyes. 'Tell us something we don't know.

Everybody is unkind to Dolly – according to Dolly. So in retaliation she walks off with your professor?'

'He isn't mine.'

But it was no use trying to keep things from the twins.

I remembered all the small irrelevant intersections that had seemed to mark out Tom for mine: the fact that our birth-dates were the same, that so many of our tastes coincided down to the tiniest trivialities, a fondness for Archimboldo, *The Gardener's Year*, and raw grated apple with brown sugar on it. For a happy nine months I, like Mrs D, had thought that by and by we would make a match of it; and so internally sure of this was I that I never made the least special effort to be with Tom, outside classes, or to engage his interest. Like those of Jane Bennett, my feelings, though fervent, were not displayed. If there was one lesson I really learned from my mother, it was how to hide feelings. Now – at least – it was some gloomy comfort to know that I need not expect a lot of pity from classmates.

'Better fish in the vasty deep,' said Elly.

'Any man that would marry Dolly is not worth a moment's chagrin,' said Ally.

'No, no,' I said. 'You will like him. Dolly chose well.'

As catharsis, I set myself to do a drawing of Lulie's bowl. It lived on the kitchen dresser at Otherland, and had accompanied her across Europe and over the sea from a small village somewhere east of Gdansk which had lost its name and been obliterated from the map. Lulie's bowl was made of thick, dark wood. It was carved by hand, flattish, almost circular but with a slight elevation, prow and stern, the curve that Dutch barges have – a most beautiful, undulant line. Generations had chopped vegetables in that bowl with a two-handed convex chopper until the curved bottom, worn paper-thin, began to leak a little. So now it was used as a catch-all; it contained postage stamps, paper clips, small change, Lulie's reading-glasses, airmail stickers, the keys of the Minor, a small flashlight, matches, candle ends (useful for lighting fires), library tickets, receipts, a wren's nest with broken eggshells, National Savings Stamps, Sellotape, seed packets, and tubes of epoxy glue. The Morningquest children had a legend about the bowl that it was like Mrs Swiss Family Robinson's bag; whatever you needed, from a Chinese yen to a razor-blade, whatever the emergency, you would be sure to find in Tante Lulie's bowl.

For my first attempt I took all the contents out of the bowl, piled it high with oranges, and produced a very boring still-life. Then I returned the oranges to the pantry, tilted the empty bowl against the white wall, and drew it again. I could hear Tom's voice: 'Much worse.' Angrily I replaced the original contents and had a third try, God's eye view this time, from above. Still not happy, I had a last attempt: Bowl Surrounded by Contents, which Lulie liked and pinned up in her room.

At the end of the week we read in the local paper that Lady Venom, down in Torquay, had died.

'From an overdose of laburnum seeds,' the newspaper story said.

'*Laburnum seeds?*' cried Lulie. 'What in the world can the poor demented *farbisseneh* creature have thought she was swallowing?'

'God, He only knows,' said Grisch.

'I shall say a *kaddish* for her.'

I wrote a lettter of condolence to Thelma Venner, whom I had known at school, but never had an answer. There had not, at any time, been much love between Thelma and her mother.

XI

'Terribly sorry, ducky, I've decided to marry Gerry Banalmond,' wrote Veronica on a postcard. 'Afraid there won't be room for you in the flat after all. But I have a chum in West Ealing who could put you up.'

Declining the chum, I went back to Cadogan Square and started flat-hunting.

But then Veronica and this Gerry – who was a news-agency man – transferred to Rome, so I took over the flat in Shepherd's Bush, although it was too expensive for me.

'She was a restless one, your friend,' said Mrs Beecham, looking at me over the tops of her diamanté glasses. 'Candidly, I never expected that she would stay here very long. How are you settling in, Miss Crumbe? I like this—' she tapped a layout of mine she was holding – 'very much indeed. Would Sir Gideon Morningquest agree to our doing a feature on him, with pictures, do you suppose? Perhaps a line drawing of yours?'

'Oh, I should think he would, certainly.' All is grist to Sir Gideon's mill, I thought. 'Only he is quite hard to pin down. He's in Budapest just at the moment. I don't think he will be back in London till November.'

'I shall make plans for November and write to him. So that would be for the March issue.'

Ton, a monthly, went to press three months ahead, and planned six months ahead of that. It was the only pocket-sized fashion journal at that period, and had a surprisingly large circulation. People – even men – found it handy to read on trains. The same size as the *Reader's Digest*, it was thick, printed on glossy paper, with fashion pictures, both male and female, photographs, no fiction, a few political pieces (slightly right of centre but tending to satire), a few poems, and a few cartoons. It modelled its laconic editorial style on the *New Yorker*. My job, which I greatly enjoyed, was organising the layout of the drawings and fashion pictures. The impressive Mrs Bo'shm was an inspiriting person to work for, ferociously intolerant of any stupidity or carelessness, but ready to encourage new ideas with enthusiasm. Where cheese could be pared, she was cheeseparing; salaries on the magazine were extremely low. It had considerable autonomy, though belonging to a large publishing stable. Remunerations to contributors were on a much more lavish scale than staff salaries. So – in order to pay for my large, uneconomic flat, which I was reluctant to share with anybody else – I fell into the habit of freelancing. Fortunately for me, Mrs B took a fancy to my line portraits and I was soon embarked on a series of monthly features – a sketch and a few lines of biography. At first, most of the subjects were friends of the Morningquest family, anybody I could persuade to sit for me, people such as Luke Rose, Sir Gervas Mostyn, Sir Lucian Hawke and Princess Natasha Bagration. Well, I did capitalise on my connection with the family. But then, I felt I was entitled to.

As soon as I could, I had moved from Cadogan Square.

In October I had been living there on my own. Toby and Selene had gone for a week to Madeira. The Morningquest reception rooms, with their velvet drapes, Persian carpets and French furniture, made me impatient and nervous; I never felt at home in them. How could the family commute so blithely between here and Otherland? Otherland, with its bare floors and farmhouse chairs, was certainly the house for me.

Danny took me out to dinner one evening, before I moved. His live-in girlfriend, plump Topsy Ponsonby, was at present almost permanently down at Aviemore, superintending the decorators, so I suppose he was slightly at a loose end. He had been amiable and accommodating when Mrs Bo'shm's secretary phoned him to suggest a profile interview with line sketch by me. (Two years later in his career he would not so have demeaned himself.) At this stage he was still quite pleased at the mild publicity and even agreed to come round to the office to be drawn. There, of course, he was fêted and made much of; all the secretaries adored his new song *Trespassing Moon*. So it was natural enough that afterwards he and I should amble along the road to a Shepherd Market pub, taxi on to Knightsbridge to eat, and then that he should see me back to Cadogan Square, though he now had a pad of his own in the King's Road.

Dan, as always, had plenty to talk about: Bow Bells TV had offered him a half-hour programme of his very own, interviews, discs, whatever he liked, and if he accepted the slot, which of course he would, he was seriously considering a change of name.

'I think I shall call myself Danny Morning. Morningquest is too long and too fancy; people don't know how to spell it.'

'Doesn't seem to have handicapped Sir Gideon so's you'd notice,' I remarked after I had politely enthused, and congratulated, and said all the right things. Sometimes I felt that was why I was there for the Morningquests: as an exclaimer. Every family needs one of these. Lulie and Grisch didn't exclaim. They were just calmly pleased.

'Well, it's different in classical music,' said Dan. 'People are *expected* to have unpronounceable names. Like *Trnka*. And then knowing how to pronounce them divides off the musical sheep from the unmusical goats.

But Gid is sure to be disgusted, anyway, at my getting into television; he'd probably be better pleased if I changed my name altogether.'

'You could call yourself Daniele Matin. Or Dmitri Kalimera.'

He appeared to give my suggestions serious thought.

'What about your mother?' I asked. 'What will she think?'

'Oh—' he said impatiently. 'Who knows what she ever thinks? Dave will make some snide comment, no doubt. Can't see any TV company offering *him* his own programme.'

Quickly I asked, wishing to steer away from the subject of Dave, when he expected to move in to Aviemore.

'Oh, I shan't ever live there,' said Dan. 'I'll keep the King's Road pad. But – as Gid is bound to cut me off with a curse over my defection to pop – I want to keep a base down there. I like Floxby. I don't want to be cut off.'

This faintly surprised me. I had never noticed that Dan was particularly wedded to country pursuits. But it seemed a point in his favour.

'How very lucky for you that the Venoms decided to move away.'

'Oh, *that* wasn't luck,' said Dan, grinning broadly at my innocence. 'That was a bit of wire-pulling on my part. Or lever-pushing, you might say.'

'What *can* you mean?'

'Didn't you guess?'

'Guess what?'

'Well you know the old girl – Lady Venom – is a bit off her trolley? *Quatre-vingt-dix-neuf* centimes in the franc? That can hardly have escaped your attention, my sharp-eyed Pandora?'

'No; certainly she is a bit odd,' I said, my heart suddenly sinking dreadfully.

'*Odd*! That's to put it in *Listen with Mother* language. She ought to be put away.'

'You know she's dead?'

That startled him.

'No? No, I didn't. Dead, is she? Well, that ought to solve a few problems for old Venom. How come she's dead?'

'It was in the Floxby paper, although they'd moved to Torquay. She swallowed a lot of laburnum seeds.'

He laughed like a kookaburra.

'What a marvellous end! You have to hand it to her. Original! I must remember that, if ever I get to writing plays; which I do have in mind for later on.'

I began to dislike Dan even more vigorously than I had before, and to be sorry that I was eating his Vitello Parmigiani. 'But what about the house?'

'Well, I was outside the public library in Floxby a while back. Odd place for me to be, wasn't it, but I needed to look up an address, so I had just come out the door and I happened to notice old Lady V, wrapped in scarves as was her wont, snitching someone else's baby out of its pram and dumping it into that wheeled shopping basket of hers.'

'You— ?' My mouth dried up completely. I gaped at him in silence. His face wore a broad, self-satisfied, remembering smirk. After a moment I croaked, 'What – what did you do?'

'Well,' said Dan complacently, 'I've never been one for nasty scenes and making a lot of fuss. I told the old girl that the librarian wanted her back at the counter for a book to be date-stamped. While she was inside I transferred the kid back to its own pram and waited. When she came out again and went off, pulling her wheely-basket, I followed her home. There I had a short sharp confrontation with her and old Venom. That *was* rather nasty, I must say,' remarked Dan reminiscently. 'Old V was *not* best pleased.'

'What did you say?'

'I told him I was aware of – had witnessed an instance of – his wife's proclivity for pinching other people's bundles of joy. I recalled that there had been several more cases in the town, over the last year or so, of babies being misappropriated; some had turned up, but at least one had *not*. And I just gently suggested that if they didn't want me to drop round to the police with this little sidelight, this little piece of local colour, they might be well advised to move away to a more salubrious climate. And I'd take the house off his hands. At a reasonable price, of course.'

'What did he say?'

'He took my point. After kicking up a bit of dust. About blackmail and so forth.'

'Which it was.'

'Oh, which it certainly was. But he hadn't a leg to stand on, had he?'

I thought of poor Ginge. My heart turned over with woe. But what can you do in such a situation? Whatever had happened to her baby was over a year ago now. If – if it was still alive, it would have been found long ago.

'The Venners gave in? Just like that?'

'Well – in the end,' said Dan. 'Yes.'

'And then?'

'Um,' he said. 'The next part of the story is rather nasty. I don't want to upset your sensibilities.'

I didn't speak. He went on, without particularly waiting.

'I remembered how the old girl used to hang about our ilex grove sometimes. And I went over there, on the quiet, last autumn, and had a sharp look round. And found a bit of ground that had been disturbed. Near the dogs' and horses' cemetery. You know?'

'Oh don't. Don't.'

'Very well. If you'd rather not! But it became abundantly plain to me that this was not the first time Lady V had helped herself to somebody else's olive branch. I assumed that, when he found out *in time*, Sir V quietly took the kids back to – to the point of origin. Or left them in some reasonably well-frequented spot. I gave him the benefit of that doubt. But there had evidently been at least two occasions when it was too late for that.'

'*Two?*'

'Gipsies used to come and camp on the other side of Thorn Hill, remember? Wasn't there some tale, a few years back, of a missing child?'

'Yes. I think there was. God almighty,' I muttered.

'And Sir V's solution to the problem – quite neatly – was to dump the evidence on *our* land – so that, if anybody was to be embarrassed or incriminated, it would be the Morningquest family. Charming, hmn?'

'What did you do?'

'Disposed of the evidence. In quite a final way,' said Dan complacently.

'Did you say anything to the police?'

'No.'

'Does anybody else know this?'

'Oh, the twins had some story once about picking up a shopping bag in the library with old Lady V's ticket and a pink bootee in it; which started them speculating. But the twins aren't really interested in anyone's concerns except their own.'

This seemed to me so wide of the mark that I let it pass. If the twins had not chosen to discuss their thoughts with Dan, they probably had some sound reason for not doing so.

We had arrived back in Cadogan Square.

'Well, that was very interesting, if nasty,' I said, in what I hoped was a final manner. 'And many thanks for the meal. I'll send you a proof of the interview as soon as it comes from the printers. Goodbye.'

'Oh, I'm coming in,' said Dan. 'I want to collect some clothes and LPs from my room.' Chronically disorganised, like Dolly, he left a trail of garments and belongings scattered wherever he laid his head.

He had his own latchkey and opened the door.

'Well in that case I'll leave you to it,' I said. 'Goodnight. I need to be at work early tomorrow because it's publication day. Congratulations again about the TV programme.'

I ran up three flights of stairs, leaving Danny below, wishing that I could expel his image as quickly from my mind. But it stayed there, smirking, cockahoop, full of self-congratulations. I flinched from picturing that interview with the Colonel, and poor mad Lady Venom.

First I'll have a long hot bath, I thought.

A hot bath almost invariably has a soothing effect. I read spy mysteries until the water begins to cool, and make plans for pictures.

There was a small odd-shaped bathroom lit by a skylight on the attic floor in the Cadogan Square house. The bath was long and deep, narrow as a horse-trough. Up there, high above the rest of the house, one had a fine feeling of bathing in a crow's nest. I filled the narrow tub with boiling water and gratefully sank under the surface, hoping to rinse away the impressions of the past two hours.

And then I heard footsteps on the stair, the door (which I had not bolted) swung open, and Dan walked in.

He was stark naked.

I sprang on to my feet in the bath, looking, I suppose, startled to death, and this seemed to amuse him greatly. He was grinning from ear to ear. It didn't suit him. Nor did nakedness. He was already becoming rather florid in colour, from high living no doubt, and had acquired a small but definite pot belly. And he had always been more solidly built, thicker, than either of his brothers. By the end of his thirties he'd have to watch out, or he might easily become obese.

'Didn't you expect me?' he said, laughing. 'Oh, come on, Pandora darling, surely you aren't *that* naïve? Get over now – shift your lovely self! I'm coming in with you.'

'No you most certainly are not!' I said.

'Don't play the sweet beleaguered innocent with me, ducky. It really isn't the least use. It doesn't impress me at all. And the water will be getting cold.'

'Look, Dan, I don't want you in the bath; or in this room; or in this house. Now will you please go?'

'Not a hope,' he said cheerfully. 'I adore arguing with girls in bathrooms. And you look cute, all pink and steamy, with your hands behind your back – I must say you've got a much better figure than poor dear Topsy.'

'What would poor dear Topsy say to your being here?'

'Shan't tell her. And you'd better not—' his grin widened still more, if that were possible. He looked like the smiling Mr Jackson, smelling the honey. 'Or I could start putting it around what you and brother Toby and sister Selene get up to alone here in the long evenings.'

'You must be mad!' I gasped.

'Not mad, sweetheart – just practical. Now come on, move over.' And he laid hold of my arm.

It was my left arm he gripped.

I brought out my right hand, into which, behind my back, I had been squeezing the entire contents of my Giant Economy tube of Morgan's Extra-strong, bright green chlorophyll toothpaste containing magnesium and electrosol disinfectant for your added protection. I slapped a lavish palmful of the powerful green goo into both his eyes, then hopped nimbly out of the bath, grabbed a towel, and beat it to my own bedroom, which had a lock on the door.

I heard him shrieking shrilly with shock, blundering about, then roaring with rage. It was not likely, I thought, that the effects of the toothpaste would last for very long; he could easily wash it off; still, I got dressed again, just to be on the safe side. But he did not come to my room. I had not really expected that he would. I heard him stomping off furiously down the stairs, shouting out some rude monosyllabic Anglo-Saxon epithet as he passed near my door. And, after a while, far below, I heard the front door slam, and, hanging from my casement, saw him walk diagonally across the road below.

Then I went to bed in my clothes and cried hard, with anger and disgust, for myself, for poor Ginge Buckley, for mad Lady Venom and for the lost darling of my heart.

XII

I didn't go back to Floxby at Christmas. My father had fallen and broken his hip while staying at Cannes with Aunt Freda, and he was still there. The hip was taking a long time to mend. A locum had been installed at the practice. The twins, thriving in Heidelberg, had no intention of coming home, and I wished to avoid any chance of a meeting with Dolly and Tom. Or with Dan. Barney, in Chicago, had suddenly announced his marriage to a botanist of impeccable New-England-Pilgrim-Father-*Mayflower* descent, so he would not be coming back to England at present.

'Priscilla Winslow, her name is. Ach, I hope he treats her better than the others,' Tante Lulie said gloomily. 'But I do not expect it. Already they have a cat, Barney writes. It is a bad sign . . . '

I had rung up to inquire about Mariana's whereabouts. She was giving a series of song recitals in Cape Town, it seemed. Dave was in Dallas. Sir Gideon was in Stockholm. The Morningquest family structure, which I had believed to be solid and firmly grounded as the pyramids or the Parthenon, seemed to be disintegrating before my very eyes. Since the episode with Dan, I had been shy of going to Cadogan Square, and therefore saw less of Toby and Selene. Sometimes we took in a concert together, but it was becoming almost impossible to persuade Selene to set foot out of doors. She stayed inside, she made a pot or two, she did exquisite embroidery, she played violin or viola; why, she demanded in a reasonable-sounding manner, should she be required to do anything more?

'Because, because – the world is beautiful, worth looking at.'

'I can look at books, pictures. I prefer to.'

'*People* can be nice.'

'I haven't found them so.'

She ate less and less.

'Selene, you really should see a doctor.'

'Oh, please, Pandora, don't bother me. I have a right to live as I choose.'

Well: she had. And I, certainly, had no right to badger her, none in the world.

Dolly, Selene told me, had come into a substantial sum of money at her last birthday, left her by some Hungarian great-aunt. With part of this fortune she and Tom planned to make a film about famous musical families. From Scotland they had travelled straight to California, looking for backers. I knew that Tom had been curious to visit Hollywood and see this crazy place for himself, though he had no ambition to live or work there.

'The film sounds a touch narcissistic,' I said doubtfully. 'More like Dolly's project than Tom's.' I felt anxious and sad, in case Tom's talent should be deflected into what sounded to me suspiciously like a Dolly-promotion project. I hoped that I was wrong.

Princess Natasha Bagration, subject of one of my *Ton* line drawings and little character-sketches, had asked me to do a full-scale portrait of her, so I spent Christmas with the Bagrations in their freezing flat in Edinburgh, getting on with it. She and her husband Andrei taught respectively Russian language and literature at Edinburgh University. For me, the temptation to pass a few days in that city, looking at all the faces in the street, was quite a strong one.

Of course I did not see my bearded man, though I attended services in several different churches, hoping to see him presiding over one of them. I rented a car, and went to spend a day in St Vigeans with Mrs D, where I put a new washer on her kitchen tap, expelled a family of mice from her pantry, and replaced the pipe-lagging which they had used for bedding.

She voiced again her disappointment that I had not married her Oe.

'Whit went wrong? He had an eye for ye. A'body could see that. And ye're a guid family lass.'

'Only because my own was so grim that I tend to get involved with other people's,' I wrote on her pad.

'That Dolly is awa' too grand for my Tom.'

'She comes from a *really* fancy family,' I scribbled. 'The aristocracy of music.'

Mrs D sniffed. Music was of negligible importance to her.

'Next time I come,' I wrote, 'I'm going to make you get yourself tested for a hearing aid.'

'Mphm.' She gave me her ironic smile.

When the portrait was completed and I went south, I left the Bagrations (who were a very nice couple, hard-up, hard-working, thirty-ninth in line, they told me, to the throne of Russia) a copy of my drawing of the bearded man and besought them, if they ever happened across him, to extract from him his name and address.

While in Edinburgh I looked up the name of my mother's cousin, Mark Taylor, in old medical registers and found him on record, but with no interesting or unusual details. He seemed to have been a worthy, respected man, that was all. He had attended medical school in Vienna.

Back in London I went round to Cadogan Square (having no TV set of my own) to watch with Toby and Selene the first of Dan's weekly chat shows 'Goodnight with Danny Morning'.

'It's a merciful thing that Mar and Gid are both overseas,' Selene said. 'They'd die of shame.'

I myself was outraged to discover that Dan was using for his signature music a jazzed-up theme from the *Serenata Notturna*, the one that we had all been whistling to each other on that carefree day-out around London. It was like, I thought, discovering your own child, all dressed up in someone else's nasty clothes, taking part in somebody's vulgar show. I would never feel the same about that piece of music, about that memory, that light-hearted time.

Toby, hard at work on his dissertation, allotted only ten minutes for the programme before pronouncing it sloppy stuff and returning to his books, but Selene and I watched it all through with disgusted fascination.

'If I hadn't had such a bust-up with Mar I'd write to her about it,' said Selene. 'But, anyway, somebody is bound to. One of her friends.'

'I'm sorry you had a row with her.'

'Oh well,' she said vaguely. 'It was bound to happen.'

She did not discuss it; nor did I inquire. But I felt sad for Mariana. Selene was her favourite child.

I myself wrote her a long, loving letter to Cape Town, describing my Scottish trip and activities on *Ton*; but received no answer.

Spring blew and pattered in with bunches of daffodils and pots of primroses on street barrows, and it seemed a long, long time since the spring of two years ago with its happy hopes. But still, spring is spring. Once or twice I went down to Boxall Hill for a weekend. My father, his leg mended at last, had decided on early retirement and had never come back to England; he was staying on in Cannes with Aunt Freda.

At Otherland the various habits and routines were happily unchanged. It was home to me now. I loved arriving without prior announcement, walking the mile from the station, taking the short cut through the chestnut wood. The house on its crescent of hillside, serene and unaltered, was like a negation of all the drastic changes that had taken place in my own life. It was like a constellation – a permanent shape, a piece of unalterable elegance, a confirmation of natural order.

The season proceeded in its accustomed orderly manner. Snowdrops gave way to crocuses around the little mossy fountain in the courtyard. Cowslips replaced primroses in the orchard and meadow.

Grisch was thinking up ideas for using old typewriter ribbons: tying up bundles of newspaper for the collectors, training sweetpeas. 'And soon we can use them for tomatoes and peonies,' he said. Dan came down to

Aviemore at weekends with some rather odd friends, Lulie reported, but he never brought them to visit at the big house.

'Odd, how do you mean odd?' I asked.

'Nothing to *sheb naches* over,' said Lulie.

'No use trying to judge others,' said Grisch, studying the reflection of his face in a copper kettle he was polishing. 'That Topsy is not a bad girl. Good-natured enough.'

'Her quilts are terrible. *Paskudne*! Such quilts I wouldn't give to my worst enemy. But yes, she's good-natured . . .'

I continued to enjoy my work at *Ton* and my life classes in Southampton Row. I had a commission to paint a portrait of Gideon's friend Stefan Bartelme the cellist, and did some preliminary drawings of him with cello. Mariana was due back from her South African tour in ten days now and I was firmly resolved on seeing her one way or another, whether in London or at Otherland. It had been too long. I was dying to tell her about life on *Ton*. And I wanted to paint her.

'Why don't you do one of Mar?' Toby had said, on one of the occasions when he was standing in for his father, and Sir Gideon, catching on to the idea, said, 'Yes-yes; a most excellent plan. You should certainly paint Mariana.'

Through the dark of winter, through cold and sadness, through spells of unappeasable longing for Tom, I had cheered myself with plans for this project. Mariana, with her white hair and sharply angled face, was a great subject; she, like her husband, had been painted several times already, but that was no bar to *my* plans. I thought I would like to do her in Lulie's room at Boxall Hill against all that vague richness of drapes and sequins, the background painted in rather loosely, and she very clear and distinct in the foreground.

And while I painted her we could talk; we could re-establish our old relations.

Toby told me that he was going to meet her at Heathrow when she flew back from Cape Town. 'Dave arrives on the same day on a Pan Am flight from Dallas, but I'm not going to wait about for *him*; he can get a taxi.'

My heart did sink at the prospect of Dave; I'd hoped he was still in the Mid-west, out of sight and out of mind.

'Will she go down to Boxall Hill for the weekend?'

No, said Toby, she had to judge a choristers' contest at Cambridge. 'She's going to Cambridge on Friday night. She won't be at Boxall Hill till the week after. Gideon will be back by then, too.'

Of course I was overwhelmingly disappointed not to see Mariana right away; after so many months the delay of seven more days seemed too hard to bear. Yet I couldn't even be sure that she would be pleased to see me. It was months since she had even troubled to reply to my letters.

Disoriented and discontented, I went down to Boxall Hill myself at the weekend and helped Toby, who had handed in his dissertation, to dig the last two yards of the tunnel.

'There! It's a bloody triumph!' he said, thrusting the final roof-prop into position. 'Heaven only knows why we did it. And nobody will ever thank us or congratulate us.'

'I daresay the twins would, if they were here. After all, they worked hard on it too. I'll write and tell them.'

'I'll congratulate you!' announced Dan, all smiles, fresh, clean, and chubby, descending the steps into the little crypt-like room below the pavilion, which had been our goal. 'Rather a lot of *mess* around, though, isn't there?'

He had a special, spiteful smile for me as he surveyed my filthy T-shirt and jeans, sweaty face and clay-filled hair.

'Is it all right for me to come down, Mopsum?' called his plump Topsy from the room above.

'No I wouldn't, not yet, Popsum. You'll get covered with dust and muck. Wait till it's all cleaned out.'

'So sorry we haven't laid down the red carpet for you,' growled Toby, who found Topsy, with her full skirts, peasant blouses and little-girl affectations, unbearably tedious. Myself I didn't mind her in small doses. She was perfectly ready to be friendly. It sometimes surprised me that Dan put up with her, since, though he often chose to play the fool, he was very far from being one; but evidently her family millions amply compensated for her lack of wit.

'Well, well,' Dan said, 'we'll bring round a bottle of fizz presently to celebrate the break-through. We're planning to come and watch the five o'clock news on your box; ours has developed glandular fever.'

'Oh – all right,' said Toby unwelcomingly. 'See you later then. I want a bath. Down tools, Pandora.'

We parked our drills and picks, locking doors at both ends to make sure that no unauthorised person could come to grief in our somewhat primitive excavations, then went indoors for our baths. Mine, in fact, was a shower in the cubbyhole installed by Grisch next door to the butler's pantry. I sluiced the grit from my hair. As I was rubbing it I heard the phone ring next door, and Lulie answer but, owing to the rush of water, could not catch what was said. But I did hear her voice rise high, in astonishment or distress. Hastily I threw Mariana's old monk's robe around me and ran out, wrapping a towel over my wet hair.

'Ach, no, *no*!' Lulie ejaculated, putting down the receiver and turning a white, shocked face. 'The most terrible news – wait, wait, it will be now directly on the television—'

She hurried next door to the ping-pong room and I followed her barefoot, trembling. '*Kriech nicht darum at borvas*,' she scolded absently.

Grisch and the others, Toby, Dan, Topsy, were in the room already, idly expectant, holding glasses of fizzy wine in their hands. The BBC news had just begun.

'—Mariana Tass, Lady Morningquest, one of the world's best-known sopranos, died this afternoon in a tragic accident in Cambridge...'

Toby's lips parted wide in shock.

We all listened, almost with disbelief, as the newsreader went on in a serious tone, fitted to such an item:

'Lady Morningquest and a companion were in Gonville Place, Cambridge, walking past a parked car which had, unnoticed, been leaking a large quantity of fuel from its tank into the gutter; a considerable pool must have collected. Lady Morningquest's companion was smoking and seems to have dropped a lighted match which ignited the pool of petrol and caused an explosion; the couple were both so severely burned that they died on their way to hospital. Lady Morningquest's companion was Mr David Caley, an American friend of long standing. She will be chiefly remembered for...'

Toby began to sob, loudly and childishly. Grisch looked stricken to the heart.

The newsreader went on cataloguing Mariana's various rôles and honours. Next door the phone began to ring again.

'It's probably newspapers,' said Dan. 'I'll go.'

He went, and through two doorways we could hear his voice, loud, assured and capable.

Topsy looked at me with large piteous eyes like peardrops. 'Darling Mariana – she was such a sweetie-pie – oh, what an *awful*, awful way to go—'

I went and put my arms round Toby, as he sobbed and shook convulsively. 'Toby, Toby, listen: somebody's got to tell Selene! She's all alone in Cadogan Square, she doesn't watch TV – does she listen to radio news?'

'Probably not,' he muttered, and visibly drew himself together. 'No, you're right. I'd better go at once.'

'I'll come too.'

'First, some kind of *tsitsebeissen* – a tisane,' ordered Lulie. She herself looked blanched and drawn, almost corpse-like.

'And we must think how to get in touch with Dolly,' said Grisch. 'Pandora, can you call the twins? Also I must get hold of Gideon in New York—'

'And David's family – does he have a family? – in Baton Rouge?'

The newspapers made a three-day event of it. The Morningquest name, Mariana's celebrity, her large family of gifted children, the fact that she had been coming up for a DBE (I had not known this), the bizarre horrendous manner of her and Dave's deaths, and his, to say the least, anomalous position in the Morningquest family, were all given full play. On it went, day after day. Also the glamorous mystery of her background. Found on the steps of a convent in Graz as a two-year-old, she had early displayed a singing voice of unusual promise as well as remarkable musical ability. The nuns at this particular convent, who were connoisseurs of musical talent and had a high reputation as teachers, kept her until she was seven. Then, guessing at her Jewish origins, for she had been found during the deportations, presumably left by parents desperate for her safety, the nuns managed to arrange for her transfer to a sister house of the same religious order in Basle, where she continued her musical education. Later, since she had no religious vocation, she was transferred to a secular school (where she had met my mother). And then the patrons who, by now, were paying for her had her sent to the Juilliard School in New York . . .

While the press publicity was still at its height, Sir Gideon arrived back in England, also the twins from Germany.

There was much discussion as to where the funeral should take place. Lulie, who looked ravaged, ten years older in the space of a week, with all the Rembrandt lines of her face dragged downwards in woe, wanted it to take place in Floxby. So did Grisch. Sir Gideon – also stricken, grey-faced and aged, argued for London. So did Dan.

'Friends will find it easier to come to a London service,' he pointed out. What he meant was, that there would be a better chance of celebrities and greater publicity.

In the end, however, Lulie and Grisch had their way, chiefly because most of the organisation lay in their hands. But a memorial service was later held in London, at which tributes were read by John Gielgud, Rafael Kubelik and enough other notabilities to satisfy even Danny. I preferred the Floxby ceremony, though it was a sharp reminder of my own mother's funeral, and, indeed, the two friends were buried within a few yards of one another.

Dave's remains were sent to a family of cousins in Baton Rouge.

At the time of the funeral I was still in shock. I could not believe, simply could not accept the fact that Mariana was gone. I had mental paralysis. I could not believe that I would never again hear her clear, bell-like voice, her sudden shout of loud, irrepressible laughter, her change from clarity to gruffness as she expressed some unexpected, trenchant opinion.

The twins, over briefly from Heidelberg, were silent also, and shocked. It was too soon for them to make any of their usual pronouncements. But at the end of three days, as they were about to leave, Elly said: 'Well, if she had to give us such a gruesome father, at least she removed him in the most expeditious way possible.'

'*He* removed her,' said Ally. 'Tired, probably, of living among a family of achievers.'

'It always seemed to suit him up to now.'

'Basically he was resentful. You know he was. All the time.'

'Most people are glad of a good excuse to feel resentful. Because everybody naturally does . . .'

'Goodbye, Pandora dear,' they said, hugging me. 'Keep an eye on Selene, if you can.'

Selene had not been to the funeral, nor to the memorial service.

But Dolly and Tom had arrived unexpectedly, the night before the ceremony in Floxby, stayed overnight at Claridges', and motored down from London next morning.

Dolly's appearance startled me considerably, when I saw her outside the church, after the service. She was so matronly. She had put on weight again – could she, I wondered, be pregnant? – but looked well and confident. Being married – perhaps being away from her mother? – had endowed her with briskness and assurance. The inheritance from the Hungarian aunt had helped, too, no doubt, I thought uncharitably. She wore dark purple, a deep damson colour, which caused Tante Lulie to mutter, 'Ach, such a *schmatte* should be worn by *nobody* under fifty, and especially not by Dolly with her colouring. But she will never learn, that one.'

Tom, who suddenly emerged from behind Dolly, gave me a total shock. I had hoped that – considering my excellent job, my growing commitments in portrait work, my busy, grown-up life – the miserable ache, the painful longing for Tom that went on inside me might be kept under control. Like a nuclear leak, safely barricaded and battened down behind concrete ramparts. But the mere sight of him made me flinch with pain.

And he was so grievously thin! More formally dressed than ever I had seen him, in dark business suit and white shirt, silent and sober, he appeared like Black Rod, sombrely observing the scene. His eyes, in deep sockets, were darker than I recalled, his cheeks were hollow and, though recently shaved, blue-grey with stubble. I thought he looked haunted. Perhaps, of course, it was just jet-lag.

Dolly was saying to Dan: 'Yes, we were able to have dinner with Strobe, from Empyrean Films, last night, so it was a useful trip. He may be offering to back us— '

I said, 'Hallo, Tom,' in a quiet voice, and it seemed to me he took a grip on himself, like a horse clenching on its bit.

In the same tone he answered, 'A funeral is a bad time to meet. How are you, Pandora?'

'Oh; all right. Sad. I'm sorry you never met Mariana. *Very* sorry.'

'I, too.'

'How are *you*, Tom? Do you like the West Coast?'

He shrugged. 'It is not where I would choose to spend my life. More and more I need to return to my root-land. To Prague.'

'Oh – but what about Mrs D? She misses you so. Aren't you going to see her?'

'Not this trip. We have no time. We must return by an afternoon flight today.'

Dolly spun round and said, 'Tom we *must* be off. We simply can't afford to miss that plane. Oh, hallo Pandora.' She gave me a sad, gracious smile. 'Come, darling, we have to fly.'

As on a former occasion she hooked her arm through that of Tom, and bore him off.

I wondered why they had stayed at Claridges'. Why not at Cadogan Square?

Three months later, when I was not even beginning to recover from the loss of Mariana, I had a letter from a firm of lawyers in the Strand: Paxley, Marwell, Floatworthy, and Ginsberg:

> Dear Madam, we are instructed to inform you that Lady Morningquest bequeathed you, in a codicil to her Last Will and Testament, dated April of last year, the Regency Carlton House writing table (1810) with brass enrichments, holly inlay etc from her boudoir at 179a Cadogan Square. Please inform us when a delivery of this article will be convenient.

I was astonished, excited, saddened, profoundly moved. So she *had* thought of me at some point, *had* remembered me. And in a way that could not have spoken to me more directly. Not money, which is impersonal, meaningless, but an article of furniture that was absolutely special to her, that she had used every day she spent in London, that was imbued with her own practical, elegant nature. I had seen her on so many mornings, after nights I had passed in Cadogan Square, settling down at that desk with her Miss Halkett, attacking the large routine pile of correspondence as briskly as a woodman applying himself to a heap of boughs.

The desk was beautiful, the colour of dark honey, with a high curved upper tier at the back, containing half a dozen drawers, and enclosed by a delicate brass rail; there were brass collars on the slender legs, a leather-lidded well in the writing area, more drawers in front and on either side. It was a mouth-wateringly desirable article of furniture, and totally unsuited to me or any of my other random and ramshackle possessions. I would never have thought of buying such a piece. I longed to show it to Tom. I still dreamed about Tom, three nights out of seven.

When I phoned the lawyers to arrange for its delivery, Mr Paxley warned me: 'The desk, I should inform you, Miss Crumbe, is a highly superior article of furniture; it was valued, of course, for purposes of probate, and we are able to tell you that it is worth many thousands of pounds; we advise you to have it insured without delay.'

I promised them that I would.

A couple of months after the delivery of the desk, I was very startled indeed to receive a visit from Dolly.

It was on a gloomy August Sunday afternoon in London; the kind of day when one's spirits are at a low ebb already. I had stayed in town for the weekend in order to get through a lot of gritty work, and was longing for distraction. My spirits perked up at the sound of the doorbell, but sank to zero when I found Dolly outside wearing what I took to be mourning: a formal grey-and-white flowered dress, a white hat. Few people still wore hats; but Dolly did.

'Dolly! What a surprise.' I could not bring myself to say that it was a pleasant one.

'Can I come in?' she said, and did so, glancing around briskly, making an inventory of my effects. I could see her mentally sorting out articles she remembered from those I had acquired since our parting.

'How is Tom?' I asked politely.

'All right. He's in Scotland. Visiting his grandmother.'

'Would you like a cup of tea?'

'No thanks,' she said curtly.

Her eye came to rest on Mariana's desk. It was covered with paper, layouts. I had been working there when interrupted.

'I came to see you about that,' she said, nodding towards it.

'Oh?'

'You probably weren't aware that Mar – that Mariana had always said it was to be mine. That I was to have it. That was always completely understood.'

'Oh?' I repeated, rather blankly.

'The boys can tell you so, or Tante Lulie, or Selene – anybody in the family,' said Dolly, emphasising the word *family*. 'Mar had always promised that it would be mine.'

'Then I suppose that she must have changed her mind,' I suggested.

Dolly gave me an impatient look, as to a backward child. 'We all know that, the last couple of years, Mar was behaving quite erratically; menopause, probably. She did lots of irrational things; and that ridiculous codicil was probably one of them. She would have changed it back later on, or cancelled it. Without any doubt whatsoever.'

'But she didn't,' I said.

'Look, Pandora, don't be difficult! Don't pretend to be stupid. Mariana didn't really mean that desk to become yours. She *couldn't*! Why, when I was quite tiny – five or six— ' Dolly's lower lip trembled – ' she *promised* it to me. It was a *promise*.'

'Dolly, I'm very sorry – but in the end, legally, in writing, she left it to *me*.'

'You don't seem to understand! You have a moral obligation to let me have the desk. It's not the monetary value— '

'Have you talked about this to anybody else? The rest of the family? The lawyers?'

'No, why should I? They'd certainly be on my side. Will you, please, do the decent thing, Pandora, and let me have the desk?'

'I'm sorry, Dolly,' I said slowly. 'But I'm afraid you haven't convinced me. OK, so Mariana did promise you the desk *once*. But that, it seems, was a long time ago. And since then she made this addition to her Will. So, somewhere along the way, she changed her intentions. Which she had a right to do.'

'But I *want* it!' said Dolly, tears spurting from her eyes.

'Just because you want it doesn't mean that you are entitled to it.'

'I know much more about it than you do! I bet you don't know about the secret drawer!'

'Well – as a matter of fact, I do.'

Enchanted by the desk, when it first arrived I had taken pains to read up all the literature I could lay my hands on about furniture of the period. At first the possibility of a secret drawer had not occurred to me but, once it had, I perseveringly poked and pulled and pushed, until I had discovered, not one, but two secret compartments under the curve of the back tier. One was empty, the other had contained a letter.

I walked over to the desk and opened the secret aperture.

'Look, Dolly. There was a letter for me inside. I suppose you'll recognise the writing?'

On the envelope was the single word Pandora. That handwriting still makes my heart put in an extra beat.

I pulled the single sheet of paper from the envelope and showed Dolly the date and the opening words. Then I put it back inside the envelope again, and returned it to the little hiding-place.

Dolly watched me in stricken silence.

Then she burst out. 'You stole her from me! You stole my mother! Because your own had died – you are absolutely without a vestige of a conscience, you came and broke up our family, you caused nothing but pain and trouble. You are a thief! That's what you are, a thief!'

'Oh, come off it, Dolly!'

'She gave you those earrings, and then the desk – that letter—'

Dolly darted one of her basilisk looks at me. I could see she was on the point of demanding to know what was in Mariana's letter. Wearily I took her by the arm and turned her round. 'Dolly I'm sure you'd like to stay here all afternoon and have a long ding-dong argument with me about it. That might make you feel better. But I haven't the time or the energy. I'm working on a job that has to be finished by tomorrow. So you just go back to Tom—'

'He's in Scotland,' she repeated sulkily.

'Well, go back to him wherever he is, and make your film; or whatever you are doing. And, if you want to go to law about Mariana's desk, feel free! But she wrote a dated letter to me, which was inside the desk, and so I conclude that she meant the desk for me, and I'm holding on to it. Now goodbye.'

Sighing, I pushed her out of the door. As she started down the stairs (my flat was the one at the top of the house) I called, 'Are you at Cadogan Square? Are you going to see Selene? She needs help – a lot of help. Maybe she'd take it from you.'

'Oh, bother Selene!' Dolly clumped down the stairs without looking up.

I returned to the desk, opened the sliding panel, and took out the envelope. As well as the letter it contained a photograph of two schoolgirls in straw hats, tunics, ankle socks. They carried satchels and smiled, screwing up eyes against the sun.

'My darling Pandora,' the letter said. 'Just for fun, and just in case I'm snatched away from all my loving friends and relatives by an air crash – which seems a statistical possibility, since I travel around such a lot – I have bequeathed you my desk and rely on your ingenuity to find this letter. Your mother was the first friend of my heart, and lit up my life with joy at a time when I was the most miserable, loveless, lonely, orphaned young female in the whole of Europe. Never let anyone tell you that the love of children can't be as deep as adult love. It can be deeper. When I lost your mother, when she was shipped off to that cousin in Scotland, I felt as if I had lost half of myself – the better half. It took me years to recover. I have had other relationships since – some strong, some deep – but none to equal the bond with Hélène. And when I found her again three years ago – but so hurt, so maimed, so scarred – it seemed as if I had suffered the same damage. If she chose never to tell us what had happened in Scotland, that was her right; and especially, no doubt, she thought it best to leave you unmarked by her trauma. I can't judge and don't intend to try. And the damned soul who did the damage is out of our reach; no doubt luckily. And Hélène herself is at peace.

'Pandora, I broke off our last conversation abruptly because I was suddenly overwhelmed by the premonition that I could soon feel for you what I felt for your darling mother. And I believed that would not be in your best interests. Dearest child, you must be free, free to make your own choices, and if we – if I approached you too closely with all the weight of history and passion and suffering that I drag behind me, your little ship might be swamped before it had even left harbour! Excuse me if I mix my metaphors – your beloved mother would have teased me for that.

'You have a good and strong talent, you have power to go your own way. In some curious sense I look on you as more my own child than any of those I gave birth to – except, perhaps, Selene.

'I will always think of you as something very precious that might have happened to me – the more precious, perhaps, because it did not.

'I love your letters. They are like jewels. I showed one of them to Argissa Montefeltro and she was very impressed. She wants you to write something for her some time. I would like you two to be friends, since you are both so very dear to me.

'Forgive me, and remember me.   M.'

Argissa Montefeltro had turned up at both the private funeral and the memorial service. She was an impressive figure, dead-white complexion, huge ravaged eyes, dressed in diamonds and sables; she edited, I knew, the international review *Phaethon*; she had had affairs with Sartre and Dürrenmatt (rumour averred), had spent time in the desert with Georgia O'Keeffe, as well as several years in Buddhist and Catholic monasteries; she was a friend of Mother Teresa. At the memorial service she had been expected to read a tribute to Mariana but had been so convulsed with grief that she was unable; dumb, choking, rigid, she had to be tenderly escorted from the podium by Pierre Boulez. I noticed that Sir Gideon looked at her with marked dislike. Rumour also had it that she had been seen stretched full-length (sables, diamonds and all) among the flowers on Mariana's new-made grave, in a total abandonment of tears.

I did not think I was at all equal to a friendship with Argissa Montefeltro, and hoped very much that she would not make any attempt to get in touch. And in fact she never did.

For months after Mariana's death I went down to Otherland almost every weekend. Thank Heaven for my absorbing, exacting job with its nonstop crises, moments of exhilaration, moments of panic and despair, but always occupation and distraction for the mind. Mrs Beecham treated me with a brisk, no-nonsense long-headedness that was supportive.

'All this nasty gossip will die away,' she said. 'Death always seems to generate it – like weeds sprouting when a big tree blows down.' And she added, with her own special brand of practical self-interest, 'It's a good thing we ran the Gideon Morningquest feature last March; if we had it *now* it would seem cashing in on all this vulgar rubbish—' tapping copies of the tabloid press which, having run through all the permutations of Mariana's relationship with Dave, and the parentage of the twins, had now moved to Sir Gideon and various of *his* past connections. Some of which had startled me considerably. The eccentric pattern of his and Mariana's lives continued to be laid bare to the public gaze and the public, apparently, found it engrossing.

My weekends at Otherland were a comfort, and I thought they were a comfort also to Lulie and Grisch who seemed, in many ways, more stricken by the loss of Mariana than her children had been. Dolly and the boys were growing away from home, had their own ways of coming to terms with bereavement, and the twins had converted grief to anger; but Lulie and Grisch were just, simply, deeply sad, and missed her all the time.

We talked about her a great deal, as I drew and painted the pair of them over and over: Lulie in her Rembrandt beret, Grisch in his black velvet vest and white polo-neck, unshaven, holding cup of coffee or glass of armagnac.

They had looked on her as a kind of younger sister, beloved, fallible, gifted, always a fertile source of interest, joy and anxiety.

'And when she found your mother again, she was so transported! Many, many times she had told me about this lost friend, Hélène, that she had loved so much at the school in Switzerland. She kept the photo always in this brush-and-comb case that your mother once made her. She had copies made of the photo, she was so afraid of losing it.'

I nodded, blinking away tears at the sight of the brush-and-comb case, faded yellowish linen, held together with cross-stitch; an ancient, childish relic, in total contrast to my mother's small handful of bleak, unsentimental possessions.

'Mariana was so angry and distressed at what had happened to your mother to change her so; at all the suffering and ill-usage that she had endured.'

'If only I knew what had happened to her . . .'

'I do not think you ever will, now,' said Lulie. 'I do not see any way in which you can discover what befell her during that period between Switzerland and when she married your father. You must try, *bubeleh*, simply to put it out of your mind.'

But I still hoped that one day I would come across the bearded man. Perhaps if I were to advertise?

And then Lulie said something that really rocked me.

'Most probably it was something to do with your mother being Jewish.'

'Jewish? My mother was Jewish?'

'Did she never tell you that?'

XIII

The second Christmas after that found me in Paris.

'We are lonely and forlorn here at Boxall Hill,' Grisch had written. 'Come down and cheer us up if you are able.' And I had every intention of doing so, but at the last minute a directive from Mrs B – couched in gracious silken language, as always, but even the slightest flicker of a demurral or disinclination would, I knew well, have put my position in peril, and I was enjoying the job far too much to risk such a loss just at present – sent me off, on Christmas Eve, to the Île de la Cité to catch and interview Daisy de Saint-Aignan, an elusive intellectual duchess who passed most of her time in a Greek monastery, but had agreed to have a line portrait done while visiting her Paris apartment on legal business concerned with pensions to elderly dependants. She proved tremendously good value, the duchess – Mrs B had an unerring eye – and I was glad to add her beaky, forcible profile, shrewd flexible mouth, and black, fierce eye, to my growing portfolio, while she talked about the problems of administering a large, ancient estate and funding the massive arts endowment which had brought her into the public notice.

Hospitable, she was not; one lukewarm cup of lemon tea was all the refreshment proffered by the black-uniformed, white-ribboned aged maid (I longed to draw her portrait as well) during my two-hour session. Millionaires conserve their millions by strict attention to low-watt light-bulbs and brief telephone calls. I have noticed this repeatedly. Through the need to catch a six a.m. plane from London I had missed breakfast, so, by the end of the visit, I was occupied with ravenous visions of a croque-monsieur. But first, since I was in Paris, I wished to visit my favourite art-supplies store, Senneliers on the Left Bank, in order to stock up with paper and paint.

Emerging from there, laden, I plunged inland into the student quarter and stopped at the first empty pavement table. Parisians, wrapped in furs and woolly mohair, were taking advantage of the crisp clear weather. And I, with my bulky parcels and portfolio, was happy to avoid struggling between café tables.

Seated, munching, swigging beer, I suddenly became aware of familiar voices.

'Bacon believed that the advancement of science could counteract the Fall of Man—'

'Bacon was an ass. He was hopelessly out of touch with reality. The New Atlantis is not – and never will be—'

'My god! *Twins*!'

'Good gracious! It is Pandora! Wearing Tante Lulie's wonderful brown velvet, you looked so elegant that we didn't recognise you!'

They rose and hugged me.

'But you must see Barney too. Quick, Ally, *quick*, run after him and catch him – he has just this minute gone off to buy tickets for a concert tonight—'

'Oh, no, no, don't chase him – he'll not want to see me—' I protested, but Ally had already sped off at a darting, dragonfly pace among the slowly strolling French.

'She'll soon catch him,' said Elly comfortably, settling elbows on the table. 'But now, do tell, what are you doing in Paris, Pandora?'

'What are you? I thought you were snugged down in Heidelberg, and Barney off in Chicago.'

'Oh, well, he needed to come over for a week and consult with a pen pal at the Sorbonne; and so he wrote to us and said why didn't we all meet. This pal has lent him a huge apartment in the rue des Ecoles. We're all camping there, having a great time.'

'Is Barney's wife here too? Priscilla?'

'No; she's not; we gather things are not too wondrous in that department. Ah, look, she caught him; Barney, Barney, see who's here!'

Barney and I had not met for a long, long time; not since Mariana's funeral, in fact, after which he had flown straight back to Chicago. But he was wholly unchanged; he still wore the same untidy corduroys and baggy tweed jacket, its pockets bulging with papers; his fair hair flopped over his forehead and his eyes tilted endearingly at the corners when he smiled.

I felt absurdly pleased to see him. And he seemed equally so to see me.

'So: what brings you to Paris, Pandora?'

I explained about my duchess, and the twins were all agog.

'She used to be a notoriously wicked lady, remember? Had an affair with Mussolini, or was it Franco? And now she's repenting of her misdeeds by ladling out money to the arts. But it will be easier for a camel to enter into the kingdom of heaven—'

'She *looks* rather like a camel,' pronounced Elly, studying my twenty drawings. 'Maybe she should disguise herself as one.'

'How long are you staying in Paris, Pandora ducky?'

'Well – I had planned to go back on the four o'clock flight this afternoon— ' I looked at my watch.

'Oh, why not wait and go back tomorrow? *Nobody* will be travelling on Christmas Day, except you and Barney. You'll have the plane to yourselves. You can spend the night with us in the rue des Ecoles – there's masses of room – and come to the concert.'

'What about you, twins? Are you coming to Otherland?'

'No, Elly and I have to go back to Heidelberg the day after tomorrow because we are directing a satirical St Stephen's Day musical which would fall apart without our hand on the tiller. But we can give you the pleasure of our company tonight. We can go out to a sumptuous dinner somewhere – can't we Barney?'

'Do stay, Pandora,' said Barney cajolingly. 'And then you and I can travel down to Otherland tomorrow. We'll phone Lulie and Grisch this evening. And Gid in Rome.'

So that is what we did. Leaving the twins to scatter the pearls of their satire before the probably unappreciative students and faculty of Heidelberg, Barney and I flew back together to Heathrow, and drove in a rented car to Floxby Crucis.

Hand in hand, a lot of the way. Which was foolish, of course, thoughtless, a mistake on almost every count; but we were both profoundly sad and lonely.

XIV

The twins remained away from England for three years.

Barney was the first member of the family they chanced to encounter, after their return, in the Marylebone Library of the Association for the Expansion of Scientific Jurisprudence. 'But what are *you* doing here in London, Barney? Did you and Priscilla definitively split?'

He invited them back to his flat in dockland.

'Cadogan Square is really too sad since Selene died,' agreed Elly, accepting the invitation. 'Old Gid doesn't really want to see us.'

'Why, why, did Selene have to *die*?'

'She just didn't want to live,' said Barney, sadly, scrambling eggs. 'She got pneumonia, and nobody noticed till it was too late. Even if they had, I don't believe it would have made any difference.'

'So what's Toby doing?'

'Working. Research on Iron-age turds. He seems to find them entirely engrossing.'

'Has he got a lover?'

Barney shook his head.

'And you, Barney? Where is Priscilla now?'

'Back in New Hampshire where she came from,' he answered shortly.

'Have you got somebody else?'

But Barney, carrying the frying pan to the sink, chose not to reply.

'Are you going down to Otherland?' he asked, returning with coffee.

'Of course. We're dying to see Lulie and Grisch. But we want to look up Pandora first. And where is Dolly?'

Barney said vaguely that he thought she was in Los Angeles still with her Czech. 'And Dan commutes between London and New York every week. He is a public person now. But his Topsy mostly stays down at Floxby. Pandora is doing a portrait of her ... I believe.'

A large tabby cat stalked into the room, glanced dismissingly at the twins, and stalked out again.

'What's his name?'

'Mog.'

'You brought him from Chicago?'

'No. That would have meant six months' quarantine.'

'I thought your cat there was called Mog?'

'All my cats are called Mog.'

'So what happened to that one?'

'I left him with friends.' Barney now sounded defensive. 'They wrote later and said he hadn't stayed with them. He ran away.'

'Pity whatshername – Priscilla – couldn't take him to New Hampshire.'

'She didn't really like cats.'

'Isn't it odd,' remarked Ally pensively, 'the way one always refers to people in the past tense as soon as one has parted from them. As if they had died and need no longer be taken into consideration.'

Barney gave his younger sister a sharp look, but said, merely, 'And you two? What are your plans?'

'We have an offer of jobs at Yokohama University. But we are going to check it out there first. A trip to Japan. Before that we have some business to transact in England.'

'You both look remarkably svelte.'

'That's the Louise Brooks syndrome.'

'It's too bad,' said Elly, 'that magazine of Pandora's folded. She was going to negotiate us jobs there.'

'Not very well-paid jobs, I'd have thought. You'll do better in Yokohama.'

'Pandora seems to be making out remarkably well with her portraits,' Ally said pensively. 'We keep coming across her name in *Encounter* and *Marie-Claire*.'

'And you, dear Barney, you're a professor now? Do all your students worship the ground you tread on?'

'Only some of them.'

'What about old Gid? Lulie writes that he is growing rather vague.'

'Mar's death really rocked him,' said Barney after a pause. 'He had that heart-block – were you there when that happened?'

They shook their dark heads.

'He just flaked out for three days. Deeply unconscious. It was fairly touch-and-go. He had oxygen and so forth. When he came to again he thought he had been off on a long journey. Afterwards, referring to the incident, he'd say, "When I was away."'

'Interesting.'

'And it changed him a good deal. He's remote now. Unreachable.'

'He was always that to us,' said one of the twins.

'Well, even more now than he was. Except when he's conducting. Then he snaps back into gear.'

'So he's still leading a full professional life?'

'Oh dear me, yes. Only Childers has to look after him a good deal more, now, and see that he gets to places on time.'

'Like a poor old shaman,' said Ally. 'Doddering about the world, waving his magic wand.'

'Well—' Barney glanced at his watch. 'I have to go off now and teach a class. Make yourselves at home, girls.'

'We'll take you out to dinner this evening. Somewhere splendid. Then, soon, we plan to go and dump ourselves on Pandora – if she'll have us.'

Barney raised his brows, said, 'I expect she will,' picked up a canvas hold-all bulging with books and students' essays, and left the flat.

'Poor old Barney,' said Ally, after a while.

Her twin did not bother to reply.

'So what do you plan to do, ultimately?' Pandora asked the twins, when they arrived at her Shepherd's Bush flat, several days later.

'Oh, ultimately, you see, we are going into politics. But not for seven years or so. Not till we have had our corners rubbed off.'

'I don't see many corners now.'

'*Besser wie gornischt,*' said Elly, grinning. 'But we have got a little problem at present. Ally has had an abortion, and is feeling rather poorly, so we do hope it will be all right if we stay with you for two or three days, Pandora?'

'Oh dear! Of course you may stay as long as you like. Is there anything I can do?'

'Nothing, apart from keep the dear girl supplied with Tampax. But we have brought a liberal supply with us.'

'Was the abortion absolutely necessary?'

'Oh yes,' said both twins together.

And then Ally explained, 'We felt it quite essential that one of us should undergo the experience. You can't really talk about things if you haven't done them, can you? Obviously it wasn't necessary for us both to do it, because our minds are fairly interchangeable. So we tossed up. And I lost. Or won; if you choose to look at it that way.'

'By "do it" you mean sex? The whole *schmear*?'

They fell about laughing.

'Dearest Pandora, we keep forgetting that now you know you are Jewish.'

'Half Jewish at least; like us.'

'Was it a shock when you learned?'

'A surprise; but a good one.'

'I have a theory,' said Elly, 'that our mothers were cousins. If you look at that early picture of them, they are quite alike.'

'No more so than any two schoolgirls of that period – the tunics, the socks, the haircut, the hats. Anyway, we shall never know. Because Mar really didn't know anything about her parents. And all the records were destroyed when that convent in Graz was hit by a bomb.'

'Did you ever get any further in hunting down Hélène's first husband, Pandora?'

'Not an inch. I tried advertising in the *Scotsman* and *The Times*. Nil results. Have you had any communications from Dave's kin in Baton Rouge?'

'Not a squeak. They received his ashes in dignified silence. A signed receipt came back, and that was the end of the transaction.'

'All of which seems to indicate strongly,' said Elly, 'that we should forget about our forbears and progenitors, and just get on with our own concerns.'

Ally nodded and, turning rather pale, made for the bathroom.

'Is she really all right?' asked Pandora. 'Shouldn't I get my doctor?'

'No, no. She's as tough as an old hickory root. It's a very good experience for us both,' said Elly cheerfully.

'Who – who was the father?'

'Oh, never mind about *him*. A person of no importance. A *nudnik*. But tell about you, Pandora? We know that you are painting the noble, and the renowned as fast as they can beat a path to your door. But are you happy with that? What about your private life? Your inner self?'

'Oh – nothing of any interest.'

'Come on. Don't be evasive.'

'It's true. I have been having an affair with a married man. It is dwindling to a close, it was never of primary importance.'

'Suspended animation,' said Elly.

'I beg your pardon?'

'That's what you are in a state of. Waiting for Prince Charming to come along.'

'Oh, *no*! Nothing of the sort.'

'We must shake you out of it.'

'I want to paint you both,' said Pandora quickly. 'While you are here. Or, preferably, down at Otherland.'

'Yes, Otherland would be best,' agreed Ally, coming back, 'What is Grisch on to now? And what about your father, Pandora? Where is he?'

Pandora began to laugh. 'Oh, he got married! Would you believe it? A widow lady that he met in Cannes. It is a great success. He is a changed person, talkative, jokey, you'd hardly know him. They don't come back to England much, he sold the house and the practice. And Grisch is OK, too. He listens to Radio Three more and more, because he is so worried about *waste*; he can't bear to think of all that free music rushing out on to the airwaves unless he is listening to it. So that gives him less time for revising English literature, which is just as well, for he has found Browning a hard nut to crack.'

'And Lulie? For whom does she make clothes now? Not for Dolly, I bet.'

'No, not for Dolly. Sometimes for me. She'll be glad to have—'

The telephone rang in the next room.

'Excuse me.' Pandora looked at her watch. 'That will be Toby. He always calls at this time.'

'Oh good, so we can speak to him. Barney didn't have his number.'

'He doesn't have one. He calls me from a box. I'll tell him you are here.'

She went into the other room and, after a while, returned, saying 'Do go and speak to him now.'

'Won't he be running out of change?'

'No, he always gives me the number and I call him back.'

Elly went through the door.

'Toby's not married, is he?' Ally inquired, looking interestedly at the tears on Pandora's cheeks.

'Oh, no. Poor Toby. No, I don't think he ever will be. He is very unhappy about Selene. But his work takes all his time. He's in line for a Nobel prize, somebody told me. He has an entirely new theory about the origins of the human race, that knocks the props from under every previous one.'

'Oh, *origins*!' said Ally impatiently. '*Destinations* is what people should be worrying about. Not origins.'

'Toby wants to talk to you!' called her sister from the other room.

XV

It would be impossible to overestimate the effect that Mariana's death had on her children. The event was so sudden, so horrible and so embarrassing. One day there she was, a powerful example of dedication and hard work, an advocate for high cultural standards and the importance of the nuclear family – Mariana's most deeply felt and frequently voiced belief was that only by the cohesion of small groups might the human race conceivably be saved; and among such groups the family was the first and strongest of all; then, next day, there she wasn't; there, instead, was a legacy of shock, scandal and vulgar gossip.

Toby and Selene had been their mother's favourites, and her death hit them hardest. Selene, I think, never recovered from it; Toby might have, was on the way to recovery perhaps, but was overtaken by misfortune. And he felt bitterly betrayed by Selene; that was what he talked of, most of all, in our ten p.m. conversations. 'She starved herself, she just let go of life. Why? She should have had more self-respect. She should have had more consideration for me.'

'But, Toby, you have to be really heroic to put somebody else's convenience above your own to that degree.'

'Well, Selene could have had heroism to that degree. Growing up is a process of slowly acquiring self-respect. If only she'd waited a little longer. We used to be so happy together. Do you remember those records you used to give us? At one time we played them such a lot; especially the Ode for St Cecilia's Day. It used to make us cry.'

'Oh, Toby. *I* can't play the Ode for St Cecilia any longer. Even thinking about the music gives me a most terrible pang.'

'Didn't you ever guess about me and Selene? We were sure you must have.'

'Guess what, Toby?'

It is no wonder that, of her sons, he was Mariana's favourite. Lulie showed me photos of him from six to sixteen; he was as innocent and beautiful as a daffodil. Even at the time I painted him he was – not handsome exactly, his mouth was too wide and too irregular – but there was a luminous quality in his face, a quality that could not be defined. I could gaze and gaze at it and never translate it in terms of paint.

The three boys reacted to Mariana's death in disparate ways. Barney applied himself conscientiously to his teaching, but, I believe, severed relations with the female sex – apart from fornication, of course – and, occasionally, reading the novels of Jane Austen or George Eliot. (Barney was the only member of the Morningquest who actually read for *pleasure*, not merely for instruction. Even the twins didn't do that.)

Dan, who, according to Lulie, had always been a dishonest and conniving little boy, attempting to keep up with Barney by cunning and trickery where he could not compete in mental and physical prowess, had been affected less than his brothers, merely abandoning any pretence of respect for morality. And yet Dan had a good brain, was shrewd and quick-witted and, of the three brothers, the most musically talented. 'One can't help remembering his wretched songs,' growled Grisch, 'even though they are such horrible trash. They do have some quality that makes them stand out from the rest.'

One of the more bizarre long-term results of Mariana's death was the conversion to Catholicism of Sir Gideon.

He had intended this to pass off quietly and without fuss, receiving instruction in Farm Street from some monsignor whom he had known for years through musical connections, and a private ceremony; but of course very few events relating to Sir Gideon ever passed off without fuss, and in any case the Pope, hearing about it, chose to take a hand, welcoming Gideon into the fold, so the newspapers ran the story most minutely and extensively. I also suspected Dan of having quite a share in the publicity; I knew he had invited his father to appear and discuss the change-over on his chat show, the message tactfully conveyed by fat Topsy who believed she was a favourite with the old boy, but the invitation was indignantly refused, Sir Gideon averring that he would sooner be dragged across the Alps by his tongue.

The ceremony with the Pope in Rome took place a month or so after the twins' return to England from Heidelberg. They and I were staying at Otherland just then, where I was at work on their double portrait. I had them posed at a small table playing chess. Ally was seen back view, in shadow, one-quarter profile; Elly facing her, three-quarter profile, with light pouring down from a high window on the left, and a mirror behind Elly reflecting her sister's face. All this took place in a room at Boxall Hill called by the family the Marble Hall which, normally, contained no furniture at all, but had large mirrors set all round the walls. At first I had made several false starts on the complicated composition, but now it was progressing well; I painted hard all day and dreamed about the picture at night, strange dreams about the chess game: that Elly's pawns were all becoming queens; that Ally's king suddenly drew a sword and began briskly defending himself. Not much, in fact, was visible of the game itself, since Ally's right elbow and shoulder formed a diagonal blocking it off, but a couple of captured pieces, white knight, black bishop, stood at the edge of the table, and the floor of the Marble Hall, alternate black and white squares, carried on the theme of chess.

Uncle Grisch used to come and potter about, cleaning the mirrors with a long-handled sponge, engaging whichever twin happened to be sitting (I took them singly) in philosophical discussion.

'Art is a method of laying claim to the physical world. You could call it the equivalent of animals impregnating trees or rocks with spray from their scent glands to mark territory. Or with urine. From that to Renaissance bigwigs defining their prestige is only a step.'

'So whose territory is Picasso marking out?' demanded Elly.

Grisch is on the right track, I thought, remembering the Advent calendars that my mother liked to find for me if she could (in those days they were not always easy to come by): calendars on which more and more little doors opened during the weeks leading up to Christmas. Did I stake my claim to the Morningquest clan by this series of paintings? Opening door after door?

Lulie bustled into the big quiet room looking moithered and put-about.

'What's up, Tante?'

'Gideon telephoned. He is coming down today with Childers and Luke Rose. He has conjunctivitis and has called off the Vienna trip. He plans to stay here a week.'

Grisch beamed with unaffected delight. 'A week! What joy! It is long since we have had him for more than a night.'

'And Childers and Rose. How shall I feed them?'

'We'll go and shop for you, Tante.'

As they grew older, Lulie and Grisch included a chicken, from time to time, in their diet. 'It is not that our principles have eroded,' Lulie explained. 'But vegetarian food entails such a lot of chopping.'

The twins were happy to shop. They had brought back a large car from Germany in which they purred smoothly to and from London. They had also fetched roofing and shoring materials from Crowbridge and made a very thorough job of completing the tunnel; and, after many telephone conversations with Toby, who was now almost as inaccessible as his sister Selene had been, they were engaged in the process of converting the tree pavilion into a monument for Mariana and Selene.

A series of curved transparent petals, like those of a tulip, separately protected the central area of the enclosure, where there was to be a glass memorial plaque, set vertically. This was being carved by one of Selene's friends, an ex-student at St Martin's, who was making a name for herself by exquisite glass engraving.

'Marsha promised she would have the slab done by this week. So we can set it up while Gid is at Otherland. He'd like that,' suggested Ally.

'Ach; poor old Gideon enjoys little these days. He is becoming an *alte kacke*,' pityingly remarked Tante Lulie who, herself around eighty, had begun to look her age since Selene's death. Her vigour and interest were, nonetheless, undiminished. She still tore into the daily papers like a squirrel, cutting out news stories, political essays, literary criticism, photographs, cartoons; still despatched these through the post in bundles. I knew now that they were sent to a cousin in San Francisco.

'Does he ever send you anything in return?' I once asked.

'Never! But he was always a poor *nudnik* of a fellow, even when we were growing up together. He would never have got anywhere in his life if I hadn't chased him up a bit, knocked a few ideas into his head.' He was, it seemed, medical superintendent of a huge psychiatric hospital. 'All that he is fit for, the poor *schlemiel*.'

Sir Gideon arrived, fending off squads of the local press, who were all eager for personal messages from him about his religious persuasions and future intentions: would he be attending mass at the tiny local Catholic church, or at the bigger, almost cathedral-size one at Crowbridge? Did he plan to build a chapel at Boxall Hill? Were any of his family planning to convert? What had the Pope said to him? Or he to the Pope? What were his views about abortion, contraception, the Latin mass, women priests?

Gideon parried the lot with his accustomed grace and saintly smile.

'He was really *obliged* to turn Catholic. So as to qualify for beatitude,' hissed Elly in my ear. 'Don't you see St Gideon gracing the side of a Perpendicular door?'

'I always have.'

But, once inside the house, the elegance and ease dropped off him. He was old, frail, tired, no more than bone and muscle covered with wrinkled parchment skin. Asked about his needs, he would answer vaguely or not at all. He was far away in his thoughts, addressing me sometimes as Selene, sometimes as Sidonie. Childers and Uncle Grisch unobtrusively took care of him every minute of the day. He listened to Radio Three, lying on a chaise longue in his large bare bedroom, where a wood fire always burned. He dozed a great deal of the time.

But – as Ally had prophesied – he was pleased and perked up at the notion of a memorial for his wife and daughter. The weather being fine and calm, he liked, in early evening, to shuffle out along the ha-ha, round the great curved saddle of meadow, fragrant with cowslips, to sit on the white metal seat at the edge of the ilex grove. Here he would gaze down over the wide empty landscape, or up at the perspex structure which now shone, mysteriously, among the dark trees. What was he thinking? I used to wonder.

Sometimes the twins would come and play Bach to him on their fiddles. He seemed more kindly disposed to them these days, perhaps because the irritant Dave was gone. Or perhaps he had simply forgotten who they were. He paid little heed to general conversation, and took no part in it unless it related to music, when he would suddenly become dictatorial. If Elly idly remarked, 'I've never liked the A Major Sonata so much as the E Major,' he would magisterially pronounce, 'Never mind about whether you like it or don't like it. With music your business is to *know* it.'

'You have to respect the old monster,' Ally admitted.

'It is of interest to see how he expands and contracts,' remarked Uncle Grisch. 'If a thing engages his attention, he can sometimes spread out, almost to his full former amplitude. And then, shrink again to the size of a pea! It is a saddening, most salutary experience to witness how an organism that once engaged the whole of one's capacity to love can so lose its faculty for absorbing love at all. Like a sponge that turns to a stone.'

'Oh, Uncle Grisch. Did you once love him so completely?'

'Unequivocally. With my whole being. He had done so much for me. And love like that is a transforming experience. Like a chemical change. You are never the same person, after.'

Had I ever loved anybody as much as that? Mariana? Tom? Many people – most? – I decided, are never in their whole lives swept through such a metamorphosis. And what could there possibly have been in Gideon to command such a degree of devotion? His own devotion to music? A bleak, unlovable quality, I'd have thought.

When plans were discussed for the Mariana memorial, Sir Gideon immediately expanded to his former dimensions and took a thoroughgoing practical interest in all the details. He even insisted on climbing the curved wooden stairway that wound up into the heart of the grove (with Childers supporting him, and Grisch vigilant in the rear) to inspect the perspex petals and the siting of the memorial plaque.

What a lucky thing, I thought, that Colonel Venner was safely off the scene, long departed to the west country. All this unwonted activity, people scurrying up and down the winding stair, would have wrought Sir Worseley into a fine frenzy. Though the stair itself could hardly have provoked his wrath nowadays; it had weathered to a gentle grey. But the glossy petals of the dome, flashing and catching the mild May sun through dark dangling ilex filaments would certainly have done so, I thought.

Toby and Barney had promised to come down to Otherland for the weekend. We planned a small family ceremony when the glass plaque would be set in place. Dolly, from Los Angeles, had cabled good wishes and regrets.

Everybody had – of course – reckoned without Dan. Working like a termite, a mole, a beaver, a prairie-dog, burrowing in every direction simultaneously, Dan organised human-interest stories in press, national, daily, weekly and local; on radio, local and national, and, naturally, on every possible TV channel.

The bluebells in the grove were soon trampled to a grey pulp by rubber-necking trespassers and photo-journalists; for days before the ceremony we had to remember to keep the house-doors locked and the sheep confined behind electric wire in the furthest corner of the orchard, otherwise some member of the press would be sure to leave the gate open and allow them to leak out into the lane.

Reporters were everywhere.

'*Stinken von kopf*,' muttered Lulie. Whom she referred to, she did not specify.

On the day itself, a battery of news cameras was trained on Sir Gideon as, helped by Barney, he tottered once again up the curved stairway and removed the *schmatte* supplied by Lulie (it was a huge yellowed piece of Mechlin lace used in preference to the red-and-blue patchwork quilt, one of fat Topsy's artefacts, which she had hopefully proffered) to reveal the slim glass tablet winking in the sun's fitful rays. Barney whipped the cork from a bottle of champagne, brilliant sparks of foam spurted among the ilex leaves. At the same instant, but much louder, a gunshot startled the rooks·in the nearby chestnut copse, several onlookers shrieked, and the glass slab shattered to smithereens.

By fantastic good fortune, nobody was hurt among the people standing on the platform – except for Toby, who suffered a slight cut on the cheekbone. Sir Gideon, nearest to the tablet, was, mercifully, wearing big screening sun-glasses, which protected his face.

Dan, down below, busy organising Bow Bells TV, was able to pounce on the marksman who – of course – proved to be none other than old Colonel Venom, alerted to the occasion by all the advance press reports. He had driven up from Torquay, starting at six a.m.

The local police (there already, keeping order) grabbed him at once, and parted him from his gun, while he, screaming vituperations, struggled, lashed out and generally gave trouble.

The burden of his grievance seemed to be that the Morningquest family were responsible for the death of his wife, who had never been the same woman since she left Aviemore; and that there was no justice in a world that put up a bloody great glass bookend in a tree for one woman while another, just as good in the eyes of Heaven, lay under a bed of granite chips in Torquay.

'Bloody bloodsuckers!' he screamed, his scanty white hair flying about; his red, chapped cheeks gleaming with sweat. 'Bloody baby-snatchers! Just you try digging under those holm oaks, that's all! Just see what you find there! Then you'll all be laughing on the other side of your faces! You'll see! Monsters! Money-grubbers! Murderers!'

And much, much more of the same. All of which, naturally, was meat and drink for the media.

And even more so when Colonel Venom, taken into protective custody, continued his wild allegations, urging the authorities to dig up the ground in the ilex grove where, he averred, they would find the corpses of the half-dozen children who had gone missing from Floxby during the last seven years.

The Chief Constable, a kindly, conscientious man called Witherspoon, came round to see Sir Gideon. He was in a great worry about all this.

'My dear man,' said Sir Gideon – it was wonderful how such a crisis rallied his wits and brought him straight back into the real world – 'my dear man, of course you must dig, since there is all this talk going around. Dig as deep as you wish, wherever you wish. I am afraid it does seem as if poor Colonel Venner has become somewhat unbalanced since the sad death of his wife. But *of course* such statements must be taken seriously.'

'Of course, sir, there have *not* been half a dozen children missing in Floxby. One, only; and an unconfirmed report of a traveller's child some years back. But babies have been mischievously removed from prams and then discovered in other places. And it does look,' Witherspoon added uncomfortably, 'as if the ground in your grove has been disturbed at some period not too long ago.'

'Then dig, my dear fellow! Dig by all means.'

And so they dug. They dug and dug.

'*Oy, veh* our poor bluebells!' wailed Tante Lulie, as more and more of the white straggly bulbs were exposed.

In the end they dug up all the ground below the trees, but found nothing except some canine and equine bones, and one damp, grey, sodden, woolly article which, inspected in a police laboratory, was found to be a baby's bootee, colour originally pink. It was shown to poor Ginge Buckley, but she disclaimed any knowledge of it.

At this point I felt obliged to relate my story of finding Mrs Venner distraught, confused and searching for something in the grove. With her wheeled shopping basket near at hand. And how I thought I had heard the cry of a child, later, coming from the Venner house.

The police were keenly interested.

'Can you put a date to that, miss?'

'Yes I can,' I said, after some thought. 'It was late winter, the day I had the cast removed from my leg. Five years ago. The hospital would have a record of it, I suppose. It was a Wednesday. I know that, because I was staying here at Boxall Hill at the time, and I was due to leave next day, Thursday.'

And we had a farewell dinner that evening, I thought. The last time I saw Mariana. Really saw her.

'Thank you, miss. That's extremely helpful.'

On that day, it was discovered by reference to police records, a baby had been purloined from its pram outside a small greengrocer's shop in Crowbridge Lane, but had subsequently turned up seven hours later on the steps of the Town Hall, wet, hungry and unharmed in a cardboard carton. What sort of carton? The sort that had once contained a dozen bottles of Australian Red Wine.

I wondered if the Venners bought Australian wine by the case; then pricked up my ears, for Witherspoon was saying to Sir Gideon:

'Due to the very particular nature of the Colonel's accusations, Sir Gideon, we had also thought of excavating the garden at Aviemore. In fact I discussed it with your son Mr Daniel Morningquest. But he tells me that when he bought the house, the garden had been so badly infested by moles that the first thing he did when he moved in was to have the entire plot excavated by a landscape gardening firm, who dug down to a depth of six feet and then laid wire mesh over the surface. And they, presumably, found nothing, or we would certainly have been informed. Naturally I have been in touch with the firm, Pedigree Plots.'

Oh, canny Dan, I thought.

'Well,' said Barney, who had stayed down at Boxall Hill for a few days to be a support to his father, 'it does look as if Lady Venner might have been the baby-snatcher. She certainly was a bit peculiar, latterly. I remember her bursting out at my mother once, when they met in the drive, saying that large families were disgustingly vulgar – just rambling nonsense, but spiteful. I suppose when the Colonel found she'd pinched a baby, he'd try to put it back, unobtrusively. I wonder if anything of the kind occurred after they moved to Torquay?'

At this, Witherspoon looked very thoughtful.

'I'll check with our colleagues there. But, in the meantime, Sir Gideon, what do you want us to do about the Colonel? After all, it was you he shot at. And your glass slab was broken. Do you wish to press charges?'

At this, Sir Gideon went into his saintly routine.

'Oh, no, no, my dear fellow. After all, he wasn't firing at me. It was at the memorial, don't you see? I'm sure there was nothing personal about it. It was like shooting at a target, really. I don't bear any animosity against the poor fellow.'

'Oh, come on, Gid,' said Barney. 'He was discharging a weapon in somebody else's grounds, yours, and certainly causing a breach of the peace.'

'And resisting arrest,' said Witherspoon.

But Sir Gideon was definite. 'The man has suffered enough already. And – I think you said? – he is in a confused mental state, needing to be kept under restraint?'

'Yes, sir, he's heavily sedated and we've shipped him off to Chidgrove.'

Chidgrove was the local psychiatric hospital.

'Well, let him stay there till he's better. I certainly don't wish to lay any charges against him. That would be most unneighbourly.'

'He's not your neighbour now!' snapped Barney.

Witherspoon seemed half-relieved, half-frustrated. 'Very well, Sir Gideon. If that's your feeling. We've plenty worse crimes to catch up on. I'll keep you informed as to any further developments.'

'Good-good,' said Sir Gideon absently, and, to me: 'Sidonie, can you be so kind as to fetch the score of *Das Lied von der Erde*? I think you may find it in the music-room.'

I nodded and went off, wondering which of the rooms in Otherland might be designated 'the music-room'. Really, they were all used for music.

In the hall Barney said to me, 'Pandora, could you possibly look after Mog for a month or so? I want to go to Denmark and see some people there. And Mog knows you, he likes you—'

'No, I'm sorry; I can't,' I said shortly. 'I'm going away myself.'

XVI

I had entered my picture *The Chess Game* for a Scottish Arts portrait contest. For several reasons I was anxious to maintain contacts in Scotland. And, having been a student at a Scottish academy for two years, I was entitled to enter the competition.

One of my reasons for wishing to return was my attachment to Mrs D. For me, she was a link with Tom. I still kept up a correspondence with her. She sadly missed her Oe, who had returned to Los Angeles with Dolly. 'Yon Los Angeles sounds a fell unchancy place,' she wrote gloomily. In another of her letters she had given me news of particular interest. 'I saw on the TV a body that looked wondrous like yon bearded picture ye once showed me in your wee drawing book. It was at the opening of a braw new hospice for dying folk; he was one of the gentry on the platform, but he didna speak. But he was as like to your picture as one pea to anither.'

Oddly enough, Grisch had seen the same programme, and said the same thing.

'I saw this face that seemed very familiar; and I remembered it was the man I had seen talking to you at your mother's funeral. The one you drew from memory later. I would say that it was definitely the same man.'

Grisch had a remarkable memory for faces, I knew; it was most unlikely that he would make a mistake. Nor, I thought, would Mrs D.

So I took *The Chess Game* to Edinburgh, travelling by train with a hopeful heart. (Unlike members of the Morningquest clan, who took to driving like breathing, I had never felt the need for a car, though I could drive if I had to.)

I stayed with the Bagrations, who were kind and welcoming, as always, and, having escorted my picture to its place on the crowded wall, went on by bus to spend a night with Mrs D in St Vigeans.

I found her in dreadfully low spirits.

'Wae's me, yon Dolly and my Oe have it advised betwixt 'em that they dinna suit after a'. Mind, I could have told them that frae the start.'

'Oh dear,' I said. 'Oh dear, what a pity.'

No news of this development had yet reached Otherland.

'Whose fault was it?' I wrote on Mrs D's pad.

'Ach, who's tae tell? But, mind ye, I'm sartain sure 'tis nae fault of my Oe, for a sweeter-tempered laddie ne'er walked the street. 'Tis that wanchancy Dolly. She's up and left Tom for some evil-doer they call a Film Director.'

At that, a great relief filled me. Oh well, I thought, Dolly always did have an eye to the main chance. And if she was continually pushing Tom into jobs that really were not his thing, he would be much better off on his own.

'Maybe he will marry some nice American lady,' I wrote down, as a sop to the malign gods.

But Mrs D shook her head even more distressfully. 'Nae chance of that! Nae chance at a'! For he lit stricht ontae a plane tae tak' him back tae Prague. He's been ettling tae do that this lang while; for his mither's no juist varra well.'

'Oh, I'm really sorry.'

'And yon Dolly, she niver wanted tae veesit Prague; I wadna wonder,' said Mrs D with one of her fearsome flashes, 'but what she was afeered that Tom's mither – my dochter Elspie – and her man wadna be grand eneugh for her genteel ways. She was aye a dink body.'

'In that case he's well rid of her.'

'Ay, mphm. Guid kens but that's so. But what frichtens me tae death is the thocht that Tom will go and get himself mixit up in the politics o'er yonder in Prague, for, syne, he's gey hot-heided. Ye remember how he used tae girn at the Dean and the Moderator.'

'Aye, I mean yes, I do.'

She gazed at me anxiously. I wrote: 'Will he stay in Prague for long, do you think? Or will he come back here?'

'It may be no sae easy tae come back; he may find that he's fixit.'

'Have you his address?'

'I send tae him at Elspie's.'

I took down Elspie's address though not certain what use I would make of it. Too many letters from the Capitalist West might be a liability for Tom, and get him into trouble with the authorities. And anyway, perhaps he might not want a letter from me.

Yet, like the heroine of *Persuasion*, when she hears that Captain Wentworth is a free man, I was filled with joy, senseless joy!

Mrs D told me about her new tenants, two canny wee lassies who were nae trouble at a', kept themselves tae themselves, but had a fearsome habit of blocking the gardy with a hantle of fozy napery stuff from the chemist's. Enchanted by her medieval usage, I promised to see to the gardy after supper, and after I had done so we spent the evening comfortably together watching television – *Evening with Morning*, Dan's chat show was on, so we were able to listen to Crusilla Fingers singing Dan's new song *Seeing-*

Eye Sunset. Oddly, Dan never sang his own songs, though he had quite a good voice. After Crusilla, Dan interviewed a famous (or notorious) art-forger, Willy Brownrigg, who exhibited his skill at turning out fake Van Goghs, but left me unconvinced.

Mrs D was greatly interested to see Dolly's brother. 'Aye, there's a likeness,' she said. 'Aront the eyes ye can see it. And yon Crusilla, Pandora, is the spit image of yourself.'

'Good Heavens, so she is! But it's partly the make-up and hairstyle.'

I wondered who was responsible for it. Was this Dan's taste in ladies? Or was it mere accident?

'But whit a skellum the man is!' said Mrs D. 'Can he no' find a more buirdly way tae make his siller?'

'But he makes such a *lot* of siller this way. The family say that already he is a millionaire.'

'Guidsakes, lass, 'tis an unjuist waurld!'

Next day I returned to Edinburgh and learned, to my total surprise, that the panel of adjudicators had chosen my *Chess Game* as the winner of that year's contest. How amused the twins would be. I must write to Yokohama and tell them.

There was a certain amount of froo-fra, a presentation ceremony, and a lunch at the Royal Caledonian Hotel. This rather cut into my plans for visiting the St Bernard's Well Hospice and one or two other places that I had marked down as possible sites for inquiry. I had also meant to go and look at one of my favourite pictures, Raeburn's portrait of an old gentleman solemnly gliding along the ice with folded arms. He reminded me of a day long ago on St Vigeans Moss.

As things turned out, missing the hospice didn't matter. After lunch, I was brought back to Ravelstone Hall, where the exhibition was hung, to have my photograph taken in front of the picture.

And there, standing earnestly contemplating it, was my bearded man. He had aged, quite a bit, I noticed instantly. His hair was greyer, and scantier; his beard was almost white. But it was the same man, narrow-faced, greenish-eyed, without a shadow of a doubt.

He began to move hastily out of the way when he saw the photographers advancing with their impedimenta. But I ran up to him and grabbed his arm.

'Oh, *please* don't go!' I begged him. 'I want – I want *so much* to talk to you. Please, please stay!'

He looked startled to death. For a moment, it was plain he had not recognised me. Then I remembered how changed I was in appearance since we had last met, at Mother's funeral. Even when I said, 'I'm Pandora Crumbe; Hélène's daughter; don't you remember?' he still seemed nervous and doubtful. 'Well – at least give me your name and address; so that I can get in touch with you.'

But at that he relented and said he would wait.

'This won't take more than a few minutes,' I said.

And, when the photographers had finished and gone their ways, I firmly took his arm and dragged him outside. 'Let's go and have a cup of tea. I do want – I really do want to hear about how you were married to Mother.'

He gave me a harassed glance. 'It's no story for a tea-shop.'

In the end we went into Prince's Street Gardens and sat on a bench there, facing a flowerbed.

He kept eyeing me in a nervous, troubled manner.

'What's your name, please?' I asked, feeling that at any moment he might break away and flee from me like a hunted stag.

'Murdoch. Ewart Murdoch.' Reluctantly he gave me a card, with the St Bernard's Well Hospice address.

How strange, I thought. The name Murdoch had no resonance for me at all; and yet it might have been mine. I could have been Pandora Murdoch instead of Pandora Crumbe. This fidgety, unhappy man could have been my father.

Suddenly my own father, with his brusque, no-nonsense dismissal of most things that interested me, appeared in my mind as a rather solid figure, reliable at least, if not particularly kind.

'How did you meet Mother, Mr Murdoch? When was it?'

'Och, it would have been 1949, or 1950; I was a theological student and she was studying languages at the university. She was living in a hostel; she had been with her cousin, who was a surgeon, but he had recently died, quite suddenly, of pneumonia. And – and she and I took a fancy to one another.'

Now he came to a total stop. He had been speaking awkwardly, with long pauses.

'We got married,' he said flatly.

He had gone very pale. The skin of his face was a greyish white under the whitish grizzle of his beard. He wore a dark suit over a Fair Isle sweater. Were these his professional clothes? Or had he taken a day off? Perhaps he was some kind of administrator at the hospice?

'You were a theological student,' I cautiously prodded him. 'Did you become a minister, then?'

'Aye. I did. Just before we married.' Again he came to a stop.

'So – you got married. Where did you live then?'

'I was to have a wee house, that went with the minister's position. In Cramond. But first we were to go on our honeymoon. To Nairn.'

The place names seemed like posts in a rail, on to which he was desperately clinging.

'How *long* were you married?' I asked.

'Just the one day.'

A silence lay between us while I took this in.

'*Why*? What *happened*?'

He gazed at me in silence, twisting his hands together. I began to wonder if he had ever told this story before, to anybody. The day had deteriorated. It was bleakly cold and grey. I shivered, being dressed for England, not Scotland. I wished I had brought a jacket, or at least a thicker sweater. We were sitting side by side on a hard, narrow bench-seat, facing a bed of lupins in hideous glaring plastic hues, pink, red and yellow. The glum sky made them seem even brighter.

At last he went on. 'She and I were to stay for our honeymoon at this little hotel, ye ken. Neither one of us had any family. There were just the two of us. My mother and father were dead already, some years. Her cousin had recently passed away.'

'So – I suppose – you sort of clung together?'

'Aye,' he said doubtfully. 'You could say that, I fancy. We did.'

'And then?'

'And then – and then – we took our dinner and went upstairs to bed – to our room. And Hélène, sitting on the bed, began to cry and say there was a thing she must tell me – must tell me before – we did anything. She had been gey silent and pale, all through dinner.'

His face had begun to work; the bones under the greyish-white beard trembled up and down, out of control. I felt a monster at continuing to press for information, but just the same I was determined to wrench the story out of him.

'Yes?'

'This cousin of hers, the surgeon Mark Taylor, who seemed to everybody such a good, kind, douce, respectable figure, looked up to and admired by all his colleagues – he was the one who had made the arrangement for Hélène to come to England from the school in Switzerland. He himself was Austrian—'

'Yes?'

'Ever since – she told me – ever since she had arrived – at the age of *twelve*, mark you – he had been abusing her. Shamefully. She told me things – terrible things, that made me sick – sick! I wouldna repeat them.

I couldna bear to. And she only a young lassie with no one to turn to! Her parents were in Europe, long gone. She never even knew where they might be buried. And this went on for years. *Years.*'

'Why didn't she – why, in the world? No. I can see why.'

I thought of her, doggedly hanging on. Bent on acquiring her education, at whatever cost. She would be terrified to tell teachers, or other figures of authority, in case she was not believed, in case she lost what little security she had. Mark Taylor was a known, highly respected figure. Whose story would they believe? And this was twenty years ago – more. Even these days, such things were the subject of horrified whispers, they were not openly discussed. What could it have been like then?

'How awful. How awful. Poor, poor Hélène.'

Tears were cascading down Ewart Murdoch's cheeks now. He was in anguish.

Trying to find some help for him, something to bring him back into circulation, I suggested: 'Were you able at all – did you manage to comfort her?'

He sobbed aloud. 'No. No! That's the waurst of all. No, I didna comfort her! I was that horrified and disgusted! I pulled away from her as if she was unclean. Well – to my mind – she *was* unclean! I told her that our marriage was a lie, a rank lie, that I would never have spoken for her if she had told me all this before. I was in a black despair. And rage. I flung on my clothes again and left the room, left the hotel, and walked about the streets all night. Oh, I am so ashamed of myself now! I – a minister of the Lord – to break down so disgracefully! I didna see at all then that my task was to comfort her, if I could, or, anyway, to talk over her trouble. To tell her that it was not her fault. I failed – I failed! Oh, I am a weak, feckless, faint-hearted, useless man.'

Furiously impatient with him, I felt he might have dwelt less, now, on his own deficiencies, and more on the state of mind of wretched Hélène; what can she have felt, left cold like that on her wedding night after she had truthfully told him her story?

Though, to be sure, her timing was not very tactful, or tactical. She chose an unsuitable moment to blurt out all that horror, about which she had managed to keep silent for so long. But she was only a girl – what – nineteen? Twenty? An orphan, a foreigner.

Suddenly Mariana's voice came back to me: 'Your mother once told me that, in the past, some disaster had befallen her because of an indiscreet revelation that she had made.' And then Mariana had gone on to say something about Hélène's relationship with my father – how severely that had been hampered by her habit of reticence.

Oh yes, I thought. *Oh yes*. Of course it would be. Once having discovered just what calamity arose from spilling the beans, she would take the greatest care never again to commit such an indiscretion. She would not make the same mistake twice. She would button herself up inside impregnable reticence.

'What happened next?'

'In the morn I went back to the hotel, thinking to pack my traps and leave without seeing her – if I could. But she herself had already gone. Packed up her own clothes and left. I never saw her again.'

'*You never saw her?*'

He shook his head, gulping, blinking. 'At the time, I was that relieved! I tell you – I looked on her as something filthy – shameful; the kind of thing you would sweep out and shovel, quick, into the dustbin. I didna see how I could even look her in the eye! So to find her gone was like a great breath of sweet, fresh air.'

I sat silent, rather wishing that he would just disappear. I did not want to talk to him any more.

But, in the end, he went on of his own accord. 'Syne I had a letter from some lawyers telling me that their client – Miss Taylor – she had taken her cousin's name when she came to England – and I suppose he had changed his from some European form— '

I nodded. I knew that.

' —Miss Taylor wished for the marriage to be dissolved, as sexual union had not taken place between us. I agreed to that, of course, through my own lawyers, and so the marriage was annulled. There was no problem about it. And I never saw her again. But a year or so later, in a Scottish local paper, I chanced to see the report of her marriage to a Mr Crumbe. And that he was a veterinary surgeon and they were moving to a town in England. And later – times – I used to travel to that town. Not to see her. No. I never did see her. But I would look up the name Crumbe in the local directory – just to see if she was still there. Once or twice I phoned the number. Just to hear her voice say 'Hallo'. Then I would put down the receiver. And I took to receiving the local paper by mail. That way I could keep in touch a little. Often there might be some mention of her – her name in some list of ladies at a meeting.'

'You felt guilty,' I said flatly.

'Aye. I reckon that was it.'

'You wanted to reassure yourself that you had done her no lasting harm. Because you knew – you must have known – that you had committed just as much of an outrage against her as the other man.'

His sad, bloodshot greenish eyes met mine.

'Aye,' he said again. 'I'd guess that is about how it might have been. But – thank the Lord – it seems I had not harmed her. She was a well-respected public person in your town. When she died she had a grand funeral – many friends. A good marriage to your father.'

Bypassing all that, I said, 'And what about you? Did you ever marry again?'

'Och, *no*! *Never*! I didna just feel that I'd be able to trust myself again in such a relationship.'

And also, I thought, you certainly never trusted any woman again. It would have been liked walking on a bog; you'd always be expecting the ground to give way under your foot. You would always be waiting for some frightful revelation.

'You left the Church?'

His clothes were certainly not those of a minister.

'Aye. I did. To me, my own character seemed too faulty – not strong enough for Holy Orders. So I trained as a nurse.'

A faint respect began to stir in me at that. At least the poor creep had done his best . . .

'And then I got into hospital administration.'

'And now you are at the hospice.'

'Aye. It's a good work. Fulfilling, ye might say.'

'Well,' I said, after a pause. 'Thank you. I'm very glad that I managed to catch up with you at last. You have – you have cleared up some dark corners for me.'

'Your mother never told you anything about this?'

'No. Heavens, no! Nor did she tell my father. I'm quite certain of that.'

'He is still living?'

'Yes, but retired now. In the South of France.'

Mr Murdoch suddenly became relieved, social, chatty.

'Ah, it's a bonny part – the South of France. Just grand for a retired person. Just grand. And is he happy, your father?'

'Oh, quite. As a matter of fact, he's married again.'

I grinned, thinking of blonde, permed, gin-and-tonic drinking, bridge-and-golf playing Reenie, my father's new wife, and how totally removed she seemed from all this grief and tragedy and sorrow. This *tsurris*.

'And now you have sorted yourself a fine career as a painter!' said Mr Murdoch, in a cheerful, encouraging voice. 'I was that interested, when I saw your name in the lunchtime paper! I said to myself, I'll just run round to the gallery and take a look. And it's a fine, well-painted, thoughtful picture. The chess, now! Ye put a lot of work into it, I can see that. I hope the gallery buys it.'

'Thank you, they have already made an offer.'

'That's grand! Grand indeed! Then I'll be able to step round, from time to time, and take another look at it.'

In my mind's ear I could hear Mr Murdoch at work, with his customers. 'Now why don't ye stay alive until Christmas, Mrs Hastie, and then we'll have a fine time, singing carols together!'

'Well; I'm very glad I met you again, Mr Murdoch,' I said, standing up, shivering in the bitter wind.

XVII

Toby flung himself into writing his book. *The Human Line*. It was presently published, with civility but no unusually sanguine expectations, by Camford University Press. And, indeed, for six months, it did no more than respectably. It was, in publishing terms, 'a sleeper'. Which is to say that after eighteen months or so, Camford suddenly woke up to the fact that it was their best-selling title and had been translated into seventy languages, including Bedouin and Eskimo.

Toby was enchanted with the Eskimo version; he used to read it aloud to me while I was working on his portrait, enunciating with special relish such words as *'inogutikarkovluggit'* – or, at least, that's what it sounded like.

'Lulie will enjoy this,' I said, painting away.

'She already does. I sent her a copy. And one to the twins in Japan.'

My picture of Toby had him untidy, in shirt-sleeves, walking with his finger betwen the pages of a book, a ruler, set-square and measuring calipers sticking out of his shirt pocket. Later on, I put in the ilex grove and tree-house, dark and gleaming respectively, in the background. It was a hasty, splashy, impressionistic painting, very different from *Selene in Yellow Dress*, which hung on the wall in his flat. The flat was not his really; it was a borrowed one near Regent's Park; it belonged to the mother of his editor at Camford Press. She was abroad for a year. He said of it, 'It will do very well, just while I finish this next book.'

He was at work on the sequel, *Peering Ahead*.

'Why don't you ever settle, Toby?'

'I want to travel, when this is finished.'

'Where?'

'I'm not sure. Bad places. Unhappy places. Places where people are at odds.' He looked up at the picture of Selene. 'To find out why.'

There was a strong likeness between his face and Selene's.

'In many ways, they were closer than the twins,' Lulie said once. 'The twins had no need to cling; they belonged together from the beginning. But Toby and Selene took a while to find one another. So – then they clung.'

Toby's first book took him four years to write, my picture of him took a week to paint. It was commissioned by the publishers for the jacket of an updated edition of *The Human Line*, the sales of which were, by now, unnumbered as the sands of the sea. The new edition was scheduled to come out around the time the Nobel announcements were made.

But then, Toby had to go and jump in the Thames, late one night, to rescue a stupid suicidal teenager who had thrown herself over the parapet of Hungerford bridge. And he was drowned. A police launch, going to the rescue of the wretched girl (also drowned) accidentally bashed his head, and by the time they hauled him out of the water he was dead.

What was Toby doing on Hungerford bridge at one in the morning? Well, he often took long walks by the river at night. He had found it hard to sleep, ever since Selene's death, he said.

I still miss his ten o'clock calls acutely. Shall miss them all my life. If the phone rings at that time in the evening, it gives me a severe pang. Mostly, I don't answer. Whoever it is can only be a disappointment.

Why, why did Toby have to go out of his way to try to rescue that silly girl? He would have written more books, he could have contributed who knows what towards the eventual salvation (if it is to be saved) of the human race.

Mariana would have been so angry if she had known about his death.

I often think that children express their parents' unfulfilled ambitions. Which, I suppose, is how we all progress; and we *do* progress, though slowly it must be admitted. But they can at least fix cataracts and appendicitis now. Mariana would have been very happy at the way Toby was shaping. She had been given a singing voice, and she put it to use, but one felt with her that she had many frustrated intentions. The voice got in her way to a considerable extent. She would have liked to do other things as well.

And, as for my mother! When I paint, I am pouring her voice on to the canvas. But anyway . . .

Poor old Gideon was really puzzled at this third loss in his family. 'Where is Toby?' he kept saying, for months and months; no explanation seemed to reach him.

Sometimes I think that life, when you get to my time of it, is like trying to use up the bits of pastry left over from cutting round the edge of a pie. What can you do with them? Start another pie?

Dolly came back to England after Toby's death.

I chanced to be at Boxall Hill just then. Lulie and Grisch were terribly stricken by the loss of Toby, and I liked to put in as much time with them as I could.

Grisch was becoming decidedly absent-minded. Only that morning I had accompanied him as he'd carried a small pot of deliquescent chicken fat out to give to the birds. (There was a constant running battle between him and Lulie about chicken fat; he declaring that it was solid cholesterol, two teaspoons of the stuff could kill you; while Lulie riposted that all her forbears had lived on nothing else and all had survived into their late nineties.) Anyway, Grisch had won this particular round, and carried the potful off in triumph. Following him with a plateful of toast crusts, I observed his attention deflected, as it often was these days, by a pale purple crocus bud appearing from a nest of dead leaves.

He said to me dreamily, 'I have been thinking about *Ozymandias*. The problem is Pandora, that word "stamped". A first-rate poem, *Ozymandias*, no denying that. But should "stamped" be taken as a straightforward verb, akin to "read"? "Its sculptor well those passions read, which yet survive, stamped on these lifeless things ..." The subject of "stamped" being the sculptor? Or, alternatively, should "stamped on these lifeless things" be seen as a clause, qualifying "passions"?'

'You got me there, Uncle Grisch,' I said, watching in paralysed fascination as he, gazing in my direction now, lifted up the pot of fat to tilt it into a coconut-shell that hung on a wire loop from an apple tree; but he missed his aim and the entire cupful of thick, liquid grease disappeared slowly down his shirt-sleeve. I was reminded of the twins pouring that green goo on to my hair.

'I'm really gravelled,' I said. 'I'll have to read the poem again before I come to a decision.'

'It is, on the whole, an excellent poem, *Ozymandias*, but for that nagging doubt – ach!' he admonished himself mildly. 'Now just look what I have done. What a very careless, silly old fellow I have become.'

'You'd better go and get straight into a bath, Uncle Grisch.'

'I believe you are right, my dear Pandora. Ach, I do not know what Lulie will say to me.'

I had a fair idea. '*Oy, veh*, what a *schmegegge!*' But she was infinitely patient about tidying him up and rectifying such mishaps.

'I'll pull out the bean sticks for you, Uncle Grisch,' I called after him, 'and make a start on the digging.'

He waved an acknowledging hand as he stomped off towards the house.

When I came back from Scotland, in a state of shock after my conversation with Ewart Murdoch, Lulie and Grisch were wonderful. We talked and talked about this disclosure.

'But that explains so *many* matters,' said Lulie. 'Why your mother lived such a buttoned-up life. She had been sent out of Europe, as it was thought, to safety, by her parents, and then her parents were lost to her and this terrible thing was done to her by her own cousin, the man who was supposed to protect her. She felt that she had nothing, and no one to whom she could turn, whom she could trust; only herself upon whom she could rely.'

'Not even herself. Because she had blurted it all out to Murdoch, and that turned out to be a frightful mistake.'

'Ach, what a hopeless man he must be!' said Grisch in disgust.

'No, just a Scot, Uncle Grisch. Scots are like that.'

'And plenty of English are, too.'

'And,' pursued Lulie, 'it explains you, too, *bubeleh*, why you find it so hard to relate to people; why you don't go halfway to meet them. Except to mend their plumbing.'

'Won't I?'

'No, you are as prickly as an armadillo!'

I thought of Tom. As so often.

'Communication is so difficult. It's rare to find people who use the same grammar. You two do. It's sad: I was remembering how I walked up through the wood with Mother – that day, the day she died – and she was saying to me – now I see why – "I do so want you to find people that you can talk to, who speak the same language."'

'She was thinking of this family. To whom she bequeathed you.'

'Yes, but they don't all speak the same language.'

'Toby did.'

'Yes, Toby did. And the twins. But they are in Yokohama.'

Pulling out the beanpoles at Otherland was a monumental job. Back in the days when the entire family of children had come down to Boxall Hill almost every weekend and all through the summer, beans, bean soup, or bean salad had formed a main staple of their spartan diet. Every autumn Lulie dried, bottled, canned or froze mountains of beans, red, white or green, and the habit still obtained, though most of the bean harvest was now given away or sold for charity. But there were still rows and rows of stakes and vines to be pulled out; first the dried tendrils must be disentangled from the poles, and the lengths of garden bast cut through that attached the poles to each other. I worked along them line by line, stacking the poles against Grisch's tool shed, raking the withered stalks into a pile, and then setting a match to them. (It is, of course, better to dig them into the ground, but I scamped that job in view of the magnitude of the whole task.)

For two hours nobody came near me except an interested robin. And in the distance I could hear a chaffinch bustling through his chatty, self-important routine of song, over and over. Do young chaffinches learn from listening to their parents? Or does the repeated phrase grow in them as naturally as their plumage?

Toby would have known the answer.

I sang a bit to myself, a thing I take care never to do when within earshot of any member of the Morningquest clan who are all, whether they care about it or not, such natural musicians. And, though I can sing in tune, it's not a voice to be proud of. I still squirm when I remember piping out 'Oh, wa ta na,' at Sir Gideon's bidding, under the eyes of the whole table. Their polite disengagement. Dolly with her red plaits and school pinafore. The dental plates of the twins. The boys looking anywhere but at me. Mariana, like the prow of a Viking ship.

A great haystack of blue-black thundercloud was piling up in the northern sky. At any minute there was going to be a torrential downpour. I was working like a Stakhanovite, hurrying to get to the end of my row, dragging out the stakes and peeling off the dry stems, tossing them on to the fitful, smoky fire, and, each time I did so, receiving a puff of white ash in my face. Undoing beanpoles is a messy occupation. I had bits of stalk in my hair and inside my shirt collar, my shoes were covered with dust, my hands were grimy and sooty. I hoped that Grisch hadn't used up all the bath water.

'Drinking treacle, drinking rum,' I sang loudly. 'Singing to de Lawd till kingdom come.'

All of a sudden, there was Dolly. Back from foreign parts.

'Hallo, Dolly!' I was startled to death. *'Es kommt a rint a bald a plugh.'*

As Tante Lulie would say. It's going to pour any minute now.

Dolly was glossy. No other word could express it. Her tailored trouser suit, lavender in hue, was the sort of thing that could have been purchased nowhere but on the west coast of the USA. She wore a lot of glittery costume jewellery and dazzling shiny black patent-leather shoes to match her whopping handbag, large enough to contain a small pig. Her hair, brighter than of yore, upswept, bouffant, added about a foot to her height. Her face was the same as ever, round, complacent, blue-eyed, but now carefully made up and no longer freckled.

'How very nice to see you, Dolly!'

And, indeed, I did feel quite affectionate. For, after all, she had been in love with me once, by her own avowal; she had pined for me, we had spent a good deal of time together. I had washed up innumerable piles of her toppling dirty dishes while she talked and talked; she was a part of my life, take it or leave it. And – very likely – she had not been at all aware of what a stroke she'd dealt me when she made off with Tom Yindrich.

'Oh, do look at the rainbow, Dolly! What a fantastic welcome home!'

A great shaft of westerly sunlight went piercing across the dusky landscape under the black dome of cloud. And suddenly a monumental rainbow sprang to meet it, with one foot firmly planted at the bottom of the Boxall Hill meadow.

But Dolly, true to form, seemed dissatisfied with things about her.

'For Heaven's sake, Pandora, you look like something out of *The Good Earth*. Do come indoors and get yourself cleaned up.'

'I'll just put these tools away.'

'Why they can't get someone to *do* all this— ' she said, as I hurled the tools into the shed and followed her. 'Why they persist in doing it all . . . '

'Well, *I'm* doing it for them now,' I pointed out.

'I mean a man, a professional.'

When we were halfway to the house, the downpour commenced.

'We'd better shelter in here – it can't last long,' I said, and whisked us both into the little pillared pavilion which concealed, below its floor, the outer entrance to our underground tunnel. And I added, 'It doesn't matter if I get wet, but you don't want that nice suit spoiled.'

The rain on the circular roof above us was making a sound like cannonballs.

'I hadn't realised how close this building is to Aviemore,' Dolly said, glancing across the top of the maze to Aviemore's mock-Tudor gables, visible just now because the Lombardy poplars in their double screening row were still leafless. 'Does Dan come down there much?'

'No, very seldom. But fat Topsy is thoroughly settled in with her quilts. And she's collecting pewter jelly-moulds now. She and Lulie have established quite a cordial relationship. They exchange stitches.'

Dolly looked disapproving. 'I cannot think why Dan married that fool.'

'To lend verisimilitude to an otherwise unconvincing narrative?'

She looked at me blankly.

'For her money? She has lots. Anyway it seems to work well enough. She doesn't seem to mind financing Dan's more dubious enterprises.'

'Really this whole place ought to be sold up,' Dolly said impatiently. 'It's ridiculous to keep it on. Who comes down here now? Does Barney?'

'Not often,' I was bound to acknowledge.

'The twins are in Japan. Gideon's practically ga-ga, and hardly cares *where* he is, I should think.'

'No, no, Dolly, that's not so. He cares.'

She shot me an angry look. Who was I, it conveyed, to pronounce judgement on Gideon's feelings?

'And what about Lulie and Grisch? And Garnet? What solution do you propose for them? Sheltered accommodation in Floxby? Or would you remove them to Cadogan Square?'

'This land must be worth hundreds of thousands; if not millions,' pursued Dolly. 'And think of what it must be *costing*, in taxes and maintenance.'

I said mildly that I believed the activities of Lulie and Grisch, still based on Mariana's original master-plan, kept the estate solvent, maybe even marginally profitable. 'There are pigs, you know, on the land over the hill, and the greenhouses are let to a man who does tomatoes and mushrooms. And the twins plan to come back from Japan in two or three years; maybe they might choose to settle here. They need somewhere to write their books.'

'Books?'

'Ally is working on a history of privacy, Elly is compiling an anthology of farts.'

'*Farts—* '

Dolly appeared even more discontented, prodding at the trapdoor under our feet with her glittering pointed toe.

To cheer up her declining spirits, I asked, 'But tell about you, Dolly? What are you doing now? Do you plan to stay in England?'

'Oh— ' she said. 'Well, that depends on Mars.'

'Mars?'

'My husband. Marston Barclay Wuppertal the Third,' she explained kindly, in her old, cream-laden voice.

'And what does Mars do?'

'He's an architect. He has done a lot of corporate work on the West Coast. Now he's over here, putting out feelers in Europe.'

'How extremely interesting. And you, Dolly, did you, do you have a job?'

'I worked for a diploma over there – on the West Coast,' she said vaguely. 'In the educational building-up of social and cultural integrationary skills. And then I worked for a while in Santa Monica effecting liaison between the various groups formed to mesh between the bodies coordinating ongoing social and psychiatrically oriented imponderables.'

'I'm sure you did it very well, Dolly.'

'And – supposing Mars finds himself an opening over here – I shall try to arrange something of the kind in this country. I daresay Barney might help.'

I greatly doubted, not Barney's ability to assist, but the likelihood of his doing so. Devoted helpfulness to contemporaries was not his long suit; though he had a reputation as an inspiring teacher.

'Is Mars down here with you?'

'No, he's seeing some people in Lóndon.'

Did Mr Wuppertal's profession, I wondered, have anything to do with Dolly's wish to see Boxall Hill sold and the land, presumably, transformed into a large estate of homes for the well heeled?

I remarked civilly that I was disappointed not to meet M. B. Wuppertal the Third, but hoped to do so soon. I could not resist adding: 'Do you hear from Tom at all? Is there any news of what he's doing in Prague?'

My latest letter from Mrs D, some months since, had expressed anxiety because there had fallen such a long gap since his last to her. And my own letter to Tom, six months before that – a card with birthday wishes, since we shared the same birthday – had also gone unanswered.

Not that I had expected any answer.

Dolly's look of annoyance deepened. 'Oh, he's in trouble,' she said. 'I knew he would be. No, I haven't heard from him – we don't correspond – but a colleague of Mars went to Prague about a possible contract for building a hotel on the Moldau, so we – I – asked him to make discreet inquiries. And he did a bit of quiet beavering and found that Tom's in prison.'

'Prison!' I said, aghast.

'Well – the *fool* – he made some satirical film about toads – *toads*! I ask you! – just before that time, two years ago, when the Russians arrived. So, can you wonder? I just knew he'd do something idiotic if he went back. I always argued against it. And that was why I wouldn't go with him,' said Dolly. 'And look how right I was.'

I made no direct answer to that. None suitable occurred to me. Instead I said, 'It's a pity Tom never met the twins. I've an idea that they would all have got on very well.'

Dolly let out a noise like a snuffle. Then she said, 'But, Pandora, what I really wanted to talk to you about was Toby's pictures.'

'Toby's pictures?'

'You saw a lot of Toby latterly,' she said in a voice that could only be described as accusing.

'No, not really, Dolly. I didn't see him. We used to talk on the phone. Well, in that way, yes, I suppose you could say I knew him.'

'You *painted* him. That picture shortly before he died.'

'Yes; I did.'

'Well, where is it? That picture? And the picture of Selene that he had? That you did? The one in the yellow dress?'

Suddenly I was reminded of the scene over Mariana's desk. Which was, come to think, the last time I had seen Dolly. Here she was again, nose down on the trail of misappropriated belongings.

'The painting of Toby,' I said, 'was commissioned by Camford Press for a book jacket. So the original is still with them. I expect Jim Lazenby has it. He's the director of the London office. And as for the portrait of Selene, she left it to Toby: I think he proposed to give it to Mrs Lazenby – Jim's mother – who lent him the flat where he was living. He hadn't any money at the time.'

'Why in the world *not*?'

'Well, he was busy writing his book – which isn't a paying occupation – and he had given a whole lot away to a Help Ethiopia fund, or something. Toby was always giving money away – so he hadn't paid any rent. The picture was in lieu.'

'Stupid *fool*!' she said furiously. 'Do you know what he did? In his will? The bulk of his estate – which must be worth God knows *what* by now, because of the way those books keep selling – *all* of that goes to charity. The only personal bequests were *things*.'

'Yes,' I said. I did know this. Toby had left me his records, LPs and tapes. But, up to now, deep sadness had prevented me from playing them.

Dolly pursued: 'His personal possessions were left to his brothers and sisters. *Personal possessions*! Some grubby clothes, some pots and pans, a few books. The only thing that's worth a penny is those pictures. Why didn't you take them, Pandora? After all, you painted them.'

'They weren't my property.'

'Are you sure he gave the one of Selene to whosit's mother?'

'Why don't you ask Toby's lawyer about it?'

'Oh, you're no help! I might have known you wouldn't be!' Dolly exclaimed in a fury. She kicked again at the ground with her pointed shiny toe. 'Why is there a keyhole in the middle of this floor?'

Then she looked up at me, her face all pink and puckered with hurt and reproach. And yes, there were tears, even, in her eyes.

'Why haven't you ever painted *me*, Pandora? You've done all the rest of us – even Barney, he says – you did drawings of him— '

'That's all they were, drawings.'

'Well, anyway. Why haven't you ever offered to do *me*?'

Dolly always had power to melt one, sooner or later by her childishness.

I said: 'I'll paint you, if you want, Dolly. But not wearing that God-awful pink pants-suit.'

XVIII

I painted Dolly over a series of three weekends spent at Boxall Hill. I didn't want her to come to my studio in Shepherd's Bush; indeed I felt quite superstitious about that. It was not that I bore Dolly any grudge exactly, but she seemed like a natural disaster – a volcanic eruption, or a plague of locusts. You don't deliberately move house to the slopes of a volcano, and you don't invite a plague of locusts into your back garden.

She and Marston Barclay Wuppertal III – who must have done well from his West Coast architectural activities – had rented somebody's studio in Cheyne Walk for a few months, but he seemed to be continually off in Brussels or Strasbourg making European contacts so she was free to spend a good deal of time without him at Otherland.

I had said that I couldn't possibly paint her wearing any clothes out of the wardrobe that she had brought with her to England; all her costumes were so sharp and stylish and brand new that the result would simply have been a kind of full-page *Vogue* advertisement. It took her a while to digest and accept this ultimatum, but finally she allowed Lulie to talk her round, on condition that Lulie provided a garment for her to be painted in. This was a great concession from Lulie, who did not make clothes for just anybody who asked her; they had, she said, to be the right shape for her elevation. No one quite knew what she meant by this but she was very firm about it. Mariana, bony and frail, had been the perfect model; the twins, too, were now approaching her ideal. However, in the circumstances, she said she would bend a point. She would like, she said, to see my portrait of Dolly. I think she felt there might be some symbolic significance in the event.

'I'll dedicate the picture to you, Lulie,' I said.

'*Tut mir nicht ķain teuves*! Don't do me any favours!'

Lulie and I consulted privately about the costume. I had told her how successful and striking Dolly had appeared in black and white as the Queen of Scots. So what Lulie produced was an impressive full-flounced long dress of stiffened cheesecloth, off-white, with grey muslin panniers and grey muslin frills round the deep 'V' of the neck, white stockings, black slippers and a huge grey broad-brimmed felt hat with a creamy plume (slightly moth-eaten) which had lain in someone's attic for seventy years until acquired by Lulie for twenty pence at a flea market.

'I shall look like a little girl dressed up for a party!' said Dolly discontentedly. But in fact the stately sweeping lines of the dress disguised Dolly's chunky, bulky outline and lent her an air of grand command. The portrait showed her in mid-stride, sporting a furled grey umbrella, approaching the little fountain in the yard. Its greens and greys, the luxurious mound of moss, the thin thread of water and the lion's heads, the grey cobbles underfoot and the almost white walls of the house in the background made – I considered – a very soothing and harmonious composition.

The two contrasting factors were the brilliant red of Dolly's hair, and her expression.

'You have painted me looking so dissatisfied!' she objected.

'But, Dolly,' said Lulie, her gentle words falling like drops of warm water on snow, 'that is the way that you almost always do look.'

'It's not like me,' grumbled Dolly. 'I just wish you could have painted me in my lilac suit. That's what I feel most myself in.'

I chuckled.

'What is it, Pandora?' Dolly asked suspiciously.

'I was just remembering that time you put your red petticoat in the machine with the rest of our things at St Vigeans launderette and dyed all my clothes pink; how annoyed I was.'

'Really?' She was surprised. 'You never said.'

'There wasn't much point, was there? It took weeks to bleach all my clothes. Some of the things stayed pink for ever.'

'Well,' she demanded, 'what's wrong with pink?'

'This, I think, is going to be a beautiful picture,' pronounced Grisch, passing by with a box of matches.

'Oh, Grischa!' wailed Lulie reproachfully. 'I send you out to buy matches, and what do you do? You come back with *one box*. Why not a packet? Two packets? We use matches such a great deal. For the garden bonfires, for the fires in the house, for the lamps.' When alone at Boxall Hill, Grisch and Lulie continued to use oil lamps and candles after about eight at night. They said they preferred the gentler light. 'What use to me is *one* box?'

Grisch looked defensive.

'I always think it is better not to get too large a size,' he argued. 'After all, we are growing old Lulie, you and I; we shall not be around for much longer. Who knows? No use to leave a lot of extra stores that other people, the children, probably will not want.'

'Everybody wants matches! And I am not such an *alte kocke*! Speak for yourself!'

'I am speaking for myself,' said Grisch. 'I just heard news about Colonel Venner. He is dead, they say, of a stroke in that hospital where they put him. He was younger than I.'

'Well I am not at all surprised he died,' said Lulie. 'Anybody, looking at him, could see that he drank far too much and probably lived also on a terrible diet. His nose was red and he had those broken veins. And then, think of his temper! I only wonder that he did not drop dead in one of his rages a long time ago. But I will say a *kaddish* for him. And I suppose I had better write a letter of sympathy to that poor girl, now left all alone, breeding dogs.'

'I don't suppose she misses him. Who could? And she had left home, after all, long ago.'

'Still, she may have better memories from before they moved here. You, Dolly, should write to her also.'

'I?' said Dolly. 'Why? It's ages since I last saw her. We haven't kept in touch at all. Why should I write to her?'

'Ach, at one time you had such a hero worship of her! You saw her at some town festival and implored me or your mother to invite her here. Well I remember it! And, later, I always thought it was you who persuaded her to encourage her father to buy Aviemore when he retired and they moved from York House.'

'I?' said Dolly again. 'Certainly not! Thelma Venner was a very boring girl. Her conversation was about nothing but dogs. I'd sooner take a walk with Ginge Buckley. Where is Ginge, by the way?'

'In Norwich. She's married.'

'Oh, that's all right then,' said Dolly, sounding like Sir Gideon.

I had been to see Ginge, after Mrs Buckley told me about her marriage. She seemed calm enough, happy enough, married to a pleasant round-faced man who ran a dry-cleaning establishment. And they had a six-month-old baby, whom Ginge addressed as 'Gubbins'.

'She's not the same as Kirk – well, never can be, can she? Just like Cyril won't never be the same as Alan. You can't ever feel *quite* the same as the first time, can you? You just have to put up with that.'

'Yes, you do,' I said.

'But Cyril's all right – he's very good to me, and he knows all about Alan and little Kirk, and it don't make no difference. He's had his troubles too – a girl what he loved got killed on someone else's motorbike. We've all got troubles, really. But I've put all that behind me. I had to; if you go on asking questions, wondering about what's past, you'd go mad. Wouldn't you? And I do love old Gubbins here, don't I, monster?'

Ginge grabbed the smiling Gubbins out of her carrycot and gave her an affectionate punch.

'I'll tell you a funny thing, though, Pandora. For three years after Kirk was took, I got sent money. Every now and then fifty pounds would come through the post, in notes. I never did find who sent it. Tell you the truth, I didn't like it; in fact I never spent it, just put it in an old cake tin. Because it felt like – well, I dunno. *Horrible*. But, in the end, when I married Cyril, I told him about it. And he said, best to spend it on Gubbins' layette. Otherwise it would just lay there and kind of fester in my mind. And I thought he was right. So that's what we done.'

'And by then the money had stopped coming?'

'Yes, about two or three years back.'

'There was no postmark on the envelope?'

'London. Just a plain brown typed envelope. Like bills come in.'

'Well, that's a mystery. But I'm glad you're all right, Ginge.'

'Yes, I'm all right. I'm not coming back to live in Floxby, though. I was too bloody miserable there. And some folk still look at me a bit old-fashioned – a bit nasty – when I come back to visit Mum and Dad. As if they thought I'd really make away with my own kid, I ask you!'

'People are unbelievable. Well, nice to see you, Ginge. Goodbye, Gubbins.'

'You ought to have one of your own,' said Ginge.

'You ought to make Dolly buy that picture,' said Tante Lulie.

'Oh, why, Lulie? I thought I'd just give it to her.'

'But, Pandora! She practically bullied you into painting it, you know that. Why give it to her? Why not keep it yourself? Exhibit it in your next show. For Dolly, the cachet of being painted by you is enough. That was what she wanted. She did not like to be left out, since you had painted the others.'

'I never painted Mariana. Or Barney. Except for drawings.'

'Everybody else you have done; even Dan.'

Bow Bells TV had approached me to do Dan after his song *Pass the Port, Polly* won a Golden Thing. I had not wanted to paint him, not at all, but compromised by doing a double of him and fat Topsy sitting side by side on an overstuffed sofa looking like a pair of Boteros. And I charged Bow Bells a massive sum, which paid the Shepherd's Bush rent for two years.

'And you have done Grisch and me so many times that I have lost count,' said Lulie placidly. 'So, naturally, Dolly felt left out. As she always does. I am afraid that is because Gideon did not look at her or speak to her till she was about ten.'

'Literally?'

'Literally. He never looked at her, never spoke to her.'

'But why not, for Heaven's sake?'

'He was just not certain that she was his child. And this was the first time he had had such doubts of Mariana. Though indeed I feel quite sure that they were unjustified then. It was at that time – when Mariana was pregnant with Dolly – that she had her great friendship with Argissa. No other man had yet entered her life.

'But, I am afraid that what Gideon did to Dolly at that age, depriving her of attention and affection, has left her with a permanent grudge. All she can grab for herself, she feels she is entitled to. The twins had the same treatment from Gideon, but they were more resilient – and had each other.'

Lulie looked at me appealingly.

'I did my best to make Dolly feel loved when she was smaller; Mariana was away so often – but my best was not enough.'

'Don't blame yourself, Lulie. I'm sure you did your best. And maybe, by and by, she will grow up some more. Growth is such a very slow process.'

It goes on for ever, really, I thought. We pass milestones – we stop peeing in the bath and stealing jam tarts from the pantry, we learn to utter false politeness and conceal our sinful thoughts, but who, ever, anywhere, can say they are truly grown up? I can remember Mariana once saying that she was not naturally good – no, no, not at *all*, not in *any* way – under the surface she was seething with wickedness, any seemingly benevolent action of hers was the fruit of intense self-discipline and control. Perhaps all goodness is simply that? Just conforming to what you think people expect of you?

I was thinking these thoughts as I painted the last frill on Dolly's neckline and she suddenly remarked, out of the blue:

'I wonder why you never married Barney?'

I put down my brush, picked up another, trailed in a thin streak of white, and said carefully, 'Firstly, he never asked me. It never came up. And secondly, I wouldn't want to.'

'Oh, why?' She seemed quite offended.

'He's far too untidy. I'm an orderly person. I couldn't possibly live with that degree of mess.'

'It's a pity, really! I quite thought you would, at one time. In fact I told Tom that you were engaged to Barney,' said Dolly artlessly.

I put down the white brush, picked up the grey one again. 'Oh? You told Tom that? When?'

'Oh, after the May Ball, you remember, that time when you made my costume. Just for a little, around then, Tom seemed to quite fancy you. Didn't he? He used to write you little poems.'

'Yes,' I said slowly. 'So he did.'

'And I thought it would just clear the field a bit if he knew you were engaged to Barney. Because it really seemed quite likely that you might be! Barney and you used to have long conversations.'

'I can't think what about,' I said, trailing a greenish shadow into a fold of Dolly's skirt.

'About books,' she said at once.

'Barney and I really don't have much in common.' Except a sense of fun, perhaps.

I thought of an afternoon when I had made, or tried to make, a series of drawings of Barney's toes – he had the most extraordinary toes, unbelievably long and bony, like those of the Mantegna *Ecce Homo* – sticking out from under the sheet. But every time he extended them, the cat Mog pounced on them ferociously. In the end, helpless with laughter, I gave up the attempt.

'It's true, Barney and I have had some laughs together,' I said. 'But no, I'd never marry him. Put that idea right out of your head, Dolly. And he wouldn't ask me. Barney has quite given up on the female tribe, I fear.'

But I was wrong, as it turned out.

Sir Gideon suffered what seemed to have been a very mild stroke, and went down to Boxall Hill for two or three weeks to recuperate. He was as tough as an old oak, really; I suppose all conductors are, because they lead such physically active lives. His retinue came with him as usual, since Lulie and Grisch would hardly have been equal to the extra work.

Grisch rang me up to say that Gideon was a bit bored, and would there be any chance of my coming down and doing another portrait of him? Portraits of old Gid were always in demand; the Hungarians wanted one to hang somewhere in Budapest. So I went down.

Old Gid greeted me kindly. 'Ah, Sidonie, my dear one! What a long time since I have seen you!'

About thirty years, I reckoned.

They had a wonderful basket-chair at Boxall Hill, with two wheels behind and one in front, and a sort of narwhal's horn. It had been acquired at a rummage-sale by Lulie, and lovingly re-basketed by Grisch, who could turn his hand to any craft.

The weather was chilly, autumnal, seldom warm enough for the old boy to sit out of doors, so I painted him in the morning-room, against one of the huge windows, reclined in the basket-chair, swathed in a fleecy rug, with the immense view beyond. It was probably not at all the kind of picture the Hungarian State Orchestra had bargained for, or would want, but I enjoyed painting it. Gideon and I held long rambling conversations while I worked. By now I knew so much family history that, whoever he thought I was, Sidonie or Mariana or Lulie, I could feed him with enough responses to keep him comfortably going.

'... And that was when the orchestra was travelling across Europe by train, from one engagement to another, and this boy, he loved me so much that he would arrange to be there, on the station platform, just for fifteen minutes' conversation when the train stopped. At four in the morning! Oh, it was such agony! We loved each other so.' Tears came into his eyes at the memory. 'But what could we do? We were young and poor in those days. And then he died – he was killed playing his viola, doing concerts for the troops – there was a bombardment. I never even knew where his grave was.'

Poor old Gideon.

To turn his thoughts, I asked him about when he met Mariana.

'At a series of concerts in Geneva. She was as beautiful as a white crocus. And Luke, already he was looking after me, Luke, he said, "Gideon, she is the one for you. She will make a frame for your life. She is the one." So I sent her, every day, a pot of white crocuses.'

Couldn't do that for long, I thought. The crocus season is quite short.

'And when you married Mariana, Sir Gideon, was that when you started to become so very saintly?'

·He gave me a wonderful smile: mischief, cunning, piety were in there, it was seraphic, shrewd, knowing, and noble, all at the same time. I *must* catch that, I thought, or die in the attempt.

'Saintliness, my dearest Sidonie, pays off every time! You are really on a winning wicket so long as you can continue to be saintly. I trust I do not confuse you with my metaphors of cricket? I know it is not your national game.'

A good deal of the time he seemed to be under the impression that I was French, and addressed me in that language.

Members of the household came in at frequent intervals with little offerings for him: titbits of toast and Gentleman's Relish, eggnog, beef-tea, brandy. He and Grisch played chess. Sometimes it seemed to me unfair that Grisch should be out and around, doing all the work on the estate, while Gideon lay in rugs and luxury, but then I reflected that Gideon's money had originally paid for all this, and he was certainly no lotus-eater; without doubt he would be up and conducting as soon as he was able. And no one could be healthier or happier than Grisch, revising *A Shropshire Lad* and doing his caricatures.

Barney came down for a weekend. Barney had always been his father's favourite; however confused and rambling Sir Gideon might be with other members of the household, he always brightened up and became quite rational and articulate as long as Barney was around. By chance on Sunday afternoon there happened to be a repeat on television of a concert that Gideon had conducted at Salzburg last summer, so we all looked at it, and it was fascinating to see how, watching his own image, active, keyed-up, and imperious on the conductor's podium, the old boy instantly sprang back to attention and became his former self again.

After the concert was over he fell asleep instantly, and Barney said to me: 'Come for a walk.'

So we walked up through the orchard, past the crumbling brick ruin the children had called 'Matilda's Tower' (goodness knows why) and down through the steep beechwoods at the back where I had once hoped to find a deep romantic chasm. A sad, autumnal walk; the leaves had begun to fall and the nettles round the ruined brick tower were draggled and wilting.

'Goodness knows what'll happen to all this when the old boy passes on,' said Barney, shivering. 'It will be a terrible worry and a trouble.'

'Who will he leave it to? You?'

'I'm afraid so.'

He ran bothered fingers through his thick fair hair, which was now beginning to turn faintly grey; bleaching really, just losing its gold. He still looked ascetically handsome; Barney had always been the most striking of the three brothers. But Toby was the kind one.

'You could split the land with Dan; he's dying to build a hundred stockbrokers' chateaux on the estate.'

'That's a *disgusting* idea, Pandora. How could you even suggest it? Anyway, what about Lulie and Grisch?'

'I wasn't serious.'

'Grisch is terrified of dying alone.'

'I know. He told me that too.'

'I worry about them. They are getting old. If something happened to one of them—'

'Yes, they really need somebody else, a third person, living here. Maybe the twins, when they come back . . .'

'Oh, who could ever rely on the twins?' he said crossly.

But I thought the twins *could* be relied on. It was just a question of engaging their attention.

'Well, Dan and Topsy are just across the garden. When Dan's at home.'

'Dan!' His tone was even more dismissive than for the twins. 'I'd hate for the old things to have to rely on *him*. He's getting mixed up with really shady characters these days – that fellow Brownrigg who claims to paint Old Masters – and some Dutchman who's always going over to Amsterdam. I wouldn't be surprised if Dan was mixed up in drug traffic.'

'Drugs?' I said, horrified. 'But why? He must make a fortune already from all the things he does.'

'For Dan, one fortune would never be enough. He wants two or three. But listen, Pandora. I want to talk to you. That was really why I came down to Otherland this weekend. Why don't you and I get married?'

I nearly fell down from sheer surprise. Which would have been disastrous, for we were winding along a muddy path which led across a steep hillside all grown over with lanky holly trees. The ground was brown and prickly with fallen leaves.

What would Dan do with this land if he got hold of it? Turn it into a ski run?

'*Married*, Barney? Are you crazy?'

'That's not very polite,' he said huffily.

'I wouldn't marry you if you were the last man on the planet. No offence – but we'd drive each other *meshugge* in a week.'

'But we get – got on very well in bed.'

'Yes, we did. Yes, it was a lot of fun.'

I thought of the fifty-odd drawings of him that I had done.

'But bed isn't enough, Barney. I couldn't, simply couldn't live with someone as messy and *schlumpy* as you. Porridge and dirty trousers and oboes all over the floor! No, thank you! If your ghost was to haunt a house, I'd know it was you, just by the ghostly mess it left behind.'

'You wouldn't be expected to pick it up.'

'I couldn't endure to leave it lying there.' And I added, 'You and Dolly are uncommonly alike in some ways.'

'But you're the only woman I've ever had a decent relationship with,' he said mournfully. 'I can talk to you about books. Remember how we used to argue about the Green Knight?'

'That was the twins.'

It was true, though, Barney was the only one of the Morningquests who read for pleasure. And I'd enjoyed our talks.

But. But no.

'It was only my shell that you liked, Barney, really; not me, myself.'

'We were friends,' he insisted.

'And you know you wouldn't be faithful to me; you couldn't. It's not in your nature. I'd never feel comfortable in my mind.'

'You like Mog! And he likes you.'

'You only want to marry me so as to have a permanent housekeeper for Mog.'

'I must say,' he said sadly, 'I do seem to love cats better than women.'

'You leave them behind too.'

'Yes,' he said, even more sadly.

'What ever happened to your wife, Barney? Miss Winslow from New Hampshire?'

'I tried to murder her.'

'What?'

'I pushed her out of a tree.'

'Why? What were you doing in the tree?'

'She wasn't hurt. Not really. She was a botanist. We were looking for oak-galls. I suddenly got fed up.'

'Well, there you are! I'm not going to be pushed out of any tree. So, I'm sorry, dear Barney, but I can't marry you.'

'Lulie will be sorry too,' he remarked gloomily.

'Why? Did she put you up to this?'

'No, as a matter of fact she told me that you'd never have me. She told me you weren't such a fool.'

'You'll have to find someone else to look after Mog. By the way,' I said, 'could I have that drawing that I did of you and Mog, the one with you in the bath and him between the taps? I'd rather like it as a keepsafe.'

'I haven't got it.'

'Rubbish, Barney, you've got them all. All those drawings. A whole portfolio.'

'No I haven't,' he said. 'I meant to ask if you'd been in and taken them. Don't you still have a key? I can't find them anywhere.'

'No, I don't still have a key. I gave it back to you, remember? And no, I didn't come and take them. I wouldn't without letting you know! Anyway I gave them to you. They are yours. But I did think I'd like just the one of Mog and the bath. If you go back and have another look, you're sure to find them somewhere, under all that mess. How about on top of the wardrobe?'

'I think I did look there,' he said doubtfully. 'But I'll look again. You couldn't have old Mog to stay at Shepherd's Bush when I go to Denmark?'

'What would I do with him at weekends when I come here? Besides,' I said, 'I shan't be in Shepherd's Bush. I'm going off to Prague.'

XIX

'So what *did* you do with Mog while you were in Denmark?' the twins asked Barney.

'Let this place to a Buddhist monk. Poor old Mog had to turn vegetarian for six months. But otherwise they seem to have got on very well. So why are you in England, twins?'

'Lawyers' business. We came into old Aunt Isadora's legacy and there were a lot of forms to sign, it seemed simpler to whizz over and do it here. Then we're going back to Yokohama for another two years. They seem to love us there. A mixture of structuralism and the Muddle Principle goes down very well.'

'Have you seen Gideon?'

'Caught him in Cadogan Square, betwen Paris and Seattle. He seems in fine form again. He could even tell us apart.'

'Funny the way he always could, right from the start,' remarked Ally.

'Perhaps because he used to dislike us so much in those days. We reminded him of Dave.'

'Whereas now we are a reminder of Mariana. Whom he did love, in his way. And he's quite fond of us, now.'

'So are you still teaching, Barney?'

'Oh yes. It's what I do best.'

'And Pandora? Still in Prague, still searching for her lost love?'

'I suppose so,' said Barney gloomily. 'She doesn't write to me. Hasn't for a year.'

'She wrote to us, just once. That he was in prison, that she was very lonely. What's she doing there?'

'Lulie said she had some kind of British Council job – portraits of the Man in the Street.'

'And schools,' put in Elly. 'Children in schools. Pen-picture pals. All friends together.'

'Doesn't sound quite like Pandora.'

'Oh, I don't know. What *is* like Pandora? How can we tell? She adapted to us. We didn't adapt to her.'

'I suppose she wanted some valid pretext for staying on in Prague.'

'Have you seen Dolly and her husband?' asked Barney.

Both twins burst out laughing.

'Yes! Dolly and her Mars Bar! He's cuddly! He's really cute.'

'She speaks about him with such bated breath – we expected a mixture of Bertrand Russell, Corbusier, and Buckminster Fuller. And out comes this darling little roly-poly fellow just like Mr Tiggy-Winkle. He's sweet and kind to Dolly, but his name isn't going down in the annals of fame. No way.'

'He makes me feel more kindly to Dave,' said Ally pensively.

'Why?'

'They had the same motive. If you can't be a unicorn yourself, get one. They both married into a family of achievers.'

'There's something about that in Marxism. The transition of quantity into quality. The interpenetration of opposites.'

'Back to Mar and Dave,' said Ally. 'He was a romantic, really. After all, he did take her to the Gobi desert. He didn't have to do that.'

'From our point of view,' said Elly, 'it would have been better if she had stayed at home and taken more interest in our diet, our characters and schooling.'

'Well, we turned out all right, didn't we?'

'Yes, but look at poor Toby and Selene.'

'Selene certainly lost out.'

'And Toby bore the brunt of that. I can remember, can you,' said Ally, 'that time she over-heated a batch of pottery in her kiln, and she was in such total despair. Was going to cut her wrists, but Toby stopped her.'

'She was quite a load for him to carry.'

'Remember how she used to copy all his speech mannerisms and how boring it was.'

'He did love her, though.'

'Of course! She was a sweetheart. Clever and funny and gentle. When we were about five, and terribly ugly, she used to be very nice to us; remember how she'd sometimes give us little picnics in her room?'

'But then, other times, ignore us completely.'

'And Toby was always remote; as if he was working out the square root of minus one.'

'Were you at home,' inquired Barney, 'when Mar found out about Toby and Selene?'

'And there was that hideous row? Of course we were,' said Elly.

'Shall I ever forget it? It was the most frightening thing that had ever happened.'

'And Selene turned on Mar and said what right had *she* to talk? Considering she'd had her fancy man in the house all that time. And after that they never spoke to each other again. Or at least Selene never spoke to Mar.'

'Poor Mar.'

'Ah well; all families have their problems.'

'"All happy families are alike; each unhappy family is unhappy in its own way,"' quoted Elly. 'Pandora didn't know what she was taking on when she took on us. I don't blame her for going off now . . . '

'Her family had its problems too. I remember she told me that, for her birthday once, her father gave her a blind kitten.'

'All kittens are blind.'

'No, but this one was old enough so that its eyes should have opened. It was *really* blind. They never did open. And he was a vet!'

'Perhaps he thought it would be an interesting challenge.'

'No. He just hadn't noticed.'

'That was why her mother bequeathed her to us.'

'And then she fell in love with the whole family.'

'*Did* she?'

'Speak for yourselves, girls,' Barney said drily.

He surveyed, with dispassion, his younger sisters sitting cross-legged at ease among the piled debris on his floor. A mirror leaning against the wall reflected their long noses, grey-green eyes and curved ironic mouths; they looked, he thought, like the masks of Comedy and Tragedy caught in the process of changing rôles.

'Lulie wonders if Mar and Pandora's mother were perhaps distantly related, and that was why they took such a shine to each other?'

'How could anyone ever possibly prove such a thing? Mariana might have been *anybody's* child, left on the steps of a convent. And Mrs Crumbe never told Pandora anything about her origins.'

'Anyway, dozens of people took a shine to Mar, or fell head over heels in love with her; that didn't mean they were her cousins.'

'If you dig far enough back,' said Barney, 'all European families are probably connected. There aren't so many groups to choose from – Normans, Celts, Magyars, Saxons, Jews. And they must have intermingled a bit. And they were decimated so often, by plagues and the Black Death. I expect we are all each other's cousins. There are hundreds of old characters all around the Mediterranean who look *exactly* like Gideon.'

'Only not so holier than thou,' said Ally.

'I'm taking a party of students to Cairo at Christmas,' remarked Barney after a moment. 'Any chance of you two still being here to cat-sit Mog?'

The twins looked at him pityingly and shook their heads.

'No way, Barney dear.'

'We'll be in Yokohama. The festive season over here is what we take pains to avoid.'

'It has too many gloomy resonances.'

'You'll just have to get your Buddhist monk back again.'

XX

My first nine months in Prague were lonely and sad.

Being sure that I had done the right thing in declining Barney's offer did not help my state of mind. I missed Barney himself and the dry jokes we used to share. Much, much more, I missed Lulie and Grisch.

But they themselves had been the warmest in urging me to go. 'Look what happened when you went to Edinburgh! What a successful journey *that* was! Who knows – Prague may be even better. Don't worry about us old things. We shall miss you, but we can always send for Topsy or Dolly.'

Still I felt guilty and anxious about them, felt that in a way I had betrayed their interests. If I were Mrs Barney Morningquest I would have a right of decision over what was done with Boxall Hill, supposing that – Heaven forbid – some catastrophe removed Sir Gideon from the scene.

Just the same, it was a considerable relief that I was not, and did not.

My friend Veronica had, several years ago, returned from Rome and risen to become a potency at the British Council. She, it was, who found me the job in Prague which gave me a pretext for remaining there for an indefinite number of months, and would go some way towards covering my expenses. Cultural Liaison and Exchange. It sounded respectable enough to satisfy the authorities. I did portraits of tram drivers and street cleaners; I went into schools and drew the children, and arranged for their pictures to be sent to English schools in exchange for similar portraits of English children. It was humdrum, reasonable, and innocuous, and I was as lonely as hell.

Prague is, I suppose, one of the most beautiful cities in the world. Even at that time in the seventies, shabby, subdued, grey and quiet, its visual charm was irresistible. I walked and walked, gazed and gazed, drew and drew. I sat on the Charles Bridge, where everybody sits, and did hasty sketches of all the faces I liked best, including the thirty groups of saints who embellish the parapet, smiling and serene like Gideon. And under-neath flowed the Vltava River, silent and dark, full of islands, swans and rats. Up on the wooded hillside above me brooded the castle and its attendant complex of buildings. And the cathedral of St Vitus (which to an English ear has a hectic ring, as if mad dances must be daily performed in its precincts, or the twin-spired edifice itself might be expected to break into a tarantella). I leaned against walls in Staromestske Square, hub of the

Old Town; I drew scaly, flaking, beautiful facades – behind many of which Kafka seems to have lived; never was there such a restless man, continually on the move; and I drew countless round, shrewd, resilient, intelligent Czech countenances. At first I wondered why they should all seem so familiar. Of whom did they so strongly remind me? Then I realised that, one and all, they recalled my mother. But was it the physical conformation? Or the expression? Both, I finally decided. Partly the shape, the outline; and partly the look of immense reticence, the air of having something to hide or, at least, something they were not going to communicate.

'I want you to find people that you can talk to,' had said my mother wistfully. Well, I could talk to Barney and Toby and the twins; once upon a time I could talk to Tom – lost Tom; but I sure to goodness couldn't talk to his compatriots. One reason for that, of course, being that my Czech was fairly minimal, though I was learning the language as fast as I could. German I had picked up from the twins, and that did come in useful; and, of course, a large number of Czechs speak perfect English. But as yet they were not getting into any conversations with me.

The British Council had installed me in a small cheap ancient hotel with cracked baroque stucco mouldings, and large spotty mirrors, and rococo metal-and-marble furniture, and wires hanging loose from non-functioning chandeliers, and dribbling taps and non-viable light bulbs. Though congenial, it was too expensive for my budget, so I moved out to lodge with a family (also recommended by the Council) in a shabby fourth-floor walk-up apartment in the southern part of the city. The family, the Kapeks, were nervous of me at first, though kind and civil; but I learned later they had thought I might be some kind of spy planted on them, maybe an *agent provocateur* of the *Statni tajni Bezpecnost* (State Security) so, sensibly, they were taking no chances. They permitted me use of kitchen and bath, and left me politely alone.

Life under a repressive administration was no novelty to me. It was what I had been accustomed to for my first sixteen years. I felt desperately sorry for the Czechs, completely sympathetic to their plight. And sometimes I wondered if this glum, mumchance, dismal regime was as needless, as foolish, almost accidental, as that of my own family; would it, in the end, just fall apart, would people realise that they might just as well be free and cheerful, and confident with one another? Or would there have to be some fearsome upheaval, a bloodbath, hundreds of deaths?

And where, meanwhile, in this grey, reticent, unfathomable city was Tom? Prisons are not marked on maps or in guidebooks. And of course I had no means of knowing whether he was in Prague at all; he might be in

Bratislava, in Brno, anywhere. And I was nervous about making inquiries, kicking up a dust; that might do him no good at all.

Meanwhile, on foot, I explored every inch of the city. This was the town in which Tom had grown up. By learning about it, I could perhaps learn something about him. I explored the Mala Strana and the Old Town; I went into galleries and churches, I wandered in the gardens on the hillsides, I crossed and recrossed bridges, climbed the Horses' Stair in the Vladislav Hall and listened to street musicians in Wenceslas Square – which is not a square at all, but a long boulevard.

My favourite part of Prague, though, was the Old Town, to which I returned again and again. Especially to the Jewish Cemetery.

I had hunted for this several times, going round and round in circles, before I found it at last, and when I did, I could hardly believe that my search was ended. It seemed so minute. One thinks of a cemetery as a fairly extensive piece of land. But the Jewish Cemetery in Prague is a tiny, odd-shaped, almost star-shaped corner of ground, the size of a tennis court, no more. It is jammed between buildings and crisscross lanes. A wall and a rusty railing protect it. Sometimes – mostly – the gate is locked. The gravestones are fitted together as close as mustard-and-cress, touching, leaning against one another. Elder trees which have sprouted between them add to the congestion. And in this place there are twelve thousand, *twelve thousand* gravestones. Or so I read. People here are buried layers deep. The place was in continuous use from 1439 to 1787.

Rain was falling when I first managed to make my way inside the enclosure. The wet gravestones shone, the sparse unkempt grass on the lumpy hillocky ground looked rinsed and clean. And the little pebbles balanced on top of the monuments shone like pearls. What in the world, I wondered, looking round me, were all those little stones? Every tomb carried several; some, dozens.

I picked up one of them. Underneath lay a scrap of paper. 'Chers grandpère et grandmère,' it said, 'We came to visit your bones. Good luck! *Mazeltov!* Jules, Rebecca and the boys Izzy and Sam. July 19 . . .' and a date, indecipherable, washed away by rain.

Each grave carried many such messages: in French, Spanish, German, Greek, Italian and plenty of languages that were unfamiliar to me. 'Dear Grandparents, we came, we were here, this is to say we have not forgotten you, will never forget you. This is to say that we are alive, that we shall carry on, that our children after us will carry on. This is to say that we love you, although we never met you.' Most of the messages, written on pages torn from diaries, on bus tickets, receipts, boarding passes, tiny scraps of paper, had already been washed out by the rain.

I found these messages indescribably moving. I could have dropped down on the ground and wept – if it had not been raining quite so hard, if there had been a spare square metre of flat ground, if the graveyard had not been crowded with other people, all silently wandering, reading the messages, many of them like myself silently wiping away tears.

The slabs, I later discovered, bore the carved emblems of family groups: an urn for Levi, hands raised in blessing for Aaron, others for Cohen, Hirsch, Kahn; an elaborate sarcophagus for Rabbi Low who died in 1609 and invented the Golem, the first man-made robot, which would go into action when he opened its mouth and inserted a slip of paper with a cabalistic message on it. Just like a car-park ticket machine really. Rabbi Jehuda ben Bezabel would have made himself a fortune today. Maybe he did back there in the seventeenth century.

I returned to the graveyard again and again. Perhaps, I thought, perhaps the ancestors of my mother and Mariana lie here, down among all the other layers of bones; though there must be many such graveyards all over Europe. Perhaps I should write a message too. 'Dear Grandparents, how I wish I knew if you were here.' What had been my mother's real name? I never knew.

One day, a bitterly cold winter day with a sprinkling of snow, I was perched against the graveyard railing, engaged in my usual occupation of drawing the people as they wandered and gazed, when a tentative woman's voice close by said, 'Hallo!'

I looked up and, after some thought, recognised my landlady, Marta Kapek. She was a teacher, and would normally have been at school, but today was a holiday.

'I did not know you had found this place,' she said. 'But my cousin, she says she sees you here many times.'

'Often, often, I come here,' I said.

We fell into cautious talk, and I invited her to come and have a coffee with me in Staromestske Square, not far away. We sat shivering at a table outside and – nobody happened to be within earshot and I was feeling unusually lonely, unusually confidential – I told her that I had once had a Czech friend, that he had been my teacher at art school, that I was fond of his grandmother in Scotland.

'A Czech, an art teacher, with a Scottish grandmother?' she said. 'Oh.'

'He makes films – used to make films,' I said.

'Oh!'

After a moment she said, 'What is his name?'

And when I told her she said, 'Oh,' for the third time, in a significantly thoughtful tone. Then she began to look restless, so I paid for the coffee and explained that I had an appointment – which was true – so we went our separate ways.

But the next day her husband, Jan – also a teacher, at the university – waylaid me on the stairs.

'Excuse that I ask,' he said, 'but your first name – might I be sure that I have it correctly?'

Forms, forms, bureaucracy, I thought, and told him. Though it seemed odd that he needed to know – surely he must already have filled it in on several forms.

He nodded, thanked me, and went on his way.

But that evening he waylaid me again and murmured that he knew of a film show which, he believed, might interest me.

For a moment I was startled to death, believing that he had in mind some *mittel*-European hard porn, but then the sheer unlikeliness of this struck me and besides, leaning even closer to my ear, he muttered, 'Films by Yindrich.'

'*Oh!*' I breathed in wonder and delight. 'Yes! But what made you—'

'Hush! Later, I tell you.'

An assignation was arranged for later in the evening in a part of the town that I did not know very well. I went to the appointed place and was picked up there in a little rattly car that smelt of petrol and dog. We shot off through dim streets – Prague is not well lit at night – soon I was completely lost. After a ten-minute drive we stopped in an unfamiliar part of town, outside the kind of bar with which I was already becoming familiar – a quiet wine- and beer-cellar with premises that seem small from the street, but which tunnel back under a vaulted roof to a most unexpected distance.

My driver came round and opened the door for me. 'Make your way far to the rear, as far as you can,' he said softly. 'Then ask for Mike.'

He smiled at me, and I realised that his face was familiar. In fact I had drawn it. He was a narrow-headed, dark man with a noticeably stiff spine, as if he had suffered some sort of injury, who had sometimes walked across the Charles Bridge when I was drawing there, perched among the street musicians and the puppeteers. Once or twice I had thought he gave me a careful, interested glance, paused, as if he had it in mind to stop and question me, but then went on his way.

Now he said, 'I go to park the car somewhere else. I may see you later.'

I made my way slowly – felt my way really, the place was lit only by tiny guttering candles – past small tables and chairs, and people quietly drinking or eating – until I came up against a door.

'*Prosim?*' said a voice. I asked for Mike.

'In here, please.' The door opened.

Now to my surprise, I felt, rather than saw, that I was in quite a large room, the size of a classroom. And, like a classroom, it had rows of chairs. A few people were sitting in them, not many, less than a dozen. A faint glow lit the place, which was draped all round the walls by heavy curtains – enough to supply Tante Lulie with winter-coat material for the rest of her life.

A friendly arm guided me to a seat, and I sat. A few more people had entered after me, then the glow of light faded and we sat in total dark. After a moment or two a screen was illuminated at the far end of the room, and the film show began.

There was no sound, no music, no voice-over. (Afterwards I was told that the films shown had originally been accompanied by sound, but in such illicit showings as this, to play the soundtrack would be to increase the risk, so they were shown in total silence except for an occasional murmur from the invisible audience.)

The first film, a cartoon, was called *Hunting Gentry*. (I was given translations of the titles afterwards.) It was a simple but cheerful piece of satire in which foxes in red jackets galloped on horseback after naked, fleeing men; bulls and cows in dinner jackets and mantillas watched while picadors and bulls with matadors' capes chased naked men around bullrings, and cheering cats in handsome folk costumes tossed naked men off the tops of towers.

'Film by Tom Yindrich,' it said at the end, among the credits.

It was followed by a surreal, Magritte-like movie about a garden. At first the place seemed charming: old-fashioned flagged paths, clumps of flowers, bird-baths, neat rows of vegetables, roses, lavender, and a lovable bearded old gardener pottering about. But soon Nature Red in Tooth and Claw took over; the flowers fought and devoured each other; worms, slugs and snails devastated the plants; ferocious birds chopped off the stalks; cats pursued the birds, and the old Adam-like gardener was finally strangled by a rampant vine.

Then there was a short, funny film called *Mine is Bigger than Yours* in which two four-year-olds tell stories to each other, their imaginations leaping higher and higher, wilder and wilder, until their fat, uninteresting mothers hale them off to bed. Both of these were credited to Yindrich.

Then there was the film about the socks and gloves, which Tom had made and shown at St Vigeans; seeing it again gave me a great nostalgic pang.

Then there was the one about toads, which Dolly had mentioned; the toads had slightly humanoid faces which, if they were recognisable as living politicians, was presumably why Tom had got into trouble. Why he was sentenced to be 'rested' from film-making, and clapped into jail.

The toad film was done with puppets which looked as if they were made from wash-leather. They were quite remarkably repulsive.

There followed another cartoon: first there was a shot of a volcano erupting, then the word 'PANDORA' slowly printed itself across the screen.

I felt as if my heart had been jolted right out of its course.

It was plain that this film, too, in its official version would be accompanied by a voice-over commentary. The audience was shown the Titan brothers, Prometheus and Epimetheus, constructing the world, modelling mountains, landscapes, trees and finally man, out of clay. Then Prometheus tiptoes up a great gleaming circular stair, winding its way through mist and cloud up to Olympus, where the Gods can dimly be seen in their glory, holding conference and drinking nectar, warmed by the eternal and dazzling rays of the sun.

Prometheus purloins a flame from the Gods' immortal bonfire, tucks it into a hollow fennel-stalk, and manages to escape from Olympus unchallenged. He passes the stolen flame to Man, who at once begins to wreak havoc with it, inventing rocket missiles and setting off disastrous forest fires.

The Gods, taking counsel together, decide to punish Prometheus for trespass and theft. They construct the girl Pandora, beautiful as the day, each god contributing some special gift to her make-up. And here I was obliged to suppress a giggle, for Pandora, no question, bore quite a peculiar resemblance to me. Even despite the fact that I am not as beautiful as the day.

Pandora is despatched down as a bride for Prometheus, with her heavy bride-chest sent behind her on a poor little put-upon donkey. She has been instructed not to open the chest.

But Prometheus, canny fellow, suspects the intentions of the Gods and their kindly gift. Feeling he has no need for a wife, he passes the favour on to his brother Epimetheus, and goes off on a long journey.

Epimetheus and Pandora settle down together, but she, after a while, becomes bored, alone in the house with not enough to do while hubby is out tending his vines.

She opens the box.

And out pour all the troubles of the world – children, creeds, diseases, cars, television, telephones that ring and ring, money, neighbours, tight shoes. Epimetheus comes home, sees all hell let loose, storms at Pandora, and stomps off to the top of the nearest mountain, there to sit and sulk.

Poor Pandora, devastated by this torrent of misfortune and abuse, picks herself slowly off the floor and sees the very last item of all in the marriage chest – *Hope*, in the form of a tiny, draggled baby bird. She picks it up, weeping, warms it in her hands and bosom, blows on it gently to dry it and looks, yearning, up to the mountain crag where Epimetheus sits and sulks. 'Oh, Epimetheus, won't you please come home?'

... Now I remembered how, one day when Tom was at his grandmother's, I had picked up a tiny house-martin which had fallen into Mrs D's yard, blown on it to warm it, and climbed up a ladder to replace it in the parental nest. Tom had held the ladder for me.

The last film of all was called *Snails*. It showed two snails crawling earnestly up a windowpane. They were seen through the glass from inside. What they were saying to each other was depicted in bubbles over their heads; and evidently it was hilariously funny, for there were subdued guffaws from all over the audience, but the Czech words flowed too fast for me to follow. The snails, though, were just as familiar as Pandora, for I remembered a wet afternoon when Tom and I had sat in Mrs D's back room and watched a pair of them do just that, straining eagerly upward, their long, intelligent horns reaching ahead of them.

'Excelsior,' I had said, laughing.

'What possible goal can they have in mind?' said Tom.

'To travel hopefully is better than to arrive,' I said.

He wouldn't let me shift them until they had reached the top. But then, as they seemed quite at a loss, he gently unglued them from the glass and carried them to a bed of London Pride in the courtyard.

After the snails film there was a long, quiet interval while, presumably, the projectionist sorted his equipment and put it away, and the audience could be heard slowly shuffling into outdoor clothes. Then, gradually, discreetly, pair by pair, people began to disperse. I, too, got up and threaded my path back through the long narrow bar, wondering how difficult it was going to be to find my way back to the Kapeks' apartment from this unfamiliar quarter of town; but, to my great relief, outside there was the stiff-backed man again, waiting to escort me.

'I have the car round the corner,' he was saying softly. 'If you do not object to walk a little way.'

'Of course not! I'm grateful to you for bringing me here.'

'So: I understand from Jan Kapek that you have known Tom in Scotland,' he said when we were alone in his car and driving. 'And that you, perhaps, have presented him with the germinal idea for the *Pandora* film?'

'I can't claim that,' I said. 'But, yes, I did know him in Scotland.'

'And you are Pandora?'

'That is my name.'

'The one he wished to marry. Instead of the one he did marry.'

'Excuse me?'

'I should explain,' he said. 'I am an old friend of Tom's parents. My name is Konrad Fischer. I have known Tom since he was born. His mother, you may know, died last summer.'

'Yes; I heard. I'm very sorry. I wish I could have met her. Poor Tom.'

Poor Tom, in prison, unable to go to her, to be with her. No wonder I had not heard for some time from old Mrs D.

'I was able to be with her when it was necessary,' said Mr Fischer. 'His father had died two years before.'

'He had a sister? Anna?'

'She married a Russian and went with him to Moscow. So Tom is alone now. Or will be when he comes out of jail.'

'But when will that be? *Where is he?*'

'Who knows? We have no very recent news. But, Miss— '

'Crumbe. Pandora Crumbe. Please call me Pandora.'

'Tom has many friends. Who love him. Who think highly of him. Some of his work we believe to be on the border of genius. His poetry. His prose writings. His abstract painting, his films – who else, living now, can cover such a wide creative range?'

'It is so dreadful that he is in prison.'

'Well,' said Mr Fischer frankly and unexpectedly, 'we, his friends, are in fact happy that he is back in this country. We think a prison, a Czech prison, may be no more confining than to be married to that demanding, foolish woman who was turning his life into a desert. In prison he has time to think, to be himself, to plan ahead. And here he is attached to his own roots. When he was over there, in exile, severed from all his connections . . . not good. Better that he has come back in time.'

'You may be right.'

'What is this expression, *fallow?*'

'To lie fallow?'

'That is what Tom does. He lies fallow. Some day they will let him out. Things will get better in this country.'

'Yes, but when, Mr Fischer?'

'Only God knows that.'

He braked, and pulled up a discreet three blocks from the Kapeks' apartment house.

'But, meanwhile, we are happy to have found you, Miss Crumbe. Pandora. In Prague is a large group of Tom's friends who will be overjoyed to make your acquaintance, with discretion and care. We know already what a great affection he has for you. And we know that you, also, are a distinguished artist. We look forward to your friendship.'

'Oh, thank you. Anybody who loves Tom – I – I can only— '

My throat seized up, I shook his hand hard and made off along the pavement, hoping that StB men were not observing my every movement.

After that, in Prague, I was not lonely.

I stayed until the evening when I came back to the apartment – not very late – to find Anna Kapek anxiously waiting for me.

A telephone call had been received from Yokohama – 'From Japan, imagine it!' breathed Anna, huge-eyed – asking if I would return to England as fast as possible. Tante Lulie had a broken hip, and was in hospital.

XXI

On the flight to London I was periodically haunted by the memory of an announcement at the BA departure gate, which had said, 'If your travel plans are flexible, BA would be grateful if you would give up your seat to a passenger with an urgent need to travel on this flight. In return you will receive a refund of a proportion of your fare.'

Well, *my* travel plans were not flexible. I had, by good luck, managed to secure the last seat, and was sticking to it. But my sympathies went out to the poor person in urgent need. I wondered if any charitable voyager had consented to stand down in his or her favour.

There had been no time to phone anybody in England. I did wonder why the twins had summoned me, rather than Dolly or Barney or Dan who, on the face of it, would have seemed more immediately accessible. Nor had there been time to check back with the twins in Yokohama. But I intended to do some intensive telephoning as soon as I reached Heathrow.

Meanwhile I sat in the plane, looked out at the winter night, and thought a great many thoughts.

I thought about the friends of Tom, many of whom had made contact with me, casually and unobtrusively, over the past few months. A man would stroll up beside me at the flower stall in the market, or in a picture gallery, or a church, and fall into conversation. Sometimes there would be a message, passed on.

'Tom says, remember the skating.'

Or, 'Tom asks if his grandmother still has trouble with her gardy.'

I sent messages back. He was allowed one visitor every two months.

'The snails are still in the London Pride.'

'Mrs D is reading Stevenson.'

She had often declared that nothing later than Sir Walter was worth reading, but I had at last persuaded her to try *Weir of Hermiston*, and she had been converted.

These frail links with Tom, seemingly so tenuous and vague, did an immense amount for my comfort and confidence. And Tom's friends, most of them living in precarious conditions, treated by the authorities with suspicion, disrespect, sometimes downright brutality, once they had satisfied themselves of my good faith, behaved to me with exquisite kindness and courtesy. They were like the aristocratic émigrés of the French revolution, earning their bread by needlework and scrubbing. Only these émigrés were in their own country. Aristocrats of the mind, university professors, film directors, poets, philosophers, they scraped a livelihood by window-cleaning, serving in shops, in bars, sweeping streets.

'But we would rather do that than leave,' Konrad Fischer told me. (He was a psychiatrist under a cloud, 'rested' from his hospital at present, working in a glass factory.) 'I have friends abroad who have been stripped of their citizenship because they chose not to return. Now they feel rootless, deprived of the landscape of home. And Tom was becoming like that, he told me. He escaped in time. He came back. It was best for him.'

Finally I had had a letter from Tom. A short note. It was smuggled out to me, at some risk, by Mr Fischer, who, as a family friend, had permission to visit Tom in order to discuss legal matters relating to the death of his uncle, his mother's brother. There would be a small legacy, a house in the suburbs, which must be let, or sold.

'Tom wishes to keep it. Then, if they let him out, in two or three years' time, who knows? he might be able to live in it.'

'How would he earn his living? They won't let him make films again?'

'Never! Not this government,' said Mr Fischer, glancing over his shoulder. We were on the Charles Bridge. 'He could clean windows, like the rest of us; or perhaps he might be allowed to teach drawing.'

'He is a wonderful teacher.'

'He gave me this for you.'

Mr Fischer removed a slip of paper which had been tucked into his hatband. Tactfully, he moved some paces away from me and inspected a stall containing hideous but interesting marionettes.

'Pandora. It warms my heart that you are in Prague. Have you learned to enjoy dumplings? Do you remember my grandmother's *tivlachs*? I so wish to see you. Tear this up. T.'

I tore it up, scattered the fragments in the Vltava. Two swans made for them, and exchanged glances of disgust.

Mr Fischer considerately strolled to the end of the bridge and back before rejoining me.

The landscape of home, I thought, as the plane trundled over Germany. What does that mean to me? I think I have no such landscape. Otherland was not my true home. Not by right of birth. Dolly's instinct was a sound one, I suspect, when she complained that I was an interloper, robbing her of her birthright.

But what about Mariana, what about Hélène? Where was their landscape of home? Was the loss of this landscape what had caused my mother's slow petrifaction? Had this gap in her life made Mariana neglect her children and slight her husband? Had this lack turned Sir Gideon into a kind of saintly charlatan?

But then, what about Lulie and Grisch? Equally deprived, they had made their own landscape, and made it for the Morningquest children as well.

I tried to sleep; but anxiety about Grisch kept me awake. I imagined him alone in that empty, echoing house. And of Lulie, impatient and worried in hospital, submitting, most unwillingly, I felt sure, to nursing discipline.

'*Tut mir nicht kain teuves!*'

The moment I was clear of the barriers at Heathrow (I had brought only carry-on luggage, a small night-bag), I made for the nearest bank of telephones and called the Boxall Hill number. No reply. It rang, and rang. Perhaps, I thought uneasily, Grisch was out, visiting Lulie in hospital. But it was late, and I knew that he disliked driving at night. Perhaps a neighbour had taken him? Worried, I tried Barney's number, and got a singsong voice, which must, I supposed, belong to the Buddhist monk.

'Mr Morningquest regretfully is not here. Mr Morningquest is at present climbing mountain Matterhorn with a party of students.'

And I hope they fall down a crevasse.

I tried fat Topsy's number at Aviemore. No reply.

So then, in desperation, I tried Dolly's number: the studio in Cheyne Walk.

Dolly instantly answered the phone. Not quite her downy, creamy self. 'Pandora! Good gracious! Where are you? You must excuse my sounding breathless; I just walked in the door.'

'Where from?'

'Cannes. We've been there for a month. I left Mars behind; he's hoping to build a stadium for the municipality.'

'*Mazeltov!* Listen, Dolly – about Grisch. I'm very worried—'

'Grisch?'

'You didn't know?'

She didn't. Hastily I outlined the situation, cramming tenpenny pieces into the slot.

'I'm going to catch the next train and go down there right away.'

'Train?' she said, already beginning to sound offended. 'Why don't we drive? I still have our rented car in the garage here.'

I could hear tension building up, as if she felt I meant to rush in where family failed to tread.

Dolly might be a terrible nuisance, but in a crisis four hands are always better than two.

I said, 'That would be *wonderful*, Dolly. If you aren't too exhausted after your flight.'

She giggled. 'I slept all the way from Cannes.'

'I'll get a taxi and be right with you.'

Replacing the receiver, I wondered if she and Mars had chanced to come across my father and his Reenie in Cannes. But it did not seem likely that they moved in the same circles.

When I got to Dolly's, we tried the Boxall Hill number again. Still no answer.

The drive to Floxby was nerve-racking. At best, Dolly was a twitchy, unsteady driver, liable to take both hands off the wheel, turn her head right round when talking to a rear passenger, make sudden decisions, change lanes without warning. Even in optimum conditions I was always nervous and keyed up as her passenger, and avoided being driven by her when possible. And tonight conditions were far from optimum. The European snow had not yet arrived but the air was freezing and foggy, visibility very bad, and the road surface glassy.

I offered to drive. This offended Dolly all over again.

'You, Pandora? No, no. You don't even have a car.'

'I can drive, though. I could spell you.'

'Not necessary.'

When we were out on the motorway and had exhausted the topic of the Cannes municipal stadium, Dolly asked carelessly, 'Did you have a good time in Prague? It is Prague where you've been, right? Did you see Tom?'

'He's still in prison.'

'Silly ass!' she said crossly. 'If he *would* make those subversive films!'

'I've met some of his friends, though. They are grand people.'

'All dropouts too, I suppose?'

'They didn't drop themselves, they were dropped.'

'Did you visit Tom in prison?'

She sounded a touch uneasy. Did she still consider Tom her property? Or was it merely the idea of our comparing notes about her? She wouldn't like that.

'No, Dolly, he's not allowed foreign visitors.'

'Talking about prison,' she said, 'Dan's in for a heap of trouble.'

Now she sounded quite cheerful, and active with sisterly malice. In the days of Dolly-baiting, Dan had always been her chief persecutor.

'Oh? Why?'

'Some man was caught with a load of stolen paintings – Old Masters –

215

and when the police started asking questions he implicated Danny. There was a lot about it in the continental *Daily Mail*. A Mafia-type ring of stolen-picture dealers. I simply hate to think what old Gid will say.'

'Where is Gideon?'

'Somewhere in Latin America,' she said indifferently.

'Oh well, perhaps it'll blow over and he'll never know.'

'He will if Dan gets arrested and tried.'

Soon after that, to my huge relief, we turned off the motorway, and Dolly slowed down. Driving conditions were now really terrible, with fog swooping at us in thick, unpredictable patches and roads covered with black ice. Dolly threaded the streets of Floxby Crucis at a snail's pace.

In fact, it was not her fault when the accident happened.

Beyond Floxby there is a long straight stretch, with a V-bend midway, where the road loops to bypass a solid complex of farm buildings. Folly Farm. *Folly Corner*, the bend is called by the locals. A lot of crashes take place there.

Dolly negotiated the corner with due care, and it was as well she did, for on the far side we encountered a tangled mess, right across the road where three motorcyclists, skidding, had fallen foul of a truck travelling in the opposite direction. Dolly braked hard and slid to a stop just in time, but we ourselves were now in a particularly vulnerable position, halted with a sharp bend directly behind us.

I said: '*Quick* – turn into that farm gateway.'

'*Why?*' Dolly's well-known, affronted, don't-you-presume-to-give-me-orders tone.

'Because—'

By then it was too late. Another truck coming along behind us, too fast, slammed into our rear, throwing us against the truck in front.

Dolly's car crunched together like a carton in the jaws of a garbage destructor.

Some instinct had made me aware of the peril just beforehand; I got my hand on the passenger door-handle, opened the door, and rolled out on to the frozen rutted mud at the road's verge.

'*Dolly!* Slide out this side – hurry!'

'It's no good,' she said. 'I can't.'

'Are you hurt?'

'No, I'm not. But I can't move.'

She was totally boxed in by bent, buckled metal.

'Switch off the ignition! Can you?'

She could, and did. I hadn't dared look yet at the annihilated vehicle behind us. Mercifully at this moment three police cars arrived, blue lights flashing, and in no time the site was swarming with official activity. There were several civilians wandering about, the motorcyclists and their passengers, as well as two people from the truck that had hit them. No one seemed badly hurt.

'Dolly, are you *sure* you're OK?'

'Yes-yes,' she said, sounding like Sir Gideon.

'Stand away from that car, please, miss,' said a policeman impatiently.

'My friend's in it.'

'She's in no danger.'

They were spraying the wrecks with fire-preventing foam. 'We shall go to her assistance as soon as we can. If *you* co-operate by not getting in the way, it will make our job easier.'

The usual irritable, patronising, official line.

'Listen, Pandora!' called Dolly. 'Why don't you just filter away? It's only half a mile across the fields from here to Otherland – less. Why don't you just *go*?'

'Are you really not hurt?'

'No, no!'

So I went. The police were too busy to bother about me.

A cart track led from Folly Farm over the ridge to join my familiar path where it emerged from the chestnut copse. The deceiving fog had lifted, or I had left it behind me in the valley; ahead of me Boxall Hill house stood out on the white, frosty hillside: clear, square, and pale against the shadowy ilex grove.

There was one light in a downstairs window.

I hurried up the slope as fast as I could, stumbling over tufted frozen grass, my lungs painfully full of ice-cold air. The night was not dark, though clouds veiled the moon. I could hear the call of an owl.

I was thinking about Grisch. The many times he had helped me, advised me, comforted me when I was puzzled or unhappy or daunted. His shrewd intelligent kindness, his percipience. His utter reliability. Grisch is my real father, I thought. It is the least I can do to be there when he needs help. If only he is still there, if only he is all right . . .

I reached the cobbled yard, where the little fountain in its collar of brick wall stood completely cased in a marble dome of ice. Without troubling to knock on the back door, I unlocked it (I had kept my key) and ran along the short passage, calling, 'Grisch! Are you there? It's Pandora!'

The house was deadly cold. It felt as if no fire had been lit there for days.

'Grisch?' I called again. And came into the kitchen.

There he sat, at the immensely long table, its only occupant. The overhead light shone down on his bald head. But I was too late. He was dead, slumped forward, his head on his arms.

Shaking, stiff with cold and dread, and fatigue, I moved closer and touched his cheek. It was icy. He must have been dead for hours.

With trembling hands, I lifted his head and recoiled in horror, for his face was streaked with blood. Then, looking closer, I saw that it was from a nosebleed.

In front of him on the scrubbed table lay a scribbling pad and a pencil. The paper was blood-spotted. He had written: 'Pandora. Dan in tun—' The final 'n' trailed away. That had been the moment when death had caught up with him. His face was contorted, eyes staring, mouth wide open. Dribbles of dried spit ran down his chin. It had not been an easy end for him.

Immeasurable guilt almost swamped me. I had failed him. Why had I not managed to get back in time? Grisch, who all his life had helped and solaced other people, borne their burdens and made their lot easier, was condemned to the very thing he had feared above all, a lonely death with no friend to see him through his final pangs.

'I would like to die listening to music,' he said to me once. 'Some friend playing the oboe, or a good record on the gramophone. *See what his love will do*, the chorale prelude, that would do well.'

The record of *See what his love will do* lay ready on his little portable player, on the worktop by the sink, but the power was switched off at the main plug; no one had played it for him.

That note. What could it mean? 'Dan in tun.' Dan in tunnel?

I struggled to remember what Dolly had been saying earlier. About Dan. Something about stolen Old Masters.

Foolishly, uselessly, I clasped the old, sinewy hand that had dropped the ballpoint, felt for a non-existent pulse. The fingers felt like frozen twigs.

Dan in tunnel?

What was I supposed to do?

The cellar door to the tunnel was always kept locked. And the outer one in the pavilion. 'So that,' Toby had once said, 'if lucky or intelligent burglars should make their way through the door in the pavilion, they still won't be able to make their way through the cellar into the house.'

God knew where the keys were kept ...

But of course – my frozen wits slowly returning to me – I did know where the key would be. In Tante Lulie's bowl. Along with library tickets, Chinese yen, razor blades and candle ends.

And there I found it – or them, rather: two heavy keys, fastened together with a twisted piece of wire. Taking a flashlight with me, I went slowly down the cellar stair. The tunnel door was concealed – another of Toby's clever ideas – behind a set of shelves, ceiling-high, which swung out on a hinge. Pulling back the shelving, I inserted the key in the hole, opened the door.

And there was Dan, blinking at my torchlight, yawning, decidedly pleased to see me.

'Pandora! Thank Heaven for large mercies! Am I happy to see you! Have the police gone?'

'Police?'

'They were here, looking for me. That was hours ago. Didn't Grisch tell you? That was why I hid down here. *Have* they gone?'

He stepped into the cellar, yawning again, and stretching. He had a roll of canvases under his arm.

I said, 'Grisch is dead.'

'*What?*' He stared at me, disbelieving. 'What do you mean?'

'He's dead. Upstairs, in the kitchen.'

'You're kidding.'

But upstairs in the cold kitchen, forced to acknowledge reality, he said, 'Oh God. The poor old boy. I'm really sorry it had to happen like this. Still, it must have been a quick end for him. He had a heart condition, you know. I'm afraid he was annoyed with me. He didn't like me coming here; in fact I had quite a job persuading him to stow me in the tunnel; we were arguing about it and he only agreed just as the police arrived. Yes; he was a bit ratty about that. I suppose all the fuss was too much for him.'

'Evidently.'

Dan glanced at his watch.

'Phew! Three a.m! How did it get to be so late? Tell you what, Pandora, it's lucky for me you arrived when you did!' He hardly, I thought, yet realised quite *how* lucky. He went on, 'It's a good thing I had the forethought to leave my car in the Silkins' cart-shed – nobody will have thought to look there. Had to come back to Aviemore, you see, for these . . . '

He pulled apart the roll of paintings and gave me a brief glimpse of dazzling dark-and-bright speckled circles, of roofs, moon, cypresses.

'My God, Dan, what's that?'

'Van Gogh drawings: about twenty of them turned up in Moscow last year, looted, you know, by retreating Red Army, lodged in somebody's attic all these years till a pal of mine found his way to them. Now they're my old-age retirement insurance.'

He gave me his naughty-boy grin, so like, yet so unlike, Sir Gideon's seraphic smile.

'Well, I'd better be off. And *you'd* better not say you saw me.'

'Why?'

'Oh,' he said jauntily, 'I've got a lot of dirty drawings of yours. Pictures of Big Brother Barney. I don't suppose you'd like *them* scattered about the world?'

'I don't care what you do with them,' I snapped, wondering when he had stolen them from Barney's flat.

'Hey – Pandora – how about coming with me? First to Jersey, then to the continent. How about it?'

'Are you crazy?'

'I always fancied you – you know that. Loved you really, I suppose. That tune you used to whistle. The *Serenata Notturna*. It really did something to me.'

'Oh, bosh, Dan.'

'No. Scout's honour! Ever since I heard you pipe out 'O Wa Ta Na' at this very table.' He gave me the grin again. 'Topsy was only a convenience, you might say. And now she's run out on me. *Do* change your mind, Pandora? Do come along?'

'Look, Dan, just go, will you? Before I change my mind and phone the police?'

I could hardly bear to look at his pink, plausible face, with Grisch sitting there, so silent, on the other side of the table.

'All right,' said Dan, suddenly quiet. And he went.

The Silkins' barn was too far off to be able to hear his car start; he just vanished away into the silent, freezing night.

I put back the tunnel keys in Tante Lulie's bowl, and started towards the telephone.

And then a small, strange and awesome thing happened. The pen, with which Grisch had written his last message, began rolling. It rolled right across the table, and fell with a soft click on to the stone floor . . .

I was sitting beside Grisch, weeping, wiping his face with my wet handkerchief, when the police finally arrived.

'You shouldn't have done that, miss,' they said rebukingly, at once. 'You should have left him just as he was.'

But I was glad that I had closed his eyes and tidied him into dignity before they took him away. At least I was able to do that for him.

And I played the record after they had gone, just in case he was anywhere still within earshot.

XXII

Next day I went to see Lulie in hospital.

After we had hugged, and cried, and commiserated, I said, 'What will you do, Tante Lulie?'

'This house, Boxall Hill, must now be shut up. I cannot in any way manage it on my own. And Gideon comes now so seldom. And you are in Prague, where it is right that you should be. You are going back?'

I said yes, that *had* been my intention, but if Lulie needed a place, how about my flat in Shepherd's Bush? It was standing empty. And I would come and go—

No, no, she said, I was right to wish to put down roots in Prague. Prague was the place for me. Maybe that was where Hélène came from.

'And let us hope that some day—'

I said that we must not think about that. One step at a time.

'Dolly has also offered me a home,' said Lulie. (Dolly was in the ward next door, suffering from shock and contusions.) 'She has invited me to come and live with her and her Mars Bar.' Lulie's face briefly warmed from hollow-eyed mournfulness to something like its old wicked grin. 'She wishes me to make her clothes for ever after. *Kinehora*! What a hope! Anyway, I shall not go there. I shall go to my cousin in San Francisco. All these years I have sent him press cuttings; now he can have me as well. I am really a city person, I shall enjoy it.'

'Travel all that way?'

'Why not?' said Lulie robustly. 'If my leg is lame, I can travel about on the cable cars.'

A nurse brought her a mug of coffee. She tasted it sceptically and made a grimace at me. '*Pischass!*'

'Oh, Lulie! Listen! If you don't like San Francisco, please come back to me. Will you promise? By then – by then – something may have happened.'

'I promise,' she said. 'But, *bubeleh* – don't *bank* on something happening. Or not for a long, long time. Years, maybe! Take your nourishment where you can get it, from walking, sunshine, from women's magazines or Proust, pop songs or Bach – it does not matter. Everything is somewhere else.'

'Oh, I know it is!'

I thought about the Morningquest family, how completely I had misread every one of them. And yet I had truly loved them, you could say that I was wedded to the whole family. *They* were my landscape. Even now – years later – to remember Toby's records, to see my name scrawled in a book in Mariana's writing – that is like a swordthrust in my heart.

'Grisch was just about to begin on the works of Browning,' Lulie told me with a wan smile. 'Perhaps it is as well that he died. Such a task might have been beyond even Grischa.'

'You and he are my real parents and I'll love you always.'

On my way out I asked the hospital authorities when they would release her. In a week, they said, all being well.

Just too late for Grisch's funeral.

Dolly's Mars Bar came up trumps for that event, he organised the whole thing magnificently, and we were all very grateful to him. Gideon came back from Santiago, and Barney from the Matterhorn. Where Dan might be, nobody inquired. Except the police, to be sure, who were still looking for him.

The twins were only halfway from Japan, delayed by bad weather.

When the funeral was over, and Lulie departed for San Francisco, Barney and Gideon set about the operation of putting Boxall Hill on the market, with outbuildings, folly, gazebo, secret passage, tree-house, pets' graveyard, and all appurtenances.

And at this moment the twins turned up, incandescent with wrath, grief, and outrage.

'*Sell* Boxall Hill? Sell our home? Over our dead bodies!'

'Well, what then?' demanded Barney, frayed to the verge of unreason.

'Keep it! *We*'ll run it. And if you dare go ahead and sell it, we shall buy it ourselves.'

'Buy it? What with?'

'With Aunt Isadora's legacy. Or the advance on Elly's book of farts.'

'What about your jobs in Yokohama?'

'That's all settled. One of us will go back and teach there till our contract terminates. And one of us will settle into Otherland. We'll fetch back Tante Lulie from San Francisco. She probably won't *want* to stay there when she's had a look at the place.'

'But are you really prepared to separate?' I asked the twins. 'You never have before?'

'Well – temporarily. The fact is—' they both grinned like Little Dog Fo. 'Elly's gone and got herself pregnant. And we've decided that we are going to have this one, and see how it turns out. Somebody new to swim in the stream, you know, and play in the tree-house, and rebuild Matilda's

Tower. It will be like old times again, the days of the Projects. In fact we can't wait!'

'Good Heavens . . . '

But I could see that the scheme had plenty to recommend it. And already Barney and Sir Gideon were beginning to look less wretched and harassed.

So I took myself back to Prague, to go on drawing faces, to wait and hope, to meet more of Tom's friends, to read the poems of Robert Browning and to wonder how Grisch might have tackled them.

I am learning how to say a *kaddish* for him.

To travel hopefully is *not* better, but it is all that we can do.

AIKEN   Aiken, Joan,
          1924-

       Morningquest.